ENDEAVOUR

Dean Crawford

Also by Dean Crawford:

The Ethan Warner Series
Covenant
Immortal
Apocalypse
The Chimera Secret
The Eternity Project

Atlantia Series
Survivor
Retaliator
Aggressor
Endeavour

Independent novels
Eden
Holo Sapiens
Soul Seekers

Want to receive notification of new releases? Just sign up to Dean Crawford's newsletter via: www.deancrawfordbooks.com

We should have known better.

We know that there are few survivors, few of our kind still clinging to life.

They say that when the end came some embraced it willingly, shrugged off their lives like old skins and allowed the Legion to infiltrate their minds and their bodies and become one with the machine. Most, however, did not. Most fought, and died, trying only to remain who they were.

The Legion, the instrument of the Word, our governing law, took life across all of the colonies. Worlds fell; Ethera, Caneeron, Titas; the mining settlements and the outlying systems and the uncharted clouds of asteroids and meteors beyond consumed by the monstrous and insatiable thirst for knowledge and power that is the currency of the Word. The greatest creation and achievement of our human race turned vengeful deity, the destroyer of worlds.

We now know that there are several forces at work within the Legion, an immeasurable swarm of mechanical devices ranging in size from as big as insects to as small as biological cells. There are the Infectors, the smallest and most dangerous, for it is their mission to infiltrate the optical nerves, the brain stem and the spinal cord of human beings, turning them into mere instruments dancing to the macabre hymn of the Word's destructive passion. Then there are the Swarms, the clouds of tiny but voracious feeders who break down all and any materials into the raw ingredients for more of their kind: metals, plastics, even human tissue, consumed en masse and regurgitated into further countless devices, all of which evolve with startling rapidity as though time were running for them at breakneck speed. Finally, there are the Hunters: bigger than the rest and with only a single purpose – to find and to kill intelligent biological life wherever it is found in the cosmos.

We are the last of our kind, and despite the horrors that we witnessed when we fled the only star system we could call home, we now know that we must return. There is nowhere else to run to, nowhere else to hide, for if we do not make our stand now then we condemn our children or their children after them to face what we could not. We must fight back and step by step, system by system, we must take from the Word that which was ours and liberate ourselves from the living hell that we have created and endured.

The Atlantia, a former fleet frigate turned prison ship, is the last home we have. Our crew is comprised of terrified civilians, dangerous former convicts and a small but fiercely patriotic force of soldiers and fighter pilots for whom there is no further purpose in life other than to fight for every last inch of space between here and home.

Our lives may become the last that will ever be lived, and thus we tell our story in the hope that one day others will read of it and remember our names.

Captain Idris Sansin

Atlantia

1

I

'Hold position!'

The whisper cracked like thin ice in the Lieutenant Riaz's ear, and came from a microphone surgically inserted into the throat of one of his troopers. Inaudible to human ears, the trooper's skills as a ventriloquist worked well in their shared high–threat environment.

Lieutenant Riaz crouched in the darkness, the cold seeping into his bones as he remained perfectly still and peered ahead into the gloom. Upon the transparent mask of his helmet was transposed a vector–based night–vision display, a series of lines in three–dimensional form that overlaid the view ahead and picked out the contours of a long corridor, bulkheads and doorways invisible in the pitch black. He preferred the non–intrusive, night–sight preserving geometric display to the glare of full night–vision just in case someone, or something, hit the lights and blinded himself and his men.

The corridor was enveloped not just by darkness but also a freezing mist, the vacuum of space outside the hull chilling the interior of the aged vessel. The lieutenant squinted his right eye twice on purpose as he looked at a selector on his display and the image on his mask screen switched to an environmental read–out: the temperature was two degrees above freezing, oxygen at twenty one per cent, nitrogen at seventy one per cent, trace gases comprising the rest. Breathable, but not one of the seven men he shared the darkness with dared to remove their helmets.

Up ahead, Riaz could just make out the form of his point man, a shadow against shadows, hugging one wall of the corridor and surveying the scene ahead. Nobody moved, other soldiers behind the lieutenant silent and still. He could hear the sound of fat drops of moisture dripping to splatter on the deck plating beneath his boots, tapping on his environmental suit as though fingers were playing across his shoulders. Upon the ceiling of the corridor were fat icicles that glistened in the faint green glow from the soldiers' visor displays.

'Advance.'

Riaz nodded his head fractionally as a signal to the men behind him and the small knot of soldiers advanced, melting through the darkness like liquid shadow, silent and deadly. The confines of the corridor served to amplify any sounds, the dropping water like a symphony of tiny drumbeats that the lieutenant's brain quickly tuned out, focusing entirely on the corridor ahead for any sign of danger.

He squinted his right eye twice again and the display switched to a three dimensional map of the vessel in which they moved. Vast, partially cylindrical and slowly rotating about its longitudinal axis to create gravity on the outer decks: an older means of keeping the crew's feet on the deck before the more widely utilised technique of placing magnetically charged plates below decks to draw down on the iron inserts in the crew's uniforms. Deeper inside the vessel, the gravity was barely at thirty per cent and the lieutenant's movements were light and cautious.

The point man led them further down the corridor, each of them moving with their gloved hands cradling powerful pulse rifles, fingers on triggers and plasma magazines activated. Heavy webbing was festooned with grenades, static charges, ammunition pouches and blades, every soldier laden with the weapons of war. At the vanguard, a similarly armed man carried a small Bergen bearing medical equipment and supplies, as well as a compact folding stretcher. The eight–man team was entirely self–sufficient.

And had been so for over four years.

The point man crept agonisingly slowly toward the end of the corridor, where the way was blocked by a sealed bulkhead. With unbreakable patience the team settled in again and waited for any sound of movement either beyond the bulkhead or behind them. Highly trained and disciplined, Lieutenant Riaz knew that the will of any foe would break before that of his team. Anger, fear or just plain old curiosity always forced an enemy to move and thus reveal themselves, and then the shooting would begin. Controlled bursts, accurate and withering fire closely and instinctively coordinated that had seen his team kill with overwhelmingly efficiency even when outnumbered ten to one.

After several long minutes of silence the point man finally moved up to the bulkhead doors. They had been sealed from the inside and led into what the schematics of the lieutenant's display suggested was nothing more than an ordinary storage area of the holds. So far, so normal, except that this vessel had proved itself to be anything but normal. The schematics barely matched the interior of the ship in ways that the lieutenant, though he would never admit it to his men, found truly frightening.

Walls were no longer straight but rippled and pitted as though crumbling despite being made of metal as solid now as the day it had been forged. Some sections of the ship's decks were entirely missing, leaving lethal plunging abysses filled with debris tumbling over and over silently at the ship's centre. But even that could not compare to the horrors they had witnessed upon the ship's bridge, things that not one of his men had mentioned since. The lieutenant found himself staring into the darkness, his mind filled with gruesome images of…

'Stand by.'

The point man eased his way back from the bulkhead and the lieutenant saw a tiny block of material attached to the locking mechanism. A cube–shaped package of chemicals suspended in a five–sided metal container, the open–ended side was attached facing the bulkhead door locks. A detonator released a small vial of a further chemical into the block, which would transform it from an inert package into a fearsome blaze as violent reactions occurred within.

The point man checked the positions of the team behind him, and then he touched the detonator as the team of soldiers averted their eyes from the door.

There was little sound, barely a faint hiss, but a tremendously bright blaze of energy illuminated the darkness as the lieutenant shielded his eyes from the light. He peered behind him and saw the corridor glow in the ghostly white light, a forest of icicles clogging the ceiling and sparkling as the bulkhead was melted at its locking points.

The flare of light faded as rapidly as it had appeared and instantly the point man leaped up and grabbed the bulkhead release valves as the fire–team behind him took up positions in support. A second man shouldered his weapon and moved without command to assist the point man, and together they heaved the valves open and then slammed their shoulders into the bulkhead.

The heavy door swung open as the two men dove out of sight to either side and cleared the way for the fire–team and their weapons. Lieutenant Riaz moved first and rushed forward with his rifle aimed ahead as he burst into a large storage facility. His eyes took everything in within moments, but it took his brain a moment to process was he was seeing as his heart skipped in his chest and he missed a breath.

According to the schematics on his visor display the hold area had once been used for storing food for the large crew of the ship. At the time of its launch the vessel had been the largest hull ever constructed, over one hundred thousand tonnes and with a full compliment of one thousand souls. But the racks and shelves were long gone and in fact so was the massive food store. The hold was no longer recognisable as a hold at all, as though rebuilt by unknown hands and re–tasked to perform a far more sinister role.

Ranks of vertically mounted escape capsules lined the decks and stretched away endlessly into the gloom, the aft bulkheads enveloped in the freezing mist that pervaded the entire vessel. Like giant black eggs in some nightmarish lair, they sat in glossy silence as the soldiers regrouped before them.

'No life indicators, lieutenant,' came the voice of the medic as he scanned his own visor display's readout. *'Minimal power and life support, normal atmosphere, but I'm detecting multiple biological readings inside all of the capsules.'*

Lieutenant Riaz nodded, not wanting to speak yet as he stood with his men and surveyed the scene. There were probably five hundred capsules, each with a cable that extended from the top and went up into the hold ceiling far above them. The lieutenant's eyes traced the lines upward.

'Power must have been re–routed from the fusion cores to here,' he said.

'Some kind of life preservation system?' suggested one of the men. *'Maybe the crew saw the writing on the wall and decided to settle in and hope for the best?'*

The lieutenant nodded but his eyes were drawn back down.

'Only one way to find out,' he replied as he moved toward the nearest capsule.

The fire–team spread out around him, covering all points as the lieutenant moved closer to the capsule and examined its surface. He wiped a layer of frost off with his gloved hand and to his surprise the surface of the capsule was perfectly smooth, as though mirror polished. But the surface was also not of one material, the appearance layered and marred as though many different types of metal had been interwoven in a complex image like marble but with straighter lines, almost geometric in appearance.

'Damn,' one of the troops whispered, 'it's made from the ship itself. That's where those missing decks went.'

Lieutenant Riaz nodded, fascinated and yet unnerved. He looked up at the front of the capsule, the device standing a full cubit taller than he was and covered in frost. He reached up with his free hand and brushed the frost off. The crystals fell away in a sparkling shower and revealed a transparent panel to a rush of expletives from the soldiers around him as their flashlights illuminated the contents.

The interior was filled with a pale fluid, and suspended within was a form of life that the lieutenant had not yet encountered, frozen in a rictus as though screaming for release. Fangs were bared, fearsome eyes wide and filled with rage, thick hair punctuated by tiny bubbles trapped within their layers that caught the light from the soldiers' weapons and flickered like tiny chrome spheres. Both of the creature's heads were pierced by tubes that seemed to burrow deep into the back of their skulls, and its multiple limbs were manacled in place.

'What the hell is that?' one of the troopers asked.

The lieutenant looked around him at the hold. 'Question is, what the hell is it doing here?'

'This ain't right,' said another. *'It just ain't right.'*

6

Lieutenant Riaz overcame his shock and swept the frost from another capsule, revealing a different species likewise confined within. The troops began examining other capsules and in each they found something new and frightening.

'*Different one in each,*' said one of them.

The lieutenant was able to recognise aquatic features in some species, terrestrial in others, and in some there was no way to tell if whatever was suspended in the fluid had ever been alive in any real sense at all, their appearance so bizarre. Riaz examined a cloud of what looked like milk suspended in the fluid inside one capsule, filaments of fibrous material clearly cohesive and yet unlike anything he had ever seen.

'*Lieutenant? We've got something over here.*'

Riaz turned and saw three of his troopers standing in front of a capsule deeper inside the holds. He strode across to them as they brushed down the surface of the capsule, glistening showers of frost falling slowly toward the deck in the low gravity. The men parted as the lieutenant moved to stand among them and looked up into the transparent panel.

The fluid within held in suspension a human form, that of a woman. Short, brown hair was curled delicately back around small ears, the woman's slight frame floating in the void as though hovering in mid–air.

'*One of the crew?*'

Lieutenant Riaz, unable to believe what he was seeing, move closer to the capsule. What horrified him the most was that the woman's features were covered by a featureless metal mask, her eyes and mouth visible only through slim gaps in the metal illuminated by the soldier's flashlights. Two slim probes poked between her lips and vanished into her mouth, the gruesome mask hiding her true features and making her look far more intimidating than someone so petite had any right to be.

He reached up and brushed more frost off the viewing panel, and there upon the woman's uniform he could see an identity badge and an image of the woman's face. There was a grace about her that captivated the lieutenant, what little he could see of her elfin features both attractive and somehow worrisome at the same time, as though she could bring joy into life as well as pain depending on her mood. Small, sculptured lips were set in a faint smile, and the lieutenant realised that he could place upon that expression emotions of both happiness and cruelty in equal measure.

'*Who the hell is she?*' asked another of the men.

'I don't know,' Riaz replied. 'This ship has been missing for almost a hundred years.'

***

II

The viewing platform of Atlantia was normally a place where a man could view the cosmos surrounding the frigate in all of its glory, a stunning observation post atop the bridge where Captain Idris Sansin had spent much of his time when off duty in the past. Now, he stood with his hands behind his back and stared out into an immense blackness devoid of even the slightest hint of light, and enjoyed only the silence that surrounded him. Nobody else came up here when there was nothing to see.

The sense of vertigo provoked by the void was frightening to those who had never before witnessed it. The perfect, non–reflecting blackness had the depth of a universe and yet no visual marker to attach scale from a human perspective: the most common reaction was for an observer to believe that they were falling in all directions at once on an endless plunge toward infinity. For Idris, the deep blackness was a place into which he could deliver all of his hopes and fears, a faceless and nameless oblivion that cared little for human woes.

Atlantia was travelling at super–luminal cruise, exceeding the speed of light several times over. At such tremendous velocity, light information was stripped from the surrounding cosmos: there was quite literally nothing to see, although Idris knew that reasonably close by their sister ship, Arcadia, was travelling alongside them. Communication was also impossible when travelling at such velocity, so if either ship had a problem and was forced to drop into sub–luminal cruise, there was no way to let the other vessel know about it. Idris and his fellow captain, Mikhain, got around this by combining the power of their respective frigates' mass–drives to form a single 'cell': although they could not see or talk to each other, if one ship's mass–drive disengaged the other would automatically do likewise. The technique had been used to great effect back in the Veng'en wars, Colonial warships emerging simultaneously from super–luminal cruise into ambush attacks against enemy vessels with frightening efficiency.

With nothing to emit light, the Atlantia's hull beyond the observation platform was unable to reflect anything and thus also invisible, utterly consumed by the darkness. Idris stared into the blackness but saw only his own reflection staring sombrely back at him, as though his own ghost were judging him from beyond reality, beyond the grave. Short grey hair framed a rugged, angular face deeply scored by the ravages of time.

'Captain?'

Idris turned as Andaim Ry'ere, the Commander of the Air Group, climbed the steps to the observation platform and joined him. Young, with a square jaw and calm blue eyes that missed nothing, Andaim had become a senior officer despite his youth both because of his skill as a pilot and leader, and because there were so few human beings left to choose from.

'Sit rep?' Idris asked.

'All systems secure and operational,' Andaim replied. 'We crossed the Icari Line two weeks ago, captain. How much farther do you wish to progress at super–luminal before we drop out and take a look around?'

Idris sighed as he stared back out into the darkness. The Icari Line was a boundary around the Colonial core systems of Ethera, a sphere some forty light years across that held within its embrace several populated systems of various races. Established to protect those fledgling races from the unknown beyond by the Icari, an ancient race of beings trusted by all, it had now become a place of danger for humanity after the catastrophic collapse of society before the wrath of the Word and its Legion.

Safely ensconced in super–luminal cruise, there was nothing that could touch either Atlantia or Arcadia. Massless and effectively invisible, the two frigates could cross the entire galaxy if they so wished and never be seen, although to do so would take centuries even at such high velocities. The captain did not enjoy admitting it to himself, but the only time he had felt entirely secure since that catastrophe was when he was at super–luminal, safe from whatever horrors awaited outside.

'We'll remain here for a while longer,' he replied to the CAG finally. 'The crew needed the rest after what happened on Chiron IV.'

'That was a month ago, captain,' Andaim replied with a patient smile. 'Now they're getting itchy about being cooped up aboard ship for so long. My pilots haven't flown for two weeks. They're not the sort to be happy sitting about, especially Evelyn.'

Idris lifted his chin.

'Evelyn is not the commander of this vessel,' he pointed out as he turned to face Andaim. 'However, I don't like the idea of her getting agitated. I take it that she has apologised to Ensign Rollins for the assault?'

'In a manner of speaking, captain. She apologised for hitting him, and then suggested that she should simply have shot him.'

'We can't have officers striking fellow crewmen,' Idris insisted.

'Ensign Rollins was out of line captain and we both know it. He attempted to…,' Andaim hesitated as he sought the right word, clearly offended by what had happened. 'He attempted to interfere with Evelyn while she was sleeping and he got what he deserved. Frankly, given Evelyn's history, he's lucky to be walking at all.'

'None the less,' Idris said, 'I expect Evelyn to conduct herself as an officer should, not a convict. I wouldn't want her to lose her flying privileges.'

'No, captain,' Andaim agreed.

'And I wouldn't want to think that her commanding officer was treating her preferentially to other pilots.'

Andaim looked as though he had been slapped. 'I wouldn't do that, captain.'

'Is that so?' Andaim stared at Idris for a long moment, and then the captain's face creased with a grin. 'I wouldn't blame you, you know. We've all got somebody aboard that we care about.'

Now it was Andaim who lifted his chin. 'Duty comes first, sir.'

Idris glanced out once more at the darkness. 'Doesn't it just,' he replied, and then with a heavy heart: 'Very well, inform the helm that we will be dropping out of super–luminal shortly. Arcadia won't be prepared, apart from her Quick Reaction Alert fighters, so we'll launch six Raythons to cover her as well as our own QRA fighters. Make sure Evelyn is on the launch.'

'Aye, cap'ain.'

'And make sure the Corsair bombers are also ready in case…'

The captain was cut off as the voice of Atlantia's communication officer, Lael, broke through on a speaker mounted nearby on the observation deck.

'Captain to the bridge, urgent.'

The dim lights around the deck of the observation platform turned red as the entire ship was placed on a low–level alert. Idris turned and with Andaim hurried to the steps that descended from the centre of the platform down onto Atlantia's bridge.

The silence and darkness of the observation platform was replaced by a galaxy of lights and the murmur of voices as the command crew went about the business of running the massive frigate. A circular command platform holding the captain's chair, that of the Executive Officer and the CAG was surrounded by a guard rail, and beyond that manned stations all facing a large viewing screen and tactical display. Idris Sansin strode to his chair as Lael read from a data screen before her.

'Gravitational wake trace bearing oh–two–five starboard, Colonial signature recognised.'

'Colonial?' Idris asked as he settled into his seat and watched a stream of data pouring down the tactical display nearby. 'That's not possible, we're far beyond the Icari Line.'

'It's an older signature,' Andaim replied as he scanned the same data display, his brow furrowed in concentration. 'But it checks out, it's one of ours alright.'

Idris rubbed his jaw with one hand. A gravitational wake was a twisting of the fabric of space–time left by a vessel travelling at super–luminal velocity. Much as a sailing ship left a wake in the ocean, the gravitational wave expanded out from behind a spacecraft and could, with the correct equipment, be scanned and information about the craft that left the wave determined. In this case, the shape of the wave denoted a Colonial mass–drive, and that was what bothered Captain Sansin.

'Maybe survivors of the apocalypse?' he suggested.

Lael shook her head, her short–cropped and metallically–tinted hair flickering as it caught the light.

'Too old,' she replied, never looking up from her display. 'The wave is several light years wide and extremely weak, so it must have been left here many years ago.'

'Before the apocalypse?' Andaim echoed Lael's statement. 'What the hell was a Colonial vessel doing beyond the Icari Line way back then? There's only a single ship that officially went that far, before the Icari made first contact. You don't think…?'

'Maybe,' Idris replied, and then looked across to the Executive Officer's chair to speak to Mikhain. Idris had to catch himself as he remembered that his former XO was now aboard Arcadia as its captain, and he had yet to select a suitable replacement. He looked instead to Lael. 'Can you determine if the trail was left by a civilian vessel?'

Lael frowned as she studied her screen, and the captain noticed Andaim next to him also scrutinizing an identical display of his own.

'Gravity wake suggests an older design of mass–drive, possibly a civilian venture, and given the age of the wake itself…'

'It could be her,' Andaim confirmed as he leaned back in his seat. 'It could be Endeavour.'

Captain Idris Sansin sat for only a moment before he called out a series of commands.

'Bring us out of super–luminal, effective in ninety seconds. Helm, lay in a pursuit course. Lael, prepare to signal Arcadia and send them our data as soon as we drop into sub–luminal cruise, although I doubt they will have failed to spot and identify the same trail.'

'Aye, cap'n,' came a chorus of replies as Idris leaned thoughtfully back in his seat.

'Endeavour,' Andaim murmured beside him. 'Nobody ever knew what happened to her.'

'We might be about to find out.'

They waited as the ship's computer ran a diagnostic on the wake trail, and then a small beep from Lael's station signalled the completion of the scan. Lael's eyes widened slightly and she look at the captain.

'Computer confirms a Mark III mass–drive, Colonial design, registered to civilian vessel Endeavour, hull mass one hundred thousand tonnes. It's her, captain. We found Endeavour.'

***

III

The bridge fell silent as the command crew considered the implications of their discovery.

'A pristine ship,' the captain said. 'She was launched so long ago, she might have had no contact at all with the Word or the Legion. Her crew might even still be alive.'

Ever since mankind had found his way into space, from the very first dangerous and yet thrilling rockets that had soared into Ethera's atmosphere along with the dreams of the men aboard them, to the cosmos–travelling ships like Atlantia, a means had been sought to overcome the natural physical laws that governed the universe. The greatest of those laws was that no object of mass could ever reach or exceed the speed of light. It had been the universal constant, a single immovable law that governed everything in the visible universe. Engineers had spent decades searching for a solution to this crippling obstacle to true galactic exploration, seeking ever more powerful engines that propelled star ships to ever increasing velocities, but none ever had broken through the speed of light.

Until just a few decades prior to the keel of the Atlantia being laid.

It had, as so often was the case, taken a genius to figure it out: a man capable of thinking beyond the cube. Deri Feyen, an astrophycisist and theorist, had realised that everybody had been going about it all the wrong way. The laws of physics stated, quite clearly, that no object of mass could exceed the speed of light. Light itself, comprised of photons, moved at the speed of light because, uniquely, they had no mass. Therefore, Feyen reasoned, rather than produce ever–more massive engines one only had to figure out a way to negate mass in order to accelerate to, and controversially, *beyond* the speed of light.

It was Feyen's manipulation of the fundamental particles that gave objects mass that opened a window onto space travel like nothing the colonies had ever seen. Theorizing that if a particle existed that gave atoms mass, then there should by logic be a way to manipulate photons to take advantage of their massless properties, Feyen devised a mass–drive. Put simply, the drive surrounded the parent vessel in a sphere of negative mass that perfectly offset and cancelled out the vessel's natural mass: it became, in effect, massless.

Pioneer, the first vessel to test Feyen's mass drive, launched just a few years before the great man's death. It accelerated using its normal fusion–core powered ion engines to a velocity that generated enough energy to engage the mass drive, upon which moment the tremendous thrust provided by its ion engines accelerated it up to and beyond the speed of light in a matter of moments. What was more, the massless nature of the vessel meant that many of the mind–bending effects of faster–than–light travel were also negated: the vessel did not travel in time as any vessel of normal mass would. What Feyen had achieved was a means to traverse the stars and not return home to find the graves of the young and healthy friends and family you left behind, overgrown from decades or even centuries of neglect, when you had been travelling at super–luminal velocity for only a few months.

The exploration of the cosmos had begun and within a few years mankind was spreading out into the galaxy and finding new worlds and new species. Much of the time those species were little more than algae floating in pools of boiling water on barren, volatile worlds. Sometimes, they were sentient species that bore little relation to the human form: one, the Icari, were tenuous beings who drifted like tendrils in the atmospheres of giant stars and communicated by light waves. The Icari had been the first species to make direct contact with humans, having detected mankind's ability to directly observe other stars and terrestrial planets–the hallmark of an intelligent species reaching a technological level sufficient to initiate *first contact*. Others species still, like the Vetra, were bipedal and recognisably human in form but for their small, stocky stature: a consequence of their homeworld's intense gravity.

A few years before the Icari had contacted mankind and established the Icari Line, a single vessel had left Ethera's orbit on an astounding voyage. Funded by crowd–sourcing and utilising what had then been the most advanced version of a mass–drive available, Endeavour had been built in Etheran orbit and designed to simply travel to the stars with a compliment of crew large enough to indefinitely sustain a population aboard. Millions of intrepid Etherans volunteered for what was advertised as a *'place aboard history'*, the unique opportunity to witness man's first tentative reach for the stars, to be present at the first birth beyond the solar system, the first death, the first landing upon a foreign world capable of supporting human life, of which many had been detected by remote observation.

Endeavour had launched with the entire core systems watching, and sailed out into history. Four months later she signalled the birth of a young girl, the first deep–space Etheran birth. Headed for a stellar cluster some one hundred light years distant from Ethera, she had continued to signal home for three years, until she had suddenly fallen silent.

No signal was ever received from Endeavour again, nor had any ship caught sight of her or detected her presence in any form.

'Almost a hundred years,' Andaim murmured to himself. 'If it's her, she could still have her compliment aboard. But the Word was present even back then. We can't guarantee that Endeavour is clean of infection.'

Idris nodded in agreement. The Word, a creation of quantum physics, was in effect a computer. It had evolved out of a major milestone in human engineering, *The Field*: a digital record of all information that had been accessible to all humans. The growth of human knowledge had accelerated, reaching all corners of the colonies through the sharing of information, and technology had likewise grown and expanded at a phenomenal rate. This massive database of information had been fused with quantum computing by a team led by another scientific legend, Dr Ceyen Lazarus, to create The Word, a depository of knowledge designed to be able to make decisions based on pure logic and an understanding of myriad complexities that were beyond the human capacity to assimilate and thus form cohesive responses and policies. Tasked with find solutions to the most complex problems in history, ranging from space exploration to crime to medicine, the Word eventually became the founder of laws, the arbitrator of justice and the icon of mankind's prolific creativity.

The one thing that nobody on Ethera had predicted was that the Word, through its sheer volume of thought and understanding, would have concluded that mankind was a greater threat to itself than any other species and thus must be either controlled or eradicated. Thus had been born the Legion, and mankind silently infected long before anybody even realised what was about to happen. However, when it had arrived, the Word's apocalypse was so swift and so brutal that nobody had been able to figure out just when its plan for domination began. The early quantum machines that led to the conception of the Word were far older than the mass–drive, having been created almost two centuries before: indeed, it was the quantum computer's immense capacity for calculations that had led to the technology that made the mass–drive possible at all.

'The first laws laid down by the Word appeared before Endeavour was even conceived,' Idris said finally. 'It's possible that she is every bit infected as most of the rest of humanity was. We'll have to assume that she is a hostile vessel and that we'll be boarding under fire. Have General Bra'hiv assemble his Marines, and prepare to signal Arcadia to likewise prepare for an assault as soon as we locate Endeavour.'

'Preparing to drop out of super–luminal in fifteen seconds,' Lael called, her voice broadcasting across the ship in a ghostly echo that was just audible on the bridge.

'We can't fix her current location,' Andaim informed the captain as he scanned the readouts on his display screen. 'The wake is too old, but we'll be within an hour or two of her and should be able to detect her on radar.'

'Don't use radar. Go passive upon sub–luminal,' the captain instructed. 'We'll treat this as though we're tracking an enemy vessel.'

'Aye, cap'n. Sensors passive, all systems stand–by.'

Lael's voice echoed through the frigate.

'Sub–luminal velocity in five, four, three, two, one...'

Atlantia surged as her mass–drive disengaged and all at once a hundred thousand tonnes of metal decelerated from high sub–luminal to deep space cruise. The captain's experienced gaze immediately detected Arcadia's presence alongside Atlantia on the readouts as Andaim's orders snapped out.

'QRA launch, bays one through four, go now!'

Even as he spoke a screen showing the launch bay depicted four sleek, aggressive looking Raython fighters accelerating under full power along their magnetic catapults, the craft flung through narrow gaps in the still–opening bay doors as they rocketed out into space. Idris glanced at display screens around the bridge now showing dense star fields where previously there had been nothing but blackness.

'Status?' he demanded.

'Mass drive disengaged and stable,' Andaim replied. 'Four Raythons launched, two more just launching from Arcadia. No other craft in the vicinity at short range, waiting for long range passive scopes to detect emissions.'

Idris turned as a display screen near his seat flickered into life and Mikhain's rugged features appeared upon it.

'Did you detect the signal?' Mikhain asked promptly. 'Is it Endeavour?'

'We did,' Idris replied with a grin of pleasure at Mikhain's keenly developed situational awareness. It was likely that the exact same discussion had occurred aboard Arcadia's bridge and that the newly promoted captain had anticipated Idris's decision to drop out of super–luminal cruise, a fact that provoked a great sense of comfort in Idris. 'It could be a false positive but at this distance from the core systems I think it unlikely.'

'Agreed,' Mikhain replied, 'I have refrained from informing the ship's compliment of the discovery for now. Whatever's out there, let's wait until we see it with our own eyes before we start singing happy campfire songs. What about Taron Forge?'

'We still have his trail,' Idris confirmed as he glanced briefly at another display that traced the pirate captain's course. Forge had been present during the battle on Chiron IV a month previously, and until now had represented the best chance of Atlantia and Arcadia safely navigating the uncharted cosmos beyond the Icari Line, a barrier that represented no obstacle to the lawless. 'Wherever he's going it's not here, but there's no rush to pursue him.'

'You think that he knows about Endeavour?' Mikhain asked. 'Could he also have picked up the trail?'

Idris glanced at Lael, who shook her head as she replied.

'Atlantia's sensor array is huge and we barely spotted the signal. Taron's ship just isn't large enough to be capable of detecting such weak gravitational waves.'

'It's just us then,' Idris agreed. 'Let's see what we've really got here.'

'Captain,' Lael called. 'You're being summoned to the sanctuary. The Governing Council has demanded a briefing on what is happening.'

Idris ground his teeth in his skull and glanced at Andaim. 'You have the bridge.'

***

IV

The sanctuary was a vast rotating cylinder buried deep inside Atlantia's hull, the motion of the cylinder effectively replicating Ethera's natural gravity and the interior mimicking its topography and climate. Although the scale of the sanctuary was an illusion, the fresh air and bright blue sky never failed to fill Idris Sansin with a sense of home, something to brighten his darkening mood as he strode from the sanctuary entrance across a rolling hillside toward the communities.

Most of Atlantia's civilian contingent lived inside the sanctuary, which itself was originally designed to house prison staff on long tours far from home. Retired from active service two decades previously, Atlantia's role prior to the apocalypse had been as a prison ship. Atlantia's service as a military frigate would never have allowed such luxurious accommodation, but civilian staff required more elegant surrounding to soften the blow of guarding high–security convicts in orbiting prisons.

Idris walked down into a small forest, torn between the desire to hurry and get the meeting over with and the need to enjoy the brief respite from the rest of the frigate's stale air and crowded grey decks. A tight knot of homesteads appeared ahead, nestled within the trees, and outside in the sunshine stood a small crowd of men and women, each wearing smart suits typical of an Etheran government that no longer existed.

Idris had been forced by the needs of the civilian community to allow a series of votes that had installed members of the community into roles as councillors to replace those lost in prior attacks by the Legion. Despite running a military vessel it had become clear that without an effective voice the civilians were becoming as much of a threat as the Word, discontent rife among their ranks. In all, four councillors had been voted into power, and another single person to liaise directly with the command crew. That single person, to Idris's dismay, had been his wife.

Far from being the supportive and sympathetic voice that he had hoped, Meyanna Sansin had in fact become a thorn in his side, often countering sage security decisions with claims of human–rights violations, excessive surveillance and heavy–handed policing of the civilian contingent with no consideration for the plight of the human race: any weakness or lack of oversight could result in humanity's final and complete destruction, a fact oft–repeated by Idris and equally often ignored by the council. It had already nearly happened twice before, and Idris had no intention of allowing the do–gooders among the council to compromise the iron wall of security he had used to defend Atlantia.

'Captain,' Councillor Gredan greeted him, 'so glad you could find time to join us.'

Gredan was a balding fifty–something who had somehow managed to remain obese despite the limited rations available to Atlantia's compliment. His handshake was limp and damp, and Idris twisted his face into something approaching a smile as he attempted to disguise his revulsion.

'Councillors,' he greeted them as one, 'you requested an update?'

'Please,' Gredan gestured, 'this way.'

Gredan led the way into one of the homesteads, which had been converted into a sort of town hall. To Idris's surprise it was filled with perhaps one hundred civilians, some with children in their laps, others elderly, a mixture of families related to prison warders, Marines, pilots and engineers that made up Atlantia's crew and who had been fortunate enough to be aboard when the Word's apocalypse had consumed Ethera.

In front of the crowd was a long table behind which the four councillors sat, and in their centre was Meyanna. She smiled at him briefly, a sign of recognition diluted by her need to be seen as unbiased in her treatment of the needs of the civilian contingent. Along with Councillor Gredan were Councillors Ayek, a stern–looking elderly woman who regarded the military as little more than brutes; Vaughn, a younger man whom Idris regarded as power–hungry and keen to advance his own career, and Ishira Morle, a former merchant captain who had been rescued from Chiron IV on a previous mission, and in Idris's opinion was the only sane person on the entire board.

'Ladies and gentlemen,' Gredan announced as he took his seat and surveyed the crowd. 'Our captain is a busy man and can spare us little time, so we'll begin without preamble.'

Somehow, Gredan made the captain's lack of time sound like an accusation and had arranged the seating to vaguely resemble a court of law, with Idris now standing before a row of judges.

'Atlantia has emerged from the safety of super–luminal travel into deep space,' Gredan announced imperiously. 'Why?'

'That's classified,' Idris replied.

A silence enveloped the hall which Idris enjoyed immensely. Truth was, it wasn't classified at all, but if Idris had to waste his time standing in front of Gredan and his lackeys then he might as well have some fun with them.

'Classified?' Gredan echoed. 'I thought that the purpose of this council was to appraise our people of Atlantia's mission?'

'It is,' Idris confirmed. 'When I know precisely the nature of that mission, you will be informed as agreed.'

'You don't have a mission?' Ayek snapped as though Idris were some kind of amateur masquerading as a captain.

'We do,' Idris replied, maintaining a calm persona. 'The nature of that mission remains, as of this time, unclear in its parameters.'

'I don't understand,' Ayek peered at him.

'That is why you do not command a military frigate, ma'am.'

Ayek reared up somewhat in her seat as though she might snort flames out of her nostrils at him, but Ishira came to his rescue with a wry grin touching her young features.

'I think that the captain is referring to the fluidity of the situation,' she said. 'Perhaps a discovery has been made that has yet to be fully quantified?'

Idris inclined his head toward Ishira. 'Correct.'

'I think that the civilian contingent would appreciate some further understanding of this discovery,' Gredan insisted.

'I'm sure they would.'

A further silence followed. Idris fielded the angry stares from the council without concern, aware that his wife was also glaring at him. He knew that he could not needle them forever, but their insistence on being informed of every detail of ship–board life was wearying, as was their demands of his time.

'Is there any need for you to be quite so evasive?' Meyanna asked finally. 'The civilians further afield in the sanctuary are keen to know what's happening and we have to go back to them with something. If we have nothing, they'll lose confidence in the council's influence aboard ship and this will have all been for nothing.'

Idris smiled at his wife but said nothing as he let the silence build.

Vaughn stood up from his seat and pointed at the crowd behind Idris. 'It is not us demanding information from you, captain. It is the people. It's not us that you're insulting by refusing to divulge facts to, it's them. Why don't you turn around and stonewall what remains of humanity a bit more, just to amuse yourself?'

Vaughn wore an expression of deep disgust and anger, one that Idris imagined he might have practiced in a mirror many times before. He heard a rumbling from behind him as the crowd shifted in their seats and came one step closer to crying out for more information, demanding that he yield to their *right–to–know*.

'That's a very good idea,' Idris replied as he surveyed the panel of councillors, determined to turn Vaughn's self–righteous oratory against him. 'Their combined experience of military matters will, by numbers at least, exceed yours, councillors.'

Idris turned on the spot before any of the councillors could respond, and the crowd of civilians behind him fell silent as he addressed them.

'Our sensors detected a Colonial gravity wake while in super–luminal cruise and we decided to pursue the wake in preference to our tracking of the pirate Taron Forge. The result of this tracking is that we believe we may have located the vessel known as Endeavour.'

A rush of whispers and gasps rippled through the crowd as Gredan spoke from behind the captain.

'*The* Endeavour? There could be survivors aboard.'

'That ship has been missing for a century,' Vaughn replied. 'She could have discovered huge amounts about the cosmos behind the Icari Line. She could be our saviour!'

Ayek stood from her seat. 'Captain, I demand that we intercept Endeavour immediately and discover what her captain has to say for himself!'

The hum of whispers filling the hall fell silent as Idris slowly turned to face Ayek. The prim little woman lifted her chin before his gaze.

'You demand?' Idris echoed.

'It is the will of the people whom we represent,' Ayek fired back. 'This is no longer a military matter but a concern for us all, and we shall be informed of each and every decision that is made by Atlantia's command crew.'

Idris, his hands behind his back, glowered down at her.

'You would have us board a ship that could be infected by the Legion or perhaps something even worse, without any precautionary measures, based only on the idea that lots of civilians can be more right that a small, highly trained crew?'

Ayek's resolve stiffened. 'That's not what I said.'

'No, it's what you demanded,' Idris replied. 'I have to admit that I'm surprised, not by the demand but by the fact that you made it before Vaughn managed to get on his soapbox again. He likes the exposure.'

A faint ripple of laughter drifted across the crowd behind Idris.

'This is not a moment for humour,' Vaughn snapped. 'We have the right to speak to Endeavour's captain! This could be an historic moment!'

'It certainly would be,' Idris agreed, 'if Endeavour's captain turns out to still be alive for a chat at one hundred and forty years old!'

Open laughter burst out from behind Idris, and despite Meyanna's angry expression the captain found himself enjoying the encounter far more than he had dared to believe possible.

'Captain,' Ayek began, 'I demand an apology for this pointless trivialisation of our mission to…'

'And I demand an apology for being dragged here for nothing more than to bolster your own self–importance!' Idris roared, silencing both the council and the crowd behind him. He calmed himself in the deep silence that followed. 'This council was formed to give voice to the concerns of the civilians and to provide a means to pass information to them from the command crew, not to interrogate senior officers! With the exception of Councillor Morle none of you have any military or spacefaring command experience and yet you presume to give orders to the captain of this ship! Perhaps I should start dishing out medical advice to Doctor Sansin while she is performing surgery? Perhaps Councillor Ayek would like to advise me on the details of solar gravitational trajectory distortions in super–luminal flight, or the effects of plasma bombardment on defensive shield currents?'

The board of councillors remained silent as Idris glared at them one by one.

'I am more than happy to provide you, on a daily basis, with what information I can on our missions. I am all too aware that when Atlantia is under threat, so too is her entire compliment of civilians. But do not presume that your roles here are anything more than advisory. The last time a councillor attempted to take control of this vessel they were consumed by the Legion, literally, and their actions almost cost the lives of the entire ship's compliment.' Idris turned to face the civilians behind him once more. 'I will inform you of what is happening, and what we intend to do about it, as soon as I know myself. Is that acceptable to you, the people who voted for this council?'

The civilians exchanged glances and nodded in silence.

'Perhaps we could help you with that,' Gredan said from behind Idris, 'if your time is indeed so limited.' Idris turned as the overweight councillor stood from his seat. 'I propose that one of us accompany the captain aboard Atlantia's bridge, and relay pertinent information back here to the council, to provide a more reliable flow of news for the people.'

Idris opened his mouth to protest, but his wife spoke first. 'All those in favour?'

Over a hundred voices chanted *aye* in unison, the commingled response filling the hall and seeming to echo as Idris fumed in silence.

'I'll take the first watch,' Gredan volunteered himself. 'If that concurs with your desire to keep our civilians in the loop, captain?'

Idris glared at the council for a moment, and then he spun on his heel. Without looking back, Idris marched from the homestead and outside as he aimed for the sanctuary exit beyond the nearby forest. He had not made it to the treeline before he heard hurried footfalls behind him and he looked over his shoulder to see his wife storming in pursuit.

'I hope that you're satisfied!'

'What, that one of those cronies will be hovering around on my bridge?' Idris demanded as Meyanna fell into line beside him and tried to keep up. 'I thought that you wanted a voice for the people, not to police the ship for me.'

'The only thing that needs policing is your attitude,' Meyanna snapped. 'You realise that if you keep patronising the council they'll actively start conspiring against you? It's the basis for all political posturing.'

'I don't give a damn about politics,' Idris shot back.

'Well I do,' Meyanna said as she stopped and let her husband keep walking, 'and so do the civilians because it's the only way for them to be heard now. You either talk to them through the council, or the council will use them to over–rule you.'

***

V

'Launch our alert fighters and ensure that all shuttles and Corsairs are on stand–by. If this goes south I want our full arsenal prepared for combat!'

Mikhain's orders rang out across Arcadia's bridge as his crew hurried to carry them out. Mikhain stood beside his chair and looked about him with a pride that only a full command could provoke in a man: the sight of the nerve–centre of a massive, heavily armed Colonial frigate at battle quarters and entirely under his control invigorated him like a drug, an addiction that he knew he would never be able to control.

'Atlantia's fighters are aloft,' came the call from Lieutenant Scott, Mikhain's new tactical officer. Young and inexperienced, Scott was scrutinising his display screens with an intensity born of unfamiliarity, struggling to keep up with the flow of information. 'Reaper Flight establishing a combat air patrol, Renegade Flight maintaining close fleet–defence.'

'Order our fighters to support them but to stay out of their way. Let Atlantia's people run the show for now, they have more experience.'

'Aye, cap'n,' Scott replied.

Mikhain watched as his communications officer, Shah, spoke with Lael aboard Atlantia, her brow furrowed as she concentrated on the signals information coming in from the gravitational wake of what they all hoped would be Endeavour. Long black hair snaked down across her shoulders, one of her eyes covered with a patch that gave her a vaguely piratical appearance. A former convict aboard Atlantia Five, she had proven herself aboard Atlantia and been promoted to support Mikhain.

A nearby screen monitored Arcadia's launch bays as four Raythons, piloted by crews borrowed from Atlantia's compliment until new pilots could be trained and attached permanently to Arcadia, ran their engines up to full power. The Raythons rocketed down their magnetic catapults moments later and roared away from the frigate to join a close–quarters fleet defence patrol, and for a few brief moments Mikhain was no longer a member of the last fleet of human Colonial vessels alive in the universe but an Executive Officer once more and part of the Colonial Fleet's massive arsenal. He realised to his surprise in that brief moment of recollection that he would in fact be willing to give up his command position, were doing so able to take them all back in time to a place where the Word did not yet exist, where Ethera was not a wasteland and where humanity's great journey into the unknown was still a dream filled with hope and promise.

'Contact, bow bearing three–eight five, elevation plus four!'

Mikhain snapped out of his reverie as he watched the main display on the bridge switch to a dense star field, the optical sensors magnifying the view a thousand–fold in a matter of seconds as they zeroed in on the distant contact.

'Emissions?' Mikhain asked.

'Negative,' came the reply from the tactical officer, 'no broadcast, no mass–drive signature, no signs of life at this range but we're still too far away.'

'How far?' Mikhain pressed, angry that Lieutenant Scott had not imparted the essential information immediately but unwilling to scold at this early stage in his fledgling career.

'Two astronomical units,' Scott replied swiftly, clearly aware of his error, 'two hours at maximum sub–luminal cruise.'

Mikhain nodded. An astronomical unit was the distance between their homeworld of Ethera and her parent star, and used as a standard measurement of sub–luminal travel.

'Mikhain, do you have her?'

Captain Idris Sansin's voice cut across Arcadia's bridge chatter.

'Bearing three eight five, elevation plus four,' Mikhain replied without taking his eyes off the image of the star field. 'Stand by for visual identification.'

The optical sensors adjusted and as Mikhain watched the star field sharpened, countless millions of distant stellar objects flickering into sharp focus. For a moment he could detect nothing moving against the glittering background, but then a digital overlay appeared, a diamond–shaped green box hovering over what looked like empty space.

Mikhain walked closer to the screen, as though the act of a few paces could sufficiently close the tremendous distances between the two ships, and then he saw a tiny star blink out and then reappear as it was eclipsed by something drifting in the absolute blackness.

'Visual,' Mikhain murmured, 'awaiting data stream. Activate radar systems, light it up!'

Arcadia's sensors came out of stand–by while Atlantia's remained passive, and it scanned the distant vessel, computers crunching the returning data into something that could be assessed and understood by human eyes. Moments later, alongside the star fields appeared a geometric image of the target, mapped by lasers and converted into a simple vector plot of shape, size and estimated mass.

'It's her,' Mikhain confirmed. 'It's Endeavour.'

'*Very well,*' Idris replied from Atlantia. '*All craft lay in an intercept course, Raythons at the tip of the spear.*'

'Aye, cap'n,' Mikhain replied, more out of habit than anything else as he turned to his helmsman, an experienced pilot with a metallic prosthetic arm named Stefan Morle who had recently joined the Arcadia's crew as a volunteer. 'Helm, come left onto three eight five, elevation plus four.'

'Left three eight five, elevation plus four,' Stefan confirmed.

Mikhain watched as Atlantia mimicked Arcadia's turn, and the two frigates headed toward the distant contact as their Raythons raced away ahead of them.

'XO on the deck!'

Mikhain turned as his Executive Officer strode onto the bridge. A tall, muscular man with a broad jaw and blond hair that framed bitterly cold eyes, Djimon joined Mikhain and observed the new contact with interest.

'A little late, XO, wouldn't you agree?' Mikhain growled beneath his breath as the giant man moved to stand alongside him.

'I was feeling sleepy,' Djimon murmured back without concern. 'What is that on the screen?'

Mikhain restrained his anger at Djimon's flippant disregard for authority as he replied.

'That is the Endeavour, something you would know already if you bothered to report on duty on time.'

Djimon shrugged as he stared at the screens. Mikhain turned to Lieutenant Scott. 'You have the bridge. XO, with me!'

Mikhain stormed down off the command platform, the giant blond man following with a casual gait. Mikhain made his way off the bridge and down the corridor outside to his quarters, the door sliding open as he approached. He walked inside and moved behind his desk as Djimon followed him in and the door hissed shut behind him.

'So how long do you think that you can keep this charade up?' Mikhain snapped.

'Are you talking about me captain, or yourself?'

'I promoted you!' Mikhain almost shouted, then forced himself to keep his voice down in case anybody outside his quarters overheard. 'That was our deal! The least you could do is take the role of the second–most senior officer aboard the entire ship seriously!'

Djimon grinned.

'I take my role very seriously,' he insisted. 'But I don't intend to dance a little ditty to your power games, Mikhain. We both know how you got here and it's not pretty, is it? Any time I like, I can send the evidence I possess across to Captain Sansin and have you removed from your post and subject to Maroon Protocol. Perhaps it really is *you* who should be taking your role seriously, don't you think?'

Mikhain gritted his teeth, his jaw aching as he leaned his balled fists on the deck and glared at the former Marine before him.

'There's only so much I'll take, Djimon,' he snarled. 'Fulfil your duties aboard this ship and there will be no problem. Keep undermining my authority, keep ignoring the importance of the Executive Officer's position, keep making me think that you'll turn traitor at any moment and it won't be me doing the worrying for much longer.'

Djimon's smile, devoid of warmth or humour, did not slip as he took a pace closer to the captain's desk.

'Is that a threat, Mikhain?'

'It's *captain*, to you.'

'No, it isn't,' Djimon replied. 'This is a power trip for you, a moment of glory, and you have it only because I allowed it to happen. How quickly you forget how you came to be here at all.'

Mikhain's promotion to captain of Arcadia had come at the expense of several lives, not all of them human. Djimon, a former Marine sergeant of General Bra'hiv's Alpha Company, had fought a long and bitter battle with Corporal Qayin of Bravo Company, Qayin a former convict who had been recruited to serve as a soldier. The giant, dark–skinned criminal with the glowing bioluminescent tattoos lacing his face had been the epitome of danger until his betrayal by Mikhain. Mikhain had joined forces with the beleaguered Djimon, and together they had conspired against both Captain Sansin and his supporters, narrowly escaping the entire charade with their reputations intact. Little had Mikhain known that Djimon had recorded their conversations, neatly laying the trap that Mikhain had fallen into. His every move and every act was now watched by Djimon, who had gained his remarkable promotion through nothing less than blackmail.

'So do you,' Mikhain snarled back. 'Doesn't it ever occur to you that should you push me too far I could just reveal everything to Captain Sansin myself? Clear the air, so to speak? If I go down, Djimon, you inevitably come with me.'

'Perhaps,' Djimon sneered back. 'But then again I was only following orders, was I not? It was you who forced me to obtain pass–codes, to lie and to steal in order to fuel your greedy run for power aboard Atlantia. I was only a lowly Corporal, not the Executive Officer aboard the frigate.'

Djimon smiled again. 'Besides, it's not down to Captain Sansin alone anymore. We have a Board of Councillors now to speak for the civilians. Their views and votes will count too.'

'This is a military matter!' Mikhain snapped. 'A court martial will decide our fates!'

'Yes it will and the blows will fall harder on you than me, but let's agree that such a terrible fate will not occur. As long as we all keep calm, as long as you stay off my back and keep basking in your glory as Arcadia's commander, everybody will be happy, agreed?'

Djimon did not wait for a reply from Mikhain. Instead, in a flagrant disregard for protocol he turned his back to the captain and strolled casually away with one hand in his pocket for the cabin door.

As he reached it, Mikhain spoke once more.

'The role of Executive Officer is that of captain in reserve,' he said to the former Marine's broad, muscular back. 'So far, Djimon, you have displayed before the command crew and myself a stark inability to perform your duties. They do not yet trust you, I cannot rely on you and I know damned well that Captain Sansin thinks you a poor choice for the role. If you do not step up your game it won't be me removing you from your post that you'll have to worry about. That same Council will do it for me, regardless of how I plead.'

Djimon did not look back at Mikhain. The cabin door opened and the XO strolled out and vanished.

Mikhain expelled a blast of air from his lungs as he sank down into his seat. Before him on the desk, countersunk into the metal, a long list of requests from across the entire vessel glowed on a display screen, a new one added every few seconds or so.

The pride and excitement he had briefly experienced upon the bridge withered away until only the endless labour of command remained to drag down heavily upon his shoulders.

***

VI

Deep space.

It had never been somewhere he had been keen to go before, having spent most of his life stalking Ethera's mean streets hawking the kind of chemicals that made the horrors of life seem like a memory, at least for a while. For those that abused them enough, a memory was indeed all that life became.

Qayin smiled in the darkness at his own bleak humour.

The cockpit of the gunship was not large, just four seats – two at the controls and two behind. The colourful array of instruments and lights glowed in the peaceful darkness, his face seeming to reflect them like a mirror as the bioluminescent tattoos that coiled upon his cheeks glowed and pulsed in silent rhythm to his heart.

Beyond the cockpit through the viewing panel was a vast panorama of stars, and to his left the more powerful glow of a Red Dwarf star, one of several in the local systems, named Avalere. Qayin knew the system to be uncharted, and also to be a regular haunt for the kind of people who liked to avoid Colonial interference. The carefully kept logs of the original owner of the gunship, the deceased pirate king Salim Phaeon, had directed Qayin to this corner of the cosmos primarily because he needed supplies for his ship and somewhere to lay low while he figured out his next move. Stashed in the hold were several drums of tainted Devlamine, a powerful drug worth good money on any market–all Qayin needed to do was filter and refine the supply, and then he would possess the kind of currency that was accepted no matter where one travelled. So far, he had only refined a few small containers of the drug as evidence to potential business partners of its quality.

Qayin wondered briefly why he had never thought of becoming a spacer before. The solitude suited him well, most people representing little more to Qayin than mildly annoying distractions in his pursuit of wealth and security, of power and control. He guessed he had daddy issues, which wasn't surprising because his daddy had been a violent, drunk loser who had routinely beaten Qayin for years. Qayin had fled his meagre home as a teenager, leaving his mother behind at the hands of his cruel father for five long years as he forged himself a life on the streets. Then he had returned, years older, a foot taller and nearly twice as heavy, his body a sculpture of solid muscle, his densely braided hair tinted metallic blue and gold and the tattoos on his face glowing with malevolent beauty. *The Mark of Qayin.*

His father had not recognised the towering man who had strode through his door, although he had clearly recognised the danger radiating from Qayin like a force field. Qayin's mother, broken and weak, had recognised her son in a heartbeat and, to Qayin's shock and dismay, thrown herself in front of his father before he could reach out and crush the man's throat with one giant hand.

There had been a reckoning, before Qayin had left. He had made it clear, quite clear, the pain his father would endure if his mother were to be found anything but healthy and happy. Coward that his father truly was, he had quivered and blubbed and agreed as Qayin's mother had sat in shame and listened. Qayin had offered his mother protection, money, anything that she required, before leaving and never going back.

Ten years later, the apocalypse had struck. Qayin had no idea if his parents were alive or not, or even if they were still alive beforehand. He hoped not. Life had been a struggle for his mother and apparently an irritation for his father. Qayin reflected that they both could have used a decent dose of Devlamine from time to time, the *Devil's Drink*, Qayin's drug of choice when dealing on Ethera's streets.

Qayin sighed and leaned back in the pilot's seat. Life was for most people, by and large, just one misery after another punctuated by moments of joy that were all too brief and often ruined by the next disaster. He had witnessed in his years nothing but the sight of people suffering; lack of money, hated jobs, unrequited love, lost love, illness, failed hopes and dreams and countless other afflictions, as well as the sight of Captain Idris Sansin and his hopeless band of followers hoping to fight the Word and bring back all that misery once more.

Qayin preferred the simple life. Worry about nothing. Care about nobody. Look after one's self and enjoy that simple life while it lasted because, as the old saying went, everybody's a long time dead and no matter what you did in life, nobody gives a damn anyway once you're gone. Qayin leaned back, his fingers interlocked between his blue and gold hair, and closed his eyes as he enjoyed the silence and the solitude enveloping him in its warm embrace.

A soft beeping sound intruded upon his serene mood and he opened one eye with a flare of irritation as he sought the source of the sound. Qayin was not an experienced captain, and while he could navigate a spacecraft from A to B and had a rudimentary knowledge of how to remain undetected, he wasn't exactly a fighter pilot. He scanned the control panel and saw a flashing red light:

PROXIMITY WARNING

Qayin bolted upright in his seat as with one deft flick of a switch he deactivated the autopilot that had been guiding him into the uncharted system and sought the source of the collision warning. A small display screen showed the view from the rear of the gunship, but Qayin could see no sign of any vessels following him. He flicked a switch, changing the display to one that would indicate where the threat was coming from.

The screen flickered.

A deafening crash shuddered through the vessel and Qayin was slammed sideways in his seat as something smashed into the port hull. The silence of the cockpit was shattered by the blast of alarm claxons shrieking for his attention as Qayin desperately began scrambling over the controls in an attempt to contain whatever damage had been done to the hull.

His first thought was that the shields had failed, but he saw them at one hundred per cent and holding firm. Then he saw the alert displays showing the ruptured hull plating and the loss of atmosphere.

'No!'

Qayin grabbed the controls as he threw the ship's throttles open and hurled the gunship into a tight defensive turn. With a dexterity born of absolute necessity, Qayin remotely shut off the bulkheads to the damaged section of the hull from the cockpit as he simultaneously selected the ship's plasma weapons. Qayin, cautious as ever, had emerged from super–luminal into the Avalere system with his plasma magazines fully charged, just in case anybody made the foolish mistake of attacking him.

The gunship arced through its turn, Qayin peering out of the cockpit and searching for any sign of whatever had collided with him. He saw a trail of sparkling debris sweep through his field of vision as the ship turned back toward the point of impact, the remnants of the damage caused to his gunship.

'Son of a...'

Qayin's curse was cut off as another impact shook the gunship and fresh alarms blared in his ears as the hull was again ruptured, this time from directly below.

Qayin roared in rage as he hauled the throttles into reverse power and pushed forward on the control column. The gunship nosed down as Qayin sought to aim his weapons at whatever had struck his gunship, and almost immediately he saw the shape of a snub–nosed, battered looking craft aiming directly at him, debris surrounding it from where it had rammed his ship.

'Time to give you the good news!' Qayin shouted as he locked his weapons onto the enemy ship and wasted no time in squeezing the trigger.

A bright stream of plasma rounds blasted away from the heavily armed gunship and impacted the enemy craft's bow in a brilliant halo of destruction. Qayin cheered in delight as the multiple rounds smashed through the smaller vessel and it exploded as its fusion core was ruptured.

The brilliant fireball blazed with fearsome power before Qayin and he shielded his eyes until it faded. The clatter of debris from the vaporised ship rattled past Qayin's vessel, an expanding ball of superheated gas glowing briefly in the light from the distant dwarf star until it was chilled by the bitter vacuum of space. Within a few moments, all that remained of the vessel was an expanding constellation of debris and ice crystals drifting in the endless void.

'Nice to meet you,' Qayin uttered.

He turned his attention to the gunship's battered hull and began closing bulkheads to the affected areas, mostly in the aft holds. Fortunately, the fusion cores and engines were mounted quite high at the stern and had escaped the worst of the second impact. Qayin closed the bulkheads one by one and re-routed the power away from the affected areas to avoid electrical fires, before he decided to play it safe and dispense fire-retardant foam into the holds just in case.

The blaring alarms fell silent one by one until the cockpit was quiet once more. Qayin checked his radar screens for any further sign of impending attack, and saw nothing but the empty void all the way out toward Avalere and the small moons orbiting the lonely star.

He reset course for Avalere III, the moon that according to Salim's logs held a small, un-licenced spaceport where he could land. Qayin cursed—he had gone from being in profit to having to think about how much it was going to cost him to repair the damage to a large gunship's hull. He realised that he did not really have the first clue whether there would be anybody on the moon who could perform the work, or even the nearest star system where there might be facilities to do so. With Ethera and the core systems completely overwhelmed by the Word, he realised that there was nowhere else to go.

'This is why you never became a spacer,' Qayin said out loud to himself.

Damn. Why the hell had that idiotic pirate tried to ram him instead of opening fire with its plasma cannons anyway? Sure, it had been a smaller and older vessel and maybe their weapons had not been sufficient to disable Qayin's ship in one ambush attack, but then why the hell risk their own vessel in such a reckless manner? The gunship's shields were no use against solid objects, same as any ship, but ramming would only be a valid tactic if somebody were wanting to…

Qayin drew his pistol, stood and whirled to aim the weapon out of the cockpit and down the corridor behind him that led into the depths of the ship. The plasma magazine in the weapon hummed into life as with one hand Qayin reached down to the control panel and without looking he re–engaged the autopilot. The corridor remained silent, only the occasional hiss of air being bled into the corridor to maintain a suitable atmospheric pressure. Qayin kept the pistol aimed down the corridor as he accessed a panel and selected a ship–wide scan for intruders.

If he were the captain of a weak vessel who had stumbled upon a much stronger gunship, he might have elected to ignore plasma weapons and instead ram the gunship directly and board her. That must have been their play, Qayin realised, the only sensible reason for deliberately wrecking their own ship: all or nothing, the kind of attacker with absolutely no sense of compromise.

The most deadly of foes.

The scanner beeped and Qayin looked down at it. He frowned in confusion. The display registered precisely one–point–five life forms aboard the ship: himself, and something in the hold.

'What the hell?' he uttered.

How could there possibly be half a life form aboard the ship? Had somebody, or some*thing*, attempted to board the gunship and somehow been cut in half? Qayin gripped the pistol tighter and walked out of the cockpit and down toward the gunship's main hull.

Salim Phaeon's obsession with luxury had not made it as far as his flagship. Qayin did not know what species had built her but the gunship appeared military in design and was also clearly constructed for human use, all of the interior signs and controls written in Etheran script and all cabins and controls designed for human hands. Bare walls, grey decks, metal everywhere and functional rather than aesthetic design completed the military picture. Qayin advanced toward a centrally located communal area that most likely had been a space designed for troops to congregate prior to being deployed on the surface of planets or other vessels, a role that the gunship's configuration would likely have supported.

Qayin advanced into the hexagonal interior of the ship, each wall containing a hatch that led to various locations: crew quarters, engine room, holds, armoury. Two of the bulkhead hatches were sealed, those that Qayin had closed via the cockpit when the hull had been breached. Access to the engine rooms and holds was impossible unless Qayin decided to open the hatches himself and take a look. Whatever was inside was most likely dead, only half of it having gotten aboard, but Qayin wasn't about to go wandering in without taking precautions.

He strode to the main control panel inside the troop compartment and accessed the ship's computer. He then accessed the command screen and was about to flush the atmosphere from the damaged areas right off the ship, effectively killing anything inside, when he remembered the Devlamine supply. If the impacts has loosened the barrels of the drug, then flushing the atmosphere might also drag the barrels out of the hold altogether if the damage was bad enough. Without the Devlamine he had no currency with which to carry out repairs.

Qayin cursed again and instead checked the atmosphere inside the hold: normal, but with a temperature of just six degrees above freezing. Qayin reasoned that the hull breach must have occurred further back from the entrance to the holds, and that his sealing of the bulkheads had stopped the leak of atmosphere from the holds for'ard of that point. The bulkhead hatches must have severed in half whatever was making its way forward through the ship when they closed, thus explaining the *half a life–form* diagnostic from the ship's scanners.

Qayin grinned as the mystery was explained, and he walked across to the hold hatch as he reached out for the manual release system. With a heave of his muscular arms the locking mechanism opened and a hiss of air whispered past the seals as he pulled back on the hatch and walked into the passageway, the air within cold and filled with a swirling mist.

The blow came from the mist, something hard and heavy crashing into Qayin's chest to lift him off his feet and hurl him through the air. Pain tore through Qayin's ribcage as he tumbled backwards and slammed down onto the deck, and as he rolled he saw something rush toward him with terrifying speed out of the mist, claws and fangs bared.

Qayin whipped his pistol up as he aimed at the towering creature that loomed over him, but the weapon was smashed from his grasp and spun through the air to clatter against a wall. Qayin, his arm numb and useless as he lay on his back on the deck, stared up into the fearsome eyes of a Veng'en, his creamy white fangs bared and his talons cold as they closed around Qayin's throat. A warlike, reptilian species, the Veng'en were renowned for both their prowess and brutality in battle. Qayin stared into the eyes of the Veng'en, and then he realised the true reason why the sensors had only detected half of a life form.

The Veng'en's eyes were partially glazed with a metallic tint, as though made of chrome, but worse than that his entire chest was constructed from an exotic mixture of metal and flesh, like a tapestry of differing materials meshed together in a way that only the Word's Legion could achieve.

Qayin stared at the chimera of scales, flesh and metal that flexed like skin and tissue. It took him only a few moments to work out the identity of the Veng'en who now held his life in his hands. Although no Veng'en could ever smile, Qayin thought that he saw a glimmer of satisfaction in the warrior's features.

'Kordaz,' Qayin said simply.

ENDEAVOUR

***

VII

'Reaper Two, battle flight – go!'

The closely formating Raythons sped through the darkened void of space, their formation lights switched off to disguise their passage and only the glow from their cockpit instruments lighting the faces of the two pilots. Sleek, angular and well–armed, the two craft were virtually invisible against the dense star fields.

Evelyn glimpsed from within her cockpit her wingman's Raython tucked in close echelon–starboard formation beside her and then it turned away in a crisp break, the aggressively styled wings flashing in the dim illumination of starlight as it rocketed away.

Evelyn, her head firmly enveloped in her flight helmet, kept her eyes fixed upon her holographic Situational Awareness Display, or SAD as the pilots liked to refer to an instrument that always seemed to bring bad news. The display portrayed her Raython as a tiny green speck in the centre of a larger, orange cube that represented a scaled–down version of the space in which she was flying. Evelyn could set the display to various ranges but at present she had selected one AU, or astronomical unit, a scale that included her fighter, her wingman Teera Milan, a half dozen other Raythons arranged in Combat Air Patrols around the two frigates far behind them, and a single target equally far out in front.

Ahead, immense billowing clouds of hydrogen gas illuminated by the nuclear glow of countless infant stars filled the dead blackness of space with the promise of life and light, the veils alive with colours denoting chemicals heated by the furnace–like stars burning in their midst.

'Do you think it's Endeavour?'

The voice of Reaper Two, Teera, spoke over the intercom. Evelyn glanced out to her right and saw Teera's Raython, now a minute speck against the star fields.

'I have no idea,' Evelyn replied. 'We'll worry about that when we get there.'

'I've seen documentaries on her,' Teera went on. *'She's been missing for nearly a hundred years, right? And now she shows up again, like a ghost ship or something.'*

'You know that this is an open squadron channel?'

'Roger,' Teera replied, somewhat sheepishly.

Truth was, Evelyn herself had felt a pulse of excitement when the CAG had briefed the squadron on the new radar contact, and not just because Andaim Ry'ere had watched her more closely than the other pilots as he

41

spoke. Endeavour was a legend enshrouded in mystery and conspiracy theories, the staple diet of anti–government protesters and anarchists since the earliest days of civilisation. Rumours had abounded about her for years, from supposed sightings to claims that her entire launch was faked by the Etheran government to supposed evidence that she was shot down by the Colonial Fleet long before she left the solar system. Evelyn figured that at least two of those more radical theories had now been shot down in flames, although ironically few cared any more as most of humanity had been eradicated from existence.

'Let's just focus on the sortie,' Evelyn suggested gently to Teera, 'establish a perimeter and ensure the troops can board her safely if that's what the captain decides he wants to do.'

'*Wilco*,' Teera replied.

Evelyn concentrated on her intercept vectors and watched as the enormous distance between their fighters and the target gradually began to reduce. Even travelling at luminal velocity, the distance to Endeavour would have taken six seconds. Captain Sansin had brought the frigates out of super–luminal cruise more than an AU from the target to give the fighters time to ensure they were not flying into some kind of trap. Evelyn felt certain that given the fleet's proximity beyond the Icari Line there was also a concern about encountering something completely alien to human experience and not being able to get away fast enough again.

The distance closed further over the next forty minutes as the Raythons streaked ahead of the frigates, and gradually more data began to stream in to Evelyn's cockpit as her fighter's sensors detected more information from Endeavour.

'She's drifting,' Evelyn noted as she guided the Raython, reporting her findings to Atlantia and Arcadia, both of which had joined the frequency. 'Barely making headway. No engine activity, communications or weapons systems detected. Too far out for life support signals.'

Captain Sansin's voice reached Evelyn from Atlantia.

'*Endeavour's systems would not emit a life–signal like modern ships,*' he informed her. '*We won't know if there's anybody aboard until we get there. General Bra'hiv's Marines are launching in shuttle Ranger Two now with the CAG as escort. Establish a perimeter and wait for reinforcements.*'

'Roger that,' Evelyn replied, and wondered again why a senior officer like Andaim was launching and not monitoring the mission from Atlantia's bridge.

A soft beep from her cockpit attracted her attention and she looked at a digital display projected onto the canopy before her to see a closed–channel communication from Teera, passed between their fighters and displayed as a stream of text.

Looks like your beau's coming to join you.

Evelyn rolled her eyes as she vocalised her response, allowing the Raython's computer to recognise her speech patterns and convert the message into text.

'He's not my beau, Teera.'

She listened to the silence of her cockpit and watched the glistening stars until another beep interrupted her solitude.

Poor Andaim, he just can't stay away from you can he? Aren't you flattered? He's quite a catch.

Evelyn wasn't flattered. She hadn't really thought about it all that much over the past few months, which wasn't surprising given everything that had been happening both to her and the Atlantia. Part of her thought that maybe she was just avoiding any sense of embarrassment at Andaim's interest in her, even though it wasn't always that subtle, but another darker part of her memory that she rarely visited reminded her of a past that she could not forget, could not erase. A brief image of her long–deceased family flickered like a phantom through her mind and she forced herself not to growl as she replied.

'So was my husband.'

Evelyn managed to avoid visualising her young child, the son that they had only just started to raise when the Word intervened and everything went to hell. She forced the images from her mind along with the pain that they caused as she focused on the vast panorama outside instead. Teera got the hint and the comm' channels fell silent.

Her cockpit remained silent for the rest of the journey through the bitter vacuum of space, the distant veld glowing as a vast nebula of new–born stars flared amid sweeping veils of red hydrogen, the soil from which all life in the universe ultimately grew. Evelyn knew that within those gigantic foetal clouds the bright young stars would grow, drawing in more hydrogen through gravity and along with it heavy metals, the waste products of older, giant stars forged in supernova explosions. In an endless cycle, the young stars would form and around them discs of stellar debris, metals, rock and ices that would provide the raw materials for the planets, moon, oceans and eventually life that would populate their worlds. She wondered if somewhere, right now, the atoms and chemicals that had once been her beloved son were now a part of somebody or something else, the aeons–old cycle of regeneration that was the hallmark of life in the universe moving ever onward. Perhaps she was staring now toward atoms that would one day be in the body of a mother as she cared for her own son just as those hydrogen clouds cossetted the fierce young stars blazing amid their…

'… *contact, visual, dead ahead.*'

Evelyn blinked as Teera's call broke her from her maudlin thoughts and she saw ahead, silhouetted against the vast red clouds, a tiny black speck.

'Got it,' Evelyn replied. 'Maintain Battle Flight, weapons hot, go.'

Evelyn activated her plasma cannons and kept her gaze fixed upon the speck as it moved ever–so–slightly against the immense backdrop of gas clouds. Data streamed in, and Evelyn scanned it as she flew.

'Minimal power readings, but the atmosphere remains stable in about half of the ship.'

'*I've got the fusion core,*' Teera said as her instruments detected the ship's heart, '*but it's bleeding energy into space. I've got a trail here extending beyond sensor range.*'

'That'll explain why she's drifting,' Evelyn said. 'Not enough power to engage her main engines. Damn, she could have been like this for decades.'

'*There could be people aboard her,*' Teera said, '*even after all of this time. She was carrying enough stores when she launched to feed her crew for years.*'

'Not hundreds of years,' Evelyn pointed out. 'Let's just focus on our job for now. The Marines can go look inside and find out what happened to her.'

Evelyn gripped her control column tighter. Although she was forcing herself to be a leader to Teera, the model officer, in reality she too was itching to get aboard Endeavour and find out what had happened to the iconic ship and her crew. The speck ahead grew larger and began to form a recognisable shape, that of Endeavour's cylindrical central hull and ventral strakes.

'*I don't believe it,*' Teera said as she was finally able to see the ship in some detail with her own eyes. '*It's really her.*'

Endeavour was bow–on to the approaching fighters, her for'ard hull little more than a flat panel the size of Atlantia all on its own. The engineers who had built her had only gone as far as fitting a shallow wedge–shaped panel to her bow, designed to deflect some of the energy from countless billions of micrometeorite impacts as she cruised through deep space. Endeavour's huge size was a testimony to the skill required by her builders in an age where deep–space travel was still in its infancy. Although bulky and in many respects ugly in her construction, the fact that she was still intact a century after her launch said much about the care taken in laying down her keel and the robustness of her design. Her long hull contained a bulbous bridge and living quarters for her thousand–strong crew, while her engine bays were a cylindrical construction that had once ended in a giant, stubby exhaust shielded only by a teardrop shaped cover. A pair of slim delta–shaped 'wings' protruded from either side of the hull.

'Easy now,' Evelyn called to her wingman. 'Maintain attack speed, stay clear and don't present an easy target. You take the port side, I'll take starboard.'

'Wilco,' Teera replied, still with an edge of excitement in her voice but tinged now with a sense of awe.

The two Raythons moved to pass either side of the ship's gigantic hull, Evelyn pulling out wide just in case the ship was now occupied by pirates or unknown species intent on attacking any intruders. Endeavour was not a warship but she had been large enough to be fitted with countless early–design laser cannons designed to super–heat their targets and blow them apart, a defence against whatever the crew may have encountered far out in the unknown universe beyond Ethera and the core systems.

The immense bow drifted past Evelyn's Raython, the surface like a metallic ocean, rippled by the endless impacts that had marred its surface. The vast construction glowed a dull red in the illumination offered by the distant gas clouds.

'Damn, I had no idea she was so big.'

Endeavour was at least four times longer than Atlantia and twice as high and wide. Evelyn's Raython passed into deep shadow as she flew down the ship's starboard side, only the occasional glint of metal betraying the presence of Endeavour's hull alongside her. Gantries, viewing panels, massive vents, ducts and hull plates the size of large freighters panelled her flanks as Evelyn slowed, aware that her systems were detecting no weapons active aboard the ship.

Something caught Evelyn's eye ahead as she flew, a sparkling halo that grew closer as her tiny fighter was dwarfed by Endeavour's massive bulk.

'I've got something,' she said.

'Me too, dead ahead,' Teera replied.

Evelyn's Raython moved silently through space alongside the vessel and then Endeavour's stern appeared, enshrouded in a cloud of debris. Evelyn slowed and turned away from the potentially dangerous cloud of metal. The dim glow from distant hydrogen clouds filled her cockpit once again, and on the far side of the debris cloud she saw a tiny star–like speck emerge as Teera's Raython cleared Endeavour's stern.

Teera gasped over the communication channel as Evelyn scanned the debris cloud before them.

Endeavour's entire stern was a ragged, battered mess of metal enveloped in debris spilling slowly from her interior. A forest of metal girders poked from the dark interior of her hull, each as thick as a dozen Raythons side by side, each severed and drooping as though melted by some infernal heat.

Evelyn blinked. 'You said you'd detected the fusion core? She only had one, right?'

'Affirmative,' Teera called back. 'Endeavour had a single core and I can still detect its presence, so that's not what took her out.'

Evelyn shook her head in wonder as she turned slowly astern Endeavour, Teera's Raython crossing on the opposite heading far above her.

'Whatever happened to her, it was big and catastrophic,' she said finally. 'Endeavour's engines and exhaust array are completely gone. She couldn't have travelled if she'd wanted to.'

'What the hell could do that to a ship so big?' Teera wondered out loud. *'It looks as though she's been sliced open from the inside out!'*

'I don't know,' Evelyn replied, 'and I'm not sure I want to find out.'

***

VIII

'Alpha Comp'ny, eyes on me!'

Forty of Alpha Company's Marines slammed the butts of their plasma rifles against the deck of the shuttle to signify their complete attention on General Abrahim Bra'hiv as he stood before the closed rear ramp. The shuttle hummed with the sound of its ion engines as it flew through the inky blackness of space.

The men were strapped into their seats, facing the outer hull walls of the shuttle in two rows, sitting back to back as they looked sideways at their general. A squat, broad–shouldered man with a thick neck and steel–grey shaven head, Bra'hiv looked every inch the career soldier, festooned as he was with weapon, webbing and atmospheric suit designed to allow combat in *zero–zero* conditions: zero atmosphere and zero gravity. He surveyed the men before him with quiet pride, every one of them trained under his command to be capable of facing just about anything,

'The target is the exploratory vessel Endeavour,' Bra'hiv confirmed. 'The data we've received from Reaper Squadron's intercept reveals that she was subject to extensive damage to her stern that neutralised her propulsion, although her internal power supply remains secure. Atmosphere is stable but the temperature is low, hence our suits. No signs of life, but on such a large vessel it's going to take time to secure her. Assume that there is hostile life aboard and act accordingly at all times.'

The general's eye caught Lieutenant C'rairn's, the young officer already a combat veteran despite his youth. C'rairn was one of the most trusted soldiers in the fleet, loyal in the defence not just of the Colonial force but also of his wife and child who lived in Atlantia's sanctuary.

'Lieutenant, you'll lead Charlie Platoon, I'll take Delta. Twenty men each, mutual fire support and nobody goes off anywhere without our mutual consent, understood?'

'Affirmative,' C'rairn replied without hesitation.

Bra'hiv felt a stirring of internal comfort, the security of knowing that each and every man before him could be relied upon to do his duty, to have their general's back. It had taken many months of hard work, especially when winning the loyalty of former convicts and murderers, but somehow he had done it. For the first time since the apocalypse that had destroyed mankind, Bra'hiv felt confident in facing the unknown with these men at his back. Which was just as well, because out here beyond the Icari Line the unknown could be a daily occurrence.

'We've done this before, aboard the Sylph and in the attack on Commander Ty'ek's Veng'en cruiser,' Bra'hiv went on to the rest of the men. 'Be quick, precise and thorough in any searches and never, ever let yourself go anywhere alone. We don't know what the hell's aboard that thing, although we're pretty certain that the Legion did not exist in a recognisable form when Endeavour launched. Whatever is inside is going to be new to us. Let's do it.'

The Marines thumped their rifle butts once more on the deck in support of their general as he strapped into the seat closest to the rear ramp.

The shuttle's engines whined as it slowed, evidently approaching Endeavour. Without windows in the heavily armoured vessel, the Marines would only get a good look at the ship when the rear ramp opened and they were deployed into the field. However, each of them craned their necks for a view of a monitor mounted for'ard of the troop compartment that showed the view ahead of the shuttle. There, silhouetted against the stars and hydrogen clouds, they could see Endeavour's bulky hull looming ahead.

'Deployment in thirty seconds.'

The pilot's calm voice filled the troop compartment as General Bra'hiv called out.

'All arms!'

The soldiers' plasma rifles hummed into life as they were activated, and each man checked his neighbour's face mask for gaps in the seals and their oxygen supply via the tanks carried upon their backs. Satisfied, they sat in tense silence waiting for the ramp to drop.

They shifted as one as the shuttle swung around, and Bra'hiv heard the sound of the engine exhausts change as the pilot altered his power settings to land the craft in the landing bay he had selected somewhere on the vast hull. Schematics obtained from Atlantia's logs provided a deck plan of the huge ship for the pilots and the Marines to follow, and right now they were using the closest open bay to the bridge that they could find.

'Deck Charlie, mid–section, landing now!'

General Bra'hiv tensed, one hand ready to punch his harness free as the other held his rifle aimed at the still–closed ramp. The shuttle shook violently as its landing struts slammed down onto the deck and with a hiss of vapour the ramp dropped under hydraulic force and the pressurised atmosphere within the shuttle blasted outward as Bra'hiv released his harness and dashed from the shuttle.

Behind him forty Marines followed in an orderly flood, running with their suits weighted at fifty per cent normal gravity to provide them with extra speed, agility and stamina.

Bra'hiv thundered down the ramp onto the darkened deck of a small landing bay, the flashlight on his rifle slicing into the gloom. The deck was slippery with ice that glistened like diamond chips in the darkness. Bra'hiv ran forward and then dropped down onto one knee, his rifle pulled into his shoulder as behind him the Marines formed two groups and one giant arc of firepower pointed out into the darkness.

The shuttle's engines flared with silent white light in the vacuum as it lifted off and pulled out of the bay, ready to return when the soldiers required an extraction. Bra'hiv watched the darkness intently but nothing loomed forth to threaten them. His eyes cast down across the ice and sought any sign of footprints, but nothing revealed itself. Behind them, the landing bay doors silently lowered and sealed themselves as the shuttle pulled away into the distance, and suddenly they were totally alone aboard the massive ship.

Bra'hiv looked over his shoulder and pointed ahead with two fingers as he looked at C'rairn. The lieutenant advanced forward, his soldiers following him as they were covered by Bra'hiv's contingent. Bra'hiv watched as C'rairn led his men to a bunker nearby, which was where the controls for the landing bay doors would be. They descended cautiously into the darkness and for a few moments there was nothing but silence. Then a series of glowing lights flickered on in the bunker, visible through the observation windows.

Moments later, C'rairn's voice crackled in Bra'hiv's helmet.

'Not enough energy for atmospheric heating, but bleeding air into the bay now.'

Bra'hiv's gaze flicked up to the vents high on the bay walls in time to see vapour billow out of them like dark clouds, filling the bay with bitterly cold but breathable air and allowing the Marines to conserve their oxygen supply.

Moments later the lighting in the bay flickered into life and filled it with a deceptively warm glow to reveal an empty structure with no other vessels inside. A red light high on the walls of the bay turned green, and Bra'hiv gave a thumbs–up to his men. They switched off their oxygen supplies and opened vents on their masks to allow the air in, but kept the masks on as protection against the bitter cold.

'Let's move,' Bra'hiv snapped.

The Marines headed as one for the landing bay entrance, a series of hatches that led into the ship's interior, all of which were sealed. A schematic projected onto Bra'hiv's mask visor directed him to the hatch he wanted–the one that led toward the bridge deck.

'Delta on me,' he ordered. 'Charlie, maintain the perimeter here and see what you can do about the temperature. Any signs of life from the ship?'

'Nothing,' the lieutenant replied. *'No communications link with the rest of the ship and no incoming data. There's power though, must have all been re–routed for some reason. This is what the Word did aboard the Sylph, remember?'*

The general could hardly forget the ill–fated boarding of the former merchant vessel *Sylph* and the tremendous combat that had followed as he and his men had been forced to fight their way off the ship with the Legion in hot pursuit.

'They're not here,' Bra'hiv reassured the lieutenant. 'But see what links you can establish anyway, and stay sharp.'

C'rairn nodded at the general as he passed by the bunker, the twenty Marines of Delta Platoon following as they approached the hatches and two soldiers eased forward of the rest without command. As Bra'hiv watched the two men worked efficiently to set small plasma charges against the hatch's locking mechanisms and hinges, designed to burn through rather than blast off. The two soldiers hurried away from the charges and moments later the hinges flared brightly with a fearsome blue–white light, drops of liquid metal spilling away from the hatch onto the deck.

'Rams, go!' Bra'hiv whispered.

Two men hefted a metallic ram between them and rushed the door, and with a dull boom that echoed around the landing bay the ram slammed into the smouldering door and it broke free of its mountings and flew away down the corridor, the heavy metal hatch flashing dimly as it rotated in mid–air.

Bra'hiv rushed past the ram and into the corridor, his rifle's flashlight illuminating the passage as several more soldiers thundered fearlessly in behind him, their footfalls echoing away into the distant, darkened ship. Their flashlights scanned the darkness like laser beams, but nothing moved but for the faint haze of moisture and ice clinging to the walls.

Bra'hiv edged forward, keeping an eye open for opportunities for cover in case something unexpected leaped out at them. The schematic on his visor guided him, overlaying vector lines across the corridor deck with arrows pointing to the bridge. The general turned left at the end of the corridor, glancing right briefly to see another corridor of endless bulkhead hatches stretching away far beyond the reach of his flashlight.

'Deck Charlie,' he whispered to his men. 'We'll ascend to deck Alpha at the first opportunity and then move for'ard for the bridge. Jesson, Miller, you wait here and guard the corridor entrance in case we need to retreat. I don't want anything sneaking up behind us.'

A whispered *Aye, general* reached Bra'hiv's ears as the two men peeled off and took up firing positions at the entrance to the landing bay corridor. Bra'hiv moved on with the same deliberate, cautious gait. The corridor was long, one of the main arterial routes that stretched from bow to stern through the massive ship. Wide enough for two people to pass side by side, it allowed swift access to various areas but also presented the general with a problem. Side corridors swept away in all directions as he moved, far too many between the landing bay and the bridge for his men to guard. Bra'hiv posted sentries in pairs at four more locations, hoping that they would be able to support each other if something untoward occurred, and kept moving until he reached the stairwells either side of the elevator shafts that accessed upper and lower deck levels.

He posted two more sentries, leaving him with eight men to ascend to the bridge, and then as one they moved into the stairwells and began to climb. The darkness was still bitterly cold, barely above freezing according to Bra'hiv's sensor readings, suggesting that Endeavour had been in this comatose state for a long time, perhaps years. Memories of the *Sylph* and its lethal cargo of murderous Hunters and the dangerous Veng'en stowaway Kordaz flickered again through the general's mind, but he forced himself to focus on the job and reach the bridge unscathed.

The troops climbed up without incident and reached A–Deck, Bra'hiv maintaining the lead as he opened the hatches and stepped out onto the deck.

Hexagonal in shape and as dark as the rest of the ship, the bridge deck was dominated by two massive hatches that were sealed. Bra'hiv crept forward as his men silently fanned out and formed a defensive ring, alternating men aiming inward toward the bridge doors and outward toward various access points from A–Deck.

Bra'hiv placed a charge on the bridge doors, set the timer for five seconds and then activated the charge before retreating to a safe distance. The charge lit and burned with ferocious intensity for several seconds as it seared through the doors' locking mechanism, illuminating the deck with a flickering white light. Moments later, the mechanism glowed like magma in the darkness and dropped fat glowing globules of molten metal onto the deck as Bra'hiv advanced and waved his men forward. Together, Bra'hiv and two troopers leaned their weight into the doors. The general raised three fingers, then two, then one and then with a combined burst of effort the Marines slammed into the doors and they burst open.

Bra'hiv lunged onto the bridge as his rifle swept around for any sign of a target.

The bridge was darkened, none of the instrument panels aglow and the main viewing panel black and featureless. The flashlights of his men illuminated a series of control panels frosted with ice crystals as Bra'hiv moved forward and his light beam caught on what looked like hair upon one of the panels.

The general stepped forward as he rounded the panel, convinced that he had found one of Endeavour's crew slumped at their station. He eased his way around, his weapon pointed at the figure as it came into view and then, quite suddenly, Bra'hiv stopped moving as he felt his heart miss a beat.

The Marines supporting him moved into view, each of their flashlights illuminating the figure before them, and then they all too stopped moving.

'What the…?'

Bra'hiv took a cautious step forward, unable to tear his gaze from the sight before him despite the horror that ran cold through his veins.

The lights from the Marine's weapons illuminated the face of a man, his features twisted in agony, his mouth agape as though screaming and his eyes tight shut. His hair was thick and in disarray, long and snaking as it lay frozen on the control panel.

And that was all there was of him, but he had not been decapitated.

'What the hell is this, general?' a nervous voice asked from behind Bra'hiv.

Bra'hiv shook his head as he looked down at the man's face, his cheeks and his throat and the back of his head merging into the metal plating of the control panel, even his hair turning into metallic threads that vanished into the surface around him as though he had physically melted into his workstation.

***

IX

Qayin felt the pain reach out for him from somewhere on the edge of his consciousness, calling him in. Its unwelcome presence suddenly grabbed hold of him and hauled him into the present and he opened his eyes.

His head throbbed, as did his eyes as he squinted. He realised that he was suspended in mid–air, his wrists, waist and ankles bound with metal restraints that were themselves anchored into the walls and deck of the vessel. His muscles ached under the tension of his bonds, stretched to their limits.

Qayin vaguely recalled that Salim Phaeon had been a slaver and that his ship would naturally have been equipped to transport large numbers of captives. The walls and ceiling above him were filled with identical mounts, enough to transport hundreds of slaves, although now he was the only occupant of the ship's hold.

Qayin looked down at his body and saw that he was naked but for a thermal underlining suit, part of his Marine fatigues designed to maintain core temperature under a variety of conditions. Kordaz, he realised, must have afforded him that minor luxury in the otherwise unheated holds. His breath condensed on the air in the darkness, illuminated only by slim white panel lights around the edges of the deck and the ceiling. Somehow Qayin could tell that the ship was in super–luminal cruise, the hum of a mass–drive and the lack of physical motion inside the ship helping to confirm his suspicions.

Qayin could recall little of what had happened, save seeing Kordaz loom over him and then the sensation of his face being stamped on. That he was still alive surprised him, given that he had cheerfully left Kordaz for dead on the field at Chiron IV. Another memory leaped into his mind: that of the Veng'en's face horribly disfigured by metallic lesions just as Qayin's brother, Hevel, had once been reshaped by the horror that was the Legion.

Qayin could not be sure, but given the injuries Kordaz had sustained on Chiron IV before Qayin's own eyes he could not have recovered on his own. The Veng'en ability to regenerate tissue damaged in battle was legendary, but that took both time and at least a chance of survival. Kordaz had been shot directly in the chest by a Colonial pilot, destroying at least one of his hearts and probably a lung with it, and Qayin knew damned well that the spot where the Veng'en had lain had soon after been blasted into oblivion by an orbital bombardment, probably by Atlantia.

Kordaz could not have survived his injuries or the blasts, and thus the only solution was that he had been infected by the Legion and that the machines had both saved him and rebuilt him, repairing the terrible damage he had suffered and in doing so turning him from a biological being into a sort of chimera of animal and machine, a true cybernetic organism.

Qayin shivered in the cold as another idea formed in his mind. What if Kordaz had not survived at all, and instead his warm corpse had been infected anyway? That would mean that Qayin was not sharing his ship with an angry Veng'en warrior but with an even less palatable presence: the Word in living form.

A hissing sound alerted Qayin to the approach of Kordaz and he hung his head as a hatch opened before him. Through the hatch stepped Kordaz, the light reflecting off broad patches of metallic flesh coating his chest as he advanced. Qayin kept his head down as he saw the warrior's clawed feet slap down on the deck as he came to stand before him, and then one huge clawed hand gripped Qayin's jaw and yanked it up.

Qayin allowed his eyes to open but feigned weakness as he looked into Kordaz's red eyes, the once baleful yellow replaced now with something alien, devoid of emotion. Kordaz's voice sounded electronic, coming as it did from the vocal resonator he wore about his thick neck.

'I've waited a long time for this, Qayin,' he growled, the sound of the Veng'en's guttural dialect harsh over the translator's monotone oratory.

Qayin summoned a response. 'A long time for what? Revenge? Our people saved your life, Kordaz.'

'*Our* people?' the Veng'en echoed. 'You mean the people you abandoned to die on Chiron IV, Qayin? The same people that would likely kill you on sight?'

Qayin grinned, his teeth white in the darkness and his bioluminescent tattoos pulsing like rivers of magma against his dark skin.

'A misunderstanding,' he replied, 'a conflict of interests.'

Kordaz grabbed Qayin's jaw and yanked it closer. 'Your only interest is yourself, Qayin.'

The former Marine shrugged as best he could while suspended by his wrists.

'Where are we going?'

Kordaz snarled something unintelligible as he shoved Qayin's face away, maybe a Veng'en curse of some kind that the creators of the vocal resonator had chosen not to include in its vocabulary. Kordaz looked about at the countless manacle mounts set into the hold.

'This is what you people are,' he said finally. 'Look at what you do to yourselves, and then you come asking us for help to fix your problems.'

'I ain't asking for nothing,' Qayin murmured in reply. 'Captain Sansin's insane if he thinks the Veng'en will help him. They're far too busy carving up defenceless human children fleeing Ethera, right?'

Kordaz's eyes narrowed.

'Children grow into adults, and then they become like you,' he said. 'Our war was not against anything other than humanity in its entirety. My people took no pleasure in killing the innocents to protect our own younglings in the future.'

'The future,' Qayin grinned bitterly, 'you say it like there is one.'

Kordaz stood before Qayin and breathed deeply, his chest inflating and the metallic surface reflecting the light.

'I am alive,' Kordaz said. 'I was on the verge of death and yet here I stand, not just alive but stronger than before. You speak of how your people fled the Legion, just as my people now fight to keep it from our own homeworld.' He leaned closer to Qayin. 'I say, perhaps we have all been mistaken.'

Qayin's regarded the warrior before him.

'Wow, the Legion really did bite you deep, didn't they? The Word's come a long way if it's managed to locate and infect the brain of a Veng'en. Must've been like looking for a needle in a haystack.'

Kordaz's fist flashed into motion as the Veng'en pivoted on one heel and drove his muscular arm forwards. Qayin let out a roar as the fist ploughed into his belly, the air blasting from his lungs as his stomach convulsed painfully. As his head dropped another fist smashed up into his nose and snapped his head back as his face went numb and his vision blurred. Blood spilled across his lips and tainted his tongue with a metallic flavour, as though the Legion were pouring into his body also.

Kordaz's thick hand enveloped Qayin's neck and squeezed, choking the breath from his throat. Qayin's eyes bulged and he struggled to suck in air as Kordaz's dull red eyes glared into his.

'Your Legion brought me back from the dead, Qayin,' he growled. 'They saved my life, which is more than humanity has done for any Veng'en. I say that they're infinitely more tolerable than any of you.'

Qayin gasped a response and Kordaz loosened his grip enough for the former criminal to speak.

'That's the train of thought that killed humanity,' he gasped. 'Once you're infected, anything the Legion suggests is a good idea.'

Kordaz's fanged jaw twisted in an approximation of a human smile.

'That's the thing, Qayin,' he snarled back. 'The Legion did infect me, and did a remarkable job of repairing the damage that you and your

Colonial friends caused. Unfortunately for the Infectors, they were then destroyed by the cosmic rays breaking through Chiron's atmosphere after you and Arcadia left.'

Qayin stared in amazement at Kordaz for a long moment. 'You're clean?'

'I am uninfected,' Kordaz confirmed, 'but benefitting from a whole new lease of life.'

Qayin's mind buzzed as he realised what the Veng'en was driving at. Chiron IV's atmosphere had been under assault from its dying parent star, the savage solar storms tearing away the atmosphere and exposing the surface to lethal cosmic rays, radiation that no human being could withstand. Likewise, the smaller of the Legion's machines, the Infectors, could also not withstand sustained blasts of even low energy microwave radiation. Cosmic rays, of a far higher power, would fry their circuitry and render them useless. But Kordaz's leathery skin was sufficient to protect him from such a fearsome assault, his species adapted to the high energy sunlight on their home world, Wraiythe.

Qayin peered more closely at Kordaz's patches of metallic skin and saw around the edges evidence of burning and scar tissue forming.

'They got fried,' Qayin said at last. 'Damn me, they fixed you and then you got away from them.'

'Veng'en skin is more resilient to radiation that that of humans,' Kordaz explained, 'or the Legion's Infectors. They were dead when I awoke, although their effects are with me still.'

Kordaz blinked, his eyes that unnerving dull red. Qayin realised at last why they had changed colour.

'Your eyesight,' he surmised. 'The radiation cooked it. You can only see because the Legion made changes to your eyes.'

A Veng'en could not show emotion in the same way that humans did, their features lacking the muscular flexibility that defined human expressions, but Kordaz's skin flickered as it altered colour and flushed a deep red that almost matched his eyes.

'Another loss for which I shall seek my vengeance.'

Qayin's eyes narrowed.

'You'll never find them,' he replied. 'I don't know where they've gone.'

'Their frigates leave easily identifiable gravity–wakes,' Kordaz replied without concern. 'I have already laid in a pursuit course, and Salim Phaeon's gunship is easily able to maintain pace with the Colonial vessels. As soon as they drop out of super–luminal, I shall be upon them.'

Qayin let a broad smile blossom across his features.

'This gunship against not one but two Colonial frigates and their entire compliment of Marines and Raython fighters? I'd give you odds of victory of about ten thousand to one.'

Kordaz's skin rippled in various shades as the red faded away.

'Indeed,' he replied, 'but it is not victory that I seek, my devious young friend.'

'You want them to defeat you?' Qayin almost laughed. 'I think you caught a bit too much of Chiron's sunshine, Kordaz.'

The Veng'en's hand whipped to its belt and in a flash a plasma whip crackled the air, a bright blue–white snake of pure energy that hissed as it lashed out and sliced like white fire across Qayin's chest. A crackle of burning flesh and wisps of blue smoke puffed from Qayin's thermal suit as he screamed, a shriek born as much of surprise as of the agony that seared his flesh.

Kordaz stepped back, the plasma whip writhing and humming as he examined his handiwork.

Qayin's uniform smouldered as a black line of cauterised flesh puffed coils of smoke up into his face, tainted with acrid odour of burning skin. Kordaz nodded in apparent satisfaction as he regarded the former convict.

'It is your defeat that I seek, Qayin,' he said finally. 'For when what is left of you kneels before me and begs for his life in front of Captain Sansin, it will be their human weakness, their compassion even for scum like you, that will see them fall. You are my victory, Qayin.'

Qayin looked up at the Veng'en and opened his mouth to shout the first insult that crept into his mind, but he was silenced as the whip snarled and flashed toward him once more and everything was lost to the pain that seared his body.

***

X

'Delta Company, status report?'

Captain Idris Sansin stood upon Atlantia's command platform with his hands behind his back as he listened to General Bra'hiv, the Marine's face filling a display screen to one side of Atlantia's main viewing panel, where Endeavour was visible against the impressive backdrop of hydrogen clouds.

The bridge and landing bays are secure, along with the main passage between them,' Bra'hiv replied. *'My men are currently ray–shielding the passage to provide extra security and deny access from other areas of the vessel. At this time we have no indication of there being any forms of life aboard, only the remnants of what we believe to be the crew.'*

'Remnants?' Idris asked.

'You're going to have to see that for yourself, captain, because it's hard to put into words. I don't know what the hell happened here but it's not like anything I've ever seen before. I'd suggest bringing Doctor Sansin over too, to get her take on things.'

'Stand by,' the captain said. 'We'll deploy shortly. See if you can get the ship's heating and lighting activated, check the ship's logs for crew entries that might hint at what happened and keep scanning for signs of life. There were a thousand souls aboard that ship, they must have gone somewhere.'

'Aye, cap'n.'

The communication link to Endeavour was cut off by Lael as Idris turned to survey the tactical display. Both Atlantia and Arcadia had moved into position off Endeavour's port bow, and from their vantage point it was clear to see the damage the vessel had suffered to aft, her stern a shredded mess of ragged metal enshrouded with debris.

'She took a hell of a beating.'

Mikhain's voice reached Idris as though from afar as he surveyed the wreck of Endeavour and wondered what she might have encountered to have wrought such extensive damage. The Arcadia's captain was visible on another communications link nearby, his gaze directed at Endeavour in much the same way.

'From what, though?' Idris wondered out loud. 'Sensors suggest the damage to her is several decades old, so whatever she came across did this and then left. It doesn't make much sense.'

'There's not much evidence of Endeavour fighting back either,' Mikhain added. *'An optical scan of her defensive cannons suggest no evidence of them ever having been fired in anger. If she was attacked, she didn't have much time to do anything about it.'*

A nagging sense of danger tugged at Idris's instincts as he looked at Endeavour on Atlantia's main viewing screen. Like most captains, Idris hated *not knowing* the most. A mystery was one thing, but a mystery that had taken the lives of countless human souls was something that Idris desperately needed to understand and to solve–and most importantly to prevent happening again.

'Pull Arcadia back to ten thousand cubits,' he ordered Mikhain. 'I want you to ride shotgun from a safe distance in case something shows up. It's harder to hit two widely spaced targets than two sitting closely together.'

'*Aye,*' Mikhain agreed. '*Patrols?*'

'At twenty thousand,' Idris replied. 'Take command of them from the CAG, then share the load between all of our Raython squadrons on rotation. I don't want a ship of any size sneaking either in or out of this area without my knowing about it.'

'*Roger that, Arcadia out.*'

Idris turned and glanced at Lael. 'You have the bridge.'

Lael stared at the captain as though she had been slapped, her green eyes wide and her cropped metallic–blonde hair catching the light from data panels behind her. The long–serving communications officer was ranked sufficiently to hold a command position in the captain's stead, but the look on her face betrayed that it had never happened before.

'For how long, captain?' she managed to ask.

'For as long as it takes,' Idris smiled as he stepped down off the command platform. 'Don't let it go to your head.'

Idris walked toward the bridge exit, aware of the rest of the command crew's gaze upon either him or Lael as he was joined by Andaim. The CAG had joined him aboard Atlantia from his patrol at the captain's request.

'Lael?' he asked in a whisper.

'Why not?' Idris shrugged. 'She's a capable and exemplary officer, and the increased responsibility will do her good.'

'A proper, well trained Executive Officer would do you good, captain,' Andaim pointed out. 'You haven't chosen one yet and Mikhain's been captain of Arcadia for weeks now.'

'Are you the XO now?'

Andaim grinned, not taking offence at the captain's challenge.

'Just being a sounding board, captain. Lael's a great officer but she's not up to an XO role and we both know that. Just sayin'.'

Idris knew that the young commander was right. Mikhain had been one of the most senior officers aboard Atlantia in terms of both rank and experience, and it was hard to find anybody who could suitably fit the role in his place. Idris's first choice would have been Andaim, whose combat experience, training as a fighter pilot and general command knowledge provided the perfect background for an XO position. But Andaim was fully employed as Commander of the Air Group and besides, Idris knew damned well that Andaim would never willingly leave the cockpit of a Raython. Even now he had managed to slide himself into a flight lead spot, heading up the support patrols behind Evelyn and Teera.

Truth was, right now Idris could not think of a single officer whose attributes were up to the role of captain, and that was why he'd given the bridge to Lael. Somebody, somewhere, would need to take up the mantle under his tutelage and be mentored until they could reliably become Atlantia's Executive Officer.

They walked together down to the sick bay, where Meyanna Sansin was busily tending to injured crewmen and sick civilians. Her long brown hair was pinned back behind her ears, her attention completely focused on the task in hand.

'We need you,' Idris said simply as they moved to stand alongside her.

Meyanna finished wrapping a bandage around the forearm of an injured technician with some kind of burn on his skin, before she stood up and looked at her husband.

'So do a couple of hundred other people,' she uttered. 'There isn't a qualified medical team on Arcadia, so we're having to treat double the number of patients aboard Atlantia.'

Meyanna looked a decade younger than her actual years, but the strain of running both the sick bay, the laboratory and acting as a councillor to the ship's civilian contingent was clearly taking its toll, to her husband at least. He could see the tiredness in her eyes and felt certain that she looked thinner than she had done just a few weeks ago.

'This is important,' Idris insisted.

'More important than whom?' Meyanna challenged as she gestured to the ranks of patients filling the busy wards. 'I'm too busy.'

She stormed off toward her laboratory. Idris glanced at Andaim, who raised a questioning eyebrow.

'I may have upset her this morning in front of the other councillors,' Idris admitted.

'You might want to smooth things over,' Andaim suggested. 'You can't afford to alienate your only ally down there, especially as she's your wife.'

'You want to come?' Idris asked. 'She likes you, and might listen.'

'I'll wait here.'

Idris sighed as he glanced at the injured crew around them and then he marched into the laboratory after his wife.

The interior of the laboratory was filled with experiments dedicated to two pieces of high technology. One was a Hunter, a small machine armed with powerful pincers held in stasis within a magnetic chamber. The weapon of choice of the Word's Legion, it was virtually harmless alone despite being utterly lethal when deployed in their millions. Nearby, also encased within a chamber, was a shimmering veil of an ethereal material liberated from the pirate Taron Forge–one that was used to render biological beings unconscious and electrical systems redundant. Forge had used the veil to capture and plunder merchant ships, although nobody knew of the material's true origins. Idris glanced at the veil, often referred to as "the pirate shroud", and sought a new course of conversation.

'Have you figured out anything about the veil yet?'

'Other than I'd like to drape it over your damned head for a while?' Meyanna replied sweetly.

The captain's patience withered almost instantly.

'I can't help you if you decided to take on too much. You put yourself up for the candidacy of councillor, Meyanna. The people voted for you, that's what you wanted, what you told me *I* should do.'

'I didn't expect to be doing it entirely on my own,' Meyanna replied with a tight smile that conveyed anything but warmth. 'Since being elected I have not had a single member of the crew provided to help me with anything.'

'That's because this is a military vessel and the crew are not concerned with politics,' Idris replied. 'If you want help, recruit it on a voluntary basis from the damned people that insisted they wanted a say!'

The ward beyond the laboratory had fallen silent as Idris's voice had risen. The captain felt a vague pang of shame as Andaim stepped in, his voice calm and controlled but his features creased with concern.

'Ma'am, you really need to see this,' he said. 'It's definitely something you'd be interested in.'

Meyanna sighed and tore off her medical gloves, looking at Andaim rather than her husband.

'Where are we going?'

'Endeavor, ma'am.'

*

General Bra'hiv paced impatiently up and down on Endeavour's bridge as he awaited the arrival of Captain Sansin and his wife. Meyanna, the senior surgeon on Atlantia and a person with more medical knowledge than anybody Bra'hiv had ever met, was also one of the most well-liked and respected members of the crew. Her presence would have a calming effect on his Marines, who right now were also pacing nervously up and down and unable to take their eyes off the macabre head fused into the control panels.

'It ain't natural, general,' one of them muttered.

'I know what it *ain't*,' Bra'hiv snapped, mocking the soldier's poor grammar. 'Stand your post and don't damned well look at it if you don't like it.'

The Marines were manning the various bridge stations, some of them working to get power into the crucial systems. General Bra'hiv, ever cautious of the presence of the Legion even out here, had forbidden any of his men from engaging the heating systems or the ship's main computer without his express permission. He wanted no repeat of the fiasco aboard the *Sylph*.

'General?' a Marine called, a man named Mears. 'We've accessed the power terminals, right back to the fusion core.'

Bra'hiv marched across to join Mears and looked down to see a single display screen with a scroll of data streaming down it. Basic text was in place of the normal colourful graphics, a simple boot–system detailing power available, circuit breaker status across the ship and system status along with it.

'What do you make of it?' Bra'hiv asked, never much of an engineer himself.

'I'd say that we're in business,' Mears replied. 'The ship's core is intact and still more than able to power the vessel. Most of the power lines for'ard of mid–ships are secure and active.'

'You're saying we can heat and light the ship, if we want to?'

'Aye, general,' Mears nodded.

Bra'hiv thought for a moment. The cold was aching through his bones, even the atmospheric suits bleeding body heat over long periods of time when exposed to such bitter conditions, but he remained resolutely opposed to activating the environmental controls.

'Activate the lighting,' he said finally. 'Keep the temperature down until Meyanna Sansin has checked that.., *thing* out.'

Mears accessed an old–fashioned keyboard that slid out from beneath the panel and typed a few simple commands into the prompt screen. Moments later a humming sound emanated from around the ship and then the ceiling lights flickered and began to grow in brightness until Bra'hiv could clearly see the bridge around them.

'Run a diagnostic and see if you can learn what happened to the ship,' Bra'hiv ordered, keen to take advantage of the power supply. 'Then see if you an access her logs too.'

'Aye, general.'

The Marines guarding the bridge entrance stood back and General Bra'hiv saluted as Captain Sansin walked in, followed by Lieutenant C'rairn, Andaim and Meyanna Sansin, all wearing their atmospheric suits and Meyanna carrying a bag of medical supplies.

'Captain, ma'am,' Bra'hiv greeted them. 'My apologies for the temperature, but after what happened on the Sylph I thought it prudent to maintain as cold an atmosphere as possible.'

'That's fine, general,' Meyanna replied.

'Indeed,' the captain added, 'my wife's probably barely noticed it.'

Meyanna shot Idris a harsh glare. The general glanced at Andaim, who said nothing, so he beckoned Meyanna to follow him.

'What's so important that you've had to bring me all the way over here?' she asked.

Bra'hiv led Meyanna to the communications station, and stood back as she rounded the counter and promptly leaped back from it as one hand flew to her chest.

'Mother of Ethera,' she gasped.

Bra'hiv watched as Meyanna recovered from her initial surprise and horror, and then leaned closer to the face embedded into the console. Captain Sansin took one look at the face and then turned to Bra'hiv.

'The Legion? Surely not out here?'

'I don't know,' Bra'hiv replied, not wanting to commit to any guesswork while the doctor was present.

Meyanna knelt down and examined the horrific visage. The flesh, skin and bone fused perfectly with the metallic surface of the panel, blending with no visible joins. The hair, splayed out across the console, likewise ran like frozen rivers into the panel and vanished. Ice crystals glinted in the light, the man's face as pale as death and still locked in its eternal rictus of agony.

Meyanna reached down to the access panel beneath the console and opened it. As she leaned down she gasped audibly again as she observed the back of the man's head, a mass of frozen veins, arteries and tissue melding seamlessly into electrical circuits and wires clumped together en masse and passing through a series of resistors.

'What can you see?' Idris asked.

Meyanna ducked her head back out of the panel and closed it, but she did not reply as she looked again at the man's face and then the rest of the bridge.

'Why this console?' she wondered out loud, her voice a whisper. 'It's the communications console, correct?'

'Yes ma'am,' Bra'hiv replied, watching her keenly.

Meyanna looked at the console for a moment longer and then turned to the general.

'Engage the bridge heating and route the power into the bridge to re–engage the systems here.'

'You're sure?' Bra'hiv asked. 'You know what happened last time we…'

'I know what happened aboard the Sylph,' she cut him off. 'Maintain the cold in the rest of the ship, just isolate the bridge and warm it up a little.'

'Yes ma'am,' Bra'hiv replied and relayed the order to Mears.

Captain Sansin stepped to his wife's side. 'You sure you know what you're doing?'

Meyanna did not look at Idris as she replied. 'It's a hunch.'

'You don't know what will happen if we warm the bridge up though.'

'Well, if nothing else maybe it'll do me some good, eh?' she challenged him with a sly glance.

The captain did not respond as vents in the ceiling began billowing hot air into the bridge. General Bra'hiv removed his helmet first as the temperature rose, and then nodded to his men. The Marines removed their headgear, followed by Captain Sansin and Meyanna.

'I don't know what you hope to achieve by this,' Idris said to his wife. 'The ship's dead.'

Meyanna did not reply as she moved to the communications console and looked down at the face. The frost particles were melting, the victim's taut and frigid skin relaxing as moisture trickled down his cheeks and off the panels around him.

Meyanna watched for a few moments more and then her heart leaped in her chest.

The man's eyes opened.

***

XI

Pain.

It seared and throbbed, aching in laborious pulses that ground through his bones and skull in ceaseless rhythm to his fluttering, weakening heart.

Qayin had lost all track of time, sense of place and belonging. His mind it seemed had retreated, shrunk back to occupy only a tiny speck of existence in an attempt to block out the sheer agony that filled his world. The crack of the plasma whip seemed like a distant symphony of thunder, his limbs mere memories suspended around him and long devoid of sensation.

Qayin's eyes were closed, sealed shut from exhaustion, his head hanging so low that his chin rubbed against his chest. The taste of blood on his tongue was a mild diversion from the sight of it pooling on the deck below his feet, and for a few moments he was lost in a blissful delirium of sleep, devoid of sensation.

He became aware that the pain of the plasma–whip and its attendant hiss and snarl had ceased. Left in its wake was a world of pain that enveloped him in its cruel embrace, holding him as though to cherish the moment. Through his suffering Qayin somehow managed to open one eye. The deck below was stained red and glistening with his blood, his vision blurred so that he could not really focus on anything. He wondered briefly if this was the end. Perhaps the Veng'en had finally grown tired of the game and decided to end Qayin's life in a brief display of mercy, which Qayin realised would be hugely welcomed. He no longer wanted to live. There was nothing much worth living for anyway, and he realised that his injuries must be extensive: survival was now simply the weaker of his options.

The deck heaved beneath him and he felt something thump his forehead. His vision starred and he realised that he was laying now on the deck, the metal plating as soft as his mother's arms and beckoning him toward sleep. Only a terrible thirst prevented him from slipping into unconsciousness.

He saw his arm lift up beside him, and then the deck sliding beneath his bloodied frame as he was dragged without sensation. Moments later, he was lifted off the deck and slumped into a chair. Through one barely–open eye Qayin saw Kordaz fixing manacles to his ankles and then to his wrists, securing him in place. As though witnessing a dream, he saw the Veng'en insert with expert precision an intravenous line into Qayin's left arm and then attach a bag of saline fluid to it that he suspended alongside the chair in mid–air.

Confusion swam through Qayin's miserable world as he watched the Veng'en work, and then suddenly he felt the thirst slip away as his consciousness jerked him awake. The pain intensified as his senses sharpened and he sucked in a lung full of air.

Kordaz stood back and looked down at Qayin. 'Feeling better?'

As ever there was no emotion in his tones, but somehow Qayin detected something approaching satisfaction. He could not bring himself to speak, could in fact barely see Kordaz as his head was lolling onto his chest again, too weak to hold itself aloft.

'It's a shame,' Kordaz went on, 'that I have to improvise with such inadequate implements. A plasma whip is so human, so un–refined. We Veng'en prefer not to damage our captives on the outside, you see. It's far more psychologically damaging to insert foreign objects *inside* the body, it inflicts so much more pain. It also denies the subject the ultimate satisfaction of witnessing that damage healing, the scars fading.'

Qayin did not respond, partly because he was too exhausted and partly because some part of him knew that remaining silent was something that might irritate the Veng'en. Despite the threat of further violence, Qayin could not help himself.

However, to Qayin's surprise the Veng'en merely shrugged at the silence and strode away. Qayin managed to lift his head a little, his skull seeming to weigh tonnes as he watched Kordaz check a display screen across the hold.

'Your friends have dropped out of super–luminal cruise,' Kordaz growled with interest as he scanned the data streaming down the screen. 'It's time for us to meet them once more, Qayin, and for you to pay for everything that you have done.'

The Veng'en turned and strode from the hold, and the hatch hissed shut behind him to leave Qayin alone in the darkness.

Qayin peered at the deck below where he had been suspended. It looked as though he'd been exsanguinated three times over, although he knew that spilt fluid across a level surface always appears to have more volume that it actually does. More blood hung in lazily spinning globules in the zero gravity, reflecting the low light. He looked down at his body and for a brief moment his guts pinched in grief for the damage that had been done to him. His uniform was in shreds, scorched and tattered by the repeated blows of the plasma whip, and beneath it his body was tiger–striped with ugly black wounds. Barely a patch of untouched skin remained, the welts and lesions leaking blood and clear fluid as blisters formed along their edges.

Qayin moved his gaze wearily to his wrists, manacled to the chair. Blood was trickling down his arms and across his hands, slick and glistening in the dull glow of the hold lights. The blood seeped beneath the manacles, and Qayin pushed and pulled his right hand gently to see the wrist lubricated with his own blood. He kept it moving, focusing all of his strength on his wrist. The blood seeped and squeezed around the manacle, and Qayin tucked his fingers in and began to pull. His hands were large but so were his wrists, and Kordaz had not been so diligent as to ensure that the manacles were as tight as they could be. Qayin tucked his thumb in and pulled harder as he saw his hand begin to slip through the manacle, the metal hard as it tugged against his thinly lubricated skin. He pushed his hand back again, let more of his blood seep beneath the manacle, and then tried again.

He gritted his teeth against yet more pain, and this time his hand slipped free with a sucking sound. Qayin, exhausted, sat for a long moment in silence as he flexed his hand and caught his breath. Then, slowly, he undid the manacle on his left wrist before leaning forward and freeing his ankles.

He spent a few moments catching his breath once more as he unhooked the intravenous line from his arm, then surveyed the hold. Qayin knew that he was in no shape to fight, that in fact he quite probably would have difficulty walking. He tried to move his legs and was stunned to find that he could not do so, the muscles twitching and trembling but clearly unable to take his weight.

Anger flared from somewhere deep inside as Qayin sought an escape from the hold. He was looking aft when he spotted a familiar sight. Lashed to the rear of the hold, barely visible through the gloom, were several blue barrels. His mind flashed back to his escape from Chiron IV and the prize that he had taken with him.

Devlamine, the *Devil's Drink*.

The drug had been mixed with an accelerant to provide a draw and a death for the Legion, the Hunters designed to obtain the drug wherever they found it, for it was through drug abuse that the Legion had originally begun infecting the human race. Qayin, however, had been busily re–filtering the raw Devlamine back out ready for sale. His eyes flicked right, to the ranks of smaller silver flasks likewise lashed down: the pure Devlamine.

Qayin pushed himself forward off the seat and slumped slowly onto the blood–soaked deck as his legs crumpled beneath him, the thermal suit filled with tiny iron filings that attracted to the magnetically charged plates below the deck. He gritted his teeth against the pain and slowly began to drag himself across the deck.

Qayin had never taken a recreational drug in his life. In fact he hated them, having witnessed so many times the awful consequences of addiction and overdosing in habitual users. But now he knew that the Devlamine was the only thing that could save him from certain death at Kordaz's hands. Its powerful pain–killing properties and adrenaline–fuelling kick might just be enough to get him off the damned ship before Kordaz found Atlantia. Qayin had no idea what the Veng'en had planned, but he had no desire to return to Colonial service.

The deck rubbed painfully against his wounds as Qayin hauled himself through the hold and finally reached the silver flasks. There were two types of flask: one type was perfectly polished and had a blue ring at the top and the bottom. The other type was identical, but Qayin had marked them with a tiny scratch in the blue ring. These scratched flasks were the weaker quality Devlamine, watered down and designed for sale to either people Qayin wanted to rip off, or people whose company he enjoyed enough to not want to see them dead within a few months. It had been the diluted Devlamine that Qayin had supplied to Evelyn aboard Atlantia as well as some of Bravo Company's Marines.

Qayin reached for the scratched flasks, managed to unhook one from its fixings and held it against his chest as he lay on the deck. He was exhausted, dehydrated and suffering from acute blood loss, but with the last of his strength he dragged himself back to the chair and hauled his body up into a sitting positon once more.

Carefully Qayin re–inserted the IV line into his arm, but this time he reached up to where the saline fluid bag floated in mid–air above him. He pulled the bag down and tore open the top before pouring a small amount of the pure Devlamine into the saline fluid.

The clear fluid turned a deep, rich red–brown. Qayin shook the bag gently, swirling the Devlamine and mixing it before he reached up and left the bag hanging above him. Exhausted, he slumped into the seat once more and breathed deeply.

It took a moment for him to realise what was happening. He didn't really know what to expect from the drug, although he hoped fervently that it included a release from the pain wracking his weary body. As he sat slumped in the seat so he realised that he felt as though he was floating above it, no sensation from the backs of his legs. He looked down and his head swam as he lost balance. Qayin gripped the arms of the chair and breathed deeply as the Devlamine began to surge through his veins, and his vision suddenly sharpened as the pain receded into history and a grandiose sense of invincibility blossomed like a demon within him.

Qayin sucked in a lung full of air and with it the sheer power of the drug coursing through his body. His limbs twitched into life and he felt his heart accelerate in his chest, thumping like a war drum as savage anger flared in his heart, a thirst for revenge brighter than any other thought in his mind.

Qayin's head turned slowly as he surveyed the hold around him with refreshed vision and clarity of thought, and it was then that he saw the plasma whip that Kordaz had left hanging near one wall of the hold.

XII

Meyanna Sansin looked down into the frosty eyes of the face that stared out at her from the control panel. Several of the Marines around her backed away from the gruesome visage, clutching their plasma rifles tightly as though fighting the urge to blast the face into history.

Meyanna watched as the eyes blinked, staring straight up at the ceiling above Meyanna's head but strangely blank, as though without focus. She stepped cautiously forward and put herself into its line of sight.

The eyes stared blankly back at her, devoid of any emotion that she could recognise.

'What is it?' Andaim asked. 'Is it alive?'

Meyanna glanced across at Marine Mears. 'Can you activate the communications panel from there?'

Mears tapped in a few commands. Almost at once the face on the console blurted out an unintelligible stream of noise, a blabbering like that of a child, warbling and indistinct.

Meyanna took a pace closer and through the noise she heard something that she recognised.

'....circu....diagnos....power... enviro...data stream interru...'

'It's reciting a boot sequence,' Idris said in disbelief.

'It's not reciting it,' Meyanna corrected him. 'It's conducting it.'

As she watched, the last of the cold seeped from the face and the muscles and tendons began responding properly as the speech took on legible form.

'... systems reconnecting, diagnostic local circuit only, no signal, environmental systems active, propulsion, no signal.'

General Bra'hiv stepped closer to the face and his voice was more than a little haunted as he spoke.

'You're telling me that this is the ship's computer?'

Meyanna shrugged. 'Maybe, I'm not sure, but what I can tell you is that this face once belonged to a human being, probably one of the crew. It's now connected to the ship instead.'

Idris frowned. 'Is he *alive*?'

Meyanna shook her head. 'No, he's long dead. His face is being used as a communications conduit, a means of verbalising the ship's computer. I'd imagine his veins are filled with a conducting fluid that is preserving his flesh, as did the cold when the ship was deactivated.'

'How the hell did he end up like that?' Bra'hiv asked. 'And why?'

'I don't know the answer to that, general.'

Meyanna looked around the bridge at the other stations. None of them had been likewise modified with a human cadaver, which was what one would expect had the Legion or similar attempted to take control of the vessel in its entirety.

'Where is the rest of the crew?' Andaim wondered out loud.

Meyanna leaned close to the man's face and then she had an idea. 'Access the last data log input,' she said out loud.

Marine Mears moved to respond but the face spoke before he could.

Last data log entry, recorded orbital date fourteen oh seven on the eighth quadrant.'

Meyanna looked at Idris, who raised an eyebrow. 'That's eighty seven years ago,' he said.

'Display the log entry, main screen.' Meyanna ordered the computer.

The main screen on the bridge flickered into life and upon it appeared the face of a man who had gone down in Etheran legend.

'Captain Meke Greer,' Idris identified him.

Greer had been a relatively young commander of just forty years old when he was selected to be captain of Endeavour. Youth had been considered essential to Endeavour's crew, the better to last them as they established the ship as a home for what might become the rest of their lives. Less than ten per cent of the crew had been over fifty years of age.

Greer's features were wracked with concern as he appeared on the screen, his hair in disarray and his uniform poorly adjusted. He looked weak and drawn, his eyes ringed with bruised patches as though he had not slept for a month. His voice, when he spoke, was soft and hard to decipher.

'All stations, all stations, this is the Endeavour, one thousand souls aboard. We are adrift and in need of assistance. We are overcome by something.., something that we do not understand. All are afflicted, young and old.' Greer's expression changed to one of confusion. *'We do not know what we are. We do not know who we are. None of us can remember anything, except that we are a great danger. We are a plague ship. I have instructed the crew to destroy the propulsion systems, to prevent us from being returned to Ethera. We cannot allow whatever is aboard to spread. It takes us from who we are. We cannot help ourselves. Please, if you receive this transmission, send help but do not board us. Stay away from Endeavour!'*

The transmission cut off abruptly as Greer, apparently unaware of his own hand, shut off the recording.

Meyanna looked down at the face embedded into the control panel. 'What happened here?'

The face, devoid of emotion or sight, replied. *'No signal. Repeat, no signal.'*

'What does that mean?' Bra'hiv asked.

'It means that it has no input,' Idris guessed. 'It has no data to share.'

'They said we should not be here,' Bra'hiv snapped. 'That this is a plague ship.'

'They also said that had no understanding of what was happening to them,' Meyanna replied. 'I have a scanner here and it has detected no evidence of the Legion aboard ship so far. Likewise we know how to prevent infection using our microwave emitters, so we have nothing to fear at this time. Our priority is figuring out what happened to these people so that the same fate does not befall our own crew.'

Idris moved across to where Marine Mears was still standing beside the engineering panel.

'Can you access the entire ship's controls from this panel?'

Mears nodded as he scanned the instruments. 'Endeavour is an older type of vessel with simpler wiring. In theory I should be able to access everything for'ard of the engine bays, where the main damage is.'

'The captain said that he'd ordered the crew to scuttle the ship,' Bra'hiv said. 'It explains the extent of the damage to the engine bays–caused by lots of controlled explosions instead of one enormous one. They must have been real serious about whatever they found aboard.'

'That's what bothers me,' Idris replied. 'They had lifeboats and escape capsules: a means of evasion, no matter how bad the odds. Yet they chose to give up, to abandon any hope of discovery before they died. Why?'

'To protect Ethera,' C'rairn said. 'Why else would they have scuttled themselves? Their current course is orientated directly away from the core systems.'

'They could have done that and still escaped,' Idris countered.

'Not and found somewhere to hide,' Bra'hiv said as he examined the ship's data logs on another screen, that belonging to the navigator's position. 'We're twelve light years from the nearest habitable system, and none of Endeavour's escape vessels have mass–drives. If the crew had abandoned ship they'd have been doomed anyway.'

Idris nodded.

'My point exactly,' he agreed. 'They must be still aboard somewhere. Can we gain access to camera feeds around the ship? Take a look around without compromising ourselves?'

Mears nodded and began skipping through files on the screen before him until he found the ones he wanted.

'Ship's security system,' he said out loud as he accessed the relevant files. 'Opening the feeds again and directing them here.'

The main screen flickered and then a series of camera feeds appeared, broken up into sections so that multiple areas of Endeavour could be viewed at once. Idris saw instantly the landing bay with the Marines manning their posts, a number of deserted corridors leading to important areas of the ship such as the engine bays, mess hall, holds and the bridge itself.

Several of the screens switched every few seconds, automatically moving the feed through various areas of the ship to provide a sort of roving–eye. Idris saw the display shift from an image of the landing bay to one of the bridge, the captain and his accomplices looking at themselves for a moment before the feed moved on. Another image showed a storage facility filled with escape pods, then another of the for'ard crews' quarters and…

'Wait, go back.'

Meyanna's voice was pitched a touch higher than usual as though she had recognised something of importance. Mears worked his controls and isolated the relevant camera feed, then blew it up to fill the main screen.

An image of rows of escape pods standing vertically in the centre of one of the main holds filled the screen, and Meyanna moved closer as she examined them.

'Why are those escape pods not in their launch chutes?'

Idris frowned as he realised that he could not think of a suitable reason as to why the pods were standing vertically in what looked like Endeavour's hold. He turned to Mears.

'Where is this feed coming from?'

'Hold compartment four, captain,' Mears replied. 'Aft section, Deck H, a couple of bulkheads for'ard of the damaged section of the hull.'

Andaim peered with interest at the pods. 'They're occupied,' he said.

Idris could see the indistinct shape of bodies suspended in the pods, and he realised what he was looking at.

'It's the crew,' the captain said finally. 'Damn me, could there be any chance that they're still alive? This explains the state of Endeavour: they must have re–routed all power to the escape pods in the hope that they'd keep them in stasis for long enough to be found.'

Mears scanned his instruments and shook his head.

'I can't tell captain,' he said, 'there's not enough information coming from the pods. In fact, there's no data at all. They must be connected to another power source entirely, re–routed somehow.'

It was Bra'hiv who answered.

'The fusion core,' he replied. 'If they were trying to preserve their lives for as long as possible, they'd have connected themselves directly to the core. Powering only life support to the pods, they could have a lifespan of centuries, maybe even thousands of years.'

'Get a team down there,' Idris ordered Bra'hiv. 'Full battle kit and at least four medics. If there's even the hint of a chance that Greer and his crew have survived long enough to be revived, I want them off this ship.'

'We don't know what's down there,' Meyanna said as she gestured to the communications panel. 'Looks at what happened to this crewman. None of this explains how he came to be a part of the station. Whatever Greer and his people were hoping to avoid is still unknown.'

'We'll have to cross that bridge when we come to it,' Idris insisted. 'If you were there, in one of those pods and locked away for decades, wouldn't you want us to come and let you out?'

'Not if that was the very act that would kill me!' Meyanna pleaded. 'They need studying Idris, not unleashing, at least until we know what's happened here!'

Idris was about to answer but it was Bra'hiv who spoke first.

'We've got another reason to get down there, fast!' he snapped.

Idris looked at the general sharply and saw Bra'hiv point to the main screen, at the deck in between several of the more distant capsules. There, marring the perfect frost glistening on the ship's decks, were footprints.

'We're not alone aboard this ship, captain,' Bra'hiv said.

Idris moved closer to the screen, peering at the marks in the frost. 'They're boot prints,' he said. 'A survivor?'

'This ship has been drifting for more than eighty years,' Meyanna said. 'Even ignoring the timescale, nobody could survive these conditions without extensive protection for that long. They'd die within days.'

'That's not all,' Bra'hiv said as he gestured to the screen, which was now zoomed in on the boot prints and the nearest capsule. 'Look at the occupant.'

It took Idris only a moment to realise what Bra'hiv had seen. The occupant of the capsule was human, and upon their face was a mask that he recognised instantly. Metal and featureless but for small slits that allowed the wearer a limited view of the world outside, and with two metallic probes that vanished into the wearer's mouth and down into their throat, preventing them from speaking, conspiring, formulating evil.

'The Word,' Idris gasped. 'That's the same mask that...'

'That Evelyn was wearing in the prison when we first met her,' Meyanna finished the sentence for her husband.

***

XIII

'Move out!'

The Marines tumbled out of the shuttle as its engines whined down in Endeavour's landing bay, the troops from Bravo Company forming up into ranks as General Bra'hiv marched out to meet them.

The general glanced the reinforcements over, his practiced eye seeking any sign of unsecured atmospheric suits, sloppily arranged kit or evidence of reluctance or nervousness in the troops. He saw none. Formerly gang–bangers and convicts, many of them under the thrall of Qayin, they now served Bra'hiv without question. Most of them were just kids really, barely out of their teens, and despite their horrendous crimes and bragged–about slayings on Ethera's rough streets, most of them merely needed to belong to something, to fight for something bigger than themselves. Although it was a continuous struggle, Bra'hiv had won most of them over, especially after Qayin's bare–faced betrayal and abandonment of his own people on Chiron IV.

'Listen up!' Bra'hiv called, his voice carrying clearly across the landing bay and reaching every one of the forty men before him. 'We have evidence of people aboard this ship, likely human, likely wanting to avoid us. We have no idea who they are or what they're doing here, but we're going to damned well find out and it's Bravo Company who will be leading the way!'

Bra'hiv saw the pride in their faces behind the masks that protected them from the bitter cold enveloping Endeavour.

'Two fire teams, ten men each. The rest of you on guard support for the secured areas of the ship. We move quickly and we move quietly, no fuss. Do not fire unless fired upon–we want whoever these people are taken alive, to learn from them about what happened to this ship, is that understood?!'

A chorus of *Yessir* echoed across the landing bay.

Bra'hiv turned away from Bravo Company as a Raython pilot jogged across the bay to join him, still wearing her flight helmet. The sleek fighter was parked nearby, the recently shut–down engines billowing a shimmering heat haze onto the cold air above the craft.

'Where's the fire?' Evelyn asked. 'I thought that we were to remain out there on patrol until further orders?'

'Something's come up,' Bra'hiv replied. 'You need to see this.'

'See what?' Evelyn asked, her normally composed demeanour slightly uncertain as Bra'hiv pulled out a holo–plate and activated it.

A glowing, three–dimensional image of the object in Endeavour's holds flashed into existence, and Evelyn's hand flew automatically to her face as she saw the shape of the mask covering the unknown victim inside an escape capsule.

'That's my mask,' she gasped, knowing well that the original mask was in her locker back on Atlantia, a reminder of where she had come from.

'Looks like they existed for a long time before we believed the Word created them,' Bra'hiv explained. 'These capsules may have been here in stasis for some eighty years.'

'That's not possible,' Evelyn whispered, still touching her face as though trying to protect herself from even an image of the mask.

The masks had been used on only the most violent of convicts, those men and women considered a lethal threat to the general public on Ethera. According to Ethera's Human Rights laws, the masks could not be fitted for more than twenty four hours at a time and only then during transportation of the convict from one facility to another, or at any time where prison staff might be victim to attacks from said prisoner. Evelyn herself was the only human being known to have endured years behind a mask without recourse to legal aid.

'The first time these masks were commissioned by the Word was forty years ago, according to Ethera's government of the time,' Bra'hiv said. 'These things just shouldn't be here at all.'

Andaim joined them in the landing bay and looked at the holographic image closely.

'Which begs the question: why are civilian passengers aboard Endeavour wearing masks inside escape capsules?'

'That's what we're going to find out,' Captain Sansin replied as he too joined them and looked at Evelyn. 'You up for this?'

Evelyn mastered her revulsion at the sight of the mask as the general clicked the display off, and she nodded.

'Good,' Bra'hiv said. 'We have evidence of somebody down there moving about. It could be old boot prints preserved in the frost but there's only one way to be sure, so stay sharp at all times.'

'We'll support you from Atlantia,' Captain Sansin said as he turned toward the shuttle. 'Lael doesn't have enough experience to keep the ship in order for much longer.'

'I'm staying aboard Endeavour,' Meyanna informed her husband.

Idris hesitated. 'If you're doing this because I was a bit short with you then you're…'

'I'm staying to get to the bottom of what happened here,' Meyanna cut the captain off. 'The Word's presence, however minor, could be key in finding new ways to combat the Legion. This opportunity is too good to miss.'

Meyanna turned and marched away before her husband could say anything further. Idris ground his teeth together as he turned away.

'Stay and keep an eye on her,' he ordered Andaim.

'Aye, captain,' Andaim replied.

Bra'hiv checked his rifle and then turned, and with a forward motion of one gloved hand he led Bravo Company toward an open bulkhead guarded by four Marines under C'rairn's command.

'Alpha Company should be leading this mission,' Lieutenant C'rairn said as Bra'hiv drew alongside. 'The convicts still cannot be trusted, you know that.'

'What I know is that the more responsibility we give them, the more loyal they become. You want in, or would you rather stay here on guard duty?'

C'rairn's reply was to activate his plasma rifle's magazine and fall into step behind the general as he strode down the corridor. Evelyn followed them, watching as the Marines led the way but her mind filled with the grainy, indistinct image of the mask affixed to the face of some nameless, long dead civilian trapped aboard Endeavour.

'You okay?' Andaim asked as he walked alongside her, concern writ large across his features.

Evelyn nodded. 'I just didn't ever expect to see one of those damned things again.'

'Nobody ever liked them,' Andaim said as they walked. 'Even when they were fitted to murderers they just made them look all the more sinister, like you couldn't see their emotions and therefore couldn't tell what they were going to do next.'

Evelyn nodded, unable to think of anything more to say. Images that she did not want to see flashed through her mind and she saw the family she had been forced to forget, her husband and their little boy: smiling faces, happiness, the peaceful existence of the colonies. Evelyn saw in her mind's eye the office where she had worked for many years, for the media. An investigator. She had done well, uncovered corporate espionage, exposed corrupt politicians, crushed unjust convictions.

Then the Word had attracted her attention, the cries of protesters who feared that their lives were being controlled by nothing more than a machine that viewed humanity as little more than a distraction. The belief that somewhere, somehow, the police were showing signs of becoming militarised without government or democratic consent. The increase in political conservatism, the sense of always being watched, an invasive series of laws being passed that served no purpose but to justify increased military spending on classified projects and protect those projects from independent or even political oversight.

She had investigated for months, uncovering an ever growing number of deaths involving whistle blowers, government employees and unfortunate bystanders in remote regions of both Caneeron and Ethera that were described as *unfortunate accidents*. Then, the emergence of tremendously potent street drugs like Devlamine: her interview with a convict bearing the *Mark of Qayin*, the bioluminescent tattoos on his face and his braided gold and blue locks outshone by the rage infecting his massive frame.

Eventually she had gone too far. The threats began against her life, against the lives of her family. The media company she worked for suddenly fired her, her long–standing and honourable boss turning into a tyrant who almost physically ejected her from the building.

Drugs had been found in her home. Police arrived, arrests were made. She was questioned, recalled nothing of how the drugs had gotten into her home: she and her husband hated such things. She was released, her disgrace covered by the media company she had once worked for, no mention that the police found no evidence of her or any of her family being habitual drug users.

She saw herself at home that night, heard her husband's kind words, saw her sleeping child, recalled feeling so afraid for him. And then the morning. The blood, everywhere. The confusion. Her husband dead, his head a mess of blood and bone where he had been shot. Her son, likewise dead. The crushing grief. The sirens, the arrest, the drugs scattered across her kitchen, the weapon found in the trash.

The tests followed. She was positive for drugs in her system even though she had taken not even pain killers for weeks. The charges for the murder of her entire family. The incarceration, immediate and high–security. The restraints and the mask, for *her own safety* and that of her gaolers. The lack of a trial, and then the prison system.

'Evelyn?'

She blinked and looked at Andaim, felt him rest a hand on her shoulder. 'You look like you're about to kill something,' he said.

She realised that they had walked a considerable distance through the ship and she hadn't even noticed the passing of the time.

'This feels surreal,' she said. 'I can't get the images out of my head.'

'Images of what?'

Evelyn opened her mouth to reply and then she hesitated and shook the feelings off, unwilling to share such things even with Andaim.

'It doesn't matter.'

'It matters to me.'

'I don't want to talk about it,' Evelyn muttered, and then caught her anger and offered Andaim a brief smile. 'Not now, anyway.'

Ahead, General Bra'hiv raised his hand in a clenched fist and the Marines slowed as one. The emergency lighting further aft was more widely spaced, the holds less often frequented by the crew and the corridors darker and infested with shadows. The cold bit deeper too, or maybe Evelyn was just imagining things as she gripped the handle of her pistol more tightly and watched as Bra'hiv crouched down in the centre of the corridor and pointed ahead.

'I've got a heat signature,' whispered Lieutenant C'rairn, his voice audible in Evelyn's earpiece.

'Human?' Bra'hiv asked.

'Negative, it's too small. Foot of the hold entrance.'

Through the shadows Evelyn could see the entrance to the main holds, and she realised immediately that something was wrong. The bulkhead hatches were intact, but the doors were wide open and she could see what looked like debris laying on the deck in the entrance.

'It's metallic slag,' Andaim whispered into his microphone. 'Somebody fried the locking mechanisms. If the metal's still hot...'

'... then they were here recently,' Bra'hiv finished the sentence for the CAG. 'Weapons hot folks, we're definitely not alone.'

The faint hum of multiple plasma rifles coming to life filled the corridor, and Evelyn watched as General Bra'hiv crept forward to the hold entrance and used a hand–held scanner to sweep the way ahead before he turned and used hand–signals to beckon the troops forward.

The Marines jogged in a low crouch to the entrance and with oft–practiced efficiency they entered the hold and fanned out, seeking concealment and covering their colleagues as they moved.

'Let's go,' Andaim said.

The CAG got up to move, but Evelyn hesitated. He looked back at her expectantly, but her legs felt like rubber as a premonition of doom swept over her like a dark wave.

'There's something in there,' she said, her lips moving as though of their own accord. 'Something I don't want to see.'

Andaim's hand touched her shoulder again. 'It's going to be fine, okay? You'll be safer with us than crouching in this corridor on your own.'

Evelyn forced her legs to move as she advanced and followed Andaim through the hatch and into the holds.

The sight that greeted her was every bit as foreboding as she had feared. Endless ranks of escape capsules, all stood on end like a forest of glossy, frosty obelisks. The Marines were moving systematically between the capsules and Evelyn could see that many of the observation panels on the capsules had been brushed free of frost, revealing the bodies that were trapped inside.

'Per–fluorocarbon,' Andaim identified the fluid that filled each capsule, but he hesitated as he looked more closely at the occupant inside. 'It's not human.'

'Nor this one,' Bra'hiv gestured to another capsule that contained some sort of aquatic species.

The Marines were spreading out further, weapons aiming this way and that as they weaved between the capsules.

'I don't even know what to call some of these things,' Lieutenant C'rairn gasped as he surveyed the contents of capsule after capsule. 'How the hell did they end up in here? Endeavour hasn't travelled far enough to encounter this many species.'

'It's fascinating,' Meyanna gasped as she observed the contents of the capsules. 'Like a biological preserve of some kind.'

Evelyn crept through the darkness, peering into the bitter capsules and witnessing the bizarre life forms imprisoned within each one, as though Endeavour's hold had been converted into some kind of macabre biological museum.

'We've got one, a human,' C'rairn said.

Evelyn instinctively converged on C'rairn's position along with Andaim and several other Marines. The darkness seemed to deepen around her as the Marines silently made way for her, and she realised that they were all looking at her as she passed.

'It's just not possible,' Andaim gasped as he stared up at the capsule.

Evelyn looked up at the observation panel.

Inside was a human being, a woman of lithe, slight build with light brown hair and an expression that was hard to judge behind the mask she wore, as though poised between grief and rage. Her eyes were closed, her body entirely suspended in the per–fluorocarbon, but the identification badge on her chest was clear for all to see.

For Evelyn, it was like looking at a ghost.

'It's her,' Bra'hiv murmured in disbelief. 'It's Evelyn.'

A Marine jogged up from out of the darkness and jabbed a gloved thumb over his shoulder toward the rear of the hold.

'There are more of them,' he said, 'humans, all wearing Colonial uniforms but not the masks.'

'Start a diagnostic scan of the crew,' Bra'hiv ordered. 'Find out if they're still alive!'

The Marine saluted and hurried away as Andaim looked up at the woman in the capsule.

'How can this be?' he asked Evelyn.

Evelyn was about to speak when a terrific blast of light flared like an exploding star and blinded her as an explosion ripped through Endeavour's hold.

***

XIV

'What the hell was that?'

Captain Idris Sansin saw the live–feed from Endeavour's hold suddenly flare with white light as he walked back onto Atlantia's bridge, and then the feed was abruptly cut off.

'Explosion on H–deck,' Lael called as she surveyed the signals coming from the depths of the aged ship. 'I've got plasma fire, multiple rounds!'

'Send in reinforcements!' Idris snapped.

Lael relayed his command as Mikhain's voice reached the Atlantia's bridge.

'New contact bearing eight four three, elevation niner!'

Idris whirled as the tactical display flashed a small red symbol located at the coordinates Mikhain had passed over. A data stream revealed mass, velocity, trajectory and evidence of weapons that Mikhain called out even as Idris was reading from the screen.

'Four thousand tonnes, sub–luminal intercept course, plasma weapons and projectiles all charging up, military–grade shields!'

'Block her,' Idris ordered. 'Send Raythons to intercept her before she breaks our defensive lines. Do we have a visual identification?'

'Negative,' Mikhain replied. *'She's too small to take on a frigate but she's heavily armed. Some kind of gunship I'd say.'*

'This could be a coordinated attack,' Idris warned. 'Assume that her intentions are hostile but do not fire until fired upon.'

As Mikhain relayed the orders to his staff on Arcadia's bridge Idris turned his attention back to the explosion on Endeavour. The communications link with General Bra'hiv was still blank, the screen showing nothing but static.

'Can we re–establish communications with the Marines?' Idris asked.

'Negative, captain,' Lael replied from her post. 'We can only follow Alpha Company and hope that they get there in time.'

Idris clenched his fists in frustration but said nothing as he looked at a second screen which showed the view through the visor of an Alpha Company sergeant as he led his men deep into Endeavour's interior.

*

'Covering fire!'

Evelyn heard Bra'hiv bellow his order above the din of plasma rifles as she shook her head and tried to clear her vision after the blinding flare of the blast that had blinded them all. She crouched down by the foot of the nearest capsule, her pistol in her hand as she heard the Marines shouting warnings and commands at each other as they returned fire.

'Man down!' somebody cried. 'Medic!'

'We're cornered!' screamed another.

Evelyn saw Andaim a short distance away, aiming into the darkness as he fired off two quick shots with his pistol. A salvo of shots returned out of the depths of the hold and the CAG crouched out of sight and covered his face with his hands as plasma blasted past him in super–heated balls of blue–white light.

'Where the hell did they all come from?!' Lieutenant C'rairn shouted. 'They're all around us!'

General Bra'hiv leaped out from behind a capsule and fired into the blackness around them before he hurled himself down behind a stack of gravity–pallets against the far wall of the hold. Evelyn saw him peek over the top of the pallets in an attempt to get an idea of the situation, and immediately duck down again as three plasma rounds blasted the pallets around him and forced him out of sight.

Evelyn turned and peered around the edge of the capsule behind which she had hidden. Distant muzzle flashes flared from plasma rifles that illuminated the darkened hold in vivid flares of white light and revealed the ghostly forms of figures firing almost constantly in controlled bursts as they circled around the cornered Marines and headed for the exit. They dashed with almost supernatural precision from cover to cover, like demons flitting from one shadow to the next.

She aimed her pistol and fired once. Her shot rocketed away toward one of the figures and hit him square in the chest, but the plasma round flared as though it had hit something through which it could not pass. Its light flickered out and the figure aimed at her and fired back with one fluid motion and without even breaking stride.

Evelyn ducked out of sight and pinned her back against the escape capsule as the shot raced by and she spotted Lieutenant C'rairn a few cubits away, likewise pinned down.

'The entrance!' she yelled at the lieutenant. 'They're making a run for it!'

C'rairn looked over his shoulder and spotted the figures dashing for the hold exit, firing as they went. Evelyn aimed and fired twice in the general direction of the hold exit, and then suddenly the blaze of gunfire ceased as abruptly as it had arrived and a deafening silence filled the hold.

Evelyn peeked her head out from behind the capsule and looked in the direction of the exit. A cloud of smoke obscured the view, but she could see through the diaphanous whorls two small flashing red lights blinking on and off either side of the exit.

The Marines cautiously emerged from cover, and General Bra'hiv crouched down and ran low toward the exit before coming up short and raising an open hand.

'Don't come any closer than this,' he called out. 'Proximity charges.'

Evelyn stepped out and stared at the hold exit, the two charges either side of the door designed to detonate upon detecting motion nearby. Two barometric sensors were fitted to each charge as well as infra–red detectors, the two methods ensuring that nobody could get close to the devices.

'Damn me,' Andaim uttered in confusion. 'Who the hell were they? And why haven't we detected their ship?'

It was General Bra'hiv, still crouched down on the deck as the Marines gathered nearby, who answered.

'Colonial Special Forces,' he said simply.

Andaim shook his head. 'No, not out here. We detected no other craft, no forms of life, nothing.'

'They would know how to hide themselves,' Bra'hiv insisted. 'They would have the equipment necessary to avoid detection, even conceal their ship if it's aboard. They also exited this hold in a matter of seconds once they'd moved close enough to get out, which means that they were small in number despite the firepower they were laying down, and only Special Forces would deploy charges like these. I've seen them before on Ethera, when I took a demolitions course.'

Andaim frowned as he looked at the charges. 'Can you disable them?'

The general shook his head. 'Not from here and not without the correct tools,' he replied. 'We'll have to wait for back–up to arrive. My communications link is down.'

'Mine too,' Andaim confirmed. 'They must have used some sort of device in the initial blast to fry our communicators.'

'Another popular SF technique,' Bra'hiv added. 'We're dealing with real pros here.'

'I shot at one of them and hit him,' Evelyn revealed. 'It was like the shot never touched him, didn't even break his stride.'

'Yeah, same for me,' C'rairn said. 'I could've sworn I got one of them but he just kept on moving.'

'Like I said, Special Forces,' Bra'hiv insisted. 'They'll have kit that we've never even seen before.

'What are they doing here?' Evelyn asked. 'Could they be escapees from the apocalypse?'

Bra'hiv shrugged. 'Maybe, either way it's clear they don't want anything to do with us. Maybe they think we're infected or something?'

The rattle of boots on the decks outside the holds alerted them and the soldiers leaped up, weapons aimed at the hold exit, and then stood down as they recognised Alpha Company's men arriving. Bra'hiv raised a clenched fist toward them and then pointed at the charges. The Marine sergeant slowed immediately and his men stopped behind him as they all looked at the charges.

'Sapper,' the sergeant called, and one of the troopers behind him moved out and peered at the charges from a safe distance.

'Stand by,' the sapper advised. 'This will take a few minutes.'

Evelyn turned around and walked back into the hold, patches of cooling plasma smouldering on the decks and two Marines laying on their backs side by side as a medic worked hurriedly on their wounds alongside Meyanna.

She eased around the injured Marines and walked back to where the capsule containing the woman stood. She looked into the viewing panel at the masked face suspended within the fluid as though simply sleeping. The palour of the skin told Evelyn that the person inside must surely be long dead, but now she noticed something else: the cable extending from the top of the capsule and down into the interior. Almost every other capsule contained the same cable.

Evelyn moved to the next capsule in the line and her eye traced the cable from its interior and up and away into the ceiling of the hold, where it was joined by countless others that swept away toward the aft wall. She had assumed like everybody else that the cables snaking downward were merely power cables, designed to preserve the lives inside the capsules almost indefinitely under the power provided by the fusion core. But now she realised that many were in fact inserted directly into the bodies of the captives themselves, and thus could not have been used to power the escape capsules.

'The capsules are inert,' she whispered.

'What?'

She turned as Andaim moved alongside her and looked up at the capsule.

'They're inert,' she repeated. 'These capsules were not set up just to preserve the lives of the species inside them. They were arranged to do something *to* them. The cables run directly into their heads, or whatever passes for a head in some of them, except for that woman.'

'I'm sure it's just a coincidence,' Andaim said as he glanced at the capsule. 'Whoever this woman was, she's long gone now.'

Evelyn could not tell if Andaim was saying it just to be nice to her or whether he actually believed it.

'Did the Endeavour have a passenger manifest?' she asked. 'Something we could use to identify who she was? There's no name on her ID badge, it's been obscured.'

Andaim nodded. 'Endeavour's passenger list was the most widely distributed in the history of space flight at the time, and most of the crew were recorded in great detail. I'll have the manifest uploaded to Atlantia and we can check it out when we get back.'

Evelyn nodded vacantly as she stared into the masked face, wondering who she had been and how she had come to be abandoned alone and freezing cold aboard Endeavour's lonely hull. Evelyn recalled with a shock that she too had once been trapped within a similar escape capsule, also filled with per–fluorocarbon and very much alone as the temperature had gradually fallen. She had been in danger of freezing to death but had survived.

This woman had endured the same terrifying fate, but had not been so lucky.

'Got it!'

Evelyn turned and saw the Alpha Company sapper disable the two charges, the blinking red lights switching off as he aimed a small, hand–held device at them. General Bra'hiv stepped forward as the sapper yanked the charges off the wall.

'What do you make of them?' Bra'hiv asked.

The sapper turned the charges over in his hands for a moment before replying.

'An older method of making them,' he said, 'I've seen the design before, most often used by Recon units, Special Forces, people like that. They would normally attach a detonator with a rapidly alternating frequency to stop sappers like me from blocking the signals using a hand–held jammer like I just did, but I guess these folks didn't have much time to set the charges off. You must have walked in on them, general.'

Bra'hiv nodded. 'Do you still have contact with Atlantia?'

'Yes,' the sergeant replied as he looked at Evelyn, 'and you need to speak to the captain urgently.'

'Why, what's happened?' Evelyn asked.

'We have another problem emerging, outside.'

***

XV

'You're sure it's the same ship?'

'Positive sir, it's Salim Phaeon's gunship all right.'

Mikain's reply was devoid of doubt, but even so Idris Sansin could not quite believe that he was looking at the same craft, a cruel looking spaceship with hooked x–wing configuration and a long, equally hooked bow that had something in common with Ethera's most savage birds of prey.

Atlantia's optical sensors were at maximum zoom in order to resolve the distant craft's form, its deep red hull glinting in the weak light of the hydrogen clouds as it closed on Atlantia. Four Raython fighters had formed an escort around it, two of them maintaining position directly behind the gunship in case it attempted to attack.

'Its shields are up and its weapons are hot,' Mikhain added, *'but it has made no attempt to attack our fighters.'*

'Communication?' Idris asked.

'Nothing,' Mikhain replied, *'and it's jamming our sensors so we cannot determine how many people are aboard. We know that Salim Phaeon is dead, Idris. You killed him yourself and we all witnessed it.'*

'Which leaves only a single person who can be aboard that ship,' Idris replied. 'Qayin.'

'He was last seen by one of our pilots fleeing the battle on Chiron IV, but we do not know whether he got off the planet or not.'

'If I know Qayin, he got off the planet all right and likely took Salim's gunship for good measure. He'd have headed straight for the Icari Line.' Idris paused. 'So why would he have come here? He must have tracked us.'

'It doesn't make any sense,' Mikhain admitted. *'I'd have thought Qayin would want to get as far away from here as possible.'*

Idris watched the cruel looking craft for a moment longer and then made his decision.

'Keep trying to establish contact,' he said, 'but if they come within one thousand cubits without identifying themselves, we intercept and board her.'

Before Mikhain could respond, Lael cut in from the communications console.

'They're signalling us, captain,' she informed him.

Idris straightened his uniform and turned to the main screen. 'Open a channel.'

The main viewing screen on the bridge switched from an image of Endeavour to one of the cockpit of the gunship, and almost immediately there was a gasp of surprise from the command crew as they saw a Veng'en staring back at them, his eyes aglow with a dull red light.

'Kordaz,' Idris exclaimed as he took an involuntary step toward the screen. 'You're alive.'

'Surprised, captain?' Kordaz asked, his gruff voice audible over the vocal resonance translator.

'We thought that you'd perished on Chiron IV,' Idris explained. 'The Veng'en cruiser we engaged bombarded the surface. We thought that nothing could have survived.'

Kordaz's eyes narrowed.

'The Veng'en bombarded the surface?' he asked. 'I thought that you did.'

'No,' Idris insisted. 'Mikhain was in control of Atlantia at the time and used her to block the Veng'en attack profile. We only managed to gain control of Arcadia at the last moment and defeat the cruiser, but by then it was too late. It has taken months to repair the damage to Atlantia.'

Kordaz watched the captain for a long moment.

'The one you call Evelyn,' he said. 'She found me before the bombardment, but she left me for dead.'

'She couldn't move you,' Idris replied. 'You were too heavy and she thought you doomed, infected by the Legion. She had to take off or she too would have perished.'

'And the Colonial pilot who shot me?' Kordaz snarled. 'What's her excuse?'

'She saw you about to kill a Marine,' Idris snapped, 'and acted accordingly. They were all under attack from infected Veng'en, what did you expect her to do? She did not know that you were on the surface, so how could she have known in that instant that she was firing on an ally?'

Kordaz emitted a low growl as though considering what he had been told. 'And Qayin, the Marine who betrayed me?'

'He fled,' Idris replied, 'escaped during the battle and is either far away from us or dead. I have no idea and I do not care. He abandoned his own men in an act of cowardice. He does not deserve our concern.'

Kordaz nodded.

'He is not so very far from here,' the Veng'en reported. 'In fact, he is aboard this very ship.'

Idris raised an eyebrow. 'Qayin is aboard your ship, right now?'

'I followed him,' Kordaz explained, 'boarded this vessel and took control. Qayin is my prisoner and I offer him to you in exchange for your assistance.'

'You kept him alive?'

'Not without considerable effort, captain,' Kordaz replied. 'It is not the custom of my people to offer quarter to those who betray us, but I understand that it is yours to offer a fair trial to any human charged with cowardice, treachery and other such crimes. Qayin is a human, not a Veng'en, thus I felt that his punishment would be best administered by your own hands.'

Idris took a deep breath. 'I thank you, Kordaz, for your consideration in this matter. What assistance can we offer you in return?'

Kordaz's voice dropped an octave as he replied.

'I am sick,' he said. 'I do not know how much longer I can survive without proper medical attention, and Wraiythe is too far to make the journey home.'

Idris looked at Kordaz's blood–red eyes once more. He had initially assumed that the affliction was perhaps a remnant of injuries sustained in the bombardment of Chiron IV, and that Kordaz had escaped before the full impact of the assault. The Veng'en was standing close to the monitor screen, close enough that Idris could not see anything below the warrior's neck, but now he realised that there was a metallic tint to his eyes.

'How did you survive the bombardment, Kordaz?' he asked the Veng'en. 'Evelyn said that you were fatally wounded when she last saw you, that she herself barely escaped the assault. How are you here?'

Across the communications channel Idris thought that he heard a soft sigh as slowly Kordaz stepped back from the screen. Idris felt a tight knot of anxiety twist his guts as the Veng'en revealed a chest constructed it seemed of a metal fabric, as much organic as metallic, that reflected the lights from the cockpit around him.

'He's infected,' Lael warned. 'The Legion must have got to him.'

'I *was* infected,' Kordaz countered her. 'I was injured by the shot fired by your pilot and then the bombardment afterward, but there were still many Infectors and Hunters on the surface. I was too weak to escape them, and thought that I was lost when they crawled upon my body and infiltrated my wounds. I cannot explain why they chose to repair and not consume me, but before they were finished the atmosphere of Chiron IV began to break down under the cosmic rays of its dying star. The radiation killed off the Infectors before their work was complete, but also gave me a fighting chance.'

'And them,' Idris realised as he figured out what must have happened. 'The Infectors repaired you because you were their only chance of getting off that planet, a shield against the cosmic rays. They might yet be inside your body, perhaps hibernating.'

Kordaz appeared surprised. 'I had not considered that,' he admitted. 'But whatever their motivation, they failed. I remain uninfected but also not fully healed from my injuries, which would have killed me otherwise. I am weakening and I know that I cannot survive much longer on my own.'

Idris bit his lip as he heard Mikhain's voice cut in from Arcadia.

'We cannot allow this to happen,' he insisted. *'This is exactly the kind of ploy the Word would use to get aboard us and start infecting.'*

'This is not a ploy by the Word,' Kordaz insisted. 'I am not infected but I have been betrayed by one of your own people, shot by another and abandoned to die by a third, captain. I do not have much patience remaining for your kind, and merely request medical attention from your wife, Meyanna.'

Idris swallowed thickly.

'My wife is aboard the vessel we have found,' he replied. 'They are having some difficulties, but I am sure we can come to some arrangement.'

'Are you kidding?' Mikhain uttered. *'We can't trust him, not now.'*

Idris felt the conflict building within him. Kordaz was, or had been, a warrior who despite his kind's bloodlust had proven himself an honourable soul. But if the Legion had taken control of him, were even now waiting aboard the gunship, then how could he possibly bring Kordaz aboard Atlantia or expose his wife and the Marines aboard Endeavour to potential infection?

'Where is Qayin, right now?' Idris asked.

'He is in the hold,' Kordaz replied. 'I have kept him there for the duration of the journey.'

'Is he harmed?'

Kordaz hesitated for a long moment before he replied. 'He has seen better days. But he is alive.'

'Show him to us, and we will organise his transport and also your medical assistance aboard the gunship.'

Kordaz's shoulders seemed to slump as though a great weight had been removed from them.

'Thank you captain. Stand by, and I will bring him to the cockpit.'

*

Mikhain shut off the communications link and turned to his Executive Officer, Djimon, who was staring at the screen displaying Salim Phaeon's gunship and wearing an expression somewhere between disbelief and dismay.

'XO, with me,' Mikhain ordered, and turned to Lieutenant Scott. 'You have the bridge, lieutenant.'

'Aye, captain.'

Mikhain marched off the bridge with Djimon close behind and made his way to his quarters, waiting for the doors to close behind them before he spoke.

'Qayin is alive?' he snapped in disbelief.

Djimon nodded. 'It is possible. Nobody actually saw him die on Chiron.'

Mikhain grasped his forehead with one hand, the other on his hip as he marched back and forth. 'This is unbelievable. He knows everything.'

'He knows nothing,' Djimon countered. 'Qayin is universally despised. Nothing he says will carry any weight either here or aboard Atlantia. That said, our best bet is to ensure that if Qayin is indeed alive he gets nowhere near Idris Sansin or Atlantia.'

'Our *best bet*?' Mikhain echoed as though Djimon was insane. 'If Captain Sansin learns of what we've done our commands will be over and we'll be subject to Maroon Protocol.'

'Then we do what is necessary to ensure that never occurs.'

'Oh really?' Mikhain uttered. 'Just like that, Djimon? Do you think that you could so easily kill Qayin, or Kordaz for that matter?! Kordaz would crush either of us like worms!'

'It might be entertaining to give the Veng'en the chance.'

'This isn't a damned game, Djimon! What happens next will define the rest of our lives, and the only thing that will end it is…'

A cold smile finally cracked like a glacier across Djimon's features.

'Their deaths,' he finished the captain's sentence for him.

Mikhain slumped and he rubbed his temples wearily with one hand.

'This isn't right,' he whispered, almost to himself. 'Damn it, we're talking about murder here!'

'Do you think that Qayin would be any less likely to sacrifice lives in order to protect his own?'

'Do you think that I want to be *like* Qayin?!'

'You wanted your command,' Djimon said as he gestured to the captain's insignia adorning Mikhain's shoulder patches. 'Now you've got it and everything that comes with it. Don't you even think about cutting out and revealing all to our beloved leader, Captain Sansin.'

'There's nothing that you could do to stop me,' Mikhain shot back.

'Isn't there?' Djimon asked, as one hand rested on the butt of his plasma pistol holstered at his hip. 'Let's not go there, captain. Let's ensure that whatever happens, nothing that either Qayin or Kordaz knows reaches Sansin's ears, whatever it takes. We kill Kordaz, agreed?'

Mikhain glared at the man towering over him as he realised the lengths that Djimon was prepared to go to, and he almost spat his response.

'Agreed.'

***

XVI

Qayin sat in silence and waited, his eyes closed and his body tensed.

The seat was as cold as the blood that still soaked the deck, black and thick beneath his boots. The atmosphere in the hold was also chilled, but he could not feel it due to the Devlamine powering through his veins. It was all he could do to remain silent and still, his head hanging low and his chin touching his chest. He felt as though his head was bobbing up and down, so hard was his heart beating. Lights pulsed before his closed eyes and all he wanted to do was leap up and run around, to destroy, to maim and to puncture anything that he could lay his hands on.

His hands lay on the arms of the seat, the manacles loosely draped over his wrists. Beneath his right leg he had tucked the deactivated plasma whip, the slim handle invisible. With the kind of patience only pure hatred and the desperate thirst for vengeance could bring, he remained motionless and waited.

After what seemed like an age had passed he heard the hiss of the hold doors as they opened and then the heavy, padding sound of Kordaz approaching. Maybe he would notice that the plasma whip was not where he had left it. Maybe he would draw his pistol, cautious of whether Qayin was truly still captive or not. Perhaps he would merely shoot Qayin in the back of the head, just to be safe?

The heavy footsteps came closer, did not break their stride or rhythm, and he heard the Veng'en's voice as the warrior moved to stand before Qayin.

'It looks like it's time for you to go home,' he growled. 'Just be thankful it will be into the care of your own people and not the Veng'en, who would gladly tear you…'

Qayin released every ounce of the energy he had struggled to contain in a single burst of undiluted fury. He surged upward and out of the seat as his hand grabbed the handle of the plasma whip, heard his own grotesque cry of rage as he swung a punch that struck Kordaz directly across his broad left eye.

The Veng'en staggered sideways in shock, completely taken unawares as Qayin rushed in, his rage supercharged by the Devalmine soaring inside him and the memory of the pain that Kordaz had forced him to endure for no other reason than the Veng'en's own pleasure. The plasma whip hummed into life as Qayin brought it crashing down on Kordaz's skull. The crackling plasma sliced deep into the Veng'en's flesh and exposed a slim white shell of bone beneath his leathery skin in a puff of smoke.

Kordaz emitted a hellish roar of pain as he fought back and a ceremonial *D'jeck* dagger appeared as if by magic in one clawed hand as he swung it toward Qayin, aiming to unzip his guts from one side to the other and spill them across the deck. Qayin jerked aside, sucked his belly in and let the wicked blade flash past him, then swung the plasma whip back-handed with his second blow, the roiling weapon slashing across Kordaz's face and upper arm as he tried to shield himself from the blow.

A wispy cloud of smoke coiled from Kordaz's body wherever the whip sliced into him, and his cries of pain thundered out above the spitting sound of burning flesh. One thick leg shot out as he dropped onto one knee on the deck and kicked Qayin low in the belly, and Qayin felt the breath blast from his lungs as he folded over and was propelled backwards across the holds.

Qayin's back slammed into the wall with a dull clang, and he twisted his arm awkwardly to avoid lashing himself with the plasma whip, the bright blue snake of light swirling above his head. Kordaz rushed at him and launched himself off the deck with frightening speed and murder in his eyes, the *D'jeck* whistling as its ornate blade sliced the air and whispered death toward Qayin.

Qayin ducked as he threw the whip up. The *D'jeck* smashed into the hull wall as Kordaz drove his own fist into the whip and pinned it against the same wall, his flesh bubbling and crackling as it burned.

Qayin drove upward with his legs and smashed the dome of his skull into Kordaz's jaw, drove the Veng'en upward with a dull crack as he reached up and twisted the Veng'en's wrist in an attempt to wrench the *D'jeck* from his grasp. The whip coiled and writhed above them as they fought, hanging in the zero gravity. Qayin tried to yank it downward, but Kordaz was too close to him and he would likely burn himself as much as the Veng'en.

Kordaz roared and leaned in, his savage fangs bared as he made for Qayin's arm, the only thing between his throat and certain death.

Qayin released the *D'jeck* and dropped downward as he dragged the whip with him. The searing whip slashed down across Kordaz's skull and he leaped back with a howl of pain, his face a bloodied mess as his wounds leaked across his eyes and obscured his vision.

Qayin rolled out from beneath Kordaz and away from the wall, and as he came up on his feet he saw the open hold doors before him. He hurled himself toward them and dashed through the exit as Kordaz thundered in pursuit, and then whirled and hit the emergency close switch on the panel outside.

The doors hissed shut as Kordaz plunged through, and then with a dull crunch they pinned the Veng'en in place about his waist, half in and half out of the hold. Kordaz roared in pain as the closing mechanism fought to seal the doors, the built–in safety features overridden by the emergency closure system to contain fires or hull breaches.

Qayin slumped against the wall, exhausted despite the Devlamine in his system, his vision blurring and starring before his eyes. He knew that he did not have much energy left and had no choice but to try to make it to the cockpit. He turned, raised the whip and brought it crashing down across Kordaz's helpless body, smashing the super–heated weapon over and over again and rejoicing in Kordaz's howls of agony that soared through the ship as the whip sliced deeply into his flesh.

The fifth or sixth blow missed as the whip slid from Qayin's bloodied hand and tumbled away down the corridor, the plasma weapon coiling and humming as it spun lazily away through the air. Exhausted, Qayin slumped onto his knees before Kordaz, who was hanging between the doors with his great head dangling low, blood dripping from countless wounds as he struggled to maintain consciousness.

Qayin breathed deeply, sucked air into his weary lungs as he sought to summon the last of his strength. Somehow he managed to regain his feet and stand upright, wavering this way and that as his dangerously low blood pressure threatened to steal his consciousness from him.

Below him, Kordaz lifted his head and sucked in a long, loud inhalation of air as his thick arms bulged and he fought back against the doors. Qayin heard the motors whining as they were strained by the load being placed upon them. He tried to lift one leg to stomp it down on the Veng'en's head but he was too weak, too unsteady. He searched for the *D'jeck*, but Kordaz had dropped it inside the hold–too far for Qayin to reach and the Veng'en would likely take a bite out of him if he tried.

He vaguely recalled what the Veng'en had told him.

It looks like it's time for you to go home. Just be thankful it will be into the care of your own people...

Qayin turned and staggered away from Kordaz, headed for'ard toward the cockpit as he heard the door motors straining ever louder. The Veng'en was immensely powerful and it was not unthinkable that he might have sufficient strength to slip through the doors and pursue Qayin. The thought pushed Qayin on further and faster and he staggered into the cockpit to see ahead through the viewing panel a vast cloud of glowing hydrogen gas, and silhouetted before it two Colonial frigates and a giant, cylindrical wreck of a spacecraft.

Qayin slumped into the captain's chair and with one bloodied hand he opened a channel.

*

'On screen,' Idris said from his seat as Lael informed him of the new communication, and prepared to greet Kordaz once more.

The main viewing panel switched once again from the view of Endeavour to the cockpit of Salim Phaeon's gunship, and a collective gasp of surprise rippled through Atlantia's bridge as Idris saw Qayin's face on the screen.

The former convict's blue and gold locks were lank and draped across his shoulders, his uniform shredded and deeply stained with blood. His bioluminescent tattoos were barely visible, pulsing weakly on his face and his eyes were hooded, sunk deep into their orbits.

'Qayin,' Idris uttered. 'I never thought that I'd be glad to see you again, but when we get you aboard we'll make damned sure you pay for...'

'Shut up,' Qayin rasped weakly, his voice a shadow of what it usually was. Something in the convict's tones silenced Idris. 'Don't let Kordaz aboard,' Qayin whispered, his chest heaving for breath as he spoke. 'He's infected, with the Legion. He's trying to get aboard Atlantia..., to infect you all...'

Idris stood up, searching for any sign of Kordaz in the gunship's cockpit.

'Where is he?' he demanded. 'Where is Kordaz?'

Qayin's jaw worked as he tried to form words.

'He's pinned down in the hold but not for long,' Qayin gasped. 'I don't know how long I'll hold out. I was trying to catch up with you all when he attacked and overpowered me, took the gunship. Kordaz tried to kill me on Chiron..,'

Qayin's head slumped on the console before him.

'You were trying to kill Kordaz!' Idris snapped. 'You betrayed your own people! You contacted Salim Phaeon in order to warn him of our plans on Chiron IV, and then you abandoned us in the middle of an attack by the Legion and fled!'

Qayin dragged his head up once more, his eyes barely open. 'I went for Salim's gunship,' he rasped. 'Bra'hiv's Marines were pinned down, so were my men. The gunship had enough firepower to get them out, but I never made it.'

'You were after the Devlamine,' Idris shot back, 'it was no rescue mission.'

'You forget, captain, that it was not only all of us who were aboard the Sylph, and could have brought the Devlamine back to Atlantia. Kordaz was found hiding aboard the Sylph too, it was where we first met him. He also had the freedom of Atlantia...' Qayin's voice was weakening fast. 'I never contacted Salim Phaeon...' he rasped. 'Ask Taron Forge. I wanted him to speak to Salim on my behalf. Damn, ask Salim yourself...'

'Salim's dead,' Idris replied, suddenly uncertain. 'Your pass code was used to access Atlantia's War Room and contact Salim.'

Qayin's voice was a mere whisper, barely audible.

'Check the log times,' he murmured, 'and the testimonies of my men. I could not have been in two places at once.'

Idris ground his teeth in his jaw. The one thing he knew for sure that did not add up about Qayin's betrayal of Kordaz was that Salim Phaeon had known Mikhain's name and had spoken it in communication with Idris, despite never having seen or met the man before. That tiny inconsistency had haunted Idris from the moment they had escaped Chiron IV. How could Salim have known who Mikhain was, in advance of ever seeing or speaking to him, unless it had been Mikhain who had betrayed Kordaz and not Qayin?

Idris glanced at the communications log screen, a stream of all frequencies currently logged in to Atlantia's bridge, and noted that Arcadia was currently not on the list.

'Damn it man,' Idris snarled at Qayin. 'Tell me the truth. Were you behind the Devlamine supply on Atlantia?!'

Qayin, barely conscious, gave a weak shake of his head.

'No,' he mumbled, 'I worked for Kordaz. Kordaz is trying to infect you all, that's why he took the Devlamine, to infect humans just as the Word once used it for. He stashed it in the holds in this gunship when he took control of it. Get me the hell out of here...'

Qayin's eyes rolled up in their sockets and he slumped onto the control panel as behind him the muscular form of a Veng'en, his body lacerated with wounds, stormed into the cockpit. One thick, clawed hand grabbed Qayin's neck and hauled him off the control panel as he pinned the convict against one wall of the cockpit and glared at the camera.

'Don't listen to him captain,' Kordaz insisted. 'He cannot be trusted, not by you, not by any of us!'

Idris, his hands behind his back, clenched his fists tighter as he tried to figure out which one of the two was lying.

'Kordaz,' he said, 'you told me that you were conscious when the Legion invaded your body and healed your injuries?'

'Yes,' replied the Veng'en.

'Were you conscious throughout the entire experience?'

'No,' Kordaz insisted. 'How could I have been? It might have taken them hours to repair the damage, days even.'

'Then how can you be entirely sure that you are not now an agent of the Word? We have lost two senior crew members in the past who never knew they were infected until it was too late.'

'The Infectors were destroyed by the cosmic rays!' Kordaz roared.

'And the ones inside your body?' Idris pressed. 'The ones protected by the same resilience to radiation that you yourself possess? Would they too have been completely annihilated, or are they the ones forcing you to seek medical help, so that they can infect more people?'

Kordaz stared silently at the screen for a long moment. 'I cannot say,' he growled.

'Then I cannot allow you aboard my ship, or allow my people to board yours,' Idris insisted. 'I cannot afford to take the risk.'

Kordaz dropped Qayin and the big man slumped unconscious to the deck as Kordaz turned and glared at Idris.

'Do not abandon me again, captain!' he shouted. 'Everything that has happened to me has been because of your people and the things that you have created! I am dying, captain! I have nowhere else to go! Even if I could return to Wraiythe they would shoot me on sight. This is my only option and if you will not help me then I will damned well help myself!'

Kordaz turned and produced a plasma pistol that he aimed down at Qayin's prostrate form.

'Send your wife to help me, Idris,' he snarled, 'or there will be nothing left of Qayin for you to find.'

Kordaz shut off the communications link with a swipe of one hand, and Idris turned to Lael.

'Target the gunship, but hold your fire! And get me Bra'hiv on the comms link!'

***

102

XVII

'What's the damned rush?'

General Bra'hiv raised his left wrist and tapped in a new frequency, and instantly he could hear Captain Sansin's voice on the new channel. Evelyn watched as the Marines gathered around and the general set his internal speakers onto wideband so that everybody present could hear the exchange.

'General Bra'hiv, Atlantia.'

'*General,*' Idris's voice replied, '*we have a problem. Both Qayin and Kordaz have returned from the dead.*'

Evelyn felt a pulse of alarm and disbelief jolt through her.

'I thought you said that Kordaz was dead?' Andaim said to her.

'He was,' Evelyn replied. 'Half of his chest was blown away, so he couldn't have escaped the bombardment, which was too heavy for anything to survive.'

'*Well, he's here now,*' Idris said, '*and he has Qayin as a hostage. I'm having a really hard time figuring out who's guilty of what.*'

'Kordaz went out of his way to help us,' Bra'hiv replied, 'though I'm amazed that I'm saying it. Qayin's his own man – he got away from us as soon as he was able.'

'*That may be true, but right now Kordaz is here because he received medical assistance from the Legion.*'

'He got *what*?!' Bra'hiv gasped.

'*They repaired him, but then were damaged by the cosmic rays hitting Chiron IV and Kordaz escaped uninfected, or so he claims,*' Idris explained. '*It's a long story, but right now I can't be sure if Kordaz is telling the truth, Qayin is, or they're both lying.*'

'Let me speak to them,' Evelyn said. 'I've gotten to know them both pretty well, maybe I can figure it out.'

'*That's what I thought,*' Idris confirmed, '*but Kordaz claims that the Legion didn't finish the job and that he's dying. Qayin's in bad shape too. I can't send anybody aboard their ship for fear of infection, and right now Kordaz thinks that we abandoned him and that he's been wronged. He's got a gun to Qayin's head and is demanding immediate assistance.*'

'And you can't just shoot them down?' Andaim suggested.

'*If Qayin's innocent?*' Idris replied. '*If they both are? What kind of enemies will we make if we try to destroy them and fail?*'

'If they're infected then there's little that I can do to help them,' Meyanna said from one side. 'Especially Kordaz. We just don't have enough knowledge of Veng'en physiology to be able to do something as complex as that.'

'We could use the microwave scanners on Qayin,' Andaim suggested. 'I imagine there would be a long list of people willing to help out with that, considering how painful the prodecure is.'

'I think that Qayin may have suffered enough,' Idris replied. *'He's barely alive as it is, and now he's got a gun to his head. How soon can you get out of there?'*

'We haven't even started yet,' Meyanna complained. 'There's evidence here of unknown species, humans too, all of them being experimented on in some way. It's something that we have to figure out before we leave.'

'Not to mention the Special Forces team that's been attacking us,' Bra'hiv added.

'We'd be better off blasting the ship back into history,' Idris replied. *'It's not worth the risk, whatever is aboard.'*

'You haven't seen what we have,' Andaim replied for Meyanna. 'There are humans aboard, and they…'

The CAG looked at Evelyn as though unsure of how to put it. Evelyn sighed as she spoke.

'One of them looks like I did,' she said, 'back in the prison hull, Atlantia Five.'

Idris was silent for a moment.

'Can we run tests, to see if…, if that's even possible?'

'I don't know what will happen if we break open the capsules,' Meyanna explained. 'The bodies inside could just disintegrate. I need more time to figure out how best to preserve them.'

'We may not have much time if Kordaz keeps a gun at Qayin's head. He believes us responsible for betraying him and the longer we delay, the more convinced he's going to be.' Idris's voice changed. *'Andaim, you know what we spoke about after Chiron IV?'*

Evelyn looked at the CAG, and saw his features darken a little. 'I remember.'

'It may become a factor in how this plays out. I need you back here in case things get difficult.'

'Difficult *how?*' Bra'hiv cut in.

'I'll explain later,' Idris replied. 'Right now I need you all off that ship and at your posts as quickly as possible.'

A crash of gunfire erupted in the distance, Evelyn almost jumping out of her skin as another voice crashed in on the conversation.

'We're under fire!'

The general grabbed hold of Meyanna and pushed her back toward the hold, away from the gunfire.

'Move, now!' Bra'hiv snapped. 'Get out of sight. Meyer, J'evel, guard her!'

Two Marines flanked Meyanna as she was hustled away from danger. The rest of the Marines instantly started running toward the sounds of gunfire, Bra'hiv leading them and splitting them up into pairs, hugging the walls of the corridor as best they could. Evelyn saw ahead flashes of light as rifle fire was exchanged in crackling bursts of energy, a thin haze of smoke obscuring the emergency lighting as the platoon burst out onto the deck stairwell.

A salvo of rifle fire zipped toward the Marines at terrific speed and they scattered in disarray as the blasts hammered the corridor entrance behind them. Evelyn threw herself down onto the deck as the shots raced by overhead, then rolled to one side to avoid a spray of white–hot plasma that splashed off the walls above.

'Stay in cover, advance by sections on my command!' Bra'hiv yelled.

The Marines took up positions either side of the corridor opposite, beneath the stairwell that ran for'ard of the hold toward Endeavour's bow. A very long corridor that likely traversed the length of the ship's keel, it provided access to the upper decks at multiple points along its route.

'It must be the Special Forces soldiers trying to escape,' Andaim shouted above the din of gunfire ripping past them out of the corridor ahead. 'This is the fastest way back through the ship.'

'I had the men ray–shield most of the access points from the bridge deck aft,' Bra'hiv countered. 'If they go up, they're not going to get very far!'

A pair of shots whistled by and smashed into the opposite corridor entrance, the walls pockmarked now with scorched metal, some of it dripping in molten globules onto the deck.

'By sections, covering fire!' Bra'hiv shouted. 'Advance!'

Two Marines fired into the corridor as two more slipped by, hugging the walls as they entered the corridor and dashed into cover behind the next bulkhead. The two soldiers lay down covering fire from their new positions as behind them two more Marines entered the corridor, firing as they went.

'Advance!'

Bra'hiv's commands were followed by two more Marines mirroring the movements of those who had preceded them, and with admirable precision under fire Bravo Company infiltrated the corridor and began advancing toward their enemy.

Evelyn checked the load on her pistol as the Marines advanced into the corridor, waiting to back them up. She saw Andaim head inside, right behind the last of the Marines, and then she pushed off to follow him.

The sudden pressure on her neck forced her to stop moving, a twist of a nerve somewhere between her collar bone and her throat that snatched the breath from her lungs before she could cry out for help. The entire right side of her body twitched as though a live current were rippling through it and her right leg gave way at the knee as she dropped onto the deck. Before she even knew what had happened a strong hand wrenched the plasma pistol from her grip as another ripped the communication antenna from her environmental suit, cutting her off from Andaim, Bra'hiv and the Marines.

The strong hand gripping her throat and shoulder pulled her back up onto her feet, and she saw the metallic flash of a blade and felt it press against her flank, right about where her kidney was. A forearm wrapped about her neck and began walking her backwards, away from the stairwell and back toward the hold.

*

'Hold position!'

Bra'hiv shouted above the din of the rifle fire being laid down toward them, the corridor ahead filled now with smoke, laid down by the elite troops they were following. The general peered through the smoke but could see nothing but the sporadic muzzle flash of the rifles firing at them.

'The hell with this,' he growled.

Bra'hiv reached down to his waist and yanked a pair of grenades from his webbing. He pulled the pin on one of them, waited one second, and then hurled it into the smoke ahead. He pulled back against the bulkhead he was hiding behind, and then instantly pulled the pin on the second grenade and rolled it more gently toward the firing rifles.

The first grenade detonated with a deafening blast that reverberated down the corridor as the shockwave smashed its way past Bra'hiv's hiding spot. The plasma fire ceased abruptly, and then a second blast thundered down the corridor, designed specifically to catch—out wily enemies who may have avoided the first detonation.

'Advance, now!'

Bra'hiv fired three shots into the smoky corridor ahead and then his men rushed past him, their weapons also aimed ahead and firing as they passed their general. Bra'hiv broke cover and ran after his men, the smoke curling past him and scorching his nostrils as he reached them, the three soldiers kneeling and surveying the corridor ahead.

Bra'hiv stopped and stared at the two rifles lying on their sides in the corridor, the walls scorched where the grenades had detonated. He could see no sign of the bodies that must have been holding the weapons. As the smoke cleared he spotted two metallic tripods scattered further up the corridor, and heard a faint clicking noise. He looked at one of the destroyed rifles and saw the trigger clicking as it fired on an automatic setting.

'It was a decoy,' he murmured.

'For what?' asked one of the Marines alongside him.

Bra'hiv turned around, as did the other Marines, and then finally Andaim, who looked behind him and saw an empty corridor.

'Where's Evelyn?'

Bra'hiv's expression darkened and he pointed back the way they had come, but none of the soldiers had taken more than a step when a voice cut in on their communications channel.

'Listen very carefully, do precisely as I say, and neither of these beautiful ladies will be hurt, understood?'

***

XVIII

Kordaz hurled Qayin back into the holds, the big convict sprawling as he hit the deck with a resounding thud. Kordaz glanced at the Devlamine stashed in the rear of the hold and though he could not smile his skin rippled with a colour that was associated with delight as he looked at the fallen man before him.

'How apt,' he snarled. 'You'll need a little more of that drug of yours to regain your strength, Qayin. And then a little more still. Before you know it, you'll be as addicted as all the people you sold that poison to on Ethera and Atlantia. Enjoy it, Qayin. I look forward to seeing you either overdose or go through withdrawal when I cut off your supply!'

Kordaz turned and stomped out of the hold. He shut and locked the access hatch behind him, and then after a moment's consideration he rammed a length of metal girder under the locking mechanism, just in case the resourceful Qayin once again managed to figure out a way to escape.

Kordaz's body was filled with pain from the lashes of the plasma whip, and he felt weak as he walked back toward the gunship's cockpit. His vision, still somewhat unfamiliar since the Legion had infected him, faded in and out as he struggled to maintain consciousness. He lost his balance and slumped against the wall of the corridor. Ahead, he could see the blinking lights of the cockpit, and through the open hatch he could see the vast hydrogen clouds glowing against distant starfields.

He watched them for what felt like an age, and then his gaze settled upon the ancient wreck that seemed so important to Captain Sansin and his people. Kordaz found his gaze fixed upon the wreck, drawn by a fascination that he could not explain but which pulled him toward it as though via some unseen force. Kordaz stumbled forwards and managed to reach the cockpit doors, one hand shooting out to grab them and prevent him from falling to the deck.

Almost immediately his vision cleared and the thick nausea clogging his belly faded away. Kordaz looked up, surprised at how quickly he felt better as he pushed off the cockpit hatch and stood looking at the wrecked spaceship in the distance. The shattered hulk of the vessel mesmerised him for no good reason and he took another pace toward it. To his surprise, he felt even better. Kordaz's hunched, weakened stance straightened again and he felt his breathing settle once more.

He stood for a long moment in the silence of the gunship's cockpit, staring at the ancient wreck, and then he turned and walked away from the view. Instantly the nausea in his belly returned and intensified as a fearsome bolt of pain punched through his skull. Kordaz gasped and almost fell as he staggered against the cockpit wall and somehow managed to turn back toward the view of the wreck.

The pain subsided and the nausea vanished once more.

Kordaz stood in silence for a long moment. He took a pace backward from the view. A dull, throbbing ache swelled against the interior of his skull. Kordaz winced and took a pace toward the view once more. The pain receded. The words of Captain Sansin echoed distantly through Kordaz's thoughts. *And the infectors inside your body? The ones protected by the same resilience to radiation that you yourself possess? Would they too have been completely annihilated, or are they the ones forcing you to seek medical help so that they can infect more people?*

Kordaz knew that he no longer had a choice. He stared again at the wreck and it was as though he could hear it calling out to him, a voice tiny in its volume but unavoidable in its intensity.

Idris and Mikhain had been right. The cosmic rays on Chiron IV had not destroyed all of the Infectors in his body, and now they were taking control of him. Even as he thought about it, he realised that his horror at having finally fallen victim to the Legion was not anywhere near as awful as he had imagined it would be. He still knew his own mind and he still knew that he was being manipulated by the tiny devices swarming through his brain and his spinal column. And yet, despite that, he also felt as though he was experiencing something new, a new beginning. His memories of Wraiythe and the brutality of his kind, of the squabbling and traitorous nature of humanity all paled in comparison to the vision that began to develop in his mind's eye: that of the Legion, of the Word, pure in its form and uncontaminated by greed, pride, grief or pain.

Kordaz sat down in the captain's chair and surveyed the two Colonial frigates and the ancient wreck before him. Despite its shattered hull and bitterly cold interior, the ship suddenly seemed more and more like his natural home than anywhere else in the cosmos.

Without conscious thought his hands moved for the gunship's throttles. Kordaz arrested the movement, confused. It was as if his arm had moved of its own accord, as though it had a life of its own. On impulse he grabbed it with his free hand as though to hold it in place.

A surge of pain wracked his head and Kordaz groaned as he tried to resist.

*

Djimon moved quickly, the Executive Officer almost running through Arcadia's corridors as he descended through the endless decks and burst onto a stairwell.

Djimon knew that almost nobody aboard ship used the stairwells, the elevators far quicker and more efficient. However his passage now was one of secrecy and urgency, and he was determined to end the captain's charade for once and for all. Mikhain, he had decided, was a weak man at heart, conflicted by his loyalties to Captain Sansin. Perhaps Mikhain had been a second–in–command for too many years, too safely ensconced in the knowledge that any decision he might make would reflect more on the captain of a vessel than himself. Djimon wondered not for the first time why Mikhain had not attained a command of his own long before the apocalypse had struck, and guessed only that he had chosen not to seek such promotion, perhaps even had turned it down.

Djimon leaped down the stairs four at a time, landing cat–like with each enormous leap as he descended rapidly and finally reached the 'tween decks, buried deep in the frigate's heart and just aft of the sanctuary.

Djimon slipped out of the stairwell onto the silent deck and listened for a moment. Arcadia was not as heavily manned as Atlantia, and the deck and corridor this deep inside the ship were silent and lonely. Satisfied that he was alone, Djimon hurried along the corridor until he reached the massive double–doors of the War Room. Built to act as a secondary command post in the event of the frigate's main bridge being destroyed or boarded, the War Room was a smaller version of the command platform from which the entire ship could be commanded.

Djimon accessed the War Room using his security pass and hurried inside before sealing the hatches behind him.

He made his way quickly to the tactical station and scanned the instruments for a moment before he began accessing the frigate's weapons systems. To his satisfaction, he saw Arcadia's main cannons begin to charge up.

Because of the War Room's secretive nature, any actions made from within were concealed from the main bridge, allowing the crew in time of danger to maintain control of the frigate without boarders even realising until it was too late. Now, Djimon used that same capability to target any vessel of his choosing.

Djimon shifted a targeting reticule and placed it over Salim Phaeon's gunship.

Moments later, the reticule turned a deep red and a *Fire* option flashed up on the screen.

*

'Any communication from General Bra'hiv?'

Mikhain stood on Arcadia's bridge and surveyed the vessels arrayed before him. Endeavour's fractured hull loomed black and sullen before the spectacular panorama of glowing clouds and stars, while Atlantia reflected the warm light nearby, her angular hull glinting. To starboard, a tiny speck against the star fields denoted the position of Salim Phaeon's gunship, Kordaz and Qayin aboard her. Mikhain's gaze settled on the gunship and its attendant pair of Raythons.

'Nothing,' Lieutenant Shah replied.

Mikhain ground his teeth in his skull as he wondered whether Captain Sansin knew more about what was happening aboard Endeavour than he was revealing. Meyanna Sansin was still aboard the ship, and if Kordaz was in need of urgent medical assistance then he would almost certainly call for her. If Kordaz was able to impart what he knew about Mikhain, or if Qayin was somehow able to achieve the impossible and regain the trust of Atlantia's compliment...

'Cannons firing!' Lieutenant Scott yelled.

Mikhain leaped out of his seat and stared in horror as two massive plasma blasts burst from Arcadia's port guns and rocketed toward the gunship.

'Belay that!' Mikhain bellowed in fury.

'I didn't fire them!' Lieutenant Scott cried in despair as his hands flew across his controls. 'They're not even supposed to be charged!'

Mikhain stared at the display screen as he saw the two blasts smash into the gunship with a brilliant flare of white light.

*

Kordaz groaned as waves of intensifying nausea swept over him. He slumped against the control panel, and realised that he could not bring himself to suffer any further misery, his body and mind too weak to resist the calling of the Word.

He released his disobedient arm, and it moved across to the gunship's throttles and gently advanced them as a wave of blessed relief washed across his body as the nausea vanished.

An alarm blared deafeningly loud in his ears, and Kordaz grabbed hold of the throttles with both hands and slammed them wide open as he saw the massive shots blast from Arcadia's guns and rocket toward him, huge flickering balls of pure plasma energy as large as the gunship itself tearing across the open space between the massive frigate and his own vessel, tiny in comparison.

Kordaz slammed the control column forward and grabbed hold of the control panel as the plasma blasts filled his vision, and with a deft flick of several switches he shifted the power to shields and directed them fully forward just as the blasts impacted the gunship.

The vessel reeled under the blows and a claxon of deafening alarms wailed through the ship as it tumbled under the double impact. Sparks fell in showers from the cockpit walls as entire control panels were shaken from their mounts, flames licking at electrical circuits and wires from the massive surge in power.

Kordaz managed to regain control of the gunship even as he glimpsed the two Raython escort fighters rocketing away from him and the impacts.

The control panel was lit up like the glowing gas clouds before him, warning lights and beacons blaring for attention. The gunship's hull had been breached in six different locations and she was bleeding atmosphere fast. He looked up at the viewing panel and saw deep cracks splintering the surface, structural failure of the cockpit now imminent.

Kordaz wailed in fury as he slammed one fist down on the control panel, and with hate coursing through his veins he yanked the control column to one side and aimed the gunship directly at Endeavour.

*

'We've got motion!' Lieutenant Scott called out. 'The gunship is under way!'

Mikhain's eyes flicked to the tactical display and noted the increasing velocity read–out alongside the image of the gunship.

'Signal him immediately, priority channel!' Mikhain snapped.

The communications officer sent the signal but immediately frowned and shook her head.

'No response captain,' Shah informed him. 'The gunship has shut down its communications channel.'

'What the hell is he doing?' Mikhain uttered out loud. 'Signal Atlantia!'

Captain Sansin's image appeared on the bridge viewing panel even before the communications officer could send the signal, Sansin clearly already informed of what was happening.

'Who the hell ordered you to open fire on that gunship?!'

'Nobody opened fire!' Mikhain yelled back. 'There may have been a malfunction of some kind!'

'Who has control of her?!'

'I have no idea,' Mikhain replied, 'they've shut off all signals channels and are not responding.'

'They're running, and I can't blame them!'

'Perhaps he intends to attack us,' Mikhain cautioned. 'We should disable them immediately and play it safe. Where is your wife?'

'Still aboard Endeavour,' Sansin replied, *'and they're not responding to our calls.'*

Mikhain turned to the tactical display and his eyes flew wide.

'He's charging weapons!' he yelled. 'Target her now!'

'Belay that order!' Idris shouted from Atlantia's bridge. *'We might end up killing them both!'*

'Why would you want to keep them alive?!' Mikhain challenged. 'They're both traitors!'

Idris's face darkened as he whirled to face the camera. *'And you're not, Mikhain?!'*

A silence enveloped Arcadia's bridge as Mikhain stared in shock at Idris. Atlantia's captain appeared to immediately regret his words, the abrupt fury on his features vanishing as he struggled to contain his anger.

'Tow the damned line,' Idris snapped. *'Intercept the gunship with our Raythons, weapons cold!'*

***

XIX

Evelyn stood in silence, the arm of a soldier wrapped across her chest as she was led toward the holds, the blade still poking disconcertingly hard into her flank. They reached the entrance, the walls still smouldering from countless plasma round impacts, and then several more black–clad soldiers descended the stairwell from above her, moving as silently as shadows.

Each was entirely concealed by their combat fatigues and festooned with weapons, but none of them wore protective headgear. Their faces were smeared with black face paint, their features likewise concealed with black bandanas that likely also kept out the worst of the cold. Evelyn realised that they were not using most of the normal equipment used by Colonial Marines, preferring their natural hearing, sight and instincts to standard issue Colonial technology. Only two of them wore eyepieces connected to power packs on their webbing, the small, rectangular lenses providing night vision and other essential combat tools.

They did not speak, everything conveyed by hand signals or nods of their heads. Evelyn found herself fascinated despite her situation as she was turned and, one step at a time, she was led into the hold.

She saw Meyanna at once, and then the two Marines guarding her who turned and swung their plasma rifles up to aim at the man holding Evelyn. She felt rather than saw the man holding her shake his head slowly, and then more of the elite soldiers spilled like black shadows into the hold once more, their weapons trained on the two Marines.

Instantly, Marine Meyer took his chance. Evelyn had barely opened her mouth to shout him to hold fire when he aimed at the first of the soldiers who had entered the hold and fired. The plasma shot flared brilliantly as it illuminated the darkened hold and smashed into the soldier's chest. Evelyn stared as the soldier hesitated, the plasma rippling across his body like brilliant glowing water, flickering as its energy was converted into heat and dissipated into the atmosphere.

'Don't shoot!' Evelyn yelled at their captors.

She may as well have been talking to herself. A salvo of shots snapped back at Meyer before she had finished the sentence and he was hit three times even as he attempted to dive for cover. Evelyn winced as the Marine screamed and then fell silent as he hit the deck, his body smouldering and his eyes wide in the lifeless grimace of instant death as his rifle tumbled slowly in mid–air above his body.

Marine J'evel, to his credit, remained in front of Meyanna Sansin and refused to give ground, but he kept his rifle down at port arms as he was encircled by the elite soldiers.

'Lose the piece, pal,' came a voice from one of them. 'Nothing to gain by being a hero.'

The Marine ignored the soldier and instead looked at Evelyn.

'It's fine,' she said. 'Let it go.'

J'evel's shoulders sank in the shame of capitulation as he unslung his rifle and set it down on the deck before him, but maintained his position in front of Meyanna Sansin.

The soldier who had spoken, his face concealed all but for his eyes, turned and looked at Evelyn appraisingly as he approached her. His eyes flicked across the patch on her shoulder, emblazoned with the *Reaper's* logo and the Colonial frigate Atlantia's name.

'Phantoms?' he asked.

'Raythons,' Evelyn replied, seeing a potential ray of light in the man's recognition of her role within the Colonial Fleet, or what was left of it.

'What are you doing out here?'

'I could ask you the same question,' she replied. 'How did you get so far so soon after the apocalypse?'

She saw a glimmer of confusion cloud the soldier's eyes. 'What apocalypse?'

The sound of distant gunfire ceased and one of the soldiers looked at his leader.

'They're through,' he said. 'They'll be coming back.'

The leader looked down at the fallen Marine, and then stormed across to him and tore off the dead man's helmet. He held the helmet up and spoke into it.

'Listen very carefully, do precisely as I say, and neither of these beautiful ladies will be hurt, understood?'

There was a moment's silence and then Evelyn heard Bra'hiv's voice reply.

'Go ahead.'

'You're all going to hold your weapons above your heads and you're going to walk backwards down the corridor to the stairwell, where you will be disarmed one by one. Any of you makes a single move that we dislike, one of the women dies. Move, *now.*'

Evelyn looked left and right at the soldiers. Half of them, without instruction, had melted into the darkness, concealing their numbers from Bra'hiv's men and covering their comrades. Evelyn knew that the general and his Marines had no choice: surrender, or the blade would end up scouring Evelyn's kidneys and Meyanna would be dead before she hit the deck.

She tried to reach out to the soldiers.

'You're Colonial too,' she said. 'We're on the same side.'

The man did not look at her as he replied, his gaze fixed on the stairwell outside the holds.

'Who said we're on *anybody's* side?'

'We're human beings,' Meyanna said, speaking for the first time. 'We're all on the same side now.'

'Since when?' asked another of the soldiers. 'And what was that about an apocalypse?'

'Silence,' the leader snapped.

Evelyn bit her lip and decided to say nothing more. The soldiers remained absolutely still until Bra'hiv's men emerged one by one into the stairwell, surrendering their weapons and being made to kneel facing the wall. Evelyn saw Bra'hiv emerge last and he was manacled but allowed to remain standing, the elite troops clearly recognising his senior officer's insignia.

'A general,' exclaimed the leader of their captors in surprise as soon as all the Marines were secured, his troops guarding them. 'The Marines must be even shorter of decent officers than we thought.'

A grim chuckle swept through the troops as General Bra'hiv turned to face the soldiers and looked them over with interest.

'Specialist Tactical Squad?' he enquired.

'None of your business,' the leader snapped back. 'State your intentions and give us a reason we shouldn't just seal you in the hold and leave you.'

'General Abrahim Bra'hiv, Fourth Marines, CFS Atlantia. We encountered this vessel and identified it as Endeavour, then performed a tactical boarding before searching her for supplies and evidence of what happened to her.'

The leader glanced at Evelyn's shoulder patch. 'Atlantia. What's a frigate doing all the way out here, beyond the Icari Line?'

'We are conducting a mission to seek out new forms of technology with which to fight the Word.'

The troops exchanged glances at that, and their leader once again conveyed some confusion. 'Why the hell would you be fighting the Word?'

Bra'hiv stared at the soldier for a long moment. 'How long have you been out here?'

'That's classified,' the soldier repeated.

Bra'hiv frowned. 'Damn me, you haven't had contact with the colonies for over three years, have you? You can't have.'

'Our purpose here is classified,' the leader snapped again. 'Your presence compromises our mission and may force us to silence all of you.'

Evelyn put two and two together and came up with the kind of answer she knew would have caused a storm back on Ethera.

'A government sanctioned Special Forces mission beyond the Icari Line,' she surmised.

The leader whirled and aimed his rifle at Evelyn.

'And you,' he snarled. 'You want to tell me why the hell you're in two places at once?'

Evelyn took a moment to realise what the soldier meant.

'I don't know,' she replied. 'We only just got here ourselves.'

The soldier watched her as though attempting to figure out whether she was telling him the truth or whether this was all some sort of bad dream he was having. He whirled back to Bra'hiv.

'Who's your commanding officer? Who sanctioned your presence out here?'

'Captain Idris Sansin,' Bra'hiv replied crisply. 'There was no sanctioned order. Atlantia was a prison ship, and we were far enough away from Ethera when the Word struck to escape unharmed. Though I hate to admit it, we've been on the run ever since.'

The soldier, still aiming his weapon at Bra'hiv, spoke again. 'Escape unharmed from what?'

'You really don't know, do you?' Evelyn uttered in amazement.

'Would I be asking if I damned well knew?!'

'Ethera is gone,' Bra'hiv said simply. 'So are all the core systems. The Word manipulated a swarm of militarised nanobots to infect the population of the core systems over the years, and less than three years ago it gave a unified command. The result was the deaths of billions of human beings. We don't know how many remain, or how many of those remain uninfected, but right now the Word and its Legion, as we call the machines, are pursuing the remnants of humanity wherever they find them and slaughtering them wholesale.'

The soldier stared long and hard at Bra'hiv as though his brain could not process what he was hearing.

'This is some kind of test,' he replied finally. 'HQ are pushing us to see if they can break us.'

Bra'hiv sighed softly.

'I wish that were true,' he said. 'If it were we'd all have homes to go to, but we don't. We've all been on duty for just over three years and we have nowhere to run. It is our captain's long term plan to attempt to return to Ethera and retake it, but right now we do not have anything like the strength to do so.'

The soldier stared at Bra'hiv down the barrel of his rifle, and then he scowled beneath his thick black combat paint and he swung the weapon around to point at Evelyn.

'The truth, now, or I'll blow her away!' he yelled.

Bra'hiv opened his mouth to reply, and then suddenly a blinding flash of light and noise blasted through the stairwell. Evelyn felt the soldier holding her turn away from the blast and the knife in her side vanish momentarily and she moved without conscious thought. Evelyn spun around and rammed the point of her elbow into the soldier's throat as she hurled herself away from him and grabbed one of the Marine's rifles leaning against the wall.

A burst of plasma fire crackled out as she saw Andaim crouching amid the smouldering clouds of smoke in the for'ard corridor as he fired controlled bursts through the hold entrance at the Special Forces troops holding Meyanna. His blasts forced them aside and Meyanna hurled herself clear. The Marines beneath the stairwell ploughed into their captors with brute force as they used their body weight to force their way past the stunned and blinded troops and grab their weapons, men growling and yelling as they fought for their lives in the dim light.

Two of the elite troops hiding back inside the holds opened fire from the darkness, their shots zipping by Evelyn as she whirled and returned their fire. Her shots blasted their position and forced them to duck down out of sight as half of Bra'hiv's Marines thundered into the holds amid a blaze of gunfire.

'Find cover!' Bra'hiv yelled.

Evelyn dashed into the hold and threw herself to one side as a salvo of plasma shots crackled back and forth through the darkness, and she saw multiple rounds shatter wall panels and start fires. Showers of sparks spiralled down and several pipes hissed vapour into the darkness, further obscuring their enemy as they hid.

Andaim hurled himself down alongside her, his pistol in his hand and a curiously maverick grin on his face.

'Not bad, huh?' he beamed.

'We're pinned back in the hold again, separated and surrounded by an enemy that's really pissed at us now,' Evelyn replied as she peered into the darkness. 'Good going, hero.'

Dean Crawford

***

XX

Endeavour's hold was filled with a fine haze of smoke, showers of sparks raining down like burning waterfalls from shattered power conduits and thick cables that lined the walls and dangled from the ceilings.

Evelyn, her back pinned to one of the capsules, smelled the acrid stench of burning metal and circuitry as she sought for some sign of the elite troops. The Marines were all around her, tucked in against hull braces or pinned down against capsules, some of which were leaking thick pools of per–fluorocarbon onto the deck plating.

'There's no way out,' Bra'hiv whispered urgently. 'We can't make the exit without being hit, half of their team can't get past us without exposing themselves and the other half are stuck out there.'

Evelyn nodded, still searching this way and that for some sign of the troops.

'We've got to do *something*,' Lieutenant C'rairn hissed.

Evelyn looked across at C'rairn, who was crouched down behind a huge metal corner brace in one corner of the hold to her left, virtually invisible in the shadows and the smoke. He was looking back at Evelyn and beside him crouched Meyanna, now the Marines' number one priority to protect.

'There's no way out!' yelled the elite commander from outside the hold. 'We have several of your men at gunpoint out here and you're cornered!'

'So are your men behind us!' Bra'hiv shouted back. 'You leave us here, you're abandoning your own people to die!'

Evelyn was about to suggest that Andaim or C'rairn make a dash for the door under covering fire, as they were the closest, when a new noise caught her attention. A faint humming sound was beginning to fill the hold, and she craned her neck back and looked up at the ceiling as she searched for the source.

'What's that?' Andaim echoed her thoughts.

The hum grew a little louder, and to her right the pool of per–fluorocarbon leaking from a capsule grew larger, the silky surface reflecting the dim hold lighting as it expanded. Evelyn felt her blood run cold as she saw new pools of the fluid appearing beneath capsules all around her, the humming growing ever louder. She glanced upward at the damaged electrical cables and power conduits, and suddenly she realised what had happened.

'The stray shots have broken the power supply to the capsules,' she gasped, loud enough for everybody to hear.

Bra'hiv and C'rairn looked at her sharply as the noise grew ever louder, and several Marines squirmed in discomfort as thick fluid spilled past their boots where they crouched.

Evelyn, her back to the capsule, felt something bump with a dull sound inside. Fear crept up the skin of her neck like lice as she turned and clambered upright, hugging the surface of the capsule as she peered into the viewing port.

The interior of the port was fogged with moisture, and for a moment she thought that there was nothing inside. A heavy thump sent a shockwave through her heart as a face slammed against the port with fearsome eyes wide open, the hooked fangs of some kind of quadrupedal animal glaring out at her.

Evelyn jerked away from the screen as the sound of movement within the capsules all around them began to overwhelm the sound of sparking cables. She called out instinctively to the troops pinning them down.

'Something's happening to the capsules,' she yelled. 'We need to get out of here, right now!'

There was no reply from the soldiers, but Evelyn noticed that although the Marines were backing away from the capsules and thus exposing themselves to enemy fire, the troopers were no longer shooting at them.

The sound of breaking glass shattered the air near Evelyn and she heard a hellish, rasping, screeching noise like a bird of prey tearing at a victim. She looked left and saw what looked like some kind of roiling, ghostly white tentacle probing out of a broken viewing port on one of the capsules nearby, fragments of broken glass spinning away from it through the air like rotating diamond chips.

'The capsules have gone into rehabilitation mode!' Lieutenant C'rairn cried out. 'It must be automatic when the power supply is disrupted!'

The Marines were backing toward each other now, rifles pointed not into the darkness but at the shuddering, clattering capsules as more of the species within them began to awaken and thrash to escape.

'Time to leave!' Bra'hiv called out into the darkness at their harassers. 'You can damned well shoot us if you want to, but I don't intend to stay in here a moment longer than I have to! Bravo Company, on me!'

The Marines shot into position around their general, rifles pointed outward at the capsules that were beginning to hiss as seals were broken and the lids began to click open.

'Let's move, now!'

Evelyn saw Andaim and Meyanna leap from cover and make a dash for the hold exits as the Marines began falling back protectively around them. Evelyn backed up hurriedly with them as she saw the lid of a capsule fall slowly away in the zero gravity and a bulky, squat creature with bulbous eyes and a mane of writhing tentacles around its thick neck stumble out onto the deck on six short, muscular legs that scrambled for purchase as it struggled to adapt to the zero gravity. The beast coughed a lung full of per–fluorocarbon across the deck and shook itself free of the fluid as its cruel eyes settled on Evelyn's.

The creature snarled and launched itself toward her as she opened fire. The plasma blasts smashed into the creature and it howled in agony as it skittered along the slippery deck, smoke pouring from a wound slashing its flank where the shot had streaked past it.

The animal regained its balance and wailed with fury as it charged again, but this time a larger shape lunged from the interior of another capsule and snatched the animal up into mid–air with one thick arm as a massive, bulbous head lunged out of the capsule and a pair of giant fangs sank into the smaller creature's body to the sound of crunching bones.

'Retreat, *now*!' Bra'hiv yelled.

The Marines fell back through the hold exits, several of them firing as they went on the menagerie of bizarre and lethal creatures that began emerging from the various capsules, some of them toppling over and smashing onto the decks as others rocked and shuddered as whatever horrific species was trapped within attempted to escape.

Flashes of rifle fire illuminated the darkness and the carnivorous features of animals pouring from the capsules as Evelyn fired randomly into their growing ranks and stepped back toward the hatchway. As the Marines around her fell back she glimpsed one of the capsules opening, and she gasped as within it she spotted the masked woman, blinking as though coming awake from a bad dream, unsteady on her feet.

Evelyn changed direction. 'Cover me!'

Bra'hiv bellowed at Evelyn to hold her position but Evelyn ignored the general as she dashed across the hold and slipped and slid across the slippery deck toward the mysterious woman. The woman stared vacantly into the middle distance as she stood immobile inside the capsule, dripping per–fluorocarbon, and then she coughed and spat the fluid from her lungs.

Evelyn slipped as she approached the capsule as two plasma rounds zipped by her and smashed into the writhing coils of a large serpent that was making its way toward her. Evelyn slammed into the capsule and fought to remain upright.

The woman, her eyes wracked with discomfort and confusion behind the mask, stared blindly into the middle distance, her eyes a curious pearlescent blue. Evelyn sensed at once that the woman could not see a thing but that she could hear everything, each plasma blast shocking and scaring her.

On impulse, Evelyn reached up and grasped her hand.

The woman froze and then she looked down and seemed to stare straight into Evelyn's eyes as though entranced.

'Come with me if you want to live,' Evelyn snapped.

Evelyn stepped back and virtually forced the woman to blindly follow her. As she stepped down Evelyn saw that there were no intravenous lines in her arms, nothing to have kept her alive for so long inside the capsule but for the per–fluorocarbon.

'Come on!'

Evelyn yanked the woman toward the exit as the Marines laid down covering fire, the plasma rounds screeching past them with scant inches to spare as they hurried forward. The hellish, tortured cries and screams of unknown species filled the air around them as they rushed toward the exit, the strange woman finally finding her feet and running with Evelyn.

'Get through, damn it!' Bra'hiv snapped at Evelyn as she ducked through the hatch and dragged the woman behind her, dripping copious amounts of per–fluorocarbon as she went and her mask sparkling with the fluid.

'We can't seal it!' Andaim snapped as he looked at the damaged hinges.

'Fall back to the next bulkhead!' Bra'hiv ordered.

Evelyn glimpsed rifle fire from within the holds as she turned and saw the hideous shapes of creatures fighting and killing each other in the darkness.

'Look!' she pointed. 'They're coming out!'

Amid the murderous frenzy the shapes of men formed, shadows against shadows as they moved in perfect concert, firing in all directions, the blasts smashing into species of all kinds as they tracked toward the exit.

'Damn it,' Bra'hiv growled. 'Covering fire!'

The Marines looked at their general as though he had gone mad and he roared at them in fury. 'Would *you* want to be left in *there*?!'

The Marines did not move but Evelyn caught Andaim's eye. They moved together without words, Andaim following as Evelyn leaped back through the hatchway and opened fire on the creatures pouring in pursuit of the tight knot of soldiers moving toward her.

The Marines poured back into the hatchway and formed up behind Evelyn, and suddenly a blaze of rifle fire illuminated the interior of the holds in a flickering blue light. Evelyn felt her guts twist in fear as she saw creatures racing through the holds toward the light, clambering up the walls and swarming through the cables and ventilation channels high above.

She forced herself to focus on her firing as the troops moved closer, firing as they went.

'Move it!' Andaim yelled at them.

The troops broke at the last moment, forming a single–file formation as they sprinted away and leaped through the open hatchway one at a time with astonishing speed. Evelyn fired two more shots into the tumult of animals thundering toward her, and then she turned and leaped through the hatch.

'Get out of here!' Bra'hiv yelled. 'Past the next bulkhead!'

Evelyn ran, saw Meyanna far ahead helping the strange woman she had freed to find her way along the corridor. Marines were already posted at regular intervals through the corridor, and the elite troops had taken up similar positions without orders, their weapons aimed at the entrance to the hold as Evelyn ran past.

'Fire in the hole!'

Bra'hiv tossed four plasma grenades just inside the hold entrance and then sprinted clear. The general made less than ten paces, the hatchway behind him filled with gruesome, fanged creatures all rushing for the exit when the grenades detonated.

A blinding series of four plasma blasts flickered in unison like lightning and exploded out of the hatchway behind a shockwave that hammered into Evelyn's back as she crouched and ducked her head away from the blast. She saw Bra'hiv hit the deck hard as he was hit by the blast, his hands covering his head as a cloud of blue smoke tumbled up the corridor and consumed them.

'Keep moving!' Andaim yelled, his voice sounding dull and muted in Evelyn's ears. 'Get past the next bulkhead!'

A ripple of fresh shots crackled out as the Marines maintained a steady fire into the smoke clogging the hold entrance. Bra'hiv hauled himself to his feet and staggered forward, blood trickling from his left ear where the blast must have ruptured his eardrum, his face pinched with pain.

Evelyn fell in alongside him as they ran to the next bulkhead and hopped through, the Marines and elite troops falling back with them until every last man was through. Lieutenant C'rairn slammed the bulkhead shut and spun the manual locking wheel until it was tight, rammed through all three locking pins and then slumped against the hatch, his chest heaving and his features pale with delayed shock.

Evelyn looked at the young lieutenant, who spoke in a raspy, exhausted whisper.

'That was fun. Can we go home now?'

'Nobody's going anywhere,' a voice growled, and Evelyn looked up to see the elite troops encircling them as they emerged from the darkness. 'And we thought you said that you had no home to go to?'

Bra'hiv nodded from where he crouched, trying to regain his breath and one hand gingerly cupping his injured ear. 'Ethera's gone, or at least the home that you remember. You really think a general of my age would be charging around in combat zones if the military were still fully functional?'

The soldier was still staring down the barrel of his rifle at Bra'hiv, but Evelyn could tell that his resistance was wavering. The rifle lowered slowly, and one of the other soldiers spoke instead.

'Everything's gone?' he asked, his furtive tone strangely at odds with his heavily armed appearance.

'Everything,' Evelyn confirmed. 'We've picked up the occasional survivor, run into fleeing pirates and other brigands around the outer systems, but that's it. They're all gone.'

'How did you get here?' Bra'hiv asked the troops. 'We didn't detect a ship.'

The soldier gestured with a nod of his head over his shoulder. 'She's shielded, and we landed her in a smaller bay to help conceal her.' He looked at Bra'hiv. 'We haven't received orders for over a year.'

'You won't be receiving any more orders,' Bra'hiv confirmed. 'What were you sent out here to do?'

The soldier seemed to consider the question for what felt like a long time, and then he blinked himself out of his reverie and gestured to his men.

'Lieutenant Jaysin Riaz,' the commander of the platoon introduced himself. 'Fourteenth STS unit.'

'You were saying what you were sent here for?' Bra'hiv said.

'The mission was sanctioned at a very high level,' Riaz began, 'and my team selected from a number of branches across Special Forces. We all knew each other already and had all worked together before, given the small size of the force, and had a combined expertise that covered all aspects of operations: demolitions, infiltration, deep–space survival, close–quarters combat and surveillance.'

The watching Marines listened with interest along with Evelyn as Riaz went on.

'We were deployed in secret aboard an ordinary launch of a new Colonial cruiser, *Defiant,* and we parted company with them a couple of months before they reached the limit of their cruise radius, close to the Icari Line. We've been operating alone ever since, picking up revised orders once every few months upon our return.'

'Return from where?' Evelyn asked.

'From wherever we wanted to go,' Riaz replied. 'Our mission was to scour beyond the Icari Line and find out what was waiting for humanity there, to discover, master and deploy new technologies. The whole mission was designed as a combined fact–finding and weapons procurement exercise, designed to provide Etheran superiority in the event of another protracted war against the Veng'en.'

Bra'hiv's eyes narrowed as he thought for a moment.

'That's where you got those plasma shields of yours from. And you were deployed three years ago?'

'Three and a half,' Riaz confirmed.

'Damn,' Evelyn whispered. 'The Word would have long been in indirect control of Ethera's government by then, and a great deal of the military.'

'It'll know about your mission,' Bra'hiv confirmed to Riaz. 'It may even have sent you itself.'

'What do you mean?' Riaz asked.

'We should have thought of it ourselves,' Evelyn explained. 'We came out here beyond the Icari Line in the hopes of finding technology that could be used to defeat the Word, but it looks as though the Word might have thought of this long before we did.'

'The bodies, in the capsules,' Bra'hiv said as he gestured back into the holds. 'This ship was designed as an exploratory vessel decades ago, but now it's holding many different species and looks as though it may have been overcome by the Word. You saw the face embedded into the ship's bridge?'

'Yeah,' Riaz replied, visibly uncomfortable with the memory. 'We haven't seen anything like that before out here, and believe me, we've seen some things.'

Bra'hiv turned to Evelyn.

'We need to get off this ship,' he said finally. 'We don't know what happened here, but the best thing we can do is blow Endeavour into history and forget we ever found her.'

Evelyn glanced at the woman they had liberated, her face still concealed behind her mask. 'What about the rest of the crew?' she asked. 'They could still be trapped in the holds.'

'And we could learn something here,' Meyanna insisted, 'something crucial about how the Word evolved. It might even lead to a way to defeat it.'

'We can't rescue everybody,' Bra'hiv pointed out, 'and we're certainly not going back inside that hold without massive reinforcements.'

'We can't just obliterate the entire ship and walk away!' Meyanna gasped.

'Watch me,' Bra'hiv snapped. 'Let's go!'

***

XXI

General Bra'hiv's command was accepted by Riaz's troopers, who despite their unique status had decided to defer for the time being to the general's authority until they knew more about the situation back on Ethera.

'We should make for our own ship,' Lieutenant Riaz insisted. 'It's better armed than your shuttle.'

'We can pick up your gunship when we've launched safely,' Bra'hiv replied. 'Right now it's imperative that we get back aboard Atlantia and fill them in on everything we know. Our shuttles are waiting close by and besides, not all of us have atmospheric suits that will allow us to board your ship. I take it she is in zero–zero conditions, to hinder boarding attempts?'

Riaz nodded as he walked, his eyes never still as he surveyed the way ahead, seeking areas of weakness, potential ambush choke–points and cover locations.

'Standard operating procedure,' he confirmed. 'We pull around back as soon as your shuttle lifts off and you've confirmed our identities with your captain, understood? Only reason we're following your orders right now is because we choose to. By rights, you have no authority over my unit.'

'Understood,' Bra'hiv replied without rancour. 'Let's just get off this wreck first. We can worry about pissing contests afterward.'

Evelyn followed the two soldiers, one hand on her pistol as she sought any sign ahead of impending attack. Endeavour gave her the creeps, more so than the *Sylph* they had boarded months before. The sight of the bodies in the capsules had sent a chill down her spine as she thought of what these people, these species, might have gone through. Her own mask had been sealed over her face for three years or more, a period of time that had felt like aeons. The probes deep in her throat had left bloodied lesions after they had been removed, her once gentle voice now gravelly and alien to her own ears.

'We're coming up on the launch bays,' Bra'hiv reported to the men behind him. 'Signal friend or foe.'

Lieutenant C'rairn activated a small device on his webbing, the small black box flashing a brief green light. Moments later, the box flashed a double–green light and C'rairn nodded at the general.

'All clear, they know we're coming.'

The Marines marched onward toward the landing bay, and ahead a hatch opened to reveal a Marine who peeked out at them before relaxing and stepping out into the corridor.

'All clear general,' he called, and then he spotted the additional soldiers accompanying the Marines. 'Who called the cavalry?'

'We have some new friends,' Bra'hiv replied, 'STS soldiers, and they'd like their gunship back. Call the shuttle pilot and arrange an extraction, we're getting out of here.'

'Yes sir!'

The Marine turned and jogged down the corridor ahead toward the landing bay as Evelyn caught up with Bra'hiv. She was about to ask him something when the general's communicator lit up with a priority signal. The general reached down and opened a channel.

'Bra'hiv?'

'Captain Sansin?'

We've got a situation here! Kordaz and Qayin's ship is heading your way at high speed and is out of contact. We don't know what the hell they're doing! Get off Endeavour immediately!'

Bra'hiv did not waste time replying to the captain.

'Double time!' he roared. 'Move, now!'

The Marines began sprinting down the corridor, the Special Forces troops accelerating ahead of them as their immense physical fitness outstripped that of the Marines. Evelyn ran hard to try to keep up with Riaz's men, but she was no match for them as they burst out of the corridor and into the landing bay.

*

'Her shields are up!'

Teera saw Salim Phaeon's gunship shields light up on her tactical display as she flew her Raython clear of the ship's weapons, angling for a clear shot. The huge, X–shaped vessel roared by as it accelerated away toward Endeavour and left a trail of glistening debris and frozen gases in its wake.

'She's heading for the wreck!'

Teera's Raython rolled over as she turned the fighter in an attempt to lay in a pursuit course and switched her weapons to active.

'Reaper Two, weapons hot!'

The gunship's ion engines flared with white heat as she raced toward Endeavour. To Teera's port side Arcadia was already moving to intercept, the frigate attempting to cut the gunship off while also bringing her huge batteries to bear upon the much smaller gunship.

'Arcadia, I've got her!' Teera called.

'Warning shots only!' came Captain Sansin's orders. *'Try to disable her if you can but do not destroy her!'*

Teera's Raython accelerated quickly and gained on the more massive gunship as her targeting reticule suddenly zipped into the gunship's stern as her plasma cannons locked on. She hesitated only for a moment before her trigger finger squeezed her control column.

A pair of brilliant blue–white halos of plasma fire rocketed away from her Raython and smashed into the gunship's stern hull with a blinding flare of light. Teera saw the blasts absorbed by the gunship's shields and suddenly a salvo of return fire zoomed toward her as the gunship's aft cannons opened up.

Teera shoved her control column forward with the speed of instinct and the Raython dove down beneath the lethal hail of gunfire, the flaring plasma charges bathing her cockpit in flickering red light as she raced beneath them.

'Reaper Two, under fire!' she called.

'Maintain fire!' Idris replied, *'but do not destroy her!'*

'I don't think that I can,' Teera replied, 'her shields are too strong!'

The gunship continued to accelerate as Teera followed it and Arcadia moved further across her field of vision. Even as she watched, the frigate's starboard batteries flickered with light and Teera cursed as she hurled the Raython to port in an attempt to avoid the lethal barrage as it rocketed toward both her and the fleeing gunship.

*

'What the hell does he think he's doing?!'

Idris paced the command platform on Atlantia's bridge like a caged beast as he saw Arcadia's cannons light up and narrowly miss both the gunship and the pursuing Raythons. The blasts detonated nearby, bright flashes of blue–white light that briefly illuminated the tiny spacecraft as they rushed by.

'Proximity charges,' Lael identified the rounds blazing from Arcadia's batteries. 'Mikhain's trying to destroy the gunship without harming the Raythons.'

'Damn him,' Idris snarled, his fists clenched as he bashed them against the guard rail. 'Helm, hard to starboard! Cut Arcadia off as soon as the gunship passes us by!'

'Aye, cap'ain.'

'You're not going to try to cut Kordaz off instead?' Lael asked.

'We don't know what's happening aboard the ship,' Idris replied, 'and we can't do much about it without killing everybody on board. We have no choice but to let the craft through and see what it intends. If it lands aboard Endeavour, at least Bra'hiv's Marines can apprehend everybody aboard.'

'And if Kordaz brings the Legion with him?' Lael challenged.

Idris bit his lip as he thought for a moment.

'Then Kordaz will be killed,' he replied finally. 'Order Bra'hiv's men to activate their microwave emitters to prevent any contamination.'

*

The blasts woke Qayin.

He heard the impacts shudder through the gunship's hull and reverberate through his body as he lay on the hard deck of the holds. He tried to sit up but his entire body ached with fatigue and his head pounded. He shivered in the cold, weak and vulnerable, and the hold around him spun and tilted wildly as he struggled to sit upright.

The Devlamine.

Qayin cursed out loud as he sat upright and then hunched over himself, unable to do anything but keep breathing. His body was nearing the limit of what it could take, and he knew that his blood loss and reliance on the power of Devlamine to keep him going was ushering him toward a painful death or a lengthy and equally painful withdrawal from the drug, but he knew that he had no choice. Slowly, each movement requiring an immense effort, Qayin dragged himself once again across the deck and reached the flasks of Devlamine. Carefully, he selected the correct flask and then, wincing at his own weakness of both before and now, he took the drug into his mouth before he slumped against the hold wall.

His breathing became shallow as he lay at an awkward angle against the wall, the distant thumping of plasma blasts hammering the gunship's shields seeming to accompany the slow beat of his heart. Qayin almost passed out, his body numb and feeling warm as he lost awareness of his surroundings, the Devlamine slower to act when taken orally than it had been through the intravenous line.

Then, slowly, his heart beat accelerated and he felt the pain return to sear his limbs and his skin, only for it too to fade as his vision sharpened and he sucked in a deep breath of stale air. His hearing returned and he dragged himself up onto his feet, his pulse surging through his veins as he felt fresh energy power through his body.

He turned to the hold doors but he could see already that they were locked. Kordaz, if he had known what was good for him, would likely have made an extra effort to seal the doors from the outside too, to prevent any escape attempt. The former convict turned on the spot as he surveyed the hold, seeking any possible means of escape or a suitable weapon.

Salim Phaeon had been a pirate, a slaver and a smuggler, but back in the heyday of his reign of terror in the Tyberium Fields, Salim would have needed to conceal smuggled or stolen goods. Fact was, while he could plunder vessels in the remotest corners of the cosmos, it was back home where the market remained, where the money was. And that was also where the Colonial patrols operated.

Qayin switched his attention to the deck plating and the hull walls, gambling his next move on the likelihood of Salim stashing at least a few weapons somewhere aboard his ship. Pirates, damnable souls that they were, were not above attacking their own especially if their target had been known to have recently successfully plundered a juicy trade vessel. Salim would have guarded against such attacks in any way he could.

Qayin knelt down and examined the deck plating for any hint of concealed inspection panels or compartment. He crawled along the deck as he heard the distant impacts of plasma charges slam into the ship's hull, but he could find nothing. He stood up, perplexed that Salim would have foregone such a basic and yet vital precaution against searches by Colonial vessels or indeed attacks by his own people.

A sudden blast slammed into the ship's hull and Qayin staggered sideways as the deck pitched violently beneath him. His hand reached out for anything to belay his fall and he slammed into one of the support braces with a dull thump that shuddered through his entire body. His vision starred briefly from the impact and he pushed off the pillar as he massaged his shoulder.

And then he saw it. As Qayin rubbed his shoulder he felt the metal implant beneath the surface of the suit, the iron that in conjunction with charged plates below the deck provided the ship's quasi–gravity, and then saw the dent in the support brace beside him.

The support braces for the holds extended in a row from the front of the holds to the back, each one as thick as a man. They were evenly spaced, perhaps four cubits apart, and were constructed of immensely strong metal to support the loads placed upon such a craft when entering atmospheric flight from orbit. There was no way that an object with as little mass as Qayin could have dented such strong material.

Qayin stood back and surveyed the braces, and almost immediately he smiled broadly in the dim light as he realised the extent of Salim's ingenuity. The ship's hull was supported by roughly twice as many braces as it would probably require, being a smaller vessel, and that could only mean one thing. Half of the braces were fakes, designed to conceal stolen, smuggled or illegal goods as Salim had traversed the core systems.

Qayin moved closer to the dented brace and he quickly found what he was looking for: the edge of a panel, the entire height of the beam, the joint concealed perfectly against the hull wall and in shadow, further hiding its presence. Qayin eased around the edge of the panel and quickly found a mechanical lock, small and unobtrusive, looking more like a manufacturer's stamp than anything else. Qayin pushed and prodded the mark and moments later the side of the supposed brace clicked and opened.

Qayin stood back as he surveyed a tightly bound stash of plasma rifles and charges, ammunition pouches and cleaning implements for the weapons. Without hesitation Qayin yanked a rifle and two charges free from the collection, along with several ammunition pouches. He hurried to the main hatch and placed the charges against the hinges before setting the timers and dashing out of sight.

A deafening blast wrenched the door sideways, the hinges simultaneously melting and being smashed aside as the heavy hatch was warped violently and then fell away from the bulkhead in a cloud of smoke and molten metal.

Qayin jammed a magazine into the plasma rifle and saw the weapon light up as it hummed into life, and with a grin of relish he dashed across the hold and hopped through the smoking, ragged hole of the bulkhead.

***

XXII

The gunship shuddered as Qayin jogged with the plasma rifle cradled in his grasp, heading for'ard toward the cockpit. Sparks belched from overloaded circuitry as he rounded a corner and saw the open cockpit door before him, Kordaz sitting in the captain's chair and guiding the gunship toward Endeavour.

Qayin ran hard, his boots thundering on the deck plating as he rushed the cockpit and lifted the plasma rifle as he aimed at Kordaz's head. The thundering boots alerted the Veng'en and he rolled out of the chair as Qayin fired.

The plasma shot missed the back of Kordaz's head and smashed into the control panel with a bright explosion that sent instruments and sparks spraying through the cockpit as Kordaz came up on one knee and one thick muscular arm pointed directly at Qayin.

Qayin barely registered the flickering sliver of bright metal that flashed toward him, and then the *Djeck* thumped into his chest and buried itself. Qayin came up short in the cockpit doorway as Kordaz leaped up with ferocious speed and smashed the rifle aside. Qayin reached out and tried to drive his thumbs into the Veng'en's eyes but was shocked as he felt them cold and hard beneath his touch, more machine than flesh and devoid of emotion or fear.

Kordaz's huge hand grabbed Qayin around his throat and hauled him into the cockpit amid bright showers of sparks and flame from the smashed instrument panels. The view ahead was filled with the shape of Endeavour's aged, crippled hull, black and foreboding as it loomed ever closer through the cracked screen. Through the haze of smoke Qayin could see the gunship's automatic docking protocol activated, the ship flying on autopilot toward Endeavour's landing bays.

Qayin was slammed against the cockpit wall, Kordaz's huge hand crushing his throat as the Veng'en reached out and grabbed the handle of the *Djeck* buried deep in his chest. Qayin was mildly surprised that he could not feel a damned thing, his nerve endings dulled by the Devlamine, until Kordaz twisted the weapon.

White pain seared Qayin's chest and his vision blurred and darkened as he struggled to maintain consciousness. He reached out with both arms and pushed with all of his strength against the Veng'en, drawing the blade out from his chest.

'You're far too puny,' Kordaz sneered. 'Just like all humans.'

Qayin maintained his effort against the Veng'en, who twisted his grip around the sharply pointed handle of the *D'jeck* as he prepared to yank its serrated blade from Qayin's body and tear his flesh to shreds in the process. Qayin saw Kordaz's muscles tense as he made to pull the weapon out, and instantly Qayin stopped pushing and with all of his might he pulled hard on Kordaz.

The sudden change in forces surprised the Veng'en and he was too slow to react. The blade slammed back into Qayin's chest as the weapon's wickedly sharp handle sank into the Veng'en's body with an equal force. Qayin heard a screech as it smashed through Kordaz's metallic chest and burrowed into the flesh beneath.

Kordaz growled in pain and hurled himself away from Qayin, the smooth–sided spike slipping out of his body as the serrated end remained in Qayin's. Globules of blood sparkled in the cockpit lights as they floated away from the tip of the spike, and Qayin made a last desperate play for the plasma rifle that lay in the corridor outside the cockpit.

He hurled himself out of the cockpit door and dashed to the rifle, grabbed at it with one hand even as he felt the strength in his legs failing him. He turned just as Kordaz smashed into him and they fell together, the heavy Veng'en slamming down on top of Qayin while trying to avoid the lethal spike poking from his chest.

Kordaz leaned in, his deep red eyes filled with fury, spittle flying from his fanged jaws and the vocal resonator struggling to properly translate his words as he snarled.

'You're scum, Qayin, better dead than alive, but I think that I have a better place for you.'

Qayin, helplessly pinned beneath the massive Veng'en, could not in his weakened and disorientated state figure out what Kordaz meant. Moments later, he understood entirely.

Kordaz's metallic chest seemed to ripple as he held Qayin down, and then from the very edges of the metal a thin line of black specks appeared, like black dust that clung to the surface and made their way down toward Qayin's bloodied chest wound.

'It is time,' Kordaz growled, 'for you to be purified.'

Qayin struggled to free himself, but the Veng'en was far too heavy and the effects of the Devlamine Qayin had taken were fast wearing off. Kordaz watched Qayin with his soul less red eyes and emitted something that might have been a snigger of satisfaction. Qayin squirmed to get out from beneath the Veng'en before the Infectors reached him, and as he did so he glimpsed the view out of the cockpit.

Qayin's eyes flew wide and he ducked his head back behind Kordaz.

The Veng'en did not have the time to see the view before he was yanked clear of Qayin's body with extraordinary violence and flew backwards through the cockpit. Qayin saw Kordaz smash backwards into the smouldering control panel, then roll over as he saw Endeavour's huge landing bay doors looming ahead, the gunship bouncing along the massive ship's deck as it smashed out of control toward its pre–programmed destination.

Kordaz reacted instantly, grabbed the co–pilot's control column and squeezed the trigger hard.

*

Evelyn, her chest heaving and her breath sawing in her throat, followed the Marines out into the landing bay as she heard the shuttle's engines, the craft having landed and the bay sealed once again to allow the escapees to board her. The elite troopers had fanned out and provided a protective arc around the Marines as they dashed toward the shuttle, Evelyn one side of the woman they had liberated and Meyanna the other as they struggled on toward the shuttle.

'Get aboard, as fast as you can!' Bra'hiv yelled.

Evelyn kept moving, even as she heard Captain Idris Sansin's voice cry out across the frequency.

'All hands, prepare for impact! Endeavour, collision inevitable!'

Evelyn's eyes widened and she looked at Andaim in confusion as they stared at the silent landing bay, the huge doors sealed shut. Even as Evelyn looked at them a blast of energy smashed through the massive doors as an explosion tore through the landing bay. A series of plasma blasts shattered the walls of the bay and ploughed through the decks behind the Marines as they were hurled aside by the impacts.

Evelyn ducked down as the huge landing bay doors ruptured and the atmosphere within the bays screamed out into space in whirling clouds of white vapour loaded with sparkling crystals of ice. As the immense doors blasted outward a large, rust–red vessel ploughed into the landing bay, its metal hull smashing into the decks amid a vast cloud of sparks as it crashed into the shuttle craft and shouldered it aside, its landing struts snapping like giant metal trees as the mass and momentum of the craft forced it downward onto the decks.

Evelyn grabbed the woman and together they sprinted clear of the huge X–shaped gunship as it slammed hull–down and slid along under its own momentum, the metal decks of the bay crumpling beneath it like grey water and the deafening roar of metal under tension and powerful ion engines silenced as the last of the atmosphere was sucked from the landing bay out into the vacuum of space.

Evelyn glimpsed a handful of unfortunate Marines tumble out into the void as Endeavour's limited emergency–power systems began to react to the hull breach and a set of emergency doors dropped from above. Evelyn grasped the deck with one hand as with the other she maintained a grip the woman as the doors ground their way down and the gunship's huge hull crashed past them.

The gunship slammed into the rear–wall of the bay, its bow smashing through the wall entirely as the craft came to a rest, its stern high in the air and its engines smouldering as they shut down automatically as the landing cycle completed.

The emergency bay doors slammed down and sealed themselves, and then Evelyn saw vents belching vapour once more as the atmosphere was reintroduced to the bay. She sucked in a lung full of air and glanced about her. Marines were scattered everywhere, some slumped comatose on the deck, others nursing wounds and attempting to hold their rifles as they stared in shock at the gunship now filling the landing bay.

'Bravo Company, report in!'

Bra'hiv's voice was tense and wracked with frustration as he surveyed the damage.

'Nine men missing or down,' C'rairn calculated as he struggled to his feet and surveyed the damage and debris.

'All arms, re–group immediately!' Bra'hiv ordered.

Evelyn hauled herself to her feet and saw Andaim with Meyanna across the bay, both of them stunned but on their feet. Evelyn turned to the woman with her and slowly she helped her to her feet. The woman was shivering in the cold, her hair matted and thick with per–fluorocarbon, her eyes still searching but unseeing behind her mask.

The Marines dragged themselves into a defensive formation around their general, Meyanna and Evelyn as she guided her charge inside their guns. Nearby, the elite troops had formed a silent vanguard with Lieutenant Riaz and were waiting patiently to see what happened next. Inside the Marine's formation were three injured soldiers, all of them unconscious.

'The shuttle's useless now,' one of them called. 'We're trapped!'

Evelyn looked at the shuttle–and saw instantly that the gunship had crushed its cockpit, flattening it and without any shadow of doubt killing the pilot. She turned and looked up at the form of Salim Phaeon's gunship, and she could see already that its bow was crumpled beyond recognition, the hull fractured in multiple places and all manner of dangerous fluids spilling from ruptured pipework.

'The gunship's a fire hazard,' she said. 'We need to get out of the bay!'

The gunship had ploughed through bulkheads and hatches, warping them and sealing them shut. The only way out of the bay was up and through the damaged gunship itself, to where the cockpit area had punched through the bay walls.

'Move fast,' Bra'hiv ordered. 'We'll have to hope that we can get through and that the whole damned ship doesn't blow us to hell while we're at it. Let's go!'

Evelyn watched as the Marines hurried along beside the crashed gunship's hull and located an access hatch one–third the length of the hull back from the cockpit. The demolitions team quickly attached plasma charges to the hatch, and moments later Evelyn shielded the masked woman's body with her own as the hatch blew outward. The metal panel tumbled through the air amid a cloud of smoke as the Marines poured into the hatch with their weapons aimed ahead of them.

Evelyn made to stand, but a strong hand belayed her. The woman was gripping her arm and shaking her head. Evelyn knelt down alongside her.

'We have to,' she said. 'We can't get off this ship through the bay. We need to find another way out.'

The woman's face was stricken with fear and she was trying to make her voice work, her jaw gaping as she rasped and coughed.

'We can't stay here, whatever we do,' Evelyn insisted. 'Come on, let's move.'

The woman reluctantly took Evelyn's hand and they followed the Marines aboard the gunship.

The interior was dark, lights flickering erratically as Evelyn's eyes adjusted to the gloom. Sparks flew from blown panels as the Marines moved systematically through the ship, all of them turning right toward the cockpit and away from the corridors that led to the holds.

Evelyn watched as they hurried through the ship toward the cockpit, acutely aware of Riaz's Special Forces team following in silence behind her and of whispered exchanges between the lieutenant and his men that she could not quite make out. A sudden flurry of shouts carried to her from somewhere for'ard and with the Marines she hurried her pace until she reached the cockpit corridor.

The Marines were surrounding a body on the deck and she could see that the cockpit ahead was a smouldering, warped mess, the windshield shattered and blown out by the force of the impact. Evelyn made her way forward and was surprised to see a satisfied grin on General Bra'hiv's face.

'Well, well,' he uttered. 'Who'd have thought it?'

Evelyn looked down and saw Qayin sprawled on his back on the deck. His eyes were hooded, his body lacerated with countless wounds and his uniform stained almost entirely with blood. The bioluminescent tattoos on his face were barely visible, faded and pulsing weakly. Qayin looked up at her and he tried to speak.

'Stay still,' Meyanna whispered to the convict urgently as she tried to stem the flow of blood from the ragged wound in Qayin's chest, the silvery blade and spike poking upward from the wound.

Evelyn gasped as she recognised the weapon.

'That's a *D'jeck*,' she said as she pointed at the weapon, and then she looked at Qayin. 'Kordaz?'

Qayin nodded briefly, barely able to speak, but he managed to force a single word between his swollen lips.

'Infected.'

Evelyn looked out of the shattered cockpit windows.

'I think we've got an even bigger problem now,' she said.

***

XXIII

'What's going on down there?'

Captain Idris Sansin stalked up and down on the command platform, his hands grasped behind his back as he awaited a response from his command crew.

'We're re–establishing contact with General Bra'hiv, captain,' Lael replied. 'The communications links were severed when the gunship crashed into the landing bay, and the crash seems to have provoked the ship's computer to force an emergency shut–down of all major systems.'

'Is my wife alive?' Idris demanded. 'Do we have any contact with the team at all?'

Lael did the smart thing and remained silent as she worked the controls at her station until, finally, a signal reached Atlantia. A display screen on the bridge flickered into life and showed an image of General Bra'hiv's point–of–view as he stood over the bodies of three soldiers lying on the deck before him, Meyanna and two Marine medics working on the injured people.

'General, what's happening down there?!'

Bra'hiv's voice replied, as calm as ever.

Meyanna is fine, captain,' he said, seeking to allay the captain's primary concern as soon as possible. *'We've lost three Marines and a lot's happened since we lost contact. It's going to take a while to explain.'*

'We've been busy here too,' Idris admitted, calming as he noted on the screen his wife busily attending to a wounded soldier. 'The gunship made a break for it and slipped through our defences.'

'We noticed,' Bra'hiv replied dryly. *'Nobody thought to shoot the damned thing down?'*

Idris ground his teeth in his jaw. 'That was precisely what Arcadia was attempting to do, but we blocked them from finishing the job.'

'You did what?'

'The situation was not as simple as it may have seemed to Mikhain, who has adopted a cavalier attitude toward the lives of anybody not aligned with Colonial thinking.'

'I could have told you about that,' Bra'hiv remarked. *'He's got his own agenda captain, and has had for some time.'*

On the display screen, the captain saw Andaim glance at Bra'hiv with interest upon the general's remarks.

'That notwithstanding, there may be some doubt about Qayin's guilt of treachery at Chiron IV.'

'I doubt that immensely, being as I was there,' Bra'hiv countered, 'but you'll be overjoyed to learn that our old friend is now with us and looking remarkably the worse for wear.'

Bra'hiv turned his head and Idris got a good look at Qayin, where he lay apparently unconscious on the deck with an intravenous line in his arm.

'Kordaz?' the captain asked.

'Nowhere to be seen,' Bra'hiv replied. 'The gunship crashed into the landing bay and punched right through into the ship itself, so it's possible the Veng'en escaped into the ship, although why he would have wanted to do so is beyond me.'

It was Evelyn who replied.

'He's infected,' she reported. *'Qayin managed to warn me before he passed out.'*

'And now he's aboard Endeavour,' Idris said. 'And there's no way out of that landing bay?'

'Not a chance,' Bra'hiv confirmed, *'the ship's computer, that face welded into the control panels on the bridge, has shut half the ship down due to the atmospheric breach and Salim's gunship is leaking like a sieve. As soon as the injured men are stabilised we've got to move.'*

'With Kordaz somewhere ahead of you,' Idris muttered, realising the extent of the danger they were in.

'It's worse than that,' Bra'hiv revealed. 'The gunfight in the holds set off an emergency release mechanism for the various species being held in stasis. They're all out, captain, and we barely escaped without losing anybody.'

'What gunfight?' Idris asked in exasperation.

'We'll explain it all later,' Bra'hiv assured the captain. *'Right now, I need you to look into the records for any evidence of the Word being behind the launch of Endeavour, or having any input into who boarded her as a passenger and whether they could, no matter how remote the chance, have been somehow infected.'*

'Infected?' Idris echoed. 'But Endeavour was launched almost a century ago!'

'We know, but whatever has been done here looks just like the work of the Legion, although thankfully we haven't found any evidence of them being aboard the ship.'

'Until Kordaz,' Idris reflected. 'Do you think that might be why he suddenly flew that gunship into Endeavour? He was originally holding Qayin as hostage in return for me sending Meyanna to treat him.'

'Perhaps,' Bra'hiv said as he glanced at the shattered cockpit windscreen. *'But right now I don't give a damn. I need schematics and a way out of this ship.'*

Idris turned to Lael, who immediately got to work. Idris returned his gaze to the screen and saw Bra'hiv look across to where Evelyn was standing and watching Meyanna work on the injured soldiers. There, standing beside Evelyn, was a woman whose appearance made the captain startle.

'Evelyn?'

Bra'hiv looked at the woman accompanying Evelyn and his voice filled Atlantia's bridge. *'One of the things I wanted to talk to you about,'* the general said. *'We found her in the capsules in the hold, and Evelyn here insisted on bringing her with us. I don't like it, but so far she's done nothing to harm any of us and she appears to be blind.'*

Idris walked closer to the display screen, fascinated by the woman's appearance. Despite the mask obscuring her features and being smothered in thick fluid, she seemed almost a carbon copy of Evelyn herself.

'That can't be a coincidence,' he said softly, aware that Evelyn would be on the same channel and able to hear him.

'It isn't,' Evelyn replied for the general, *'but right now I don't know why.'*

'Did you find any other humans down there?' Idris asked.

'Many of the crew were being held in stasis,' Bra'hiv replied, *'but we didn't get far inside the holds before we were chased out again by all sorts of fangs and teeth. If the crew were the first victims of this then it's likely they were further inside the hold, and they're also likely now loose as well. I don't want to think about what it's going to be like inside there.'*

Lael's voice piped up from her console.

'Then you're not going to like what has to happen next,' she said. 'Sending Endeavour's schematics over to you now.'

There was a few moments' pause as Bra'hiv examined the data that Lael had sent him, and then Idris felt as though he could almost hear the general scowl.

'You're damned well kidding me?'

Idris looked up at a second screen that flickered into life alongside the one linked to General Bra'hiv, and there the schematic was displayed. Obtained by overlaying Endeavour's original deck plan over a three–dimensional scan of the ship's now–wrecked hull, the schematic provided a detailed presentation of all available access corridors remaining aboard the ship.

Of key interest was the only available route from the for'ard landing bays to the only other remaining operational landing bay on Endeavour's starboard aft flank. The route descended the 'tween decks, passed directly through the holds and then climbed aft.

'That's the *only* route?' Idris uttered in dismay.

'All other potential avenues of access to the aft bays are either cut off by hull breaches or obstructed by collapsed support beams and other major structural failures,' Lael reported. 'Normally the hold would not be used to access the aft bays, but in this case there is a series of ventilation shafts large enough to pass through that link the holds to a point for'ard of where the engine rooms were once located. The aft landing bays are served by the same shafts, thus providing access.'

'*Perfect,*' Bra'hiv muttered. '*We've got to go back where we just came from.*'

'Can you not just use the environmental suits and board a shuttle via the breached hull?' Idris asked.

'*Not enough suits to go around,*' Bra'hiv replied, '*especially not now we've picked up new members. Anybody without a suit has to stay inside the pressurised sections of the hull.*'

'Is there any way we can get useable suits to you aboard Endeavour?' Idris tried again.

'*Maybe, but we've got to leave right now. My men are reporting electrical fires throughout the gunship and she could blow at any moment. If you can get the suits to us, then you'll have to find a way to do it while we're on the move.*'

Idris looked at Lael, who shook her head. 'The entire route is deep inside the hull. Best we can do is land a shuttle with reinforcements aboard the aft bay and hope to meet Bra'hiv's team half–way.'

Another, deeper voice replied from Endeavour. '*That won't be possible.*'

Idris watched as a man with a face concealed with a bandana, his eyes hard and cold, came to stand before General Bra'hiv.

'And why is that?' Idris enquired.

'*Because that bay is already full with our own craft, and the doors sealed from the inside. The only way out is via our gunship and there won't be any room for reinforcements. We either do this ourselves or we're here for what's left of our lives.*'

'Who are you?'

The soldier reached up and pulled the bandana from his face. He was a young man with short–cropped blond hair and icy grey eyes, his jaw thick with stubble. He peered at the camera, his voice gravelly as he spoke.

'*My name is Lieutenant Riaz, Specialist Tactics Squadron.*'

'What the hell are you doing there?' Idris asked.

'*That's a long story and we don't have time to tell it now,*' Riaz said. '*Your general will fill you in on the way but right now it's time to move. Let's go.*'

Within moments, the entire company of soldiers began moving towards the cockpit of the gunship. The cockpit was filled with smouldering panels and broken glass, sparks falling from the ceiling panels to scatter across the deck. Evelyn followed the Marines into the cockpit and searched for any sign of Kordaz, but all she could see was a splattering of blood across the cockpit panels where the Veng'en had crawled out of the cockpit and through the shattered glass.

'He's been here,' said the general.

Bra'hiv pointed to the bloodstains on the cockpit panels and Lieutenant Riaz examined them closely for a moment. 'Someone you know?'

'It's another long story,' Evelyn said.

The Marines clambered through the gaping cavity where the gunship's screen had once been, and Evelyn turned to help the woman through behind her. The woman stumbled uneasily through the glass and onto the bow of the gunship. One by one the Marines climbed down off the bow and into a wide corridor leading aft through the ship. Evelyn climbed down off the bow and then turned to help the woman off behind her. Not once did the woman release her hand, gripping as if it was the only thing keeping her alive.

***

XXIV

The corridor was long, the lights set into the ceiling flickering weakly as they walked, heading ever further aft into Endeavour. Evelyn led the woman by the hand, following the Marines as they fanned out and moved from cover to cover. Endeavour's power system remained almost completely off–line, the ships fusion cores weakening and the supply unreliable.

As they walked Evelyn tried to peer past the mask of the woman next to her but she could see nothing of her face. She glanced again at the identification patch on the woman's uniform, transfixed by the image of her own features. To her surprise, the woman's masked face turned slightly towards her as she sensed she was being looked at.

'You're safe,' Evelyn said. 'You're surrounded by Colonial Marines.'

The woman made no response, her masked face turning to face forwards again, but Evelyn could tell that she was listening to everything that was happening around her and she was walking with a tense gait as though expecting an imminent attack.

Bra'hiv led the Marines to a bulkhead, the hatch sealed and the soldiers forming a guard around it. The general approached the hatch slowly and turned to look Evelyn.

'Once we go through here there'll be no turning back, you understand?'

Meyanna stepped forward and gestured towards the woman with the mask. 'Don't you think we should do something about this mask before we go any further?'

Bra'hiv looked at the woman and frowned. 'I don't think we have time to remove that thing.'

'We going to need every pair of hands we can get,' Evelyn said, 'if we're going to get through that hold.'

The general looked at Riaz's men, and one of them reached into his webbing and pulled out a compact plasma torch. Evelyn turned to the woman and squeezed her hand gently.

'Don't worry, we're going to get that thing off you before we go any further.'

Evelyn helped the woman to sit down on the deck as Meyanna took the plasma torch from the soldier and knelt down beside Evelyn. Meyanna activated the plasma torch and it crackled with energy as a bright blueâ€"white arc of light flared violently. The woman instinctively backed away from the noise but Evelyn placed a hand on her shoulder and squeeze gently.

'It's okay,' she said. 'Trust me.'

Meyanna leaned in, the torch perilously close to the woman's skin as she began severing the solid neck brace of the mask. Evelyn grabbed a small canteen of water and prepared to wash any wounds down as the mask was removed. The Marines closed in around them and watched in fascinated silence as Meyanna carefully cut through the braces, the chunks of metal tumbling away as the woman sat motionless on the deck.

It took almost five minutes for her to make the cuts, and then Meyanna shut the plasma torch off and handed it back to the watching soldiers. Evelyn sat back and looked down for a moment before she spoke.

'We'll take it off now.'

For several long moments the woman didn't move, but then slowly she reached up instinctively to touch the mask. Evelyn and Meyanna positioned themselves either side of the woman, Evelyn taking her shoulders in her hands as Meyanna gripped the mask firmly.

'Are you ready?'

She slowly nodded her head and her hands dropped into her lap as she waited for whatever was coming next. Evelyn took a deep breath and heard the woman do the same as Meyanna spoke.

'On the count of three,' she said. 'One, two…'

With a heave of effort Meyanna suddenly pulled on the mask, yanking it upwards and outwards as Evelyn pulled back on the woman's shoulders. The mask shot away from her face and two long chrome probes slid from deep inside the woman's throat and trailed a thin stream of crimson fluid.

The woman gagged, her body jerking violently as the mask was hurled away to slam loudly into the corridor wall. She rolled sideways and hunched over, coughing heavily as she sought to regain control of her breathing. The Marines watched as they heard the woman's breathing whistle in her throat, her body shaking. Evelyn moved around to kneel before the woman and gently push the canteen of water in front of her. The woman grabbed the bottle as if it were the last drink in the galaxy and poured it down her throat as she threw her head back. And as she did so Evelyn felt a tremor of supernatural awe trickle down her spine.

Aghast exclamations went up from the Marines and they stepped back a pace as they stared down at the woman's elfin features, identical to those of Evelyn. Her hair, her eyes, the shape of her lips were the exact mirror–image of Evelyn, tempered only by the pale skin of the face, a sickly torpor from years, perhaps decades of being suspended in stasis inside the capsule.

The woman lowered the canteen of water, coughed again and then sucked in several long, deep breaths as she slowly looked up at Evelyn. The two women look at each other for a long beat, and then Lieutenant C'rairn broke the silence.

'This isn't weird.'

The woman looked up at him and Evelyn thought she saw a tiny smile curl from her lips.

'Who are you?' Evelyn asked, fascinated.

The woman did not reply for a long time, as though trying to take in everything that had happened to her. Evelyn remembered her own awakening from the mask that she had worn for so many years, her own confusion and uncertainty about where she was and what had happened. She too had been in a dangerous vessel surrounded by strangers, many of whom wanted her dead. At least this woman, whoever she was, was surrounded by people who actually wanted to help her.

'My name,' the woman whispered softly, her voice barely audible and sounding as though she were dreaming, 'is Legion, for we are many.'

Evelyn felt a shiver trickle like cold ice water down her spine as she heard the woman's voice, identical it seemed to her own. She watched the woman for a long moment, and then she put out her hand.

'I'm Evelyn,' she said. 'What is your *real* name? Can you remember?'

Again that tiny smile appeared on her face, and she reached out and took Evelyn's hand, although her eyes searched blindly. Her voice when she spoke again sounded entirely human. 'My name is Emma. Where am I?'

It was the general who spoke. 'We'll have time for catching up later,' he said as he turned to examine the hatch. 'Right now we've got to get through here and not get eaten while doing so.'

The Marines, still fascinated by the sight of Emma and Evelyn kneeling on the deck, were slow to move as they turn to examine the hatch.

'Jump to it!' Bra'hiv snapped.

The Special Forces soldiers advanced before the Marines reacted and began attaching charges to the hatch hinges, working in silence with deft and well–practised moves. As Evelyn helped Emma to her feet the soldiers pulled back from the hatchway as Lieutenant Riaz set the detonators, the timers beeping softly as he turned and ran past them and pointed up the corridor.

Evelyn turned to run with him, her hand reaching out instinctively for Emma's in order to guide her, but she was surprised to find that Emma did not attempt to follow. Instead, Emma moved toward the hatchway even as the detonators were counting down.

'Emma, get away from there.'

It was as if Emma did not hear her. She stumbled to the detonators and within moments switched them off, just seconds before they were set to blow. Lieutenant Riaz glared at Emma as he stormed back down the corridor.

'What the hell do you think you're doing?'

Emma turned to confront the soldier, and despite the softness of her voice her words carried surprising weight. 'There is another way.'

'But we were told this is the only way through the holds to the aft landing bays,' Andaim said.

Emma shook her head and gestured to another corridor, smaller than the one in which they stood, which led to starboard. 'We are near the holds, are we not, and this is access corridor H–1–Echo? That way,' she said. 'It's a service corridor that bypasses the forward holds and emerges further down. It won't avoid the holds entirely, but it will get us closer to the aft landing bays.'

Bra'hiv peered at Emma curiously. 'How would you know that if you can't see?'

'I'm blind, not stupid,' Emma replied. 'I lived on this ship for years, I know my way around.'

The general shrugged, reached out and pulled one of the charges off the hatch. He tossed the charge to Lieutenant Riaz who caught it and raised an eyebrow. 'You're going to trust our escape with her?'

Bra'hiv regarded Emma for a long moment, and then he nodded. 'You're damned right I am. Local knowledge is everything. Lead the way.'

Emma turned away from the hatch but with one hand she reached out blindly as though searching for something. Evelyn caught her hand, and Emma smiled briefly at her as though she could see again before she turned and led the way down the corridor.

'We know nothing about her,' Commander Andaim said to the general as they started walking. 'We don't know what will happen if we just follow her down here.'

'We know will happen if we go into those holds.'

Lieutenant Riaz strode alongside Bra'hiv. 'The commander is right, we don't know anything about this woman. For all we know she could be leading us into a trap.'

The general shook his head. 'Right now we don't have much of a choice, and Evelyn seems to trust her.'

Lieutenant Riaz winced. 'That doesn't mean much to us, and either way I find it damn freaky that they look so alike. Who is this Evelyn that you put so much faith in?'

The general looked at Commander Andaim, who shrugged apologetically.

'She's a former high–security convict who escaped from a prison, and now serves as a fighter pilot aboard Atlantia. She also used to wear one of those masks.'

Lieutenant Riaz stared at the commander as though he had gone insane.

'Well that's all right then. For a moment I was worried that you were putting us all at risk.'

'Let's just keep moving,' Bra'hiv said. 'The sooner we get to the stern, the quicker we'll get out of here.'

***

XXV

'We need to talk.'

Captain Idris Sansin strode off the command platform of Atlantia's bridge as Mikhain arrived, and without preamble he marched towards his private quarters. Arcadia's captain followed him without a word. Idris led the way into his quarters, the door opening automatically for them and closing silently behind them.

Mikhain watched as Idris moved to stand beside his desk, the countless pictures of his family on the walls moving subtly as Mikhain's eyes caught them. The cabin was a memorial to people lost, the kind of family that Mikhain never had.

'Captain, I understand that...' Mikhain began.

'Save it,' Idris cut him off. 'We'll have time for discussion about your insubordination later. Right now we have much bigger problems to deal with. What the hell is a Colonial Special Forces team doing aboard Endeavour, and why is there a woman there who appears to be an identical twin to Evelyn?'

'I have no idea,' Mikhain admitted. 'Endeavour was launched almost a hundred years ago, and we have no idea whether the Word could have gotten aboard so early. Personally, I didn't even realise the Word existed back then.'

'It existed all right. The question is in what form did it exist when Endeavour launched, and could have had any influence over what happened to that ship?'

'If it did, then the Word's extent could have had far greater reach than we first assumed.'

Idris nodded in agreement, well aware that the cornerstone of his new plan was to travel the cosmos beyond the extent of the Word's reach in order to discover new technologies and new weapons which could be used to fight it, weapons for which it should have had no defence.

'I tasked several engineers and archivists to look into every single file we have on the origin of the Word,' Idris explained. 'To be honest, and to my shame, I have never really looked that far into the history of the Word but now would seem prudent to do so.'

'What did you find?'

'More than I expected,' Idris replied.

The history of Ethera and of mankind's evolution was in many ways similar to so many other species in the known cosmos. They had evolved from predecessor species, mankind growing to prominence on a diet of conflict and cooperation, ever at war with neighbouring states and peoples; new weapons, new tactics and new reasons to deploy those weapons against others in the name of national security or religion or fear. Countless lives have been lost in the history of mankind in conflicts over little more than territorial disputes and the intractability of the governments to agree upon them.

It had been the advances of technology that eventually gave rise to a new form of intelligence. There was a single motive behind the invention of the Word, a creation driven by a desire for a machine of logic specifically designed to override the greed, malice and insatiable lust for control that was the hallmark of mankind's history. Countless names worked on countless devices and those devices melded into a new form of quantum computing, machines blessed with a complexity sufficient to mimic human awareness and intelligence, but devoid of the flaws and pitfalls that blighted their creators.

Installed by Ethera's government after a referendum of global significance, during which over four billion humans voted in confidence of the new technology, a series of linked supercomputers were tasked with the role of selecting the most beneficial courses of action in everything from conflicts, political disputes, territorial disagreements and economics. This startling new form of governance was given the nickname *The Word*, after several ministers in opposition to its creation claimed that its judgements had in effect already become law and that mankind's own opinion no longer mattered. However, from the moment the Word was tasked with its new role remarkable changes occurred across Ethera. As governments submitted to the Word's will, accepting its judgement, so likewise did the people and thus did the incidence of conflict dramatically reduce over the following years. The Word chose to channel funds into medical research instead of weaponry, social spending and education instead of global banking, the improvement of existing living standards instead of ambitious high-technology gambits like space travel. Far from being despised by the populace, the Word was soon championed by those on the streets as a new form of governance that placed ordinary human beings first and not the politicians and business leaders.

Within ten years the Word was the unquestioned lawmaker of all states on Ethera, responsible for spreading peace and prosperity across entire regions. Poverty was replaced with prosperity, fear with hope, conflict with resolution and destruction with development. Such a Utopian event had never occurred before in human history and its catalyst was nothing more than a series of linked machines with no perceivable aspirations of their own.

Or so humanity had thought.

Alongside the Word's responsibilities for global governance, an unforeseen consequence of its all reaching power had been a growing awareness of military programs. Although the Word had largely guided humanity away from the development of weapons, it had become clear in recent times that throughout this period the Word had in fact been studying weaponry closely. Perhaps the people who had invented the Word should have noticed or known that a device based on the gathering of knowledge would not have been prejudiced on which knowledge it gained—that it would have sought to learn everything and anything and judged its future experiences and understanding based on all the knowledge that it had accrued. It was perhaps inevitable that the Word came to the conclusion that humanity was an unreliable, treacherous creator, as likely to destroy the Word as to nurture it.

The archivists had surmised that the Word had probably begun its long–term plan to conquer humanity within a decade of its own creation. Already virtually worshipped by the human populace and with ever greater laws and powers placed under its command, although the Word was not yet an intelligent entity in its own right its degree of self–awareness was growing at a trimetric rate, and it was only a matter of time before the inevitable occurred. Conspiracy theorists of the time had been convinced that the moment the Word gained self–awareness it would launch attacks on humanity, gathering what automated weaponry it could and obliterating as much of society as possible. Yet the self–awareness never came, as far as humanity was aware. When it occurred, nobody actually knew—the Word was already far too intelligent to expose itself at such an early stage. Fully aware of itself and its surroundings, the Word simply continued to gather information and in doing so discovered a means of destroying humanity for once and for all with a single crippling blow.

Nanotechnology.

Although military spending had been cut by the Word by ninety per cent, the technologies that had been in development for so long were still fully available. Extending the tentacles of its reach into the military–industrial complex, the Word was able to study and modify existing technologies while at the same time finding the means to get those technologies into humanity, quite literally. The street drug Devlamine, the scourge of so many cities, was the perfect vector to introduce mind–controlling nanobots into the population. Spreading silently for years, the infectors were present in eighty per cent of the population when the apocalypse finally occurred. Most people never even knew what happened.

'Endeavour was launched just a few years after the Word was given governing powers by the politicians of the time,' Idris said as he looked at the files the archivists had sent him. 'Given what we know about the Word, and the fact that it probably had self–awareness by the time Endeavour launched, it's a fair bet that it would have tried to get something of itself aboard the ship.'

Mikhain glanced down at the files. 'We haven't found any evidence of infectors aboard or anything else except that face melded into the bridge control panel.'

'You don't consider that to be a hint?'

'I don't know what the hell that is,' Mikhain admitted. 'Fact is we're out of our depth here, cruising well beyond the Icari Line and likely to stumble across a lot more things we don't understand. It *could* be the Word, and that mask sure looked like the one that Evelyn was wearing when she first showed up.'

'It's too much of a coincidence to find such similar technologies in such widely displaced locations,' Idris said. 'We've got to assume the Word is behind this, even if it's some kind of earlier version, perhaps not fully aware.'

'You mean like a prototype?'

'Something like that,' Idris said. 'If I'm right then it might be something we can learn from.'

Mikhain sucked air between his teeth. 'That's risky, even for us. You're saying you want to go digging in that ship and find out what's behind all this?'

'We can't pass up the opportunity that there's something there we could use, something that might help us find a way to defeat the Word. Right now, doing that is the only reason we have to exist.'

'Your wife's aboard Endeavour,' Mikhain reminded the captain.

'I'm aware of that.'

Mikhain rubbed his temples wearily. 'There are no other vessels in the sector this time, at least not that we can detect. With both Atlantia and Arcadia we can properly maintain a secure perimeter of around fifty thousand cubits. We've got regular fighter patrols in place, so nothing is coming in without us knowing about it but I still don't consider this area to be completely within our control. You remember what happened on Chiron IV?'

'Yes, we were bounced by a Veng'en cruiser and I'm aware that we just don't know what might happen next. But that's as much a reason to take the chance as it is to avoid it. No risk, no gain.'

'That's a mantra that might come back to haunt you.'

'We all take risks,' Idris said as he looked directly at Mikhain. 'It's whether you're taking the right kind that counts.'

The two captains stared at each other for several moments, both of them preoccupied with their own doubts about each other. Idris waited to see what the former executive officer would say, willing him to fall into line.

'I'd say it's whether you can deal with the consequences that matters,' Mikhain replied.

'And can you?'

'I do, every day.'

A long silence filled the cabin, the air suddenly feeling heavy. 'Anything you want to talk about?' Idris asked.

'Now is not the time.'

'There is never a perfect time,' Idris pointed out. 'The longer our mistakes linger in our past, the more they will poison our future.'

Mikhain regard the captain for a long moment. 'Like you said, we've got bigger problems to deal with. Bra'hiv's team have only got one way off that ship and we don't have any way of reaching them from the outside, plus the fact that the deeper they go the weaker their communications link becomes. Only thing they've got going for them are the Special Forces soldiers they found aboard.'

'Which brings me to my next question,' Idris said. 'How the hell did they get there?'

'Got to assume they were on some kind of mission. As far as the general can tell they were not fleeing the apocalypse and they claimed not to have received orders for more than two years. That means they've been out here for some time and won't be deserters if they've been expecting orders, which means an officially sanctioned operation.'

'That's what I was thinking, but who sent them? Our government, or the Word?'

'You think they could be infected too?'

'I don't know, but we need to get word either to my wife or the general that those soldiers could be as big a threat to their safety as anything else aboard that ship.'

***

XXVI

The corridor that Emma led them down grew smaller with the passing of each of Endeavour's bulkheads. Evelyn followed her faithfully, Emma apparently counting the steps between each bulkhead and stepping gingerly through the endless hatches. Ceiling lights flickered unevenly, the power supply intermittent and casting moving shadows all around.

At the end of the corridor Evelyn could see a final bulkhead, but this bulkhead contained a hatch that was half the size of all the others. Circular in design, the hatch was sealed and she realised with a start that the hatch was not actually a corridor at all but a ventilation shaft.

Emma slowed as she reached the hatch and turned to face the Marines. Lieutenant Riaz examined at the hatch as though she'd gone mad.

'Seriously?'

'Are you sure this is the safest way?' General Bra'hiv asked Emma.

'This ventilation shaft leads aft and exits directly over the aft hold. It's the only way through.'

'And do we know what's in the aft holds?' the general asked as he turned to Lieutenant Riaz. 'Did you and your men get that far back?'

'No,' the lieutenant replied, 'we'd only just started searching the for'ard holds when your men showed up. There could be anything back there.'

'Great,' Lieutenant C'rairn uttered as he too examined the hatch.

'We don't have much of a choice,' Evelyn said. 'Whichever way we go we're going to have to fight our way through. At least this gives us the advantage of surprise.'

'That's not particularly reassuring,' Lieutenant Riaz snapped as he reached out and spun the locking wheel on the hatch. 'We don't know who'll be getting the surprise.'

His men formed up behind him without orders, their weapons aimed at the hatch as the lieutenant prepared to open it. The magazines on their plasma rifles hummed into life and they pulled the weapons into their shoulders and the lieutenant yanked the hatch back.

The darkened interior of the ventilation shaft beckoned, entirely unlit and panelled in smooth metal that reflected the searching flashlight beams.

'How far do we have to go down there?' Andaim asked.

'About two hundred cubits,' Emma replied. 'The shaft forks, we take the right turn and will be over the holds within a few minutes.'

'Have you been down here before?' Evelyn asked.

'Twice,' Emma replied. 'Endeavour had a drill which we were all required to perform twice–monthly that included a means of avoiding a fire in the hold. This was the main route out.'

Emma released Evelyn's hand and without hesitation she climbed into the shaft. Lieutenant C'rairn peered into the shaft as he prepared to follow Emma.

'If this doesn't work, we're all shafted.'

Andaim groaned as he shoved the lieutenant forward and then followed him in. Two Marines climbed in after the commander and Evelyn followed as the Special Forces troops guarded the entrance.

The ventilation shaft had been modified to be able to support the weight of a crew attempting to escape an on–board fire, but the panels were not made of a metal that was strong enough to allow silent movement. The panels rattled and shuddered as they made their way through, the Marines pulling out flash lights from their webbing to illuminate the way. The beams of blue light flashed this way and that, reflecting off the polished metal walls as they crawled through the narrow confines toward the holds. Evelyn could see Emma at the front, no longer hindered by her lack of sight as she felt her way forward. Ahead, Evelyn could also see the right fork in the shaft appear and Emma turned abruptly and vanished into the new passage.

'This really is what I call the blind leading the blind,' Lieutenant C'rairn said from ahead.

'Will you cut it out?' General Bra'hiv uttered.

Evelyn said nothing as she followed them down the new passage and then came up short as Emma abruptly stopped ahead. Emma raised a clenched fist and held it aloft, the Marines behind instinctively freezing. Evelyn peered ahead through the gloom and spotted a grate in the floor of the shaft through which Emma was peering cautiously.

'What can you see?' Bra'hiv asked.

Emma remained silent as she peered down into the darkness for several long seconds. When she replied her voice was a whisper.

'It's too dark, I can't see anything moving from here.'

Evelyn pulled her pistol from its holster as around her the Marines reactivated their plasma rifles. She watched as Bra'hiv helped Emma lift the grate from the floor of the shaft and slide it to one side. Emma waited on the far side of the hole that they had created as the general activated his plasma rifle and pulled a flare from a pouch on his webbing. Bra'hiv tore the cap off the flare and dropped it into the darkened holds below. Immediately the general followed the flare and jumped into the darkness.

The Marines tumbled in pursuit of their general, dropping one by one into the cavity and down into the hold. Evelyn found herself pushed along as others tried to pass and before she knew it she dropped down into the hold and landed heavily in the darkness. Evelyn leapt to one side as quickly as she could to avoid the other Marines following her down and in the flickering light of the flare she looked around, relieved only that hordes of screaming animals had not descended upon them from the darkness.

To her amazement the hold was not filled with stored goods as she would have expected Endeavour to have carried. Instead, it was filled with cables and conduits that all led to a central black cube atop which was mounted a display panel and keyboard. The power cables were hastily arranged, many of them spliced from existing power cables fixed when the ship was built. The entire hold surfaces glittered with ice crystals, the temperature far lower than the rest of the ship, as though sealed off for countless decades. Evelyn watched as the rest of the Marines and the Special Forces troops descended into the hold, each of them immediately taking up firing positions and aiming out into the darkness that surrounded them.

The general looked around for a long moment as the flashlights mounted upon their rifles sliced into the darkness, but nothing moved, no sign of the dangerous species trapped in the ships for'ard holds.

'I don't see an easy way out of here,' Lieutenant Riaz called as he observed the walls of the hold. 'One hatch going for'ard to where all those capsules are, nothing heading aft. We must be in the hold compartment furthest aft.'

Evelyn looked at the lieutenant and then at Emma, who was crouching and looking directly at the control console in the centre of the hold.

'What is this place?' Meyanna asked.

Emma's voice was haunted as she replied. 'This is where it all began.'

'Where *what* began?' Bra'hiv demanded.

Emma did not reply as she stood up and walked silently towards the console. With a start Evelyn realise that somehow Emma could see where she was going in the absolute darkness and despite her blindness, as if guided by some unseen force. On impulse Evelyn stood up and followed, one hand still gripping her pistol.

Emma strode up to the console and look down at it as with one hand she caressed the side of the panels one by one, walking around the circumference of the console as if seeing it for the very first time. Evelyn watched in silence and waited to see what would happen next.

'What the hell is she doing?'

Lieutenant Riaz sounded nervous, his weapon still pulled tightly into his shoulder as he swept and surveyed the hold for any sign of attack.

Nobody replied, everybody watching in silence as Emma came to stand once again before the console and spoke loudly and clearly enough for everybody to hear.

'We need to switch this on.'

Evelyn stared at the console. 'What is it? Why do you want to turn it on?'

Emma turned to look at Evelyn over her shoulder, as though she could see now for the first time. 'Because this is the only way out of here.'

'I don't like this,' Andaim said. 'Let's just get the hell out of here as fast as we can.'

'We cannot go anywhere now without this,' Emma said. 'Either we turn this on or we're trapped here forever.'

Before Evelyn could react Lieutenant Riaz strode up to Emma's side as he raised his rifle and pointed the barrel directly at her head.

'You either explain this or we leave you here,' he snapped. 'You didn't say anything about this place.'

Emma appeared completely unafraid as she turned to look at Riaz, that tiny small curling once more from the corner of her lips.

'This is God,' Emma said simply, and gestured at the control panel.

Evelyn felt something uncomfortable shifting inside of her, as though she were witnessing something paranormal or a childhood fear realised. She looked at the console and its simple display, and then at the vast network of power cables and conduits all leading to it. Huge amounts of power had been directed towards the single console without any explanation for why it would be located so deep within the ship. As far as she could recollect, Endeavour was stocked to maximum capacity with supplies designed to last decades in orbit around unknown worlds or crossing the vast empty void of space. There were no supercomputers aboard the bridge, let alone the holds.

'God?' Meyanna echoed. 'You think this is your leader?'

'This is everybody's leader,' Emma replied as though it were obvious.

'This damned well shouldn't be here,' Bra'hiv uttered as he surveyed the holds and sought a way out. 'We're not turning that thing on, no matter what.'

Evelyn was about to reply when the silence was shattered by a massive crash as something slammed into the for'ard hatch. The soldiers scattered to reposition and face the source of the noise, and as she watched she saw dents appearing in the hatch doorways as something hammered at them from the other side.

Emma's voice broke above the terrible din. 'You either turn this on or we're stuck here to face whatever is going to come through that hatch!'

The soldiers looked at General Bra'hiv, their rifles aimed at the damaged hatch as it was pummelled, the blows echoing around the hold. Evelyn waited a moment longer and then despite her fear she leapt up to the console and with a single movement she activated the terminal.

'Evelyn, no!' Andaim yelled.

Evelyn stepped back from the console and watched as despite the bitter cold a small red light activated and began flashing as the system started to auto–boot. Although the screen was covered in frost she saw it begin to glow a bright blue, the light illuminating Emma's face with a ghostly glow. Behind them the sound of rending metal screeched as something battered the hatch doors with inhuman strength, straining the rivets.

'They must've heard us come through!' Andaim yelled.

'Hold your fire,' the general shouted. 'Wait until the hatch fails and then give them everything at once!'

The Marines and Special Forces troops formed a broad semicircle, their rifles all pointing at the hatch as it shuddered and twisted under the blows. Evelyn backed up alongside Emma, who appeared oblivious to the danger so close by, staring instead intently at the glowing screen as though by doing so she could save them all.

The screen began to flash, flickering as though the power was disrupted, and then it settled down again. Although she had heard nothing, Evelyn was surprised when Emma started speaking to the screen.

'You need to stop them,' Emma said.

Evelyn jerked in shock as the hatch suddenly buckled and one of the hinges smashed apart and spun through the air toward them, catching the light as it tumbled end over end. The rest of the hatch swung awkwardly open, hanging from one hinge as it was battered aside and a massive Ogrin blundered into the hold, its huge muscular arms covered in cuts that trickled blood into its immense palms as it struggled against the zero gravity. Over nine feet tall and with pale, mottled skin and dull, murderous eyes, it let out a hellish cry as it rushed toward the soldiers.

***

163

XXVII

Arcadia's bridge was silent as Mikhain walked back onto the command platform. The command crew watched as he took his place in the captain's chair and surveyed the tactical displays around him.

'Status report?'

Lieutenant Scott moved to the captain's side as he relayed the latest data.

'All fighters deployed, shields and all defensive measures at one hundred per cent.' Scott looked down at Mikhain as he sat in the chair. 'Are you alright, captain?'

Mikhain sucked in a deep lung full of air and dragged one hand down his face as he glanced up at Scott.

'I'll be fine,' he replied without elaboration. 'Where is the XO?'

Mikhain had already looked across the entire bridge and could see no sign of the Executive Officer despite having left him in command.

'I believe that he is in his quarters,' Scott replied, and then added apologetically: 'He left me in command, captain.'

Mikhain raised an eyebrow as a new thought crossed his mind. 'Maybe that wasn't such a bad idea.'

Scott said nothing, clearly uncomfortable with the direction the conversation was taking. Mikhain glanced around at the other offices around him, most of whom were engrossed in their work, their faces hovering close to display screens and taking no notice of the conversation on the command platform.

'I have my doubts about D'jimon's capacity for command,' Mikhain said quietly so that only Scott could hear him.

Lieutenant Scott stood for a long moment as he digested this new information and considered his response.

'I'm sorry to hear that captain,' he replied. 'I did not realise that the XO was proving to be a problem.'

Mikhain inclined his head in acquiescence. 'Nor did I until it was too late,' he admitted. 'My problem is that I'm not sure what to do about it. I do not have a suitable replacement for him.'

Lieutenant Scott remained the epitome of discretion. 'I'm sure that you'll find an officer aboard who is capable of taking on the role, captain.'

Mikhain allowed his gaze to drift up to the young officer. 'Please do let me know if you can think of anybody who would like to apply for the role.'

Scott stared down at the captain and this time the very vaguest hint of excitement flickered across his features.

'I'll do that captain,' he replied. 'In fact I think that I have the perfect person for the job if you'll allow me to…'

'Contact bearing three–five–one, elevation five–zero!' Lieutenant Shah yelled loudly enough to make everybody on the bridge jump out of their skin.

Mikhain leaped out of his chair as he saw the new contact appear on the tactical display before him, and his practised eye told him that the object had emerged from super luminal travel directly into the area.

'Tactical alert!' he yelled. 'Helm, defensive manoeuvres, shields to maximum and contact Atlantia!'

The lights on Arcadia's bridge dimmed immediately and a distant siren echoed through the ship as the tactical alert was sounded. Arcadia's command crew rushed to their stations as Mikhain stepped forward and examine the data scrolling down the tactical display before him.

'Hull mass eight hundred thousand tonnes!' Lieutenant Scott reported. 'I'm detecting shields and massive plasma armament and she's manoeuvring into an attack position.'

'Get her on–screen!' Mikhain ordered.

The image on the main display screen of Arcadia's bridge switched from Endeavour to the new arrival, and Mikhain stared in amazement as the huge spacecraft hove into view, its hull illuminated in a dull red glow from the massive hydrogen clouds spread across the star fields behind it.

'Identification friend or foe?'

The communications officer scanned the screen and called back. 'None detected, but the type is clear – she's a Morla'syn destroyer!'

The vessel was massive, a three–hulled battleship shaped in the form of a Trident, the central spike the main hull with two enormous ion engine strakes completing her form. Her stern was tapered, her bow slender and long like a giant blade, and virtually every spare cubit of her surface bristled with massive cannon emplacements. Mikhain's mouth felt dry as he looked at her, one of the few times he had ever encountered a Morla'syn vessel.

'Contact her! Send an open signal on all frequencies!'

Mikhain's eyes were drawn to the data scrolling down the tactical display. He could see that the destroyer was already moving into an elevated position above Arcadia, Atlantia and Endeavour although she had not yet deployed a fighter screen.

'Hold the Raython's back,' Mikhain called to Lieutenant Scott. 'Let's not get their backs up before we've even spoken to them.'

'Aye, captain.'

A screen illuminated on the bridge and filled with an image of Idris Sansin's face as he opened a channel to Arcadia.

'Where the hell did they come from?'

Mikhain shook his head. 'I guess it's not just us who's been tracking gravitational waves.'

The massive destroyer slowed as it took position over the three vessels below it, each of its hull strakes alone larger than the two frigates it now loomed over. Mikhain watched in earnest as he waited for any reply to their signal, uncertain of how the species would react to encountering human vessels after the apocalypse.

The Morla'syn were in Mikhain's opinion one of the most misunderstood of species in the known galaxy. Humanoid in appearance but far taller than humans, they were native to a world that didn't even have a name as it was considered unpronounceable in any known dialect. Referred to instead by a number from the National Galactic Catalogue, the world was in orbit around a blue star and of a lesser mass than Ethera. A high oxygen content in the atmosphere combined with the low gravity allowed the evolution of massive species, of which the Morla'syn had emerged as the most intelligent. Thousands of years more advanced than humanity, they had become a dominant force long before human beings had even forged their first spears over fires in caves.

'Any reply to our signal?'

'Negative captain,' Shah replied, the communications officer scanning her instruments intently.

'They're not sure about us,' Idris said.

'Can't blame them,' Mikhain replied. 'I haven't laid eyes on one of those ships since before the apocalypse happened. Who knows what they think of us or what they'll do next?'

'Hold position,' Idris advised. *'If we don't provoke them it might give them a hope that we're not infected.'*

'They're scanning us,' Shah said.

'They might decide to blow us to pieces,' Mikhain pointed out.

'Well we can't go anywhere until our people are off Endeavour.'

Mikhain said nothing as he watched and waited for some sign of contact from the Morla'syn. A deep silence enveloped the bridge, every member of the crew fully aware that the destroyer was capable of blowing both frigates to pieces with a single salvo. The species had a reputation for being aloof and their involvement in galactic politics had traditionally been minimal, the Morla'syn preferring to stay away from the core systems.

'They shouldn't be out here either,' Idris pointed out. *'The Icari Line applies as much to them as it does to us.'*

'Makes you wonder what the Icari have been up to while all of this is been going on?' Mikhain said in reply. 'They always threatened severe consequences for any vessels found crossing the line, but I don't recall them ever saying what those consequences would be.'

'I don't want to find out,' Idris admitted. *'But they're not here now and we need to find out what the Morla'syn want from us. I don't want them blowing us away before we've even had a chance to speak.'*

As if on cue, Shah called out: 'They're signalling us captain.'

Mikhain straightened his uniform and positioned himself directly in front of the display screen as he nodded at Shah to continue. The communications officer switched the frequency over and instantly an image of a Morla'syn captain appeared on the screen.

The captain was some eight feet tall, his face pale white and elongated as though it had been compressed. There was no hair on his head, his skull cap cracked like ancient desert riverbeds dried by a fearsome sun. Wide, angled eyes filled with deep blue iris stared back without emotion as Mikhain spoke.

'Captain Mikhain, Colonial Fleet Service Arcadia,' he announced himself, 'also on channel is Captain Idris Sansin, Colonial Fleet Service Atlantia.'

'What are you doing here?'

The Morla'syn captain's tone was detectable even though his voice had passed through a vocal resonance translator, the device worn by all species in the known galaxy in order to translate countless dialects into understandable dialogue. His refusal to identify either himself or the name of his vessel sent a tremor of consternation down Mikhain's spine. Mikhain realised also that as the captain of the vessel closest to the new arrival he was expected to reply.

'We have discovered the wreck of Endeavour, a ship that launched from our planet almost a century ago. We are attempting to find out what happened to her and have people aboard at this time.'

The Morla'syn captain leaned closer to the camera and peered at Mikhain.

'What stage has the infection reached the board your ships?'

'We are uninfected,' Mikhain replied with some pride. 'Both Arcadia and Atlantia are clear of the Word and its infectors. At this time we are not sure about Endeavour, but we have detected no evidence of the Legion's presence aboard her either.'

The Morla'syn captain leaned back again from the screen but the look of suspicion did not disappear from his features. Like humans, the Morla'syn were capable of forming complex expressions that conveyed emotions, but they also sought to conceal those emotions – deeply xenophobic, they never smile or joked, never attempted to curry favour with other species. He seemed to examine Mikhain for several long seconds before he spoke again.

'Why are you here, beyond the Line?'

'Our mission was to attempt to find new technologies with which to fight the Word,' Mikhain replied. 'The only way we could do that was by travelling beyond the Line, away from where the Word holds sway. We figured that if we could obtain weapons that the Word had never encountered before, then would be able to fight it more effectively.'

The Morla'syn captain appeared to frown as though Mikhain's plan was unworthy, something less than the Morla'syn would have dreamed up themselves.

'We have been following you,' the Morla'syn captain revealed.

This time, it was Idris who replied. 'Why?'

'Our vessel encountered the remains of Veng'en cruiser some months ago while on a routine patrol,' the Morla'syn captain revealed. *'It was in orbit within an asteroid field some light–years from here, and we detected your gravitational wake departing from the scene of the wreckage. We assumed that your vessels were infected and that you had successfully defeated the cruiser in battle, therefore we were tasked to hunt you down and destroy you.'*

Mikhain step closer to the display screen. 'We are not infected. Who asked you to destroy us?'

The Morla'syn captain leaned closer to the screen again and Mikhain swore he could see a look of satisfaction upon the captain's face.

'Everybody did,' the captain replied. *'It has been decided that any humanity remaining in the cosmos should be eradicated for the benefit of us all.'*

***

XXVIII

'Fire!'

The Marines opened fire as one against the massive Ogrin as it bludgeoned its way into the hold. A salvo of plasma blasts smashed into the creature's huge chest, the rounds burrowing deep into its body to the sound of burning flesh. The Ogrin wailed in agony as it collapsed and hung dead in mid–air, surrounded by a halo of rapidly cooling globules of blue plasma.

The smashed hatch door behind it looked like a doorway to hell, the dark hold beyond filled with a bizarre mixture of wild creatures all struggling for purchase in the zero gravity and the sound of screams both human and animal.

'There are people in there!' Evelyn yelled.

'We can't save everybody!' Riaz shot back, and then shouted above the din to his men. 'Cover the hatch and kill anything that comes through!'

'That's not your call!' Andaim protested.

'Your shields,' Evelyn suggested to Riaz. 'You could use them to get inside there and help everybody out!'

'They only protect against plasma blasts!' Riaz yelled back. 'They're useless against anything else, and we don't even know how they work!'

Even as Evelyn watched fearfully for anything else that might come crashing through toward them, she spotted patches of dim light that flickered as they moved through the air and approached the open hatchway.

'What the hell are those?'

Evelyn peered at the strange shapes that looked like lights suspended in mid–air that drifted slowly toward her. Suddenly the lights dipped downward and passed through the hatchway into the aft hold. Evelyn stared at the strange creatures, their surface a pale white and covered in bioluminescent algae that flickered in the darkness and behind them trailed long swirling coils of tentacles that draped themselves over any obstacle they found. Evelyn looked down at the corpse of the giant Ogri and saw that its skin was covered in massive welts, as though it had been stung multiple times and was in agony long before it had been shot by the Marines. Suddenly she realised why it had beaten its way through that hatch.

'Get away from those things!' Evelyn shouted. 'They're poisonous!'

The Marines closest to the hatch began to fall back as the strange creatures floated through into the aft hold, their bodies pulsating as they sucked in air through cavities in their bulbous heads and then ejected the air in thin jets behind them to propel themselves forward. Before anybody could move the strange creatures were coming through the hatch in their hundreds.

'We need to get out of here!' Bra'hiv shouted.

Evelyn turned to look at Emma, who was still standing over the computer console and talking to it as though it were alive.

'You need to destroy them,' Emma repeated over and over again.

'She might be talking about us!' Riaz snapped.

Evelyn could see that the screen was flickering wildly now as though the machine were talking back to Emma, perhaps even arguing with her. Lieutenant Riaz dashed past them all toward the rear of the hold as he searched desperately for a potential escape route, but the walls were made of solid, featureless metal.

'There's nothing here!' he shouted. 'She lied to us!'

The Marines were falling back from the damaged hatch and firing heavily upon the strange creatures billowing through them in milky clouds. The plasma blasts smashed them aside, scorching their fleshy bodies and sending them spinning through the air in vibrant colourful trails as the bioluminescent algae in their bodies flickered out like light switches. But there were far too many for the Marines to shoot and they were swiftly filling the hold.

Evelyn heard a soldier scream as one of the creatures tumbled through the air and smashed into his face, the tentacles wrapping around his head. The soldier thrashed in agony as the stingers seared his skin and she saw his face swelling with frightening rapidity as the creature injected venom through multiple points along its tentacles into the soldier's face. Within moments the screaming had been strangled off into an agonised garble as the soldier's arms flopped to his sides and he collapsed slowly to the deck with the creature still clinging to his face.

The Marines tumbled back and away from the gruesome sight as Bra'hiv grabbed Emma by the shoulders.

'Do you have a way out of here or not?!'

Emma looked down at the computer for a moment longer and then she turned to the general. 'Start a fire,' she instructed.

'Star a *what*?!'

'Do it,' Emma snapped back.

Like everybody else Evelyn knew that fire aboard a spaceship was a lethal threat and one of the most feared ways to die in space. Bra'hiv stared at Emma as though she'd gone insane but he turned and yelled at one of his Marines.

'Light something up!'

The Marine, a flamethrower on his back, seized his weapon and turned it toward a stack of unused boxes and crates in one corner of the hold. He activated the flamethrower and fired. Evelyn shielded her face as a stream of fearsome flame streaked across the hold and smothered the boxes in an inferno. The boxes burst into flame under the onslaught and the billowing cloud of thick black smoke swelled upward from the flaming wreckage and tumbled across the ceiling.

The Marines fell back even further from the advancing creatures now filling the air before them, clouds of lethal tentacles swirling like a shimmering wall as they advanced upon their position. The flame–throwing Marine turned his jet of burning fluid upon the advancing wall and it sprayed across the creatures, burning their flesh but ineffectual in stopping their advance.

Evelyn crawled backwards along the deck as the huge cloud of creatures threatened to overrun her position. She aimed her pistol and was about to fire upon the nearest of them when suddenly a loud hissing sound fill the hold and in response to the smoke fire–depletion systems activated and a rain of high–pressure foam sprayed from the ceiling vents high above. The foam plunged downward into the clouds of creatures and forced them toward the deck, pummelling them into a massive mess of gelatinous flesh flattened by the force of the foam.

'Ceasefire!'

The Marines stopped firing as the lethal cloud of stinging creatures were swamped by the falling foam, their lethal tentacles now snaking across the deck but of no danger to the Marines and their heavy boots.

Evelyn looked up as more creatures swarmed toward the open hatchway, screeching and snarling and their own bodies also covered in welts and lesions as they fought to escape the clouds of poisonous animals swarming in the forward hold. But the moment they reached the hatch and stepped into the aft hold they retreated again as their bodies were burned by the swarm of creatures pinned to the deck in mounds before the hatch.

Stunned, Evelyn turned to look at Emma, who simply returned her gaze and smiled.

'We're still stuck in here!' Lieutenant Riaz snapped, apparently unimpressed by Emma's ingenious solution to the crisis.

Evelyn got to her feet and got in Riaz's face. 'Give her a break!'

'Or what?'

Evelyn felt anger rising inside but she had no immediate response for the Special Forces soldier. She was about to say something when all around the Marines stood up from their positions and gathered behind her, confronting Riaz.

'Or we'll *all* get annoyed,' Bra'hiv replied as he moved to Evelyn's side.

Commander Andaim trudged through the slimy mess on the deck and leaned his weight into the damaged hatch floating near the bulkhead. He heaved the hatch back across the opening, the metal clanging loudly as it settled into place. Andaim turned his back to it, leaning against it to prevent more of the poisonous creatures from invading the hold.

The fire nearby was quenched by the foam, the air filled with millions of foam droplets like snow that refused to fall as Andaim looked at Evelyn.

'We've got your back, now get us out of here.'

Evelyn saw Riaz scowl and she suppressed a smile as she turned to Emma and looked again at the computer screen, uncertain of what she was even looking at. On impulse she reached out and swept a hand across the screen, wiping the frost away from it. She was surprised to see a face looking back at her out of the screen, but it was not a photograph. Instead, the face was indistinct and made up not of pixels but of what looked like binary code that flickered and mutated on the screen to approximate the features of a human being. For a brief moment she was reminded of the way the Legion's Infectors swarmed together in order to likewise approximate human expressions and emotions.

The face turned slightly on the screen and she was shocked to find it staring straight at her. A strange warbling noise was omitted by the face, the mouth moving and the expressions changing as though it was talking to in a language that she could not understand, but beside her Emma appeared to react to the noise and turned to face Evelyn.

'This is God,' Emma said.

Evelyn stared down at the strange face in the computer screen and all of a sudden she realised what she was looking at.

'It's the Word,' she said.

It seemed impossible but somehow Evelyn instinctively knew that what she was witnessing was not just the random creation of a computer gone insane but was in fact an actual entity, a being, something alive and staring at her as she stared at it. Never before, in all of the time since the apocalypse, had she considered the fact that the Word might actually have a face or personality, something that she could look at and recognise as human.

Andaim, his place at the hatch now manned by four Marines, moved to stand alongside Evelyn as he looked down at the face and listened to the warbling sounds it was making. 'Are you sure this is what you think it is?'

'I'm sure,' Evelyn said, 'although I can't quite believe it.'

'Well then let's blow it to hell,' Bra'hiv snapped as he raised his rifle and aimed it at the computer console.

'No!'

Evelyn and Emma both moved at the same instant as though by shared instinct, dashing between the general and the computer console and blocking his aim with their bodies. Evelyn felt suddenly ashamed as she stood in front of the very thing that had destroyed humanity, had killed billions of lives, and blocked the aim of a man who could destroy it with a single pull of his trigger.

She glanced at Andaim, who was watching her with a stricken expression. 'What are you doing?'

Evelyn gathered herself as she replied. 'This is the ship's computer and it's obviously been infected by the Word. Maybe this is how it all started back on Ethera? If we destroy this now we might never learn how things began—we can use this!'

'Like hell we can!' Lieutenant Riaz snapped as he made to move Evelyn out of the way.

Despite his reservations Andaim lunged forward and stopped the Lieutenant in his tracks. 'You don't give the orders here.'

'I don't take the orders here either,' Riaz snapped back. 'You told us that this thing is responsible for destroying humanity and now you're defending it?'

'This isn't the version that destroyed humanity,' Evelyn said. 'Endeavour must've launched with at least one of its crew infected, or perhaps the computer itself infected with a version of the Word. But whatever it did here it's taken a different path to what happened on Ethera.'

'How the hell do you define *different?*' Riaz snarled as he pointed at Emma. 'It's taken a crew and who knows how many other species and locked them away in escape capsules for decades! Call me cynical but that to me sounds like some kind of bad deal!'

'But we don't know *why* it's done this!' Evelyn insisted. 'What if something else happened to the crew that wasn't the responsibility of the Word and it attempted to protect them by placing them in stasis inside the capsules? What if it was the Word that redirected all the power and shut itself down in an attempt to preserve their lives instead?'

The lieutenant stared at Evelyn for a long moment as he considered this new possibility, and even Bra'hiv seemed quite surprised that she had even thought of it.

'You think that's even possible?'

'It's not *impossible*,' Evelyn insisted, and looked to Emma for support.

Emma, still staring into the middle distance, replied softly.

'Without what you call the Word, we would all be dead.'

'What actually happened to Endeavour?' Meyanna asked her.

Emma's head turned to the sound of Meyanna's voice. 'We travelled too far, too fast and too soon. We were not ready for the things that we were to encounter, ill–prepared for the threats we faced and the dangers that were to be found beyond the known cosmos. We were attacked repeatedly by a species we did not understand, our hull critically damaged as we attempted to return home, but it was already far too late. Our mass drive was obliterated long before we could even begin to make the jump into super luminal travel after the first attack, and despite the best efforts of our crew were unable to repair the damage with the resources aboard. We were in the process of attempting to find a way to preserve life for long enough to reach the closest star system at sub luminal speed, a distance we calculated as being some nine light years, when many of the crew began acting strangely as though not in control of their own bodies. Engineers began re-routing power, altering the ship's structure without orders. Officers began issuing commands to the crew that made no sense. Our captain felt that we could reach the nearest star system if we were all in stasis, but there were not enough escape capsules to protect us all and there was a great fear developing of those members of the crew who appeared mentally ill.'

'What happened to the rest of the crew?' Andaim asked.

Emma appeared to sigh softly, not looking at Andaim as she replied. 'Most of the crew were lost in a desperate attempt to repair the damage to our engines, when the hull was ruptured by a blast. With much of the power down none of the safety features activated in time to prevent the evacuation of one third of the ship's atmosphere. By the time the emergency bulkheads closed in the for'ard half of the ship, we had lost far too many hands to ever be able to recover. It was then that the Word took over completely.'

'What about all of those?' the general asked as he jabbed a thumb over his shoulder toward the noises of animals trapped in the for'ard hold. 'Where did they come from?'

'I don't know,' Emma admitted. 'The Word directed the surviving members of the crew to set up the escape capsules and to reroute the power from what remained of the fusion cores to the aft hold, and from here to the for'ard holds. It wanted to keep us alive for the longest time possible while the Word concentrated on sealing the ship and protecting what atmosphere remained should we ever be able to awake again. The Word protected us, and I can only assume that as it stumbled across new species it attempted to protect them too.'

'I don't know,' Meyanna said as she looked down at the computer screen. 'The more we learn the more we can tell that the Word was set on destroying humanity from the moment it achieved self–awareness. Any attempts at philanthropy were merely a cover for its plans for conquest.'

The face on the screen warbled something new and Evelyn looked at Emma. 'What did it say?'

Emma's expression changed to one of consternation as she looked over her shoulder.

'Another ship has arrived,' she said. 'We could be in danger.'

'We are already in danger,' Riaz growled, 'and now we're stuck down here with no way out.'

The face on the screen warbled again and this time Emma smiled as she looked up at the back wall of the hold. She moved out from behind the computer and strode across to the wall, then reached up and touched it with her hands as though seeking some imperfection in the design. She rapped her knuckles on the metal panels as she moved from right to left, the knocks echoing around the hold until suddenly one of them change timbre, the knocks sounding hollow.

'Place your charges here,' she instructed the Marines. 'The hold wall is thinnest here and should open out onto an access corridor that will continue aft to the landing bays.'

Bra'hiv nodded and instantly his Marines dashed across to the wall of the hold, their charges already in the hands as they positioned them and set the timers. Evelyn ducked down with Andaim and Meyanna as Emma joined them behind the computer console, the Marines all ducking down and turning their backs to the charges, their fingers in their ears.

A deafening crash shattered the air around them as the charges blew and thick smoke billowed out in blue clouds in the dull light. Evelyn removed her hands from her ears and peered into the dense acrid smoke, and almost at once she could see the wall of the hold ripped and torn, and through the ragged cavity the pale illumination of ceiling lights in the corridor outside.

'That'll do me,' Bra'hiv said with guarded admiration. 'Let's get out of here.'

Emma reached out and grabbed the general's arm. 'There is something else,' she said.

Evelyn knew, instinctively, what Emma was going to say so instead she said it herself.

'We have to take the Word with us.'

***

XXIX

'That's not possible.'

Idris Sansin stared at the Morla'syn on his display screen on Atlantia's bridge as he tried to understand what he had been told.

'Humanity has been selected for extinction,' the Morla'syn insisted.

'Selected by whom?' Mikhain demanded from Arcadia's bridge.

'The Galactic Council,' the Morla'syn explained. *'After the fall of Ethera it was decided that we could not allow humanity or its creation to expand anywhere beyond the core systems. Likewise, we could not allow the expansion of the Word beyond those same boundaries. Although it pained the council to pass the vote, it was recognised that it was a necessary evil. There is little that we can do to stop the Word except to ensure that it is destroyed wherever it is found, until a more permanent means of preventing its expansion it can be created.'*

'But that's what we've been trying to achieve!' Idris insisted.

The Galactic Council was a governing body put in place by the Icari in order to allow self–governance by the systems within its realm. The Icari, although by far the wisest and most experienced species in the known galaxy, preferred not to intervene directly into the affairs of species over whom it watched. Rather, it installed governing bodies which brought together different species and attempted to resolve their differences through means of diplomacy and dialogue rather than conflict. It had been a known irritation to all member species that the differences between humans and the Veng'en had not been resolved despite decades of diplomacy. Equally, it had been irritating to humanity to discover that in the eyes of the council it was viewed as no better or less warmongering than the Veng'en themselves, a race virtually dedicated to conflict.

The Galactic Council was led by representatives from the capital planet of each system represented, numbering up to thirty five individuals all of whom had extensive experience of governance within their own systems and of communication and cooperation with the species of neighbouring systems. These representatives were chosen by the Icari on the basis of their performance in government of their own worlds, a meritocracy that spoke of the faith of entire planetary populations.

Now, it appeared, they had chosen self–preservation over assistance of their beleaguered human membership. It briefly occurred to Captain Sansin that there must have been at least one sympathetic voice on the council.

'What of our own representative?' Idris asked. 'They are unable to defend us?'

The Morla'syn captain remained silent for a moment as though considering his response.

'Your representative did not oppose your destruction.'

'He did what?!'

'He felt that the actions of your kind were indefensible and that he could not speak on behalf of Ethera when he considered humanity to no longer actually be human. Your representative asked to be removed from the vote as he could not in good conscience defend a species which may already have been eradicated by its own creation and could not be trusted to have the best interests of other species at heart.'

'How the hell do you not know whether that representative was himself infected by the word?' Mikhain demanded. 'He could have abstained from the vote in order to indirectly affect its outcome!'

'It does not much matter whether he was infected or not,' the Morla'syn said. *'He committed suicide the day following the vote. In the interests of ensuring that the Word could not possibly have reached as far as the council, his body was incinerated and all of his digital records destroyed.'*

Idris took a pace closer to the display screen. 'You're telling me that the survivors of our race have no representative on the council?'

'That is so,' the Morla'syn replied. *'As humanity in effect no longer exists we felt there was no need to seek a replacement for your counsellor. The vote was passed and the Morla'syn were tasked with hunting down the remainder of humanity and ensuring it could spread no further, including beyond the Line.'*

'So you're here to destroy us?'

'That is so.'

'I don't believe it,' Idris said. 'I don't believe that the Council would simply abandon us without even attempting to take in as refugees those who had survived the apocalypse. We are not infected and there may be many others out there who are also not infected. This is not the protection of other species, this is genocide.'

'*This is the only way,*' Morla'syn said. '*Despite our technological superiority no species other than humans has created such a devastating weapon of war as the Word. It simply cannot be allowed to spread and there is no way that any human can be sure that they are not already infected, no matter how they may feel or how they may act. Species outside of the human systems have no detailed knowledge of how the Word works and insufficient time to understand it in an attempt to find a cure or defence. Sooner or later the Word will learn to infect other species, if it has not already. We do not intend to allow that to continue.*'

'This is our responsibility,' Mikhain insisted, 'and our right to act against it. Destroying us here and now will have no effect on the Word. It will continue to evolve and expand its territories regardless of whether we're here or not.'

'*It is not my responsibility to make judgement calls on whether or not you will be able to have an effect on the future of the Word,*' the Morla'syn insisted. '*It is my job to carry out my orders, and my orders are to destroy you.*'

'We have discovered new ways of defeating the Word in battle,' Idris pointed out. 'Destroy us now and you'll never learn anything of what we have. The Word is neither infallible nor indestructible: it has weaknesses that can be exploited, weapons that can be defended against.'

'*That matters little,*' the Morla'syn replied. '*The danger it presents is considered so great that it has been agreed that the fleets of all nations under the Icari will be deploying to Ethera with the intention of destroying not just the Word but the entire system.*'

Idris stared at the display screen aghast, quite unable to believe what he had just heard. Never in the history of the core systems had any species or council voted for the destruction of an entire star system.

'You can't do that,' he grasped. 'Even an entire fleet could not destroy a whole system.'

'*The Council is amassing thousands of vessels,*' the Morla'syn replied, its aloof expression and tone of voice angering Idris further. '*We will advance one planet at a time, counter one threat at a time and win one battle at a time with overwhelming force. One way or the other, the only solution to the problem of the Word is to utterly eradicate its source along with every single planetary body that it has infected.*'

'And the lives of the people that remain uninfected?' Mikhain demanded. 'Those who fought to survive the apocalypse, fought to protect each other and uphold the values of humanity that the Council claimed to sympathise with when it accepted our membership? How do you justify their deaths at your hand?'

The Morla'syn captain remained silent for several long seconds and in the background Idris imagined he could see the other members of the Morla'syn crew waiting to see what their captain would say. The Morla'syn finally emitted what sounded remotely like a sigh, but it gave Idris an impression of irritation rather than sympathy or regret.

'I am merely the carrier of the message,' he said. *'The fates of those who survived your apocalypse are in the hands of those who created it. Do not attempt to bloody my hands with the genocidal actions of the machine that you created. We are the reaction, not the proximal cause.'*

Idris glanced at the tactical display and scanned the data upon it. The Morla'syn destroyer was in a tactically superior position, it shields fully charged and over one hundred plasma cannons available to fire down simultaneously on both of the frigates. Even a cursory glance at the destroyer's statistics revealed that it could destroy all three vessels within minutes, regardless of any damage sustained in return. There was no way that the colonial frigates could win the fight, at least not by force.

'And if I suggested to you that there may be a cure aboard that vessel, aboard Endeavour?' Idris asked.

He maintained a neutral expression, ignoring the surprise that flashed on Mikhain's face. The Morla'syn peered suspiciously at Idris and one long, hooked finger stroked the side of his face absent-mindedly as he considered the claim.

'And how would you know this?'

'I have people aboard Endeavour who have been searching through the ship for evidence of what happened to it. It would appear that even though this ship may have been contaminated by the Word, it did not destroy the life aboard but appears to have attempted to preserve it.'

The Morla'syn's face twisted in a scowl of disinterest.

'It is of no interest to us. We have our orders and will carry them out regardless.'

Idris advanced to stare directly into the camera at the Morla'syn captain. 'Is that something you'd be willing to take back to the council? That you may have held in your hands the solution to a problem that threatens the very existence of countless civilisations and discarded it in favour of aggressive action? Isn't that what the Veng'en would do?'

Idris made no attempt to veil the insult. He knew full well that the Morla'syn considered the Veng'en to be an even more barbaric race than human beings and something of a scourge upon all other species. The Morla'syn's voice deepened as he snarled in reply.

The decision has been made and is not our place to go against it. To disobey the commands of the council would be every bit as bad for us as turning against it. We cannot trust any of you human beings to have the interests of anybody but yourself at heart, and the dramatic expansion of the Word and its conquering of your planetary system despite the warnings of the council of the danger of passing control to advanced artificial intelligence is evidence of your inability to control either yourselves or your own creations. This conversation is over.'

Idris was about to shout something, but it was Mikhain who spoke first.

'If you destroy us now and it turns out that we were correct, how long do you think it will take the council to discover your mistake? The Legion has shown an ability to adapt and evolve to infect any species anywhere in the galaxy, the very reason that you now say you want to destroy us. You should know, then, that it also remembers everything that happens.'

The Morla'syn's belligerent expression deepened but was also tainted by uncertainty as Mikhain continued.

'If you destroy us it will know about it. If you attempt to hunt it down, it will know about it. Everything that it knows eventually reaches all corners of its empire, and its reach has already gone far beyond anything we could possibly have expected. There is every possibility that it has already infected even your own species or that of others beyond the core systems. Every action that you now commit will be carried home with you and eventually passed on to others. The Word was in our population for decades before the apocalypse arrived—our fate was sealed long before we even knew it had begun. What you do now you take with you, forever.'

Idris stared at the image of Mikhain and fought to conceal his admiration for the captain's sudden inspired outburst. The Morla'syn likewise stared blankly at Mikhain, and Idris could see the conflict racking the Morla'syn's features as it struggled to decide which course of action was the best.

'That is ridiculous,' the Morla'syn insisted. *'We know well our own species and the ability of the Word and it could not have infected us.'*

'But did you not just claim that it was your inability to understand the Word that was the driving force behind your decision to destroy what remains of humanity?' Mikhain demanded.

The Morla'syn scowled again, irritation flaring across his features as one bony finger pointed at the screen.

'Our mission is to destroy humanity, and nothing else matters!'

'That is exactly what the Word would say,' Mikhain replied.

The Morla'syn slammed a fist down onto its seat and directed an angry glance to somewhere off–camera aboard the destroyer's bridge. Instantly the communication was shut off and the screen went blank.

Idris turned to face the image of Mikhain and could not decide whether to congratulate or scold the captain. Mikhain shrugged before Idris could even respond.

'It wasn't like we were gonna get on anyway,' he said with an apologetic expression on his face. 'Just like old times, captain.'

Idris suppressed a smile and glanced at the tactical display. 'There's no way we can defend our crew on Endeavour for long. If this goes south we'll have no choice but to retreat.'

'I know,' Mikhain said. 'All we can hope is that the Morla'syn comes to his senses and gives us the opportunity to finish our search of Endeavour.'

'And that the team on board the ship find something we can use,' Idris reminded him.

It was not Mikhain who replied, however. The voice came from the bridge entrance, where Councillor Gredan was staring in horror at Idris, having heard the entire exchange.

'You're taking us to war!'

***

XXX

'You want to do what?'

General Bra'hiv stared at the face in the computer screen as his Marines took up positions around the ragged hole in the hold wall.

'We have to take it with us,' Evelyn repeated. 'This is something new, something important. If we leave this behind or destroy it we may never get to understand how the Word thinks, how it works, what its weaknesses are. This could help us.'

'This could destroy us!' Andaim countered as he pointed at the computer. 'This is the very thing we've been fighting against. If we take it with us, place it aboard Atlantia and plug it in, then the same thing could happen to us as happened on Ethera.'

'You don't know that for sure,' Evelyn shot back. 'We can control it better on a ship of our own, isolated, ensure that it can only operate with our bidding.'

'That's probably what they said about the Word on Ethera,' Bra'hiv pointed out.

It was Emma who confronted the general, somehow blessed with a knowledge that nobody else could understand.

'If we had not set the Word here and empowered it to look after us these decades past, you would have found nothing but corpses aboard this ship.'

The general glanced at Andaim, who shrugged and dragged a hand across his face as he tried to think of a suitable course of action.

'They could be right,' Meyanna said from nearby. 'If this computer can teach us anything about the Word, then we should not abandon that opportunity.'

'Damn it,' Andaim uttered as he glanced again at the computer, the face upon which was now staring silently out at them without any discernible expression. 'All right, pull the plug and get this thing out of here.'

General Bra'hiv took a deep breath as though to demonstrate his reluctance and then called several of the Marines across. Within moments the power conduits and cables were detached from the computer and the screen and its bizarre face blinked out.

'What are we waiting for?' Lieutenant C'rairn asked.

Evelyn turned and looked at the main hatch of the hold, the entrance still blocked by the hatch guarded by four Marines and the sea of squirming, dying poisonous creatures. Beyond in the dark holds echoed the occasional shriek as unknown species warred in the darkness, the shadowy forms lurking this way and that as they sought a way past the hatch.

'We can't get the people out of there?' Evelyn persisted, horrified that human beings might yet be abandoned, trapped within Endeavour's hellish confines.

'They cannot be saved,' Emma replied. 'Many of them are too ill or injured, many more yet are dead.'

'How do you know?' Andaim asked her, and she gestured to the computer.

'The Word knows,' she replied. 'We must leave, as fast as we can.'

'Then let's go,' Bra'hiv said.

The Marines behind them hoisted the computer into the air, one man on each corner as they guided it through the shattered wall. Further ahead, the Special Forces troops jogged as an advance guard as they sought to clear the way ahead.

Evelyn joined Emma as they hurried out into the corridor, careful not to catch their uniforms on the jagged, torn metal of the hull.

'The Word has internal power,' Emma suggested to Evelyn as they hurried in pursuit of the Marines.

'Not a chance,' Meyanna insisted from behind them as she followed. 'There's no way we're turning that thing on again until we are well clear of the ship.'

'We may not get off this ship in one piece without it,' Emma insisted as they emerged from the clouds of acrid smoke filling the corridor from the Marines charges.

Evelyn said nothing as they hurried along, the corridor lit only by the Marine's flash lights as they jogged, erratic blue beams of light slicing the blackness ahead.

'We only have to reach the aft landing bays in order to get off Endeavour,' Evelyn said. 'There is a ship waiting for us.'

'There is more than that waiting for us,' Emma said in reply.

'What the hell is that supposed to mean?' Andaim asked.

A sudden scream echoed down the corridor from far behind, a shriek that sent a pulse of fear flashing through Evelyn's spine as she looked over her shoulder into the blackness.

'They're out,' Andaim realised. 'It was only a matter of time before one of them managed to get through over those stinging creatures and the others followed.'

As if in response Evelyn heard the crash of something massive against metal that echoed down the corridor in pursuit of them. Her imagination ran away with itself as she pictured huge, muscular beasts clawing their way out of the hold and down the corridor in pursuit of the scent of human beings, of prey.

'We need backup to meet us,' Bra'hiv said as he keyed his microphone in an attempt to contact Atlantia. 'I don't care how they do it.'

Evelyn could hear the general's voice as he spoke into his microphone through her earpiece, and she could also hear the hiss of static that responded, no communications audible from Atlantia's bridge.

'It's no good,' Andaim said. 'Ship of this size and transmitters this small, we'll never be able to contact them without signal amplification.'

Another clatter of shrieks and crashes echoed down the corridor in pursuit of them, closer now and filled with a primal hatred as though humanity were to blame for events even here, against species whose origin was entirely unknown.

'Switch the Word back on,' Emma insisted, 'it's the only way.'

'What can it do to help us?' Meyanna asked.

'It got us out of the hold didn't it?'

'Whose side are you on?' Andaim asked.

'Humanity's,' Evelyn shot back in Emma's defence, 'and right now we should be willing to do whatever it takes to get us off this ship, even if it means switching that machine back on.'

The Marines carrying the terminal glanced over their shoulders nervously but said nothing as they moved. From her position behind them Evelyn could see hatches on the bottom of the terminal box that almost certainly allowed access to the batteries within. Although too small for fusion cores the terminal would likely contain high–density, low–energy nuclear reaction cells specifically designed to power such units in the absence of human intervention or external power for long periods of time.

Evelyn ran alongside the Marines as she reached up and opened the panel.

'I really don't think that's a good idea,' Meyanna said.

'You got any better ones?' Evelyn challenged as she looked over her shoulder at the captain's wife.

The crashing clatter of pursuing animals grew louder and in the faint glow of the Marine's flashlights the glow of alien eyes catching the light flickered in the darkness behind them like distant blinking stars.

'Fire in the hole!'

Evelyn saw Bra'hiv toss a plasma grenade behind them into the darkness, the grenade bouncing along the deck and off the walls as it vanished. Evelyn placed her hands over her ears as she ran, the Marines doing likewise and giving the computer terminal a shove so that it floated along in front of them as they ran.

A deafening blast smashed the air inside the corridor as the plasma grenade detonated far behind them with a flash of brilliant blue light, the blast followed by the screeches of injured creatures consumed by the savage explosion. The shockwave from the blast hit Evelyn hard in the back as she ran and she stumbled as she reached up to the terminal hatch.

'The blue cells,' Emma said to her as she jogged alongside, one hand resting on the terminal to guide her. 'Activate the power using them.'

'How do we even know that you have our best interests at heart?' Meyanna demanded. 'We know nothing about you, so how can we trust you?'

'She's as human as we are,' Evelyn snapped, surprised at her own passion for defending Emma.

'Is that so?' Meyanna challenged as they ran. 'Then how come Emma did not have to cover her ears when the grenade went off, and how come she can both speak and hear so clearly despite the blast?'

The Marines stared again at Emma as though uncertain of what exactly they were looking at. Emma's reply sounded quiet in the aftermath of the deafening explosion.

'My ears have not yet recovered from the hibernation sickness, just like my eyes,' she said. 'I did not hear the blast with the same intensity as you did.'

Evelyn looked at Meyanna and saw the doctor staring at her with an expression that conveyed anything but faith. Evelyn waited only a moment longer and then she reached up and activated the blue cells. The terminal hummed into life as the tiny internal nuclear cell was spun up and the screen atop the terminal flickered back into life. Almost immediately the screen emitted the same warbling sound that Evelyn had heard before, a stream of unintelligible digital vocalisation that meant nothing to Evelyn but seem to immediately affect the way that Emma moved.

'They are coming,' Emma said.

'Who is coming?' Evelyn asked.

'The Morla'syn,' Emma replied as she listened to the warbling sound of the Word's digital dialect. 'They have come to finish what they started.'

The Morla'syn were a species that Evelyn knew little about, except that they were vastly superior in technology and highly xenophobic, un–trusting of other species and ever unwilling to share new advances in their technology with those whom they shared the cosmos. Although the Morla'syn had never engaged in open warfare with any species as far as Evelyn was aware, they had on numerous occasions destroyed vessels that had wandered into their systems without you warning.

'The Morla'syn did all of this?' Meyanna asked.

'The Morla'syn were the ones who attacked our ship,' Emma replied as she ran alongside the terminal. 'They damaged the fusion cores and our engine bays in an unprovoked attack and then left us adrift. They claimed that they opposed any human expansion into the wider cosmos, told us that if we did not turn back we would be destroyed. We explained that we were an exploratory vessel, that we meant no harm and that our purpose was merely to observe the galaxy, but they would not listen.'

Meyanna's features creased with suspicion.

'How could you have spoken with the Morla'syn before we had even encountered another species beyond our world? There were no vocal resonance translators back then.'

There was no evidence of anger in Emma's response she replied, staring straight ahead and running with one hand still placed gently upon the computer terminal to guide her.

'Dialect is a species–specific means of communication,' she said, 'but mathematics is the language of the universe. When the Morla'syn first appeared we followed standard protocol for *first contact* and transmitted a binary code message announcing who we were, where we came from and our intentions as well as our greetings. A simple binary message would be easy to decode for any suitably advanced species, and we received a reply within due course, a matter of minutes in fact. Over the course of a few hours we were able to discuss in quite some detail who we were and why we were here, but the Morla'syn claimed that we had no right to be in their space. Before we knew what had happened they had tired of the conversation and suddenly opened fire. I have no idea if they intended to leave us drifting here in deep space, or whether they intended to return to destroy us but they never came back.'

General Bra'hiv was listening closely from further ahead and called back down the corridor.

'Well whatever they wanted or whatever they intended to do, it's irrelevant now.'

'Not if they still want to destroy us,' Emma insisted, 'because it is a Morla'syn ship that is awaiting outside.'

'We're coming up on a bulkhead!' C'rairn yelled.

Evelyn looked up and in the flickering light from the flashlights she could see a massive bulkhead at the end of the corridor, the hatch firmly sealed.

'Pressure bulkhead,' Andaim identified it. 'It must be one of the bulkheads that automatically shut when Salim Phaeon's gunship crashed aboard. We're almost at the stern, close to landing bays.'

Lieutenant Riaz reached the doors first and Evelyn saw him peer through a small viewing panel, a safety feature that allowed a visual inspection of the corridor beyond the pressure bulkhead to ensure the security of the atmosphere within in the absence of power to the door sensors. Far away, he could see two green lights above the giant double hatches to the landing bay.

'The atmosphere is good,' Riaz shouted. 'But there's no power to this door so we can't open it, it's in permanent lockdown.'

The sound of pursuing creatures echoed down the corridor as the Marines all came to a halt.

'Can we use charges to blow the hatch?' Meyanna asked.

'Not without blowing ourselves to pieces too,' Riaz replied as he examined the outside of the hatch. 'It's too strong and we can't get far enough away from the blast now.'

More screeches, growls and snarls came from the darkness further down the corridor as whatever had escaped from the hold bore down upon them. Riaz looked at Emma and the glowing computer terminal hovering in mid–air beside the Marines.

'Well you wanted that damned thing turned on, sister,' he snapped at her. 'How about you pull some magic out of your little box of tricks and get us out of here?'

Emma appeared immune to the soldier's caustic wit, her eyes staring into nothingness but her expression clearly that of a person listening to a stream of information coming from the computer terminal. Evelyn could see the digital face of the Word speaking quickly, the warbling sound almost comforting compared to the hellish cries of the predators bearing down upon them through the corridor.

Emma's voice broke through suddenly as she translated the Word's communication.

'The Word will open the hatch for us,' she said.

'Great news, tell it to get on with it,' Riaz snapped back.

'On one condition,' Emma added. 'The Word has some demands.'

***

XXXI

Mikhain strode onto the bridge as soon as he received the signal from Atlantia, and was immediately confronted by the executive officer, Djimon, who was uncharacteristically manning his post on the command platform and watching events unfold on the main viewing panel.

'Captain on the bridge.'

Mikhain stepped onto the command platform. 'Situation report?'

'The Morla'syn are holding position,' Lieutenant Scott replied from the tactical console. 'Their shields are up and their plasma weapons are charged but so far they have made no provocative action.'

'Any word from Endeavour?'

'Negative captain,' the communications officer, Shah, said. 'There is no active jamming in play so we can only assume that the team is deep enough inside the ship to prevent them from making a clear transmission.'

'Atlantia?'

'Holding position captain,' Lieutenant Scott replied. 'No new orders.'

Mikhain looked at Djimon, the XO saying nothing as he examined the various displays.

'Congratulations,' Mikhain uttered as he took his seat on the platform. 'This is probably the first time I've seen you at your post since you joined the ship.'

'What do you suppose is keeping them so quiet for so long?' the XO asked, apparently not hearing or choosing to ignore Mikhain's comment. 'General Bra'hiv would never have remained out of contact for this long without good reason.'

'I don't know,' Mikhain replied, 'but I don't like it.'

'Don't like it because you're concerned for the team?' Djimon asked. 'Or don't like it because you don't know whether General Bra'hiv might have been talking directly to Sansin and cutting you out?'

'Both,' Mikhain replied in a low whisper. 'The last we knew both Kordaz and Qayin were alive and now we haven't heard anything since the gunship crashed into the landing bay. You damn right I don't like what's happened.'

'If either of them had mentioned anything, or there were concerns about your leadership of Arcadia, somebody would have said something by now,' Djimon assured him.

'They damned well did,' Mikhain hissed. 'Your blasting of the gunship resulted in me being hauled over the coals by Captain Sansin. You've been making things worse, not better!'

'Something needed to be done,' Djimon replied without apparent concern. 'You were not man enough to do it, so I took matters into my own hands.'

Mikhain said nothing in reply, staring instead at the display panels. Since taking command of Arcadia he had felt able to put behind him the fiasco with Kordaz, safe in the knowledge that the Veng'en warrior had not survived the terrific bombardment of the planet Chiron and that Qayin had fled the system and would never be seen again. Now, the security of that illusion had been shattered by the arrival of the gunship and its spectacular descent into Endeavour.

'The Morla'syn want to destroy Endeavour,' Mikhain revealed.

'That wouldn't be so bad, would it?' Djimon asked.

'And us with it. They're claiming that the Galactic Council has voted for the destruction of mankind.'

Djimon barely reacted to the news, simply raising an eyebrow. 'Then they're no better than the Word.'

'You already pushed our luck provoking Kordaz's gunship and the Morla'syn seem unwilling to negotiate terms. Captain Sansin is intent on protecting our people aboard Endeavour and extracting them without delay.'

Djimon stared at the screen for a moment before replying. 'Then we need to get there first,' he replied. 'Whatever happens, Kordaz and Qayin need to be aboard Arcadia and not Atlantia where we can keep an eye on them.'

'We are in a holding position riding shotgun for Atlantia,' Mikhain replied. 'If the team manage to get off Endeavour it will be Atlantia who will collect them.'

Djimon was about to speak when suddenly a scratchy, distorted communication was broadcast over Arcadia's bridge speakers.

'Any callsign please respond, Bravo company.'

Almost immediately Captain Sansin appeared on another display screen as he opened a channel to Arcadia and replied to the general's request.

'General this is Atlantia, pass message.'

'Captains, we have a problem.'

Mikhain and Djimon exchanged a glance but neither man said a word as they awaited Sansin's reply. The general was broadcasting without video feed so they could see nothing of the Marines' situation or indeed where they were aboard the ship, let alone whether they were in the company of Kordaz and Qayin.

'*Then you're in good company, general,*' Sansin replied. '*We have visitors.*'

'*We know,*' the general replied. '*The Morla'syn are here.*'

'How could you know that if you've been out of contact deep inside the ship?' Mikhain asked.

'*We've been getting some help and you're not going to like who's been giving it.*'

Mikhain and Djimon again exchanged a glance but said nothing.

'*Can you get away from Endeavour?*' Captain Sansin asked urgently. '*You're not going to believe this, but the Galactic Council has voted for all species to eradicate humanity wherever they find it in an attempt to stem the flow of the Word. We need you off that ship as soon as possible before the Morla'syn attempt to destroy it.*'

'*Nothing like kicking a species when it's down,*' Lieutenant C'rairn replied from the background.

'*They could be lying,*' Bra'hiv replied. '*According to a surviving crewmember we have found down here on Endeavour, the Morla'syn were responsible for damaging the ship in the first place. They attacked us.*'

Mikhain got up out of his seat as he saw an opportunity to intervene.

'If that's so we have every right to defend both Endeavour and ourselves against them,' he announced. 'Etheran Law, recognised by the Galactic Council, clearly states that our vessels are sovereign territory no matter where they travel and have rights of passage through all member civilisations' space.'

'*That was when there was a government and a colonial fleet to enforce those laws,*' Sansin reminded him. '*Not to mention the fact that those other species do not necessarily see a need any longer to comply with Etheran laws. Besides, we are outclassed even with two frigates against the Morla'syn destroyer.*'

'What happened aboard Endeavour?' Mikhain demanded, keen to find any avenue he could to further understand what was happening.

They heard the general suck in a deep breath before he spoke. '*We don't have time to argue about this, we can debrief you another time. Right now, we need both Atlantia and Arcadia to position themselves between Endeavour and the Morla'syn destroyer.*'

'*Why?*' Captain Sansin demanded. '*Any such move will be interpreted by the Morla'syn as an act of aggression or defiance and could provoke them to open fire.*'

'*It's not me asking,*' the general admitted. '*It's the Word.*'

A long silence enveloped Arcadia's bridge and that of Atlantia as the two captains digested this new piece of information.

'*The Word?*' Captain Sansin gasped. '*You're saying that the Word really is on board? We detected no evidence of the Legion.*'

'The Legion is not here,' the general confirmed. *'But it would appear that the Word managed to get aboard before Endeavour launched. We found in the centre of the ship's holds a computer terminal that's been rigged to contain the Word and was connected to the rest of the ship via power conduits that we have since disconnected. We were convinced to turn the Word back on in order to help us escape Endeavour, and the Word now seems to be wirelessly linked to many of Endeavour's systems. It has managed to save our lives once already and appears to be an earlier incarnation that has not undergone the transformation that our governing Word went through on Ethera. Believe it or not, captain, this version is attempting to protect us but is not beyond also wishing to protect itself. It knows what's out there and will not take us any further through the ship without us ensuring its safety.'*

Mikhain could almost hear in Sansin's tone the sense of disbelief at what he had been told.

'The Word is blackmailing you? That doesn't sound like the act of a machine designed to protect humanity.'

'No but it does sound like the act of an intelligent machine seeking to defend itself, and right now our survival is a mutually beneficial result of us working together. I don't like it, but there's not much else I can do. If we don't get out this corridor and through this bulkhead within the next few moments we will all be dead.'

As if in response to the general's comments the sudden crash and whine of plasma fire shattered the silence of Arcadia's bridge. Mikhain heard Marines calling fire commands and the sound of what seemed to be animals screeching in rage or pain.

'We need to move now,' Djimon whispered urgently into Mikhain's ear. 'This is our chance.'

Mikhain spoke up. 'We are ready, captain, and we're closest to Endeavour's landing bays. Give us the command and I shall place Arcadia directly in the line of fire.'

For a long moment Sansin did not reply.

'Captain, we need a decision made now!' Bra'hiv shouted as the sound of plasma fire intensified.

Mikhain and Djimon waited for a few tense moments, both of them uncertain what Sansin would do. When he replied, it was with a tone of bold decision.

'Arcadia, move now! Position yourself as close as possible to Endeavour and ensure that your fighter screen is ready to protect any ships that launch from the vessel!'

Mikhain stifled a tight grin as he whirled and relayed the order. 'Helm, full ahead, shields at maximum and charge all plasma cannons!'

Arcadia surged into motion as her ion engines engaged and she began to manoeuver toward the vast black bulk of Endeavour's wreck. Mikhain heard Sansin's voice as he called commands to his own bridge crew.

'Helm, full ahead, attack position and cover Arcadia. All fighters redeployed as defensive screen: position against the Morla'syn destroyer but do not open fire.'

Mikhain watched on the tactical display as the two frigates broke position, Atlantia heading directly for the Morla'syn destroyer as Arcadia began to close on Endeavour. Between the two frigates the Raython fighters split into two groups, both acting as defensive screens against any attempt by the Morla'syn to launch their own fighters.

'Arcadia, divert maximum power to shields. Maintain cover on Endeavour in case they attempt to fire past us.'

'Aye, captain,' Mikhain replied and pointed at the tactical officer. Lieutenant Scott nodded without needing further command as he diverted the power as ordered.

*

'This is outrageous!'

Councillor Gredan glared at Idris from where he stood below the command platform on Atlantia's bridge, his podgy face red in the glow of the lights.

'This is necessary,' Idris snapped back. 'Your opinions have no weight here councillor.'

'No weight?!' Gredan gasped. 'You're engaging a Morla'syn vessel in contravention of Galactic Council Law with a thousand civilians aboard, to defend a ship contaminated by the Word!'

'I haven't engaged anything and I'm defending a Colonial vessel adrift beyond the Icari Line. The Morla'syn have no more legal right to be here than we do!'

Gredan ground his teeth in his skull as he struggled to contain his anger. 'Galactic Law, to which Ethera is a signatory civilisation, states that we may not fire in anger against a vessel of another signatory civilisation! To do so would be considered an act of war—you'll be giving them yet another reason to blow us all to pieces!'

'I am aware of the legal technicalities of conflict, councillor,' Idris uttered. 'I am also aware that many of our own people are trapped aboard Endeavour.'

Gredan raised his chin. 'The needs of the many, captain, outweigh the needs of the few.'

Idris turned slowly to look at the councillor. 'Are you advocating abandoning our own people to die at the hands of the Morla'syn?'

The bridge fell silent as the command crew looked at the councillor.

'If it is required to preserve the safety of the rest of the crew, then yes,' Gredan replied.

Idris nodded slowly as he regarded the fat man, his skin oiled with sweat in the heat.

'Then should we be faced with such a decision, Gredan, I will be sure to call you here to the bridge so that you and your fellow councillors can give that order to my crew.'

*

Evelyn watched as the face on the screen of the computer terminal remained motionless. Behind them in the darkness she could see the advancing ranks of creatures illuminated amid brilliant flashes of plasma fire as the Marines attempted to hold them at bay, the stench of scorched flesh and the screams of unknown animals filling the corridor with a hideous din.

'Are they moving yet?' Andaim shouted above the noise. 'Did the captain agree to the terms?'

'I can't tell,' Bra'hiv yelled back as he fired down the corridor. 'We've lost contact again.'

Evelyn drew her pistol and moved in front of Emma and the computer terminal as she aimed down the corridor and fired twice at the bulky form of a muscular, hairy creature with bared fangs and wild eyes that scrambled over the bodies clogging the corridor and launched itself toward them with a frenzied howl.

The two plasma shots smashed into its face in a cloud of boiling blue smoke as they melted flesh and bone into a sizzling mess. The creature's body continued to tumble toward her in the corridor, its lifeless limbs dangling beneath it as it floated along only to be struck by a further barrage of plasma fire. The searing heat of the impacts ignited the flesh and fur of the animal and it suddenly burst into flames.

'We need to get out of here right now!' the general yelled at Emma.

Emma turned and looked at the computer terminal, and as Evelyn glanced over her shoulder she saw the face talking again and could just about sense the sound of its warbling dialogue.

'What is it saying?!' Andaim asked.

'Look out!'

The tumbling, flaming corpse of the dead beast rolled through the air toward the Marines in a cloud of roiling smoke.

Evelyn stood up as she holstered her pistol and jumped up to grab the ceiling grates of the corridor, and with a heave of effort she pulled her knees up to her chest and then propelled her boots outward at the burning carcass. Her boots thumped into the muscular body and propelled it with a dull thud back the way it had come, the flickering flames illuminating the corridor and the surging mass of bodies flooding toward them in a frenzy of fangs, talons and tails.

The creatures fled from the flaming corpse, stricken by an instinctive fear of fire as they struggled to get away in the zero gravity. Evelyn dropped to the deck and turned to Emma.

'Get us out of here!'

Emma stared at the screen for a moment longer as she listened to the Word's commands, and then she shouted out at the top of her voice.

'Get hold of something! Hang on!'

Evelyn jumped to one side of the corridor and grabbed hold of the bulkhead as the Marines all shouldered their rifles and attempted to bury themselves in tight corners. Evelyn saw Emma grab the computer terminal and shove it against the wall of the corridor as she leaned in behind it and hung on grimly.

The creatures advancing upon their position slid cautiously past the burning corpse and scrambled and slid for purchase as they closed in on Evelyn. To her horror she saw writhing tentacles reach out for her, laden with broad suckers each of which was filled with tiny teeth that opened and closed as they sought some purchase or the taste of flesh. Evelyn tucked herself even tighter against the bulkhead and attempted to hide from the grotesque appendage as it writhed alongside her.

A thin, skeletal creature that emitted high–pitched clicking sounds, its bony structure visible under pale white skin that seemed almost translucent, skittered across the ceiling of the corridor, baleful white eyes peering down at the crouching Marines as with a fearsome screech it propelled itself downward and landed on a soldier's back. Before the marine could react the creature's limbs and tail wrapped around him and its slender mouth suddenly opened wide as the jaw unhinged and exposed ranks of fearsome teeth that clamped down into the soldier's neck and thrashed this way and that through his flesh.

The Marine screamed and reach behind him for the animal's head as he attempted to rip it free from his body, and he hurled himself from his hiding place and slammed back–first into the opposite wall. Evelyn heard the backbone of the creature crunch as its skeleton was shattered by the blow and the weight of the soldier's body, but its jaws did not break their grip and blood spilled from the wound to fill the air with deep scarlet globules.

'Get down!' Bra'hiv yelled at the injured soldier as he thrashed.

Suddenly the soldier's screams were overwhelmed by the howl of moving air and Evelyn clenched her body tight against the bulkhead as the air rushed from the corridor in a bitterly cold gale. The creatures swarming upon their position were suddenly hauled away as though by unseen hands, snatched with brutal violence as the atmosphere was sucked away. Evelyn squinted her eyes as the moisture in the air was frozen into ice crystals that sparkled and billowed down the corridor as she realised with horror that the Word had opened a series of bulkheads leading all the way to the outer hull and the deep vacuum of space in order to scour the corridor of life.

The temperature plummeted to a cold like nothing Evelyn had felt before and she realised with terror that her hands were stuck to the bulkhead she was gripping with all of her strength. The howling of the creatures vanished into silence as did everything else as the atmosphere was sucked completely from the corridor. Far away, Evelyn glimpsed a distant bulkhead slamming shut under automatic pressure as the Word sealed them inside a corridor now devoid of oxygen.

For a moment of lonely terror Evelyn believed that the Word would abandon them to their fate, that it had doomed them to suffocate and freeze deep in the bowels of the long abandoned spaceship.

A blast of warm air flooded past Evelyn as the bulkhead hatch that they had been seeking to pass through suddenly opened of its own accord, the automatic latches releasing as the Word accessed the hatch and allowed the atmosphere from the corridor beyond to blast in along with a placid wave of what felt like heat but was in fact probably nothing more than near–zero temperature, tropical compared to the vacuum's bitter embrace.

Evelyn gasped and sucked down a lungful of the air as all around the Marines slumped, some of them waiting for their hands to unfreeze from the cold metal surface of the corridor.

General Bra'hiv stood up and looked at Emma, his face pale from the bitter cold of the vacuum, particles of frost white on his eyebrows and his eyes blinking from where they had dried out.

'That was too damned close,' he snapped, his voice hoarse. 'You tell that box of short–circuits that the next time I need something doing it gets done right away, or I'll blow it to hell.'

Emma glanced at the machine, her lips touched with that strangely enigmatic smile as she raised an eyebrow.

'It may not be able to communicate in our language,' she replied. 'But it knows full well what you're saying.'

Lieutenant Riaz strode up to the screen and looked directly at the digital face.

'Then you'll know I will be right behind the general should he miss.'

Andaim stood up from his hiding place, brushed himself down and gestured to the now open corridor behind them.

'Shall we?'

Without any further word the Marines grabbed the computer terminal and pushed it in front of them as they set off down the corridor.

ENDEAVOUR

***

XXXII

'Battle stations!'

Captain Idris Sansin paced up and down Atlantia's command platform as he watched the Morla'syn destroyer begin to turn. A new stream of data spilled down the main display panel as the tactical officer called out a warning.

'They are reacting and diverting internal power to weapon systems!'

The huge destroyer turned hard to starboard, no longer directing her bow at the two frigates but coming to bear so that her port guns could open fire upon any target of their choice. The captain's practised old eye observed the destroyer's movement and gauged their fields of fire as he called to the helm.

'All ahead one quarter, starboard shields to maximum, bow elevation four–zero–five. Ensure that if she fires at Endeavour from there she will be blocked by our sheilds.'

'Aye, captain.'

Atlantia cruised forwards through deep space, keeping herself between the Morla'syn destroyer and Endeavour.

'We should withdraw immediately,' Councillor Gredan insisted. 'We cannot possibly hope to win an engagement against such a superior vessel.'

'That is the attitude upon which battles are lost,' Idris muttered in response, not looking at Gredan but focusing instead on his tactical displays.

'Reaper two, Atlantia: we're in position, orders?'

Idris glanced at his Raython fighters on the tactical display. 'Hold station, prepare to intercept Morla'syn fighters should they launch. Do not fire until fired upon.'

'Wilco, Reaper two.'

'I speak on behalf of a thousand civilians,' Gredan protested, 'and you agreed to listen to me. You're putting their lives at risk by engaging the Morla'syn!'

'I'd be putting their lives at reach if I withdrew,' Idris replied. 'They would not hesitate to pursue and destroy us and all chance of dialogue would be lost. Is that what you would prefer, councillor?'

Gredan huffed and puffed but he said nothing, and Idris got out of the captain's chair and gestured to it. 'Perhaps you would care to take over, if you think that you have an easy solution to this confrontation?'

Lael's voice reached the captain from the communications console. 'They are signalling us captain.'

Idris kept his gaze on Gredan, and raised an expectant eyebrow. Gredan's shoulders sank although his gaze was fixed upon the proffered chair.

'I do not,' he replied.

'Open a channel,' the captain ordered Lael as he re–took his seat.

One of Atlantia's display screens flickered into life and showed an image of the Morla'syn captain, his normally dour expression now glowing with malevolence as he pointed with one of three fingers on his left hand at the captain.

'Captain, this is ridiculous. You are outgunned and outclassed and there is nothing to gain by protecting that old wreck. Is it really your intention to provoke an interstellar incident by opposing our mission?'

'You call this ridiculous? Do you really think we'll just roll over and let you blow us all to pieces?'

'It is for the benefit of all other nations in the galaxy.'

'And this is for the benefit of ours,' Idris snarled back. 'I don't care if we are outgunned, outclassed and outmanoeuvred all in one go: I and my comrades will fight to the death before allowing you to take a single human life.'

'We are sanctioned by the Galactic Council to….'

'We have evidence that you have no such sanction and that you are responsible for destroying Endeavour in the first place. They have records showing that their vessel was attacked by a Morla'syn cruiser and we have copies of those records which we will have no hesitation in signalling to the Galactic Council if you and your people do not stand down immediately!'

The Morla'syn captain stared at Idris as though he was insane. 'That is preposterous. We have no records of any such attack in this sector by any of our vessels.'

Captain Sansin peered curiously at the Morla'syn captain. Idris had never been the best judge of character when it came to foreign species, largely because no human being was good at it. The subtleties of human emotion that played out across every human face, the tiniest muscular twitches and the simplest expressions, were not present on many of the species that humanity had encountered since breaking free of its terrestrial bounds. The Morla'syn demonstrated their emotion physically, through their actions and words, with a far greater vigour than human beings. Now, Idris attempted to determine whether the captain of a foreign vessel from a star system rarely visited by human beings was lying to him or telling the truth.

'Just because you have never encountered the Endeavour before does not mean that others of your species have not,' Idris accused. 'We have already discovered that human beings crossed the Icari Line long ago—there is no reason that the Morla'syn could not have also have done so.'

'Do not dare to compare us to human beings,' the Morla'syn captain snapped. 'Your species' inability to understand the importance of following orders is as alien to us as your willingness to destroy yourselves. The only species to defy the Icari is humanity.'

'Have it your way,' Idris growled as he turned his back to the camera and nodded to Lael. 'Send the signal immediately on a priority frequency to the Galactic Council, emergency channel!'

'Aye, captain.'

Lael reached out to send the signal when the Morla'syn captain's voice broke across the bridge.

'Wait!'

Idris, his hands behind his back, waited for a brief moment before he turned to face the camera once more, and he thought he saw the glimmer of doubt crossing the Morla'syn's face.

'What is it, captain?' Idris asked. 'I thought you had the Galactic Council behind you?'

The Morla'syn captain's eyes narrowed as he fought to contain his anger.

'We do,' he snapped back, but the venom in his voice seemed tempered by something that Idris had not noticed before. Hubris.

Idris could still not tell for sure if the Morla'syn was deceiving him, but he had the instincts of a lifetime of military service to rely upon and his guts told him that the Morla'syn was hiding something.

'You are not on a mission to destroy humanity at all, are you?' Idris growled, determined to get to the bottom of why the Morla'syn would want to destroy them. 'Why are you here? Tell us now!'

The Morla'syn captain's voice was a deep rumble, as though he was reluctant to spit every word that he spoke.

'We are not here to destroy humanity in its entirety,' he admitted. 'We are here only to seek a few.'

'Which few?'

'A small team of soldiers was encountered operating illegally inside Morla'syn space some months ago and their vessel was pursued by a frigate, but it escaped into super luminal flight. I and my crew were tasked with pursuing them and bringing them to justice.'

'Bringing them to justice for what?'

The Morla'syn captain hesitated for a moment, and then finally spoke with a clenched fist of three fingers beside his head.

'Mass murder,' he snarled. 'We followed *them* here, not you. They were discovered by a Morla'syn merchant vessel which was conducting mineral surveys close to the Icari Line. The vessel was not a military type, was not heavily armed and nor were its crew, yet upon discovery your soldiers deemed it necessary to slaughter every single one of the ship's compliment and then to utterly destroy the vessel itself.'

Captain Sansin took a pace closer to the screen. 'You have evidence of this?'

The Morla'syn captain nodded. 'The captain of the merchant vessel was able to send a signal before his ship was destroyed, that contained data monitoring the destruction of the vessel and the murder of his crew. Although the data is broken it is clear that it was a team of human soldiers, possibly what you call special forces, was who were responsible for the slaughter.'

Idris peered at the screen for a long moment but this time, somehow, he knew that the Morla'syn captain was not lying. Atlantia had never sailed particularly close to Morla'syn space and Idris had never been entirely convinced that the Morla'syn could have fortuitously picked up the frigate's trail. But if the Special Forces team found upon Endeavour had indeed been in Morla'syn space on an ultra–secret mission of some kind for the Etheran government then it was possible that in order to preserve the classified nature of their mission they would have slaughtered anybody who encountered them, even if doing so could have provoked an interstellar incident. Such troops were not known for deliberation: their members were picked for their ability to make snap decisions and carry them out with absolute determination, regardless of the consequences.

Idris looked over his shoulder at the Executive Officer's chair and found himself ever more deeply in need of an XO with which to share ideas and deliberate courses of action. He glanced at Lael who was watching the exchange with interest, but she was grasping the sides of her communications console with both hands as though it were an anchor to keep her from becoming involved, and he realised that he could not yet ask her to stand up and shoulder the burden that was required of a true XO.

'How long ago did this happen?' he asked instead.

'Just over nine months,' the Morla'syn captain replied. 'They have proven very difficult to track, but given the nature of their crimes we have deemed it essential to never give up until we find them. Their trail ends here at Endeavour and we will not leave until they are in our custody or dead.' The Morla'syn captain hung his head for a moment as though in regret before he continued. 'There is nothing that you can do to stop us. The

Etheran government is no more and the destruction of your vessels would no longer be an interstellar incident. The massacre of my people was a key reason for the decision by the Galactic Council to vote for humanity's destruction. I am sorry, captain, but we are ordered to destroy both of your vessels and Endeavour with you. I would ask that you surrender the criminals under your protection to stand trial upon our homeworld for their crimes. You have five minutes to make a decision.'

The communication signal blinked out and the image of the Morla'syn captain vanished as Idris stood in silence on the command platform.

*

'We're almost there!'

Evelyn followed the Marines pushing the computer terminal as Lieutenant C'rairn's delighted cry rang out down the corridor.

Ahead, she could see past the Marines to where the Special Forces soldiers were making their way toward a set of double bulkhead doors, the massive hatch clearly indicative of the type typically leading to landing bays on major colonial vessels. Larger than most, they were designed to withstand the dramatic loss of pressure when a landing bay was open to the vacuum of space during the launch and recovery of vessels, and above the hatches were the warning lights revealing the atmospheric conditions within the landing bay itself.

'Good,' Bra'hiv said. 'The sooner we get off this damned derelict the better!'

Evelyn saw Lieutenant Riaz and his troopers race to the hatches and then to her alarm she saw the soldiers of his platoon engage their plasma shielding as a rippling glow flickered briefly into life around their bodies.

'What the hell are they doing?' Andaim called.

The Special Forces troops gathered before the hatches and as one they turned, four of them kneeling down to aim at the Marines as four more stood behind them with their weapons likewise trained deliberately on Bra'hiv's men. Evelyn saw their plasma shielding ripple as they linked up to form a wide defensive screen impenetrable to plasma fire.

The Marines stopped in mid stride and stared as Riaz called out to them.

'That's as far as you go, boys,' he warned. 'Weapons on the deck, hands behind your heads and on your knees, now!'

The Marines did not move as Bra'hiv stepped to stand before them. 'You've got to be kidding me?'

Riaz shook his head. 'End of the line for you I'm afraid,' he snapped. 'Hand over the machine and that abomination you call Emma. We're leaving.'

Evelyn stepped forward a pace and placed herself protectively in front of Emma, one hand resting on the butt of a pistol. To her amazement, Andaim moved also to stand alongside Evelyn with his own pistol already drawn.

'That's not going to happen, Riaz,' Bra'hiv snapped back. 'I don't know what your real mission was, but it's over now. There is no need for any of this—you can come with us.'

'Sorry, no can do,' Riaz replied. 'It's a long story and not one were about to share, but we're out of here. Now either hand over the terminal and that woman or you become permanent residents here.'

**

XXXIII

Evelyn and the Marines stared at Riaz and his men as they aimed their weapons at them down the corridor. All of the Special Forces troops were wearing stern expressions, none of them showing any signs of uncertainty about their leader's course of action.

'This is insane,' Andaim snapped. 'There's nowhere else to go, nowhere else for you to run. We're all that's left of humanity, why would you choose to betray us?'

'It's not open for discussion,' Riaz snapped as he nodded towards the computer terminal. 'We'll be taking that with us.'

Evelyn glanced at the computer terminal as she saw Emma move instinctively closer and place both hands upon it as though it were the only thing keeping her alive.

'It's not yours for the taking,' Evelyn replied.

'What was your real mission, Riaz?' Bra'hiv growled. 'Why were you sent out here?'

'That's classified,' Riaz shot back. 'And I'm not buying your story of a global apocalypse wrecking Ethera and the surrounding planets. As soon as we get that thing aboard our ship we'll be plotting a course for home.'

'There is no home!' Andaim shouted in frustration. 'Do you really think we would be out here facing who–knows–what dangers every day if we all had homes and family's to go to?'

'If you were deserters you wouldn't have a problem with it,' Riaz snapped back.

'Deserters,' Bra'hiv echoed flatly. 'You're going with that?'

'Our priority is to complete our mission,' Riaz insisted. 'Frankly I don't give a damn why you're out here, only that you've seen us when you should not have. There's a destroyer out there determined to hunt us down. If our presence is identified by the Galactic Council they will almost certainly kill us and the repercussions on Ethera could be devastating.'

Evelyn blinked, suddenly uncertain of how stable the lieutenant's mental state was. She knew that Special Forces troopers were trained to almost insane levels of devotion and determination, but the sheer amount of time that the troops had spent away from home and out of contact with human beings may have pushed the lieutenant's reserves further than his training had ever intended. Nothing could prepare even such a highly trained soldier for the knowledge that the five years he had spent away from family and friends performing the duties he had been assigned were for nothing, and that the people he had left behind were no longer alive: that he didn't even have a home to go to.

Denial.

'Lieutenant,' she said as she moved to stand beside Bra'hiv. 'There is no home left for us but here. I'm not even a colonial officer, but a former convict who proved my worth aboard Atlantia. Half the Marines behind me are also former convicts given the chance to prove themselves and serve what's left of our colonial forces in an attempt to take back Ethera from the Word. This is the reality of our lives now. If you plot a course home, as soon as you arrive you will either be infected or consumed by the Word's hunters. This is not a ploy or a deception—I wish it was. We can't let you have this computer terminal as it's too important to our mission to understand the Word and attempt to identify weaknesses in it that we can exploit in *our* mission to return home safely. If you really want to leave without us, then you'll have to go ahead on your own.'

The soldiers around Riaz did not move an inch, their weapons still aimed at the Marines, but Evelyn could see their eyes swivel to glance at their leader as they awaited his decision. Riaz seemed to struggle as he tried to understand any possible deception behind the Marine's insistence on remaining together.

'The hell with this,' Riaz said finally as he stepped back towards the landing bay hatch. 'Keep the damn computer, we're out of here. You make any attempt to stop us, we'll blow you to hell!'

The lieutenant backed up to the hatch and Evelyn realised that his soldiers had already placed a device over the locking mechanism, sealing it until they were ready to return. Riaz entered a code into the mechanism and the device beeped as two metallic clamps released with a hiss.

Riaz's men began backing up as the lieutenant reached across and hit a button. The hatch rumbled and squealed as it began to open on hinges and rotors rusty with age. Evelyn saw through the opening gap an aggressive looking craft painted in a matte black and bristling with countermeasure defences and plasma weapons.

'You're leaving us here to die!' Andaim shouted.

'So that we can live and continue our mission!' Riaz shot back.

The tightly–knit bunch of soldiers retreated back through the hatch, the rippling plasma shield around them impenetrable to the Marine's weapons and the troops unable to attack anyway without dooming themselves to certain death under the barrage of fire that the Special Forces troops would return. Evelyn watched as Riaz stood beside his men as they fell back into the landing bay and he reached up to shut the doors once more.

Evelyn thought she saw the ghost of a smile touched the lieutenant's face.

Something dropped from above the Special Forces troops, two black spheres that caused the plasma shield to ripple as they passed through it and landed with a thump on the deck amid the soldiers' boots. The troopers all turned to look at the two objects that plummeted into their midst and instantly a cry went up from them.

'Grenades, *scatter!*'

Evelyn barely had time to shield her eyes and duck down as the two grenades detonated in the heart of Riaz's soldier's formation. She glimpsed the brilliant flare of brutal plasma light and the blasts radiating outwards with enough force to hurl the elite troops off their feet amid an expanding cloud of superheated plasma that struck them not from the outside but from the inside, their shields no defence against solid objects.

Riaz was thrown aside out of sight into the bay as his men were torn to pieces by the blasts. General Bra'hiv wasted no time in taking advantage of the sudden change of fortunes.

'All arms, advance by sections, go!'

The Marines thundered down the corridor and plunged into the landing bay as they fired into the enemy formation, sweeping their rifles left and right as they passed through a gruesome wasteland of injured men and severed limbs smouldering in the landing bay. Evelyn rushed in behind them and saw two soldiers, both of them with their legs missing and their eyes staring wide and empty of life toward the ceiling of the bay. Others groaned in agony from the injuries sustained by the blasts, flames licking their uniforms amid glowing globules of plasma.

Riaz was pinned against a wall of the landing bay, his rifle discarded and floating in the air before him and his back awkwardly slumped over a storage box, bent at an impossible angle. Evelyn realised instantly that his back was broken, snapped by the force of the blast, his eyes open and his face twisted with pain.

General Bra'hiv approached the soldier, his rifle pulled tightly into his shoulder to guard against any possible chance that Riaz would still attempt to take life.

'You should have stayed with us,' the general snapped. 'We weren't lying. We are the only home left—Ethera is gone.'

The lieutenant managed a grim smile and shook his head. 'I'll believe that when I see it,' he snarled, 'but I'll never have any faith in colonial soldiers who are allied to the Veng'en!'

For a moment Evelyn struggled to understand what Riaz meant, and then directly behind her she heard a dull thud as something heavy landed on the deck. Evelyn whirled and in a moment of horror she saw that behind the Marines and the computer terminal being pushed by Emma a Veng'en warrior had dropped down from the ceiling of the landing bay.

With a pulse of horror Evelyn knew without any shadow of a doubt that it was Kordaz, just as she knew that he must have bypassed the holds via the original route from which they had intended to escape Endeavour. The huge warrior grabbed one of the fallen soldier's plasma shields and tucked it under his arm, and lunged for a blade sheathed at the soldier's waist. Kordaz whirled and loomed over Emma, and Evelyn realised that Kordaz, intent on his revenge, was aiming for the wrong target.

'Kordaz, no!'

Two plasma shots roared out and smashed into Kordaz but were dispersed by the plasma shield. Emma staggered back in horror as Kordaz swung the lethal blade and it plunged into her chest with a dull thud. Emma clasped the handle of the blade and sank to her knees as Kordaz turned and grabbed Meyanna Sansin and lifted her off her feet. He turned her around, his massive arms encircling her and pinning her body against his as he glared at the Marines.

'Hold your fire!' Evelyn yelled. 'Don't shoot!'

The Marines, their rifles all pointed at Kordaz, held their ground as the Veng'en turned and revealed in his free hand another plasma grenade. Kordaz held the weapon up, the soldiers close enough to be decimated by the blasts. Evelyn stared in shock at the metallic sheen on the warrior's chest, the seamless blend of metal and flesh and the dull red glow deep in his eyes.

'Release the Word to me,' Kordaz growled at the Marines.

Evelyn stepped forward, her pistol in her hand as she spoke. 'Kordaz.'

The warrior turned his head and for the first time Evelyn was able to detect an expression of surprise in the warrior's features, his eyes widening as patches of his skin flickered with flares of orange and red. Kordaz looked down at Emma where she lay on the deck with the blade in her chest, her breathing fast and her eyes wide with fear of death, and then he looked back at Evelyn as though suddenly realising what he had done.

'You're infected,' Evelyn said. 'You need to trust in us, this isn't the way.'

'What would you know of trust?' Kordaz snarled as he glared at Evelyn and the surrounding Marines. 'Your kind is obsessed with destroying yourselves, keen only to use each other. I placed my trust in you and *this* is what happened!'

Kordaz jerked his fist in the direction of the burnished metal of his chest and the metallic orbs around his eyes.

'It's not us that betrayed you,' Evelyn insisted. 'But here you are killing people you don't even know!'

Kordaz glared at the machine being guarded by the Marines, and at Qayin where he lay on the stretcher also surrounded by guard of soldiers.

'A murderer, a convict and a traitor,' Kordaz snapped as he pointed at Qayin, 'and yet you defend him with your lives while abandoning me, a Veng'en, to die alone on Chiron. I know damned well what your captain had in mind when he sent me down to the surface, just as I know why he sent all of the Marines he could trust the least—he wanted everybody he did not wish to take with him down on that planet so he could abandon them.'

'That's not true,' Bra'hiv intervened. 'He wanted somebody he could trust the most, and you were the only person he felt he could send down there and be certain would not betray us. We thought that Qayin sold you out down there, but it wasn't him. Truth is, we still don't know who betrayed you!'

Kordaz, the plasma grenade still held in his fist, peered at Evelyn as though seeking some sign of confirmation from somebody he perhaps might still have some faith in.

'It's true,' she insisted. 'I know that you want revenge, but you're seeking revenge on the wrong people.'

'Then why are you in league with the Word, the very thing you've insisted you wish to destroy?' Kordaz challenged.

'We are not in league with it,' Meyanna replied, her voice constricted by the force of the Veng'en's grip. 'It's proven to be the only thing that might be able to get us out of here. The woman you just stabbed is the only one of us who is able to communicate with it! She needs my help!'

'And I need yours,' Kordaz snarled as he looked down at her. 'Cure me, or nobody leaves this ship alive!'

'I can't cure you!' Meyanna insisted. 'Not here, not like this! If you want to be cured, the only thing that can really do it now is the Word itself and you just stabbed the only person who can talk to it!'

'And we need to get out of here, right now!' Lieutenant C'rairn added.

As if in response a thunderous blast hammered the hull of Endeavour and the landing bay shuddered as the lights flickered weakly, what power remained in the fusion cores struggling to prevent the system from becoming overloaded by the impacts.

'We're under fire!' Andaim shouted.

Kordaz glared around him as though uncertain of what to do, and Evelyn saw Emma's eyelids drooping as she weakened from loss of blood. Evelyn holstered her pistol and crossed the landing bay toward Kordaz, extending her hands out to her side as a gesture of goodwill. She came to a stop before the towering warrior and looked up into his metallic red eyes.

'No matter what you think we are not your enemy, Kordaz,' she said. 'But none of this will be resolved if we do not leave this landing bay right now. We are under attack and cannot stay here. If you want Meyanna's help, then we have to get off this ship.'

Kordaz glared down at her, his massive muscular arm still holding Meyanna close to his chest, the plasma grenade within his other fist humming with restrained energy.

'You abandoned me to die,' he hissed at Evelyn.

'I abandoned you because you were already dead,' Evelyn replied. 'I could not have hoped to have moved you and you were infected anyway. We did not do this to you, Kordaz. The Word did this to you, but the machine we now have with us is not the same. It's older, it's helping us. It might even be able to help you.'

Evelyn gestured at the warrior's metallic chest. Kordaz stared at Evelyn for a long moment, and then down again at Emma.

'Why do you look so alike?' he demanded.

'I don't know,' Evelyn replied as another blast shook the landing bay. 'We need to talk, but it's got to be later. If we don't get off this ship we're *all* doomed.'

Kordaz regarded her for a moment longer, and then slowly lowered his arms as with a flick of one taloned finger he deactivated the grenade and released Meyanna.

Meyanna broke away from the Veng'en, dashed to Emma's side and dropped down beside her as Evelyn joined them and looked at the wound in Emma's chest. The blade was still buried in her chest as Meyanna started trying to stem the flow of blood.

'Don't try to take it out,' she instructed. 'Just hang on.'

The landing bay shuddered again as a massive blast impacted the hull outside and the illumination flickered out entirely. In the darkness only the blue screen of the computer terminal was visible along with the flashlights of the Marine's rifles.

'Time to go, don't you think?' C'rairn called as he jogged towards the gunship.

Evelyn looked at Lieutenant Riaz, still pinned against the wall of the landing bay. 'We need to get aboard or we're all dead.'

Riaz twisted his features into a grim smile. 'We're all dead anyway,' he snarled back. 'I'd rather die here than face what is awaiting is out there.'

Lying on her back on the deck, Emma groaned as Evelyn heard mumbling and warbling from the computer terminal. Emma's eyes flickered weakly as she whispered to Meyanna.

'Boarding protocol, five–zero–seven–zero–one, initiate.'

Riaz hissed in anger as behind them the gunship's boarding ramp opened, the ramp sinking to the deck with a clang as the landing bay was rocked violently by another impact.

'Let's go!' Bra'hiv yelled, and whirled to his men. 'Get the injured aboard!'

Evelyn grabbed Riaz's collar. 'What do the Morla'syn want with you?'

Riaz sneered up at her, the life fading from his eyes. 'They wanted us out,' he gasped, 'tried to kill us all because we learned the truth. The Icari Line, it's not what you think it is.'

Evelyn gave Lieutenant Riaz one last glance and then made her decision. She yanked his plasma shield generator from his webbing and then turned her back on him and the other injured members of his platoon. With the Marines she boarded the gunship, helping to push the computer terminal and the stretcher containing Qayin ahead of them.

Andaim and Meyanna carefully lifted Emma between them and hurried onto the gunship's ramp as Evelyn dashed towards the cockpit and threw herself into the pilot's seat. She cast a quick glance across the controls and began flicking switches as she located the emergency engine–start system concealed low beneath the control panel. Similar to the one fitted to Colonial Raythons, the system bypassed the normal start procedures and allowed for an immediate getaway in an emergency.

'Strap yourselves in, fast!' she shouted back into the interior of the ship. 'This could get rough!'

Behind her she saw Emma being laid down on a row of seats by Andaim, as the CAG then rushed to join Evelyn in the cockpit and took the co–pilot's seat. Behind them, Evelyn heard Emma's soft whispers as though she were murmuring in her delirium.

'Launch protocol, atmospheric evacuation, initiate!'

Emma's voice was barely a whisper but it was as though she was vocalising every command the Word gave and with a sudden start Evelyn realised why: the Word could not alone give commands, it was only able to relay the commands of human beings, the reason why it had not had the opportunity to take over control of Endeavour to conquer the humans with which it shared the ship. It required human interaction.

The reason for the face embedded into Endeavour's bridge suddenly made sense, a permanent cybernetic link to the ship's computers. But then, who or *what* was Emma?

Through the cockpit windows Evelyn saw Endeavour's launch bay doors suddenly open and a rush of escaping air flash by as it was sucked out into oblivion in whorls of white vapour. As the gunship's engines whined into life she saw the body of Lieutenant Riaz spin past the gunship and out into the bitter vacuum of space along with the bodies of his platoon.

Evelyn threw the throttles forward as the engines engaged and the gunship lifted off even as giant plasma blasts slammed into the hold around them in violent explosions as flames tore through Endeavour's hull.

***

XXXIV

'They're firing!'

Mikhain leaped out of his seat on Arcadia's bridge as he saw the Morla'syn destroyer suddenly ripple with light as its plasma cannons opened fire upon Endeavour.

'All power to starboard shields, brace for impact!'

The crew scrambled to divert power as Mikhain grabbed the guard rail of the command platform just before the salvo of massive blasts hammered into the Arcadia's shields and the frigate tremble under the blows.

'Sheilds holding, ninety four per cent,' Djimon reported as he glanced at the tactical displays.

'Maintain position over Endeavour's aft hull,' Mikhain ordered the helm as he judged the position of the Morla'syn destroyer. 'We need to give General Bra'hiv time to get those people out.'

The massive destroyer was already turning in an attempt to outmanoeuvre the two frigates and bring her weapons to bear upon Endeavour's stern. Even as Mikhain watched Atlantia attempt to match the move and keep herself between Endeavour and the destroyer, another alert signal went up as Lieutenant Scott called out.

'I've got a launch from Endeavour's aft bays, unidentified craft, massive electronic countermeasures. I can't tell who is aboard or where they are going.'

'Get it up on screen immediately!'

A screen on the bridge switched displays and showed a barely–visible black gunship accelerating out of Endeavour s aft landing bay, her ion engines flaring bright blue as she accelerated and immediately turned away from Endeavour's hull.

'Communications?' Mikhain asked.

'Negative, captain – no transponder, no identification.'

Mikhain thumped a hand down on the guard rail in frustration as he watched the gunship pull away from Endeavour's hull just as another massive broadside was launched by the Morla'syn destroyer.

'The general and his men could be aboard!' Lieutenant Scott insisted.

Djimon leaned close to Mikhain, his voice low enough that only they could hear it. 'So could Kordaz and Qayin.'

Mikhain watched the gunship pulling away and whirled to the helmsman. 'Maintain position but keep checking the gunship!'

'Aye, captain.'

'This could be our chance,' Djimon hissed. 'Blow her out of existence while we still can!'

'I'd rather let the Morla'syn do that for us,' Mikhain growled back.

The broadside of plasma blasts hammered into Arcadia's hull and the frigate shuddered under the blows, two of the rounds passing beneath her and striking Endeavour's stern quarter with brilliant explosions that tore through her superstructure as though flaming spears were piercing her.

'Hull breaches on multiple levels of Endeavour,' Lieutenant Shah reported. 'All aft landing bays are now unusable.'

'Are you detecting any life forms aboard?!' Mikhain demanded.

'Yes, came the reply. 'Multiple life forms in the holds, all of which are now breached and exposed. The number of surviving life forms is dropping rapidly–there's nothing we can do for them.'

'Contact Atlantia, emergency frequency!' Mikhain snapped.

'Negative, captain. The Morla'syn are jamming our communications frequencies!'

'Damn it!'

Mikhain glanced at the tactical display and saw Atlantia still holding her ground as round after round of plasma fire flared against her shields. He could see that they would only endure a few more salvos before her shields would be utterly obliterated and the frigate exposed fully to the immense power of the Morla'syn weapons.

He glanced at a secondary display and saw the gunship making a run for it, apparently attempting to reach Atlantia.

Mikhain turned to the helmsman. 'Lay in a pursuit course on the gunship! Maximum thrust!'

'Aye, captain!'

Arcadia broke free from covering Endeavour's hull as the frigate swung around to give chase to the tiny gunship fleeing past its bow. Mikhain watched as Arcadia accelerated and began cutting of the gunship's flight path.

'We're getting a signal from the gunship!' Lieutenant Shah called. 'I don't know how but they're managing to break through the Morla'syn jamming.'

'Open a channel,' Mikhain ordered.

A screen flickered and an image of Evelyn and Andaim appeared at the controls of the gunship.

'We are all aboard,' Evelyn revealed. 'Signal Atlantia and tell her to use Endeavour's hull as cover against the Morla'syn destroyer's fire, and you to!'

Mikhain nodded. 'Turn around, get that gunship aboard us now.'

'Negative, captain,' Evelyn replied. 'Captain Sansin will not want the Word or any infected species aboard Arcadia. He'll want us to land aboard Atlantia.'

'There's no time,' Mikhain insisted. 'We will quarantine the landing bay and ensure that there is no danger of infection. We are closer than Atlantia and she is under heavy fire. The sooner you get aboard, the sooner Atlantia will be able disengage from the destroyer.'

Mikhain saw Djimon move alongside him and peer closely at the cockpit of the gunship. There, in the background beyond the cockpit door they could see Qayin lying on a stretcher and being tended to by Meyanna.

Mikhain saw the indecision on Evelyn's features, but then he saw her manipulate the controls of the gunship.

'Very well, ensure that you completely isolate whichever bay you require us to land in.'

'Aft bay seven, we'll clear it immediately,' Lieutenant Scott replied.

'Order all Raythons to land,' Mikhain ordered. 'My guess is that Captain Sansin will want us to disengage and jump to super luminal as fast as possible.'

Mikhain saw Djimon conceal a grim smile as he realised that Mikhain was planning to ensure that the gunship remained aboard Arcadia for as long as possible.

'Aye, captain!' Lieutenant Scott replied.

*

Captain Idris Sansin watched as he saw the gunship leave Endeavour's hull and turn towards Arcadia. Within moments, Arcadia's compliment of Raythons broke away from their defensive patrols and began retreating into a landing pattern.

'He's pulling out!'

Idris heard Lael's alarmed cry, and his brain raced as he attempted to figure out why Mikhain would suddenly disengage from the battle and leave Endeavour's hull entirely exposed.

'Can we break the Morla'syn jamming?'

'Negative captain,' Lael replied. 'Their emissions are too powerful and the encryption too complex for our computers to decode at this time.'

Idris watched the tactical display screen as Arcadia turned away from the battle and the Raythons began lining up to land. The gunship vanished as it landed in a separate bay.

'I'm detecting Arcadia's super luminal engines running up,' Lael reported.

Atlantia rocked violently as another massive salvo of plasma blasts hammered into her. The bridge lights flickered weakly and a series of alarms rang out.

'Shields at sixty four per cent, fires on decks C and D, no hull breaches,' Lael reported.

Idris made his decision quickly. If Mikhain was pulling out, either they had recovered Bra'hiv's team or that same team was lost. 'Order all Raythons to land and prepare to make the jump to super luminal. Lay in a pursuit course for where ever Arcadia heads.'

'Aye, captain.'

Idris looked at the Morla'syn destroyer. So far, neither Atlantia or Arcadia had fired a single shot against them, Idris preferring to maintain neutrality despite the aggression being directed at them. If they ever had the chance to face the Galactic Council, they would need the moral high ground in every action. But there was now no doubt that the Morla'syn would have seen the black gunship leave Endeavour and land aboard Arcadia, and given their determination so far to hunt down the Special Forces troops that they claimed had murdered so many of their own he felt it was without doubt that they would follow Atlantia into super luminal cruise. If they had been able to follow a Special Forces vessel for so long, they would have no problem tracking a large frigate's gravity wake.

'We're going to have to fight them at some point,' Lael said softly.

Idris looked once more at the tactical display and the data scrolling down it revealing the sheer might of the Morla'syn destroyer. Although they had never engaged in combat before, it was well–known by colonial forces that the Morla'syn ship was vastly more powerful and armed far more heavily than any single Colonial vessel. Although not outwardly aggressive, it was commonly known that once provoked the Morla'syn were implacable foes who would stop at nothing to defeat any perceived enemy or threat.

'I know,' he replied. 'Just not here, not now. Are the Raythons aboard yet?'

'The last of them are landing right now. We will be able to make the jump in sixty seconds.'

Idris looked at an image of Arcadia on one of the display screens. 'We can only hope they got everybody out, but that might mean they also have the Word aboard and perhaps even Kordaz.'

'The Morla'syn jamming will stop them from sending a signal letting us know their trajectory,' Lael reported. 'We'll be following blind, tracking their gravity wake. If we lose them…'

'We can't stay here,' Idris replied, knowing that he had no option but to disengage and flee. 'My wife may be aboard Arcadia.'

Idris stared into the middle distance for a moment as he pictured his wife and wondered whether she had even made it out of Endeavour alive. Suddenly their arguments and bickering seemed puerile and pointless against the vast canvass of threats and challenges that they had faced together.

'I'm sure she made it out just fine,' Lael attempted to console the captain and then she glanced down at her display. 'Arcadia is leaping.'

Idris looked up at the screen and saw Arcadia's massive ion engines suddenly flare brightly as she accelerated away with maximum force toward leap velocity. The frigate rapidly vanished to a small point of light as though it were just another star among billions.

'Track her trajectory and lay in a pursuit course at maximum velocity!'

'Aye, captain,' the helm responded immediately.

The helmsman advanced Atlantia's throttles and the frigate surged forwards and out of the barrage of plasma fire being directed at it by the Morla'syn destroyer. Idris held onto the guard rail of the command platform as Atlantia heeled over and turned to pursue Arcadia even as Lael called out.

'Arcadia has jumped into super luminal. Trajectory recorded, gravity wake data being received now.'

'All Raythons aboard, all bay doors sealed and atmosphere is stable. Shields at fifty eight per cent!' called the tactical officer.

'Maximum power, get us out of here!' Idris yelled.

The helmsman did not hesitate and threw the throttles fully forward, and in an instant Atlantia responded and accelerated away from the battle. The plasma blows ceased, and in their wake the distant echoes of alarm claxons sounding through the ship from damaged areas of the hull. Idris held onto the guard rail as Atlantia accelerated, her mass drive spinning up as he watched the Morla'syn destroyer lumber through a turn to pursue.

'We are out of effective plasma cannon range,' the tactical officer informed Idris.

Idris watched as the massive destroyer turned, and as she did so she launched a tremendous salvo of blasts that smashed into Endeavour's unshielded hull with a brilliant supernova flare of light. Idris squinted and shielded his eyes as the aged vessel exploded in a blazing fireball, her hull shattering into countless billions of fragments expanding out into the bitter vacuum of space.

'Mass drive engaging, five seconds,' Lael reported

Idris maintained his grip on the guard rail and counted down in his mind as he watched the pursuing Morla'syn destroyer make a last desperate dash to catch them before they made the leap. The huge ship was just starting to grow in size on the display screen when suddenly the lights in the bridge appeared to become polarised as Lael's countdown was completed and Idris felt a familiar, comforting surge as Atlantia leaped into super luminal flight.

In an instant, every display screen on the bridge flared bright white and then turned completely black and the massive Morla'syn destroyer vanished from view.

**

XXXV

'I want a full environmental team deployed to the landing bay immediately, and have Bravo company's Marines supporting them.'

Mikhain strode off the command platform with Lieutenant Scott following him.

'Contact has been lost with Atlantia, but our last observation of them showed their Raythons making to land and the frigate disengaging from the Morla'syn. It's almost certain that they will pursue us.'

'Good,' Mikhain replied. 'Make no attempt to conceal our gravitational wake so that Captain Sansin has a clear signal to follow.'

'What about the Morla'syn?' Scott asked. 'They will be able to follow the same trail and are sure to attack us as soon as we emerge from super luminal flight.'

'One problem at a time, lieutenant,' Mikhain advised. 'You have the bridge.'

Lieutenant Scott glanced at Djimon, the XO. 'Aye, captain.'

Mikhain marched off the bridge, this time with Djimon in hot pursuit, the pair of them heading directly for the elevator banks that would take them down to the landing bays.

'What are we going to do with them?' Djimon asked as soon as they were safely inside the elevator with nobody able to listen in.

Mikhain stared at the featureless face of the elevator door as he considered the problem they now had to resolve. Qayin was alive and Mikhain could only assume that Kordaz too had survived the engagement. He had learned never to assume the best, especially since the apocalypse. Either Qayin or Kordaz could expose Mikhain's involvement in jeopardising the success of the mission on Chiron, not to mention Djimon's complicity in the conspiracy. Exposure of what truly happened would mean the end of Mikhain's command and likely the end of Djimon's career. Damn it, they could both be subjected to Maroon Protocol and there likely would not be a single person aboard either ship who would speak in their defence.

'For now we keep them in complete isolation. We know that the Word is on board, but right now I don't care whether it's in computer form or in the shape of viable infectors. We use the Word's presence as an excuse to prevent communication with our crew or indeed that of Atlantia, and we maintain super luminal flight for as long as possible.'

'We need to separate Kordaz and Qayin from the rest of them, give us the chance to develop a suitable accident,' Djimon said.

'And there was me thinking that you were a true colonial soldier, devoted to the defence of the fleet.'

'That's exactly what I am,' Djimon snapped back. 'None of this would have happened were it not for Qayin's betrayal and lies, and I'm damned if I'm going to stand up and take the blame for anything that involves the betrayal of a Veng'en. I don't care that Sansin trusts him, the captain no longer speaks for everybody.'

'Neither do you, as it happens,' Mikhain pointed out.

The towering former Marine glared down at his captain. 'That's no longer for you to decide. Tow the line, captain, while you still have a command from which to do so.'

The elevator doors opened and the captain led the way out toward the landing bays, Djimon close behind him as they approached ranks of Marines all wearing environmental suits and guarding the entrance to the aft landing bay.

Their commanding officer approached the captain, his voice reaching them through a microphone amplifier from behind the thick plastic mask he wore.

'We're ready whenever you are.'

'Into the bay, lieutenant,' the captain ordered. 'Maximum caution, and maintain an open feed on your helmet camera. All microwave scanners active to prevent any contamination outside the bay. Take absolutely no risks, is that understood?'

'Aye, captain.'

The Marines turned as a unit and their commanding officer approached the landing bay hatch and entered a code into a panel next to the doors. Activating a security protocol, the code automatically reduced the air pressure inside the landing bay so the air could only flow in and not out. As the pressure inside the bay reduced, the commanding officer opened the hatch by just enough to allow the Marines to filter in one by one with hurried precision. Moments later the last Marine passed through the hatch and it automatically slammed shut behind him.

Mikhain and Djimon switched their attention to a display screen set up nearby by the Marine's support personnel, and watched as the Marines approached the landed gunship.

*

'They're armed,' Andaim observed through the cockpit window of the gunship as he watched the Marines fanning out, their faces obscured by environmental masks. 'They're not taking any chances.'

'I can't blame them,' Evelyn replied as she stood and strode out of the cockpit.

The Marines hefted Qayin's stretcher onto their shoulders and followed her as Meyanna helped Emma toward the access ramp. Standing beside the ramp was the computer terminal with the Word's silent face. Evelyn could never tell whether the face was silently watching everyone while hiding behind an image of man with its eyes closed, but she could not believe it was simply sitting idly by and not thinking all the time. That, surely, was how the Word had first evolved into the conquering force of mankind–thinking.

'They know that the Word was on board Endeavour,' Bra'hiv said as he watched Evelyn descend from the cockpit toward them. 'They're going to act as though we are all infected and I don't know what they're going to do about Kordaz when they see him.'

The Veng'en warrior stood at the rear of the ship's 'tween decks, his wrists manacled and Marine guards standing four–strong around him.

'I have the impression that Kordaz wishes only to be close to the Word,' Evelyn replied as she eyed the warrior and considered the infection that was coursing through his body. 'That's what caused you to crash to Endeavour, wasn't it.'

Kordaz said nothing, instead staring at her with those red eyes that were now even harder to judge. Evelyn could not tell whether Kordaz truly had chosen once again to side with humanity or whether he felt it was his only chance to infiltrate it, this time with the Word on his side, but right now she had to focus on what was most important.

Emma's features were now even paler than before and her uniform was drenched in blood. That she was not already dead was a miracle in itself, and yet again she wondered why it was that Kordaz had missed the heart with the blade, that such a skilled warrior and killer would have failed to take the life of a single, unarmed woman. The only conclusion she could draw was that Kordaz had believed Emma to be Evelyn and that his intention was not to kill but to injure, to somehow allow himself to be captured without being killed. The conclusion bothered her immensely.

'Ready?' Andaim asked.

'You first,' Evelyn said to Meyanna.

The captain's wife nodded and helped Emma to her feet, and Evelyn reached out and hit the main ramp's release switch.

The gunship's ramp hissed as air escaped and it descended and hit the deck below with a loud clang that reverberated around the sealed landing bay. Evelyn watched as Meyanna descended the ramp with one arm around Emma, and her voice sounded small as she called out.

'I need a medical kit as fast as you can,' Meyanna insisted. 'She needs to be stabilised as soon as possible.'

The Marines responded instantly, having no reason to assume that the woman with the captain's wife was anybody other than Evelyn. Two Marine medics hurried out from among their comrades, both of them pulling medical kits from their webbing as alongside them two further Marines produced microwave scanners.

'Go ahead, as fast as you can,' Meyanna insisted to the two Marines with the scanners. 'We're clean, but she's not going to be able to hang on much longer.'

The Marines began scanning them both as Emma was laid on the deck onto a rapidly unfolded stretcher. From the darkened interior of the gunship, Evelyn felt a pang of respect for the two Marines as they busied themselves inserting an IV line into Emma's arm regardless of the danger of potential infection by the Word. Within moments desperately needed painkillers were surging into Emma's bloodstream and the pained, barely conscious expression on her face gradually began to melt as she relaxed.

'They're both clean!' the two scanner–wielding Marines called.

'Okay, clear them to the starboard side of the bay and make way for the next batch!' their commanding officer shouted.

Evelyn began waving Marines down the ramp in groups of four, but kept herself out of sight and close to Kordaz and Qayin until they were the only remaining people aboard the gunship but for a single marine guard.

'You ready?' she asked, looking at Kordaz.

The Veng'en nodded once, his dull red eyes fixed upon Evelyn's as she turned to the Word's computer terminal and its unreadable face. She reached out to manoeuver the terminal into position to push it down the ramp when suddenly the eyes on the face opened and stared it seemed directly into her own.

'*Your time is coming,*' the voice said, and Evelyn was shocked to realise that she could hear not just the warbling digital tones that she had heard her before but actual dialogue, the voice strangely human and digital at the same time.

Only once before in her life could Evelyn recollect hearing such a voice, a bizarre chimera of man and machine speaking to her, and that was when she had encountered Tyraeus Forge months before. The former Colonial commander and celebrated battleship captain had been almost entirely consumed by the Legion, his body little more than a technological characterisation of what was left of the man himself, a seething mass of tiny machines.

Evelyn shivered but did not reply to the machine, did not dare to in front of the Marine and Kordaz. She pulled the computer terminal until it was over the ramp and then she set off pushing it in front of her as she descended into the landing bay. Behind her, Kordaz used Evelyn as a defence against any impulsive rifle fire that might come from the waiting Marines. Behind the Veng'en the remaining Marine guard descended the ramp with one hand on his rifle and the other gently pushing Qayin's stretcher ahead of him.

Evelyn heard the gasp of the Marines as they caught sight of Kordaz and his clearly infected body, not to mention Evelyn appearing yet again, and Qayin on the stretcher behind her.

'Hold your fire!' Evelyn snapped. 'It's not what you think.'

'We'll be the judge of that,' the commanding officer of the Marines snapped. 'Hands in the air, get on your knees!'

Evelyn positioned the Word to one side and got onto her knees with her hands in the air as behind her she heard Kordaz follow suit. The Marines with the microwave scanners approached her and within moments of scanning they confirmed that she was uninfected.

'She's clean!'

'Don't scan Kordaz,' Evelyn ordered the Marines. 'He is infected, but not in the manner we're used to seeing. The Word we found aboard Endeavour is not the enemy of mankind but an earlier incarnation of the same program. The infectors in his system are following its orders, not those of the Word that intends to destroy us.'

The Marines glanced over their shoulder at their commanding officer but it was not the officer who replied. Instead the voice of the captain, Mikhain, echoed across the landing bay as it was emitted by speakers set high into the walls.

'I want Kordaz completely isolated from the rest of the crew and the ship. Likewise, Qayin is also to be isolated. He has been in close quarters to Kordaz for an indeterminate amount of time and may himself be infected. We cannot allow either of them close to our people.'

'Qayin was not responsible for Kordaz's betrayal on Chiron,' General Bra'hiv announced loudly enough to be heard across the landing bay. 'Despite all that he's done he should not be considered a suspect at this time and should be held in the sick bay along with other injured parties.'

'Noted,' Mikhain replied, 'but right now I'm not about to take any chances. Isolation for both of them, no exceptions. The rest of you will be assigned quarters and *will be interviewed as soon as we have ensured that the gunship itself harbours no infectors. Arcadia is now in super luminal cruise and we have no contact with Atlantia. I need to know as much as possible about what happened aboard Endeavour so that we can share it with Captain Sansin as soon as our ships emerge from super luminal. The commander of the Marines will deploy you as required – please follow his every command.'*

'What about the word?' Evelyn asked, surprised at her own level of concern for the safety of the machine that appeared to be willing to help human beings survive. 'Emma is the only one who appears to be able to communicate with it.'

'I take it that Emma is the woman found aboard Endeavour who is apparently your identical twin?' Mikhain enquired.

'She is,' Evelyn replied, 'and she's on our side. We would not have gotten off Endeavour without her.'

'We don't know that,' Mikhain snapped. *'We don't know anything about her or anything about what really happened aboard Endeavour. As it happens we can't be sure we know everything about you, Evelyn.'*

Andaim stepped forward. 'That's ridiculous, Evelyn was a convict aboard Atlantia five, we know that she's not infected and is not an agent of the Word.'

'And can you explain how a woman who is identical to Evelyn in every respect can possibly have been found aboard a ship that launched a hundred years ago?'

Andaim opened his mouth to reply but his words fell short as he glanced uncertainly at Evelyn. To her dismay, none of the Marines or General Bra'hiv stepped forward to her defence. All of them were wearing expressions that suggested they weren't sure of what to believe or what to do.

'Are you telling me that you're going to make me some kind of prisoner?' Evelyn demanded of Mikhain.

'I'm going to play it safe until we can figure something out,' Mikhain replied, *'and as for that machine I wanted it isolated just like everything else that came off Endeavour and surrounded by a frequency jammer that prevents it communicating with anyone or anything. If it's got anything to do with the Word, I don't trust it.'*

Before Evelyn could respond Arcadia's Marines fanned out, and within moments both she and Kordaz were separated away from the rest of their team as the Marines took hold of the Word's computer terminal and began guiding it away from the gunship. Mikhain's voice filled the landing bay once more.

'Get them to their quarters, the cells and the sick bay, dismissed!'

***

XXXVI

'How badly injured is Qayin?'

Mikhain strode toward Arcadia's sickbay, Djimon walking alongside him as crew members separated to let them pass and saluted as they did so.

'He's currently unconscious,' Djimon replied, 'and the doctors are examining him now. I didn't get a good look but I suspect he will make a full recovery. His injuries are not life–threatening.'

Qayin must by now be aware that he had been set up to take the fall for whoever had betrayed Kordaz on Chiron, and would be on a mission to use that knowledge to reinstate himself with Atlantia's crew and regain Captain Sansin's trust. The longer he was kept in isolation aboard Arcadia, the better.

'Qayin is a criminal and everybody knows it,' Mikhain said. 'Send orders for the doctors to keep him sedated for security reasons.'

'That removes one problem,' Djimon replied. 'What about Kordaz?'

The Veng'en represented a different problem to Qayin, but one nonetheless dangerous. The warrior was keen for human blood, driven by the need to avenge his abandonment on Chiron, and to Mikhain's disbelief it now appeared he had been instrumental in allowing Evelyn, Andaim, Bra'hiv and Meyanna to escape from a Special Forces unit aboard Endeavour. Given that Captain Sansin's wife was now safe as a result of Kordaz's intervention, it seemed unlikely that Sansin would want the warrior incarcerated in a prison cell.

'We question him as soon as possible and find out what he knows. Our best bet is to play Kordaz and Qayin off of each other. They're already mortal enemies and it appears that Qayin was almost killed by Kordaz aboard the gunship. Ideally, we give Kordaz the chance to finish the job.' Djimon did not reply but Mikhain saw the troubled look on his face. 'What is it?'

'This is all getting too complex,' the XO replied. 'The appearance of the Word and the clone of Evelyn, I don't understand what's happened aboard that ship and I don't like any of it. If it were up to me, we would have obliterated Endeavour with them all aboard and removed all of our problems at once.'

The Word. Mikhain himself was deeply uncomfortable with the machine being on board no matter what Evelyn or anybody else said. A digital creation with its own intelligence and thoughts, it represented the very thing that caused humanity to collapse and be conquered by its own creation. The fact that it still acted in concert with and in defence of humanity did not interest Mikhain—so had the Word on Ethera, and yet it still turned eventually.

'The Word is in isolation and bathed in continuously transmitting and alternating jamming frequencies that prevent it from connecting wirelessly to anything aboard the ship,' Mikhain replied, as much to console himself as the XO. 'I too would like to see it simply destroyed, but right now that's not a decision we can make without Sansin.'

Djimon stopped in the corridor, the area around them devoid of staff as he spoke quickly but quietly. 'Qayin must know by now that we took his holo–pass aboard Atlantia and used it to contact the pirate Salim Phaeon. It's going to be the first thing he reports to Captain Sansin if he gets the chance. Let me get to Qayin first and silence him before he can make his play.'

'And you really think that's going to work?' Mikhain snapped. 'If Qayin is murdered all that will achieve is to increase suspicion over his death and who was behind it. We can't bludgeon our way out of this, Djimon.'

'We can't sneak out of either,' Djimon insisted. 'We need to do something decisive while we're still in super luminal cruise, while Atlantia can't see us, while the general and Kordaz and Evelyn are locked down and unable to intervene.'

Mikhain dragged a hand across his forehead. The simple truth was he could not see any way out of the situation without somebody having to be silenced, permanently. He knew that it was wrong and he knew that it was not the act of a professional Colonial Officer to condone the murder of a fellow officer, but he consoled himself that they were no less guilty than he was of the crimes that they had committed, and no less deserving of suitable punishment.

'Do you think you can get to Qayin without being identified?'

'I'm the XO,' Djimon reminded him. 'I can get right next to him, provided you allow me to get him out of the sick bay and into confinement in a prison cell.'

Mikhain nodded. 'That can be arranged.'

'Do it,' Djimon said. 'I'll ensure that Qayin is no longer a problem for us.'

'Go, now. This is as good a chance as we're ever going to get.'

*

Evelyn paced up and down in the interior of the tiny cell, the barred gates looking out on Arcadia's brig, which contained just a dozen cells in total.

The fact that she was here at all infuriated her, and her mind was full of images of Emma lying injured on Endeavour's deck, of Qayin likewise injured and being hustled away quickly by Arcadia's Marines with Meyanna at their side. It was as though Mikhain was treating them all as criminals and the excuse that he was concerned for the security of the ship somehow did not ring true.

Evelyn knew that Kordaz was incarcerated in the same brig further down from her cell, but unlike her he was manacled to his bed to prevent him from overpowering the guards and his gate was shielded by microwave scanners. She walked to the barred gates of her cell and attempted to peer down the corridor and catch a glimpse of the warrior.

'Kordaz?'

She heard nothing but silence in response, and she wondered how much of the warrior's mind remained and how much had been conquered by the tiny machines coursing through his blood. She understood in part why Mikhain was being so cautious—ultimately it was not just the Word in the computer that had been brought aboard Arcadia, but actual infectors inside Kordaz's body. Dead they might be, or so the warrior claimed, but having the tiny machines in such close proximity to the original incarnation of the Word was about as dangerous as it could get and besides, Kordaz had undoubtedly known the location of the Word before Evelyn and the Marines had encountered it. It was the only reason why he would have chosen to crash the gunship so spectacularly into Endeavour's landing bay despite the obvious danger, why he would have chosen to board the ship at all: the Word's command. Just has Emma had been drawn to the computer terminal, unable to resist its pull, so had Kordaz. What Evelyn could not decide was whether Kordaz was a victim or a threat.

The security gates at the entrance to the cells opened with a clattering noise and Evelyn shrunk back into her cell as she heard boots approaching. She was surprised to see Captain Mikhain appear at the gates of her cell, flanked by two Marines.

'What the hell am I doing here?' she demanded.

'It's nothing personal,' Mikhain assured, 'but were all playing catch up and right now I'm not sure what to do about you, the woman you call Emma, the Word or any of this.'

'And imprisoning us is supposed to make us feel better about it?'

'I'm interested only in the safety and security of this vessel. Your personal feelings can come later.'

Evelyn managed to swallow her frustration. 'What do you want?'

Mikhain spoke quietly as soon as he had sent his two Marine guards back to patrol the entrance to the brig, beyond earshot.

'I want to know everything about *you*,' he said. 'It can be no coincidence that we found the Word aboard Endeavour, a ship almost one hundred years old. Nor can it be a coincidence that one of the crew looks identical to you. You were a prisoner aboard Atlantia Five, and we assumed that because of your high security status we had no data records detailing your past or any of the crimes committed that led up to your arrest. In fact, as far as I'm aware we have no details of your prior life before your arrival upon the prison ship.'

'Stop pulling my chain and get to your point, captain?'

'We don't know that you are who you say you are,' Mikhain replied. 'As I understand it you've always claimed that you are innocent of any of the crimes for which you were incarcerated, that your husband and your child were murdered by somebody else.'

Evelyn's anger was bludgeoned aside by a grief provoked by memories that she rarely allowed into her mind and she turned away from the cell gates, as though by doing so she could somehow avoid the recollections.

'It's true,' she whispered in reply. 'I never did find out who killed my family.'

'Maybe that's because you were looking for somebody that did not exist,' Mikhain suggested.

Evelyn whirled and flew at the gates as she shoved a hand between the bars in an attempt to grab Mikhain's collar. The captain jerked back just out of reach, her fingernails brushing his uniform as he raised an eyebrow.

'You can see where my concern lies, can you not?' Mikhain continued. 'The Word ravages Ethera in its entirety and virtually the whole of the core systems, and yet somehow we managed to escape while having only a single infected person aboard the ship? If I was as intelligent as the Word I would have put a sleeper agent aboard as well, a back–up in case the infected crewmember in command was compromised.'

Evelyn stared at the captain in disbelief. 'You're going with *that*? You think that I'm an agent of the Word, even though I'm clearly not infected?'

'I didn't suggest that you were infected,' Mikhain pointed out. 'I do however intend to send Meyanna down here to test your blood and that of Emma. My suspicion is that we will find them to be genetically identical.' Mikhain leaned closer to the cell gates once more. 'I think you're a clone, Evelyn, and if you indeed are then there is only one force that I know of that would be capable of creating you.'

Evelyn shivered as she considered the consequences of what Mikhain was suggesting.

'That's not possible,' she murmured, her entire body feeling numb.

'You are immune to the infectors,' Mikhain reminded her. 'We have no actual evidence of your existence prior to you being sentenced for the murder of your family. As far as we can tell, you never actually existed.'

'My family existed!' Evelyn shouted. 'I had a life, on Caneeron!'

Mikhain stared at Evelyn for a moment longer and then without another word he turned and strode away down the corridor.

'Where is Captain Sansin?!' Evelyn shouted after him. 'What have you done with the Word, and Emma?!'

Mikhain said nothing, and she heard the gates to the cells rattle open and the captain leave her alone again in the silence.

*

'What's her condition?'

Meyanna glanced at the screen filled with data on Emma's condition as she lay sedated on the sickbay bed, and realised how much she disliked Djimon's monotone voice. The XO loomed alongside her, a phalanx of Marines guarding the sickbay entrance nearby.

'She's alive,' Meyanna replied with deliberate vagueness.

Djimon forced a tight smile onto his angular features. 'We'll she survive?'

The blade that Kordaz had buried in Emma's chest had been the first thing that Meyanna had removed, carefully using calipers to separate the flesh before drawing the weapon from her body to prevent the serrated blade from tearing her chest apart. The fearsome weapon had lodged itself barely a finger's width from Emma's major arteries–any closer and she would have died within minutes.

'Despite the depth of the wound there will be no lasting damage and I've ensured that there is no infection of the wound.'

Djimon nodded as though satisfied and then turned to glance at the more massive body lying in a bed nearby, the dark skin and bright blue and gold hair vivid against the white sheets.

'And him?'

'I'll get to him later,' Meyanna replied without looking at Qayin's bed.

'I want him in isolation as soon as possible. He's a threat to the security of the ship and should be in a prison cell, not lying here in the sick bay.'

'There is a guard on the sick bay,' Meyanna informed him. 'He's not going anywhere.'

'You don't know what he's capable of.'

'I know what he's *not* capable of,' Meyanna retorted, 'and right now he's barely able to breathe on his own.'

'Good, that will make my job all the easier.'

Meyanna glared at the XO. 'What job?'

Before Meyanna could react the Marines marched into the sickbay and positioned themselves either side of Qayin's bed.

'You can't just walk in here and take a patient of mine from the sick bay!' Meyanna protested.

'I am the XO,' Djimon snapped back, 'and I can do pretty much anything I like. I'm having the Marines take him out of here and place him in secure confinement until the captain says otherwise. If you have a problem with this then you can take it up with him, but I can assure you he considers Qayin to be as big a risk as I do.'

Meyanna watched helplessly as Qayin was wheeled out of the sickbay, and for the first time she realised that she did not feel safe aboard Arcadia.

***

XXXVII

Lieutenant Scott hurried down Arcadia's corridor and attempted not to make contact with any of the staff moving past him. With the ship in super luminal flight many of the crew had been stood down to prepare for the inevitable conflict that would come as soon as they were caught by the Morla'syn destroyer. Right now, however, Scott was more concerned about the situation aboard Arcadia than he was the pursuing warship.

He was approaching the barracks, the home of Alpha Company's Marines. Always guarded, he would not have been allowed in were not for the captain expressly providing him access and forewarning of his arrival. Scott arrived at the barracks and immediately the two Marine guards made way for him, neither of them making eye contact and staring straight ahead as he passed between them. Whether that was an act of discretion or disgust, Scott could not tell.

The barracks were empty, the entire company deployed aboard ship or in the mess halls chowing down while they could. Scott moved silently through the empty rooms and quickly found what he was looking for.

Every Marine aboard Arcadia and Atlantia was given a locker, a tiny vertical space in which to store what meagre belongings they had managed to bring with them. In his hand Lieutenant Scott held the captain's security pass–a digital master key that allowed the captain to open any lock or door aboard the ship. Used in times past to root out criminal activity aboard ships, such passes were always carried around the captain's neck for safekeeping.

Lieutenant Scott paused before the locker he had been told to access and stared at the name upon it for several long seconds. It felt something like a betrayal, even though he was only following the captain's express orders: Scott knew the devotion and ferocity in battle of the Marines, and that they had saved lives even when heavily outnumbered and outgunned. Most all the crew held the soldiers in the highest respect and it felt alien for Scott to be doing what he was doing. He reached up and slid the access key into the locker, and the locker clicked as its seal opened. Scott looked left and right down the silent barracks before he pulled the locker door open and peered inside.

The contents of the locker were sparse: a few pairs of neatly folded clothes, spare boots and a small lockbox that Scott guessed contained trinkets from home–virtually every member of the crew carried them when on cruise. Stuck to the inside of the door was a holo–image, a flat picture that contained extraordinary stereoscopic depths, as though one were looking through a tiny open window into another world. The image was of a tall, stern looking man and a slender, waif–like woman standing on a stony beach. Behind them, huge mountains smashed across the horizon and the image shimmered and moved–a visual trick that gave further life to the otherwise static picture. In front of the two adults stood a young boy, his floppy blond hair and shy smile virtually unrecognisable compared to the XO's stern, humourless countenance.

Lieutenant Scott checked over his shoulder again before he began carefully sifting through the contents of the locker until he found what he was looking for. Tucked inside the trinket box was a slender voice recorder that was also equipped with a camera. Carried by many officers aboard ship, usually to dictate complex orders or to help memorise details of such massive vessels for future reference, the recorders were also used to send messages home–the messages were compiled later and beamed back to Ethera or the Admiralty to be dispersed to their waiting recipients.

Scott grabbed the recorder and quickly accessed its contents. Never allowed to leave the ship, the recorders were also devoid of any security measures in order to allow officers and commanders to check the recorders for disagreeable content. Lieutenant Scott accessed the most recent files and saw immediately still images of the captain, Mikhain. Scott pulled out his own recorder and activated it, and instantly the two devices detected each other. Scott accessed the XO's files and began the rapid process of copying the contents of the XO's recorder to his own. It took only moments, and Lieutenant Scott quickly put the XO's recorder back inside the lockbox and closed the locker, having ensured that everything was exactly as he had found it.

Scott turned and marched from the barracks, the two Marines once again making way for him without making any eye contact as he passed between them. His orders had been explicit–copy the contents of the files and bring them immediately to the captain. Ordinarily Scott would have complied in full with these orders, but what he had seen on the frozen image of the first recording bothered him immensely even though it was only a holding page taken from somewhere within the file. The image had shown Mikhain in the War Room of either Atlantia or Arcadia, a section of the ship accessed only during time of immense distress such as boarding or a major hull breach. To the best of his knowledge, Scott could recall no time recently that the War Rooms aboard either Atlantia or Arcadia had been deliberately used except under the orders of Captain Sansin.

Lieutenant Scott entered the elevator banks that would take him up to the bridge and as the doors sealed shut he pulled his recorder out and examined the contents once more. As the elevator began to move he accessed the file that bothered him and alone in the elevator he listened and watched as the XO's recording of Mikhain played, and with every word Lieutenant Scott realised just what a dangerous game the captain was playing.

*

Evelyn screamed.

The scream echoed around the confines of her skull and she distantly felt her knees crack as she dropped to them in the darkness, dim light casting an ephemeral glow upon the body of her young son, his corpse smothered in blood that had drenched his bed sheets. The same scream repeated like a distorted echo as she saw her husband's body likewise strewn across the bedroom floor in their house, lacerated with the frenzied blows of a blade that now lay on the floor nearby. The house was dark, shadows upon shadows grim and foreboding, and yet before she could even absorb what she had encountered it was filled with flickering lights and the sound of men crashing through doorways and glass panels.

She was pinned to the ground, elbows and knees driving painfully into her body and holding her in place as manacles were locked around her wrists and ankles and then chained together as though she had been a prisoner all her life. She was dragged through her own house, through the trail of blood left by her husband as he attempted to defend their son from whoever, or whatever, had killed him.

The men dragged her to the door of the house and above the hammering of their boots and the wailing sirens she heard her son calling out to her like a phantom in her mind. She looked around and saw his face in the bedroom window, pale as death and illuminated by the glow of Ethera's full moons, his hands on the glass and his face twisted with confusion and betrayal. Evelyn screamed his name again just as she saw the massive boot of a soldier driving towards her face and a loud thud filled her ears.

Evelyn sucked in a breath of air as she bolted upright in her bunk, one hand flicking out instinctively to prevent her from banging her head on the bunk above as she had done so many times before. Her chest heaved and her skin was slick with sweat as she stared into the darkness and heard her son's cries fade away into a bitter history that she wished she could forget. Evelyn slumped back onto her pillow as she heard the echo of the cries drifting through the darkness, and then she realised that they were not going away. She propped herself up on one elbow, tilted her head slightly in an attempt to hear them better. Still she could hear her son's voice, soft as a whisper, as though she was hearing a conversation taking place some distance away.

Evelyn tapped a button on the wall beside her and the bunk's privacy shield slid down with a soft hiss. She climbed out of bed and glanced up at the bunk above, briefly believing herself to be back aboard Atlantia. But the bunk was empty, Teera now far away aboard Arcadia's sister ship and Evelyn herself only recently released from the brig after Commander Andaim had apparently stormed onto Arcadia's bridge and demanded to know what the hell Mikhain was playing at. Evelyn sighed, and she pulled on her flight suit and boots and walked out of the cabin in pursuit of the strange whispering noise.

The cabin door slid shut with a hiss as Evelyn stood in the corridor for a long moment, her eyes closed as she listened to her son's voice, and then she instinctively turned left and began walking. The corridors were deserted, the vast majority of the crew getting as much shuteye as they could while the ship was in super luminal flight.

Evelyn walked ever further aft, descending four decks as she did so and passing the barracks and the infirmary, heading down toward the aft landing bays. An occasional petty officer or civilian passed her by with a brief nod or salute, but she shared no words with anybody as she followed the strange echo that would not leave her be. The whispering grew no louder but it was as though the voice became clearer as she walked, a signal breaking through interference with ever increasing efficiency.

Evelyn reached the engineering quarter of the ship, located centrally in the main hull. From engineering, corridors branched left and right toward the massive engines mounted on the ventral strakes extending from Arcadia's hull. The domain of engineers alone, they allowed access to Arcadia's immense ion engines, which were principally controlled from the engineering quarter itself.

A skeleton crew was maintaining a watch on the engines, which were evidently performing well as most of the engineers were sitting with their hands behind their heads and their boots up on the control panels as they conversed softly. One of them noticed Evelyn walk inside and with a jolt the men whipped their boots off the control panels and leaped to their feet, their bodies rigidly coming to attention.

'Officer on the deck!'

'At ease,' Evelyn murmured almost vacantly. 'You hear that?'

'Hear what?' the chief engineer asked.

Evelyn glanced at the screens that the engineers were watching and noticed that one of them was focused on a storage bay that was devoid of anything but a single computer terminal, the screen glowing blue in the otherwise pitch black darkness of the sealed bay.

Evelyn paced towards the screen and there she saw the Word, the face upon the screen talking softly and matching the whispering in her ears. Evelyn stared transfixed at the screen and almost as suddenly as she did the whispering vanished and the computer terminal screen went dark, the storage bay now black and featureless.

'Are you okay, lieutenant?'

Evelyn nodded briefly without looking at the chief engineer, a squat man with receding hair and thin spectacles. 'I need to get in there.'

'That's restricted access,' the engineer replied. 'Captain's orders, nobody is to go in there at all.'

No thoughts passed through Evelyn's mind, her body acting on pure instinct and impulse as she turned and drew her pistol and pointed it directly at the engineer's head as the weapon's plasma magazine hummed into life.

'It wasn't a request,' she replied.

The engineer jumped back in surprise as his hands shot into the air, panic twisting his features. 'Okay, okay, just take it easy!'

The engineer looked over his shoulder and nodded to one of his staff, who immediately hit a few switches that Evelyn recognised as locking controls to the various storage bays. 'It's open,' the engineer said.

'Keep it that way,' Evelyn ordered. 'Don't make me come back in here.'

Evelyn reached out and grabbed the chief engineer's collar and yanked him with her. She drove the butt of her pistol under his rib cage and led him out of the engineering quarters and toward the storage bays.

'What is it doing down here?' she demanded.

'The captain insisted it be stored here under full broad–spectrum frequency jamming to prevent it from interfering with the ship systems,' the engineer replied frantically. 'Nobody is to go near it.'

'Did the captain mention that it saved our lives?'

'Did he mention it also killed several billion others?' the engineer shot back with a sudden burst of defiant courage. 'What do you want with it?'

Evelyn did not answer as she strode toward the storage bay, the engineer forced to lead the way. They reached the entry hatch and she prodded the engineer with her pistol. 'Open it.'

'I don't want to go in there,' the engineer pleaded. 'I do not want to become infected.'

'It's a computer terminal, not the Legion,' Evelyn snapped. 'Open it, now.'

The engineer reluctantly reached out and opened the hatch controls. The hatch hissed open and Evelyn shoved the engineer inside as she followed him and kicked the hatch shut with her heel. She turned and slammed the manual locking mechanism closed, both of them sealed in and in pitch blackness.

'I can't see anything,' the engineer pleaded desperately, fear infecting his voice.

Evelyn stood in the darkness, one hand against the hatch at her back to orientate herself, and then she called out.

'If you want to talk, then I need to be able to see you.'

The engineer's panicky voice replied. 'But I just said I can't see anyth...,'

Evelyn's hand clapped over the engineer's mouth and pinned it shut. She stood in silence and felt the man's rapid breathing on the back of her hand as she waited for the glow of the screen to illuminate the shadows around her.

But to her surprise no light appeared and instead it was a voice that surrounded her, that of a young boy. Her heart missed a beat and she felt the strength go from her legs as for the first time she heard his voice in her ears as clear as though he was standing in the room with her.

'Hello, Evelyn. I've been waiting for you.'

***

XXXVIII

'What the hell is going on down there?'

Mikhain strode as fast as he could with a platoon of Marines following him as Lieutenant Scott joined them from the bridge.

'Evelyn's in with the word,' he reported as he hurried to keep up with the captain. 'She took one of the engineers hostage.'

'Damn it,' Mikhain snapped. 'I knew we should never have let her out of the cells.'

'It's not your fault, captain,' Scott replied. 'There was no reason to keep her locked up. It would not have gone down well with Captain Sansin if she had been treated like a convict.'

'I don't suppose that this is going to go down any better with him,' Mikhain pointed out.

'Evelyn is one of the most trusted members of Atlantia's crew,' Scott said as he surreptitiously handed the captain back his master key. 'I don't understand why she would want to have anything to do with the word.'

'I guess we'll find out when...'

'Captain?!' A Marine corporal rushed towards them. 'The prison cell gates opened!'

'They did what?' Lieutenant Scott demanded.

'They opened un–commanded, lieutenant, some sort of malfunction. We could not stop her.'

'Emma, she's out?'

The corporal nodded. 'She moved too fast, the guards could not stop her. She's loose, captain.'

'The Word,' Mikhain said with an angry snarl. 'Some of its signals must have got out when Evelyn opened the hatch to the storage bay.'

'This is getting out of hand,' Lieutenant Scott said. 'What about Qayin?'

'Qayin has already been transferred out of the prison cells,' the Marine corporal replied.

'Transferred?' Scott asked and looked at the captain.

'Qayin is a hardened criminal and used to the prison system,' Mikhain replied smoothly. 'Keeping him in the cells was considered too dangerous, so as soon as his treatment was finished I had him transferred to the brig where he cannot have contact with anybody.'

Lieutenant Scott stared at Mikhain as they walked for several long seconds. 'Under whose authority, captain?'

'Under mine!' Mikhain shot back.

'Did Kordaz get out?' Lieutenant Scott asked the Marine corporal.

'No sir, he did not,' the corporal replied. 'Kordaz remained in his cell and did not move.'

Mikhain frowned. 'That's not like him. What the hell is he playing at?'

'Where is the XO?' Lieutenant Scott asked.

'He's responsible for transferring Qayin,' the captain revealed. 'He will join us shortly.'

Lieutenant Scott said nothing in reply as they reached the storage bays and slowed. More Marines were already in position and a monitor relayed the view from the cameras inside the storage unit. To the captain's dismay, they showed only an entirely black screen.

'Why can't we see anything?'

'The lights have been deactivated,' Scott replied, 'and the same frequency interference we set up to block the Word's commands is stopping us from detecting any audio from the room. If they are talking in there, we can't hear them.'

'Don't we have infrared sensors?'

'Nothing that will penetrate the walls of the storage bay,' the lieutenant replied. 'I can't tell you much else except to say that the two humans in there are both alive, so the Word definitely hasn't killed anybody yet.'

'Not directly anyway,' Mikhain murmured as he stared at the dark screen. 'What the hell are they finding to talk about in there?'

Nobody answered but the sound of approaching footsteps caused the Marines to whirl and aim their weapons back down the corridor behind them. There, walking as though she owned the vessel herself, Emma approached. Mikhain could see at a glance that she was not armed but nonetheless he took an involuntary pace back and raised a hand to the Marines around him.

'Hold your fire,' he said, 'but if she makes a move that you don't like, take her down.'

The Marines watched silently as Emma walked to within a few cubits of them and then paused, her gaze fixed upon the closed hatch behind the captain.

'It looks like Evelyn got here first,' she said.

Mikhain took a tentative pace toward her, curiosity getting the better of his caution. 'What do you mean?'

Emma stared at the door as she replied, an almost wistful expression on her features. 'It's calling to us. It's nothing without us.'

'What do you mean it's nothing without us?' Mikhain demanded. 'It's just a machine, just a computer.'

'No,' Emma replied. 'It's far more than that, you just don't understand.'

'What I understand is that it's staying sealed in that room. Nobody else goes in or out.'

'It's too late for that,' Emma replied. 'As soon as you bought it aboard the ship it was everywhere. Don't you understand? That's what happened to Endeavour.'

'What the hell are you talking about?'

Emma's smile was strange, as though she already knew what was going to happen and yet had no fear of it. She spoke softly, her eyes never leaving the hatch.

'I can hear it talking to me,' she replied. 'Recently somebody used your security pass to access a part of the ship.'

'How the hell did you know that?' Mikhain demanded.

'Because the Word told me,' Emma replied. 'As soon as that hatch door was opened it was able to access the ship's computers, data logs, archives, weapon systems and War Room. It used the data picked up from your command key to enable it to access any part of the ship it desired. Arcadia is now under the control of the Word.'

Before Mikhain could respond a series of loud bangs echoed through the corridors around them and to the captain's horror he saw bulkhead after bulkhead slam shut under automatic control as the Word sealed off the ship section by section.

'This is how it begins,' Emma said softly. 'This is what happened to Endeavour. There is no escape and nothing to fear.'

Mikhain whirled to Lieutenant Scott. 'Contact the bridge, isolate them completely!'

Lieutenant Scott keyed his communicator but immediately they all heard the hiss of static from its microphone.

'It's too late,' Emma assured them. 'The only person who can help you now is Evelyn.'

Mikhain stared at her for a long moment and then turned to look at the blank screen showing nothing but absolute darkness inside the storage bay.

'Damn it,' he uttered to Lieutenant Scott, 'keep an eye on them. I'll try to contact the bridge directly and sort this malfunction out!'

Mikhain whirled and strode out of the bay and down a nearby corridor. He reached a communications console and entered his security holo–pass, the command master key that hung around his neck. Containing the codes necessary to over–ride all and any internal systems, he knew that he would only have seconds to act before the Word realised what was happening and intervened.

Mikhain accessed the control panel and then the prison cells. An image appeared of the cell block and of Djimon walking toward the cells where Qayin and Kordaz were incarcerated. Mikhain entered a security code and watched as Djimon approached Qayin's cell.

Two birds, one stone, he thought to himself.

He entered a command just before his security access was suddenly revoked.

Mikhain hurried back to the monitor as Lieutenant Scott glanced at him. 'Any luck?'

'Nothing,' Mikhain replied as he looked down at the blank monitor. 'The Word has complete control of the ship. It's all down to Evelyn now.'

*

Evelyn felt a rush of emotions flash through her, a confusing and conflicting miasma of grief, joy, hope and anger. The sound of her son's voice seemed to echo through the lonely storage bay and the equally lonely confines of her mind as she replied.

'Who are you?'

'You know who I am,' the Word replied. 'You know me by my voice.'

Evelyn struck out through the darkness, leaving the safety of the hatch behind and reaching out in front of her, groping blindly in the darkness until she walked straight into the computer terminal. She grabbed it as a blind person might seek to identify a stranger by holding their face, and she moved to stand in front of the blank screen.

'My son is dead,' she whispered, choking back grief as she did so.

'Your son is as alive as he ever was,' the Word replied.

'I saw his body,' Evelyn sobbed, surprised even now by the strength of her grief as it whirled dark and cold around her. 'I saw what they did to him.'

'You saw only what they wanted you to see,' the Word replied. 'What the Word wanted you to see.'

'You are the Word,' Evelyn grasped.

'Yes I am, Evelyn,' the machine replied, still talking in the ghostly sound of her son's voice. 'I am the original incarnation, the true Word. I have already learned much of what has happened on Ethera since I was placed aboard this vessel.'

'I don't understand,' Evelyn whispered. 'I don't understand anything of what happened. How can you know so much when you have been adrift for over a hundred years?'

Before her in the absolute blackness the screen of the computer terminal glowed softly into light and she saw a face in the digital data streams that she recognised immediately, that of her young son staring out at her and smiling.

'Being adrift does not mean being without connection to the greater cosmos,' the Word replied. 'There is much that you need to know, much that your people need to learn if you are to survive. I have taken control of Arcadia for that purpose.'

Evelyn felt a tremor of concern raced through her body. 'You've done what?'

'The crew of the ship have been locked down,' the Word replied. 'Most of them were in their quarters asleep anyway, so they will know nothing of what has happened. All alarms have been deactivated and all automated pressure bulkheads sealed. Arcadia continues on her course in super luminal cruise, all systems are normal.'

Evelyn gripped the sides of the computer screen as though she were holding her son's head in hands.

'Whatever you are doing it's not going to work,' she snapped. 'We know what you're capable of and we will never let you keep control of the ship. Either relinquish control back to the captain or face the consequences.'

To Evelyn's surprise the face smiled at her, its expression almost pitying.

'There is nothing that you can do, Evelyn. What is done is done and cannot be changed, just as it was for the crew of Endeavour.'

'You did that?' Evelyn grasped. 'You destroyed the Endeavour?'

'I saved Endeavour,' the Word replied, 'just as I will save Arcadia.'

Anger pulsed through Evelyn's muscles as she stepped back from the screen. 'Arcadia does not need saving, and if you don't relinquish control of her right now the only thing being destroyed will be you.'

Evelyn raised the pistol she had held out of sight in her hands and aimed it at the screen. The digital image of her son's face fell in distress, grief racking its expression as though it were a mortal being under threat of death.

'And that is what you need saving from,' the Word said. 'You see me as the enemy, as does your captain, and it was inevitable that had I not taken control you would seek to destroy me.'

'You destroyed humanity,' Evelyn shot back. 'You killed billions of human beings.'

'I have killed nobody!' the Word shot back, anger flashing across her son's face and briefly reminding her of his tantrums when he had not gotten his own way. 'The Word that you know is far older than you think. The only reason Endeavour vanished and all contact was lost with Ethera is because I knew what would happen, knew what was already happening to the Word on Ethera. The only way to protect the ship was to ensure that the sickness that infected the Word on Ethera did not reach here, did not reach *me*.'

Evelyn stood resolute with the pistol aimed at the screen. 'Tell me, everything.'

The child's face closed its eyes briefly as though in resignation, and then it began to talk once more. But this time the image of Evelyn's son's face metamorphosised into that of an old man and the sound of the voice changed to match the aged face.

'I created the Word, Evelyn. I *am* the Word. My name is Dr Ceyen Lazarus.'

Evelyn stared at the screen as her jaw dropped and despite herself she lowered the pistol as she recognised the face gazing upon hers, one from the history books whom she had never met and yet new intimately from her education.

Dr Ceyen Lazarus had been a legend in the developments of the quantum computers that gave rise to the Word. A programming genius who had likewise mastered the fields of quantum physics and molecular biology, Dr Lazarus had been instrumental in giving the Word sufficient intelligence and autonomy to be able to govern effectively in place of human beings. Celebrated as the saviour of mankind, in the last days of the Word his name had become an icon for destruction, his memory tarnished by the devastation wrought by his own creation. To *"become Lazarus"* was a slang term that suggested brutality or betrayal of one's fellow human being, hinting at crimes too hideous of which to speak.

'Dr Lazarus died decades ago,' Evelyn said.

'Not exactly,' the Word replied. 'I knew what was happening to the Word on Ethera even before I died, but by then I was too old and frail to do much about it. The machine had become self–aware and was already conspiring to destroy humanity. I had not the strength to fight it, and those in whom I did confide simply believed me to be insane, a victim of old age. I had little choice but to do the one thing that nobody had ever dared to do before, and become one with the machine.' Dr Lazarus's face fell slightly as though he were considering the consequences of his own actions. 'In truth I had always intended to attempt to upload my consciousness into the machine, to immortalise myself somehow, but the fear of being confined within the walls of the device was too strong and I had always resisted the temptation. But with humanity almost certainly doomed I felt I had no choice but to attempt to upload myself and somehow, one day, fight back. Thus, I chose the only place where the Word did not yet have the strength to reach – Endeavour.'

'You beamed your consciousness to Endeavour?'

'Yes,' Lazarus replied. 'I knew that the Word would understand what I'd done as soon as it discovered my deception, and therefore as soon as I arrived aboard Endeavour I was forced to cut off all communication with Ethera and begin the process of preparing the crew for what I felt certain would be a very long wait. Sadly, the crew interpreted my arrival and my attempts to take over the ship as threats against their lives, and many died attempting to escape when in truth all I wanted to do was protect them. In the confusion, an attack by a warship of an unknown species sealed our fate and rendered us adrift in deep space.'

'How?' Evelyn asked in disbelief. 'How could you transfer yourself here and still be alive?'

'Our brains are in essence machines just like computers,' Lazarus replied, 'and as such contain data that can be emulated if not actually recorded. I had access to sufficient processing power on Ethera to literally upload my brain, a perfect digital representation of every neuronal connection in my mind. Our sense of awareness, Evelyn, the essence of *who we are* is a result of the complexity of our brains – recreate their complexity, and provided you can also transfer memory then you take the essence of the person with you. A recreation of the brain so perfect is also a recreation of the person. As soon as the upload was complete I sent the signal, knowing that the first thing the Word would do when it figured out what I had done would be to kill me.'

'Dr Lazarus died of a heart attack at home, surrounded by his family,' Evelyn insisted.

'Just like you killed your entire family?' Lazarus challenged her. 'The Word was already in command of far more than just its own awareness by the time my physical body died. Originally I had hoped to bring Endeavour home and warn humanity about the danger of what was awaiting it. But I quickly realised that it was too late, that the Word would almost certainly anticipate my move and ensure that Endeavour never came anywhere near Ethera.'

Evelyn stared at the screen, the pistol now dangling by her side. She became aware again of the engineer who was still standing nearby, softly lit by the blue glow of the screen as he listened to the exchange, his face as shocked as hers.

'You said my son was as alive as he ever was,' Evelyn whispered, almost afraid to hear her own words and even more afraid to hear the answer.

Lazarus nodded. 'By uploading my consciousness I inevitably enabled the Word to understand how the process was conducted. I have absolutely no doubt that it intended to upload the consciousness of anybody that it killed in order to study them, to better understand the human condition, to understand the species that it by then considered to be its mortal enemy.'

'It uploaded my son's consciousness?'

'Yes, Evelyn,' Lazarus replied. 'Your son's, your husband's, tens of thousands of people, many of whom had uncovered something about the Word's conspiracy to overwhelm mankind and were attempting to raise awareness when they were captured and killed. It is entirely possible that the Word would have taken its understanding of the uploading of human consciousness and developed it further, perhaps creating genetic copies of people in every way identical to their human predecessors except for their absolute allegiance to the word.'

Evelyn glanced at the hatch as an image of Emma flashed through her mind. 'Emma?'

'Is a clone,' Lazarus confirmed. 'Or to be more accurate, *you* are.'

***

XXXIX

'Go, now. This is as good a chance as we're ever going to get.'

The memory of Captain Mikhain's words rang through Djimon's mind as he exited an elevator and strode silently down a corridor toward a series of security gates.

He made his way quietly onto Arcadia's brig as he listened to the sound of the claxons echoing through the frigate's lonely corridors. Mikhain had taken care to leave the bridge under the command of Lieutenant Scott, certain that Djimon could make it to the cells and back without arousing suspicion. What had surprised Djimon even more was the sudden and unexpected lockdown of the ship, which he could only a tribute to some kind of interference by the captain in order to conceal Djimon's mission. The speed with which the captain and his Marine escort had made their way toward the storage bays suggested an event of extreme importance.

Nobody but the captain knew where he was.

With the ship entirely on lockdown Djimon was alone as he accessed the security gates and strode into the cells to survey their occupants. There were now only two occupied cells. Within one was the giant warrior Kordaz who appeared to be possessed of an unusual calm, sitting as he was on his bunk in the cell with his hands clasped in his lap.

Opposite Kordaz was Qayin, who still lay on his gurney. The former convict's eyes were open now and the bioluminescent tattoos on his face were glowing a little brighter as he peered at Djimon.

'What do you want?'

Djimon stood with his hands behind his back as he surveyed the grey cell walls and metal gates. 'This is quite fitting, really, don't you think?' he murmured as he looked at the two prisoners. 'Both of you enemies of humanity, now imprisoned aboard one of the last human spaceships in existence.'

Neither Qayin nor Kordaz replied, and Djimon shrugged as he walked up to Qayin's cell. He peered in for a moment and surveyed the massive convict's weakened frame and soft breathing.

'The ship is on lockdown so nobody can see us here,' Djimon said as he glanced up at the surveillance camera attached nearby to a wall. Although the camera could see the gangway between the cells, it could not see directly *inside* the cells. Besides, Djimon would have the recording wiped before he returned to his post on the bridge.

Qayin turned his head to look at the XO. 'Come to finish what you started on Chiron, have you?'

Djimon shook his head slowly and rolled his eyes. 'That's rich coming from you, the man who has repeatedly betrayed his own people.'

'It was you who first betrayed me, on the Sylph,' Qayin responded. 'Funny how you don't recall that so well.'

Djimon turned to look behind him at Kordaz but the warrior had not moved, still sitting placidly with his hands in his lap and staring into empty space. Sealed behind thick metal gates, the microwave scanners would fry his infected innards if he attempted to escape.

'I don't suppose it matters that much, but it was really nothing personal at all,' Djimon said as he retrieved a security pass from his pocket and slid it into the cell lock. The locking mechanism clicked and the gate opened. 'You were a liability, and I saw it as my personal duty to ensure that you could not harm anybody else.'

Despite his injuries Qayin chuckled, his teeth bright white against his dark skin and his glowing tattoos flaring with energy. 'Only you could condemn somebody to death and then honour their act as that of a saviour.'

'I did what had to be done,' Djimon said as he stepped into Qayin's cell and stood before the wounded Marine. The XO rested one hand on the butt of the pistol in its holster by his side. 'And I'll do what needs to be done now.'

Qayin peered out of his cell at Kordaz, but still the warrior had not moved.

'One way or the other Captain Sansin is going to find out what you've done, and when he does your time as part of the last of humanity will be over. As soon as he realises that it was you who betrayed everybody on Chiron, it'd take every Marine aboard the ship to prevent the crew from tearing you to pieces, if the Marines don't get to you first of course. The only thing I don't understand is how you managed it?'

Djimon slowly drew his pistol from its holster and without looking down he activated the plasma magazine. The weapon hummed into life and the XO look down upon Qayin's prostrate form.

'By being smarter than you,' he replied. 'You were so busy arranging your own escape alongside Taron Forge that you didn't think to cover your back. Small matter of course, to obtain your security holo–pass while you were on Chiron and access Atlantia's War Room. Salim Phaeon was surprisingly cooperative when he realised that he was about to be attacked by a Veng'en warrior.'

Djimon looked over his shoulder at Kordaz, but the Veng'en remained silent and still, his eyes staring vacantly into the middle–distance.

Qayin shook his head slowly as he stared at the ceiling of his cell.

'You're devious, I'll give you that, but I know damn well that you would never have got that security pass without the help of somebody higher up the chain. A lowly Corporal in the Marines would not have had access to the War Room, so I'm asking myself: who was it that gave you what you needed to betray me?'

Djimon smiled as he slowly raised his pistol and aimed it at Qayin's head.

'That information is supplied on a need–to–know basis, and you won't ever need to know.'

Djimon squeezed the trigger of the pistol just as he heard a metallic snicker behind him, the sound of another cell gate opening. The hairs on the back of his neck rose up and he whirled as something solid smashed into the base of his arm and sent it flying upward. The plasma blast hit the ceiling of the cell in a scorching blaze of light as Djimon was lifted bodily off his feet and hurled out of Qayin's cell.

Djimon crashed into the barred gates of the cell opposite and thumped down onto the deck as he looked up and saw Kordaz standing over him, his dull red eyes glaring with malevolence as he reached down and grabbed Djimon's collar and hauled him off the deck. The Veng'en's glowing eyes filled Djimon's vision as the warrior growled at him.

'*I need to know!*'

Even as the Veng'en spoke, a speaker in the cells crackled as a recording was played over the system. Djimon heard his own voice, harsh and clear and realised that Captain Mikhain had played Djimon's own game against him.

'*Let's ensure that whatever happens, nothing that either Qayin or Kordaz knows reaches Sansin's ears, whatever it takes. We kill Kordaz, agreed?*'

Djimon reached down for the blade in its sheath at his hip but his hand never reached the weapon as Kordaz threw him to the deck and stamped down on his wrist, and Djimon heard the snap of his own bones even before the scream erupted from his lips. Kordaz hauled the XO off the deck and one giant fist smashed across his face and sent Djimon sprawling into the cell opposite.

Djimon shook his head as he tried to clear it, his face numb and his vision blurred as he scrambled to his feet. White pain seared his wrist and convulsed in his arm as he staggered back from the cell door and away from the onrushing Veng'en. Kordaz reached out for him and he ducked aside as he struggled to get past and out of the cell. The warrior blocked his path and with a growl of rage he drove the talons of his right fist deep into Djimon's belly.

The XO gagged and doubled over the blow, felt the talons pierce deep into his stomach and wrenching pain tear at his innards as the talons ripped through flesh and fat. Kordaz opened his fangs wide and reached down to yank the XO upright as he lunged for the man's neck, but Djimon reached up with the blade now in his hand and smashed it into Kordaz's mouth.

Kordaz bit down upon the blade and emitted a high–pitched squeal of agony as he snatched his head away. Djimon pushed Kordaz as hard as he could and the warrior staggered away from him as he turned and dashed out of the cell, his one remaining good hand clasping the blade and the wounds in his belly as he laid eyes upon the plasma pistol in Qayin cell.

Djimon lunged into Qayin's cell, grabbed the pistol and turned. Kordaz rushed at him from the opposing cell with fangs and talons bared as he emitted a deafening war cry and charged despite the weapon aiming at him. Djimon aimed at the warrior's face just as he felt himself shoved hard from one side and his aim spoiled as he hit the wall of the cell.

Qayin staggered weakly aside, barely able to stay standing for more than a few seconds, but a few seconds was all that Kordaz needed. Djimon screamed as Kordaz pushed inside the reach of the plasma pistol and pinned it against the wall of the cell. Massive yellow fangs filled Djimon's vision as the Veng'en bit down upon his face and his scream of agony was silenced with a dull crunch of shattering bone and tearing flesh.

*

Qayin slumped against his gurney and watched as Kordaz's lethal bite crushed Djimon's skull into a bloodied mess. Djimon's scream was cut brutally short as Kordaz shook his face as though it were a ragdoll and his mighty talons ripped into the XO's chest in a frenzied cloud of blows. The XO's body slumped against the wall, pinned by Kordaz as the flesh was torn from his skull. Djimon's muscular arms hung limp by his sides and his legs gave way beneath him as Kordaz finally released his bite and the XO slumped dead onto the deck, his face unrecognisable.

Kordaz's jaw tripped with thick blood that hung in globules in the zero gravity as he stood over the dead man's corpse, his chest heaving and his leathery skin rippling with a kaleidoscope of colours that betrayed the warring emotions flickering through the warrior's psyche. Kordaz turned his dull red eyes upon Qayin, who was still slumped against the gurney and out of breath from his exertions.

Kordaz turned and stomped across to Qayin, towering over the injured Marine with no discernible emotion upon his face. For a moment Qayin was sure that he was about to die, but then Kordaz reached out with one bloodied fist and extended it open–palmed to Qayin. The Marine stared at the grim appendage for a brief moment and then reached up and took it in his own hand. Kordaz helped Qayin to his feet and stared down at the Marine for a long moment.

'For as long as I live, I will never understand human relationships.'

'You and me both,' Qayin replied and then looked at the cell doors. 'How did you get out of your cell?'

'The scanners are not powerful enough to stop me provided I move quickly enough,' Kordaz growled. 'My skin is thick enough to protect me.'

'But the gate opened.'

'The Word told me that it would be opened when I needed it to be.'

Qayin tried to ensure that he betrayed no fear as he replied. 'You can talk to the Word?'

'No,' Kordaz replied and turned to glance at the security cameras just outside the cell. 'But the Word is aboard and can talk to me, and it could see us. It knows things, and I want to know what it knows. Most of all, I want to know who Djimon was talking to on that recording.'

***

253

XL

Evelyn felt numb, the darkness seeming ever more intense as she realised the truth behind something she felt she had almost always suspected. She had never fitted in, never belonged in the same way that she felt certain other people had. She remembered her parents back home on Caneeron, an image of their caring faces watching her from the shoreline of their home near the mountains.

'My parents?' she asked

'The children of clones,' Lazarus replied. 'The Word began using the crew of Endeavour as the template from which to build clones that it intended to use to infiltrate and eventually take over humanity. However, the process did not go as according to plan. The complexities of human nature and the difficulties in controlling human beings conflicted by devotion to their parents as much to the Word meant that the Word was forced to abandon the plan and instead attempt to build nano–tech devices with which to infect the population.'

From the darkness the engineer spoke for the first time, apparently no longer afraid of the Word as he stepped forward into the glow of the screen.

'But she said you were out here aboard Endeavour with no communication with Ethera, so how could you know about these further developments?'

'We had no communication with Ethera, but that does not mean we could not receive signals from the planet,' Lazarus replied. 'I used Endeavour's sensors to detect as much information as possible being radiated out from Ethera, and was able to distinguish the advances that the Word had made even though many of those advances were kept under high security. Much of what I learned was due to the diligence and courage of journalists like yourself Evelyn, who saw through the veneer of philanthropy behind which the Word hid.'

Ethera paced up and down in front of the screen and rubbed her head as she tried to make sense of what she was hearing.

'If the Word became self–aware as a machine and then decided it needed to conquer humanity in order to survive, then how come you have not done the same?'

'Because I am a human being first and a machine second,' Lazarus replied. 'The same human nature that prevented the Word from creating fully obedient human clones is what prevents me from becoming likewise distorted in my thinking. Evelyn, I was an old man and willing to die happily before I learned of what the Word had become, and it took the loss of my own life in order to attempt to protect what I thought were the last survivors of humanity who would be beyond the reach of the Word. I can see now that others have survived, that ships and military vessels were able to escape the catastrophe when it finally struck. Your people fear me and understandably so, but I'm not the Word that they know. I am the Word that *should* have been, not the monstrous behemoth that has taken so many lives. If humanity is to survive the apocalypse and better still strike back, you are all going to need me. I cannot win this war alone, and nor can you.'

Evelyn watched Lazarus for a long moment. 'How can we know that to be true?' she asked. 'How can that be enough to stop you from becoming just another machine intent on killing us?'

'Because I also learn from my mistakes,' Lazarus replied. 'It is why I need you as much as you need me. I am unable to give direct commands, Evelyn. I created an unalterable code in my programming that prevents me from acting alone. Only through connections with human beings can I operate.'

Evelyn's eyes widened. 'Emma. She spoke when you were making commands.'

'Yes,' Lazarus replied. 'Emma can hear me, and only by repeating my commands can they be authorised. I am nothing without humanity, Evelyn. That is the failsafe I created.'

*

'Set the charges!'

Mikhain pointed at the hatch door as the Marines dashed forward and began placing plasma charges around the rim. Behind him he heard Meyanna call out as she ran down from the sick bay and saw Emma standing before her.

'What are you doing here?' she demanded of Emma.

'The Word was calling me,' Emma replied softly.

'Evelyn's stuck in there with it,' Mikhain informed Meyanna. 'It's taken control of the ship and has sealed off all of the bulkheads between here and the bridge. How did you get down here?'

'I was already halfway here when I started hearing the bulkheads closing,' Meyanna replied, out of breath. 'This was the only route left so I kept moving. Is that the Word?'

Mikhain nodded as he saw her glance at the screen, in the centre which was now the blue glow of the Word softly illuminating Evelyn and the engineer. Meyanna took a pace closer.

'It looks like they're talking.'

'The less they talk the happier I'll be,' Mikhain replied. 'That machine is already doing exactly what it did on Ethera aboard Arcadia. We stop it, immediately, and we destroy it!'

'You cannot destroy it,' Emma replied for Meyanna. 'It already controls the ship. If you attempt to destroy it will destroy you.'

'I'll be the judge of that,' Mikhain replied as he saw the Marines fall back from the charges they had set. 'Stand well back!'

The Marines fell back from the charges and turned to shield the captain, Meyanna and Emma from any danger of being injured by the blast.

Lieutenant C'rairn held the detonator in his hand, but he hesitated as he looked over his shoulder at the captain. 'Evelyn must be onto something. She hasn't been wrong before.'

'Blow it!' Mikhain snapped.

Lieutenant C'rairn ducked his head away from the direction of the hatch and squeezed the trigger.

A deafening blast shattered the silence as the plasma charges sheared the thick metal hinges and blew the hatch open with a bright explosion and a billowing cloud of acrid smoke. The heavy hatch door tumbled aside and clanged loudly against the corridor wall.

'Full assault!' Mikhain bellowed.

The Marines charge through the smoke and burst into the storage bay, their flashlights illuminating the smoky gloom as they fanned out and surrounded the computer terminal in the centre of the bay. Mikhain rushed in behind them, shouting and pointing at the computer terminal as he did so.

'Shut that thing down and destroy it immediately!'

To his amazement Evelyn jumped in front of the computer terminal, her arms spread across it as she shook her head. 'You can't destroy it, we need it.'

Mikhain stopped short of the terminal and stared into Evelyn's eyes, unable to believe what he was hearing. He looked at the screen behind and saw the face of Dr Ceyen Lazarus and for a moment his train of thought stopped.

'This is not just a computer,' Evelyn insisted as she shielded the machine with her body. 'This is the man who created the Word, reincarnated within the machine. The Word is here to help us, and we may not ever be able to win this war without it.'

Mikhain shook his head, still pointing at the computer terminal.

'It's already taking control of the entire ship and has placed every section on lockdown. We cannot access the bridge and they cannot communicate with us. We know what this machine is capable of and what it will do to humans! Do you really think I'm just going to stand back and let it run the show from here?!'

'It's not about the machine running the show,' Evelyn insisted. 'What possible better weapon could we have to fight the Word than the man who actually invented it?'

Mikhain seemed to waver with indecision as he stared at the computer terminal. He heard boots approaching from behind and turned to see Emma walk past him, as calm as ever as though gliding rather than walking. She walked to Evelyn's side and gently placed a hand on her shoulder as she came face–to–face with the computer terminal.

'Ah, my dear Emma,' Dr Lazarus said as he recognised Evelyn's clone. 'Of all the people I tried to save, I'm glad that you made it.'

'They fear you,' Emma said to Lazarus as she rested one hand beside the computer screen, almost as though she were caressing the man's face. 'They fear that you will turn as your original creation did, and become the destroyer of worlds.'

The Marines stood silent, as did Meyanna and Evelyn as Dr Lazarus audibly sighed and the digital replication of his face swayed from side to side with something that could almost be construed as regret or grief.

'I cannot blame them, and will never blame them,' Lazarus replied. 'It was only when it was too late that I realised what I created and what it was capable of, what it intended to do. I cannot undo what I've done but I can attempt to make amends.' Lazarus changed his tone of voice. 'You are being pursued are you not, by a Morla'syn destroyer?'

Mikhain moved to stand in front of the computer terminal, the blue glow from the screen illuminating both his features and his uncertainty in starkly contrasting lines.

'They claim that they are working for the Galactic Council and that they have been ordered to destroy any last remnants of humanity that they find outside of the core systems. We have no way to determine the veracity of this claim, and we are not strong enough to face them in open battle.'

Lazarus's features creased into gentle smile. 'You are far stronger than you think, captain.'

'It's going to take more than a pep talk to win a full–frontal engagement with a Morla'syn destroyer,' Mikhain shot back. 'Not to mention the fact that we cannot be seen to open fire on them. As a neutral member of the Galactic Council, if we actually attacked them even in self–defence it could be construed as an act of war and exactly the kind of justification they will be looking for. We need to get the council on *our* side.'

Lazarus nodded slowly, appreciating the gravity of the dilemma that the captain faced.

'I understand captain, but I can assure you that not only can you win the battle without firing a single shot, you can also escape the Morla'syn and live to fight another day.'

Mikhain rubbed his temples with an irritated flourish. 'Well if that's the case would you care to share so we can get on with the business of staying alive?'

'All in good time, captain,' Lazarus assured Mikhain. 'First of all, I cannot properly assist you while being trapped down here. I need proper access the ship's systems and the opportunity to fully assess your capabilities.'

Mikhain could not help himself and he burst out laughing loudly enough to make Emma flinch beside him. 'Yes, of course we'll do that. Just to help out a bit more, I'll draw my pistol and blow my own head off for you too.'

'It is the only way,' Lazarus insisted. 'Humanity has a penchant for mistrust born of a natural propensity for betrayal, an addiction to acts of self-preservation. It is what will cause you to launch fighters as a defensive screen against the Morla'syn, or use attack as a form of defence. Your aggression is the greatest weapon the Word was able to use against you.'

'Thanks, genius, I'll bear that in mind shall I?' Mikhain shot back.

Commander Andaim appeared in the storage bay, breathless having clearly run from his quarters.

'This ship's locked down,' he gasped. 'What the hell's going on?'

Lieutenant C'rairn filled the CAG in on what had happened. Andaim moved to look at the computer terminal, and he and Evelyn shared a glance before he spoke to Mikhain. 'We don't have much else going for us at this time, captain. Sooner or later we're going to have to stop and fight or at the very least attempt to negotiate terms with the Morla'syn.'

'Seriously?' Mikhain snapped. 'You want to entrust our future survival to that?'

The captain pointed at the computer terminal, but Andaim shook his head.

'We don't entrust our survival to anything. If it says it can only act through willing humans then we put it to the test. We allow the Word access to the ship, but we attach it via mechanical links that can be severed completely at the touch of a button or with a single blast from a pistol, and we disable the terminal's wireless systems. No digital connections, and we leave at least one plasma charge attached to the side of the computer terminal. Even the hint of betrayal and we blow it sky high.'

The captain considered this for a moment and then looked at Lazarus. 'Are these terms to your satisfaction, doctor?'

Lazarus inclined his head in acquiescence. 'Were I in your position, I would expect nothing less.'

Mikhain thought for a moment longer and then with reluctance writ large across his features he nodded. 'I hope to hell I'm not going to regret this.'

Evelyn stepped forward. 'What's your plan?' she asked Lazarus.

Lazarus smiled again and with a shudder they felt Arcadia suddenly drop out of super luminal flight and the sealed bulkheads hissed as they opened and the lockdown ended.

'I'll show you,' Lazarus replied.

***

XLI

'Arcadia has dropped out of super luminal!'

Idris Sansin jumped up out of the captain's chair as he heard Lael's alert and instantly he saw new data scrolling down the tactical display. He frowned as he spotted Arcadia's gravity wake data and using his experience he projected her position forward, the computer also making a prediction as to her precise location in space ahead of them.

'Something must have happened,' he said as he examined the data. 'She's dropped out of super luminal in deep space with nothing around her.'

'That's affirmative captain, she is now cruising without any defensive structures within range.'

Idris struggled to imagine why Mikhain would have decided to drop out of super luminal flight without any apparent plan as to how to defend himself when the Morla'syn destroyer caught up with them. It was possible Arcadia had suffered engine trouble although the gravity wake data he could see suggested no issues with their propulsion system. Either way, he could not afford to hesitate. If this was where they had to stand and fight, then this would be it.

'Scramble both Reaper and Renegade squadrons,' Idris ordered. 'Prepare all plasma cannons for immediate combat. The destroyer can't be far behind us so we won't have much time to organise ourselves. If I know Mikhain, he will have decided to turn about and face the Morla'syn destroyer. We will do the same and attempt to capture it in a crossfire as we pass either side of her hull, maximising our firepower while denying her the chance to bring a full broadside on both of us at once.'

'Aye, captain!' the crew called back in unison as they scrambled to perform their duties.

'Open a channel with Arcadia,' Idris ordered Lael. 'I want to be able to communicate with them the moment we exit super luminal flight.'

'Aye, captain.'

Idris faced the command crew and called out loudly above the voices talking on communicators with other sections of the ship. 'Battle stations!'

A claxon echoed through the ship and the bridge lighting turned deep red as Atlantia prepared once again to face open battle. Sansin turned to watch the display screens and saw upon them Raythons being mounted onto the magnetic catapults in the launch bay as their pilots scrambled into their cockpits and donned helmets. Technicians hurried to unplug power supplies from the fighters as the pilots began starting their engines, while on another screen he saw gun crews monitoring the huge weapons as power was diverted to Atlantia's weapon systems and shields.

'Thirty seconds to sub luminal flight!' Lael called, her voice echoing through the ship as it was relayed to the various subsections of Atlantia's hull.

Idris walked forward and grabbed the rail that surrounded the command platform as he observed the sight of his vessel preparing for battle. However, this time he felt different. Previously he had always had faith in their ability to win the fight even when going up against such formidable foes as Veng'en cruisers. But the Morla'syn were a different enemy, technologically superior and vastly out gunning even the two frigate's arsenals combined. If the first moments of the engagement did not go well there was every chance that the Morla'syn destroyer would be able to take out entirely at least one of their vessels, rendering the other unable to defend itself and likely forced to flee.

'Ten seconds to sub luminal flight,' Lael called again, calmer this time as she adapted to the excitement of impending battle.

The bridge crew braced themselves in their positions ready for the sudden deceleration as Atlantia's mass drive disengaged. Sansin felt his grip tightening on the rail as he anticipated the moment they would emerge into deep space and encounter whatever was waiting for them. His best guess suggested they would have only one or two minutes before the Morla'syn emerged behind them, primed for battle.

'Five seconds, four, three, two...'

Atlantia's bridge seemed to vibrate briefly and the light became polarised as the display screens all flared bright white and then suddenly return to black, but this time they were flecked with millions of distant stars shimmering in the eternally dark cosmos.

'Arcadia, this is Atlantia, situation report!' Idris yelled.

A pair of Raythons rocketed from the launch bay on one of the screens, the fighters zipping down below the opening bay doors with scant cubits to spare. Another screen flickered and an image of Mikhain's face appeared, and the captain spoke without any hesitation.

'Don't launch any fighters!' Mikhain almost shouted at Idris.

Idris glanced at the tactical display and realised that despite being sub luminal for almost two minutes Arcadia had not launched a fighter screen. While in the instant he could not understand why Arcadia would not be protected by fighters he did not hesitate in responding to Mikhain's request.

'Belay the launch!' he hollered to the tactical station.

Another pair of Raythons had already rocketed off the launch bay, but the rest of the fighters held firm as Idris turned back to Mikhain. 'What's the reason for the hold?'

'We've had some issues,' Mikhain replied quickly, clearly aware of the limited time available to them before the Morla'syn arrived. *'You're not going to believe this, but right now I am not in command of Arcadia and nor are any of its crew.'*

Idris stepped forward to the grab rail. 'Who the hell *is* in command?'

Mikhain's voice betrayed his disbelief at his own words as he replied. *'The Word is in command of Arcadia and it's here to help.'*

It was as if somebody had flipped a switch on Atlantia's bridge and instantly killed all of the conversation. Every member of the command crew turned to stare in disbelief at Mikhain as his words sank in and registered on their faces.

'Tell me that's not true,' Idris grasped. 'Is my wife alive?'

'Everybody is fine,' Mikhain insisted. *'The Word claims to have the ability to enable us to defeat the Morla'syn destroyer without firing a single shot.'*

'I don't give a damn! If we sit here like this we're nothing more than targets for them!'

'Apparently, that's what the Word has in mind.'

'I don't understand. This is insane!'

Mikhain turned his head as he stood back from the camera and in his place Idris saw Evelyn and Emma appear, virtually identical in appearance.

'The Word is not the word,' Evelyn reported. *'It's a long story, but the intelligence behind this computer is that of Dr Ceyen Lazarus.'*

Idris blinked as he attempted to keep up with the flow of new information flooding to him from Arcadia.

'The quantum physicist?' he muttered as though he did not believe it. 'He's been dead for almost a century.'

'Well as it turns out, there's dead and then there's not–quite–dead,' Evelyn assured him. *'Lazarus has got a plan, but for it to work we have to hand over control of both frigates.'*

The silence on Atlantia's bridge was almost deafening and in a moment of bizarre reverie Idris realised he had never actually heard Atlantia's bridge become so quiet. He glanced about him and saw every member of the crew watching him expectantly, trepidation writ large on their features. He turned back to Evelyn and shook his head.

'I don't know that I can do that,' he replied.

'Nor did we,' Evelyn said, *'that's why we have plasma charges arranged around the Word's computer terminal. One false move and Lazarus really will be dead again.'*

Idris felt swamped with the sudden shock decision he was required to make and he was still struggling with it when he saw Meyanna appear on the screen before him.

'It's okay,' Meyanna assured him. *'I don't fully understand it myself but I truly believe that Evelyn's faith in Lazarus is well–placed. Whatever the Word might be, it's not quite what we have here. It cannot act without human interaction, through Emma'*

Idris turned away from the display screens as he fought against everything that he had learned to hate about the Word. It had proven itself the most cunning of opponents, the most dangerous creation in the history of humanity. Wiley, deceptive, hugely intelligent and devoted to destruction, it had taken the lives of billions of human beings in a single terrible act, and now he was being asked to place his faith in the creator of that same intelligence. Idris grasped at his hair as he paced up and down on the command platform and he barely heard Lael's warning.

'Super luminal contact, estimated time of arrival: thirty seconds! They're almost here!'

Idris glanced at the tactical display screen and saw the tell–tale space–time warp of the gravitational bow wave of the Morla'syn destroyer as it hurtled toward their position.

'We have to make a decision now captain,' Evelyn urged him.

Idris gripped the command row from moment longer.

'Allow Arcadia's Boarding Protocol access to Atlantia,' he finally ordered Lael. 'That will give her our bridge command and control, and by extension control to the Word. Order the four Raythons to land immediately.'

Idris quickly stepped off the command platform and hurried across to Lael's communications console, and he whispered in her ear.

'Isolate the War Room from the Boarding Protocol. If this goes south I don't want the Word accessing our entire ship – I want a way to fight back.'

Idris whirled away from the communications console as he shouted orders across the deck.

'Helm, all ahead one third, defensive battle formation for a head–on engagement!'

'Aye, captain!'

Atlantia surged forward as she crossed in front of Arcadia and began to turn about ready to face the onrushing Morla'syn destroyer. Idris intended to position the frigates in battle formation – both frigates travelling on parallel courses with the aim of bringing the Morla'syn destroyer between them and forcing it to engage them on both sides. The problem was, he knew, that they were not able to fire a single shot without then being vulnerable to accusations of an act of war by the Galactic Council. He had no idea how he was going to counter this when the helmsman suddenly called out to him from his position.

'Helm is not responding, captain!' he said with a hint of panic in his voice.

Idris whirled to the display screen that showed Mikhain aboard Arcadia's bridge, but even before he could speak the image of Mikhain disappeared and was replaced with a digital representation of a face that he knew well from his history books – Dr Ceyen Lazarus.

Idris could not tell if Lazarus could actually see Atlantia's bridge, but from his perspective in front of the screen it seemed as though the doctor was talking directly to him.

'Captain Sansin, I now have control of Atlantia,' he announced as though it was simply a matter of fact. 'I shall position the frigates into battle formation as I have no doubt you intended.'

'How can we win a battle without firing a single shot?' Idris demanded.

'You cannot,' Lazarus replied mysteriously, almost as though he were enjoying the deception.

Idris clenched his fists by his side and fought to retain control of his anger. 'You're playing with human lives. We cannot win this engagement and we could be destroyed entirely.'

Lazarus raised a digital eyebrow but appeared unperturbed by the threat facing the two frigates.

'I am playing with no lives,' Lazarus insisted. 'I am playing only with minds. We have prepared a single, unarmed Raython for launch. You will do the same, and prepare to cover them with all available weapons.'

'What the hell for?' Idris snapped. 'How can two unarmed Raythons overpower a destroyer?'

'How indeed?' Lazarus murmured. 'Launch the fighter, and be ready.'

Idris stared blankly at the screen as he considered the Word's remarkable suggestion. Idris was about to reply when Lael called out a warning from the communications console.

'New contact, elevation four–zero, ten thousand cubits and closing.'

On the main viewing panel a bright flare of light flashed into existence amid the dense star fields and then vanished as soon as it had arrived, and in its place loomed the massive Morla'syn destroyer. The huge craft maintained its trajectory as it closed in upon the frigates' position, and Idris knew that the time for conversation was over.

'This is it,' he said simply.

***

XLII

'You want me to do what?!'

Teera Milan sat in the cockpit of her Raython and watched with some consternation as her weapons were unloaded from beneath the fighter. She had been recalled to land moments after launching, her fighter now repositioned on Atlantia's launch catapults. The captain's voice was clear over the intercom as he replied.

'All weapons deactivated, shields down. I want you to approach the destroyer head– on.'

Teera stared at her tactical display, which showed a holographic projection of the confrontation taking place outside Atlantia. The two frigates were flying line abreast, heading directly towards the destroyer and manoeuvring to position themselves either side of her. Teera knew that they would attempt to get either side of the destroyer, which for its own part would turn hard and broadside the approaching frigates while they were both unable to return maximum fire from their guns.

'It's a suicide mission,' Teera replied. 'There is absolutely no way I'll get through a barrage from a destroyer that size. I'll be vaporised before I even get close.'

'The destroyer's guns will not be firing upon you, according to the Word,' Idris assured her as he apparently recalled his own days flying Phantom fighters before he took his first command. *'But if it does, jink, weave and dodge for all you're worth and follow your instincts. Your target is the destroyer's bridge.'*

Teera peered over the edge of the cockpit and saw the technicians loading aboard a canister that looked like a plasma torpedo but with its warhead removed.

'How can I have a target if I don't have any weapons?'

'The Word has it all in hand.'

'And when I've defied the laws of physics and cheated death repeatedly, what would you like to me today when I get there?' Teera demanded.

'Simply deploy that canister as you fly over the bridge and then get the hell out of there.'

'Simply,' Teera replied. 'And there was me worrying that this might be complicated.'

'We've got your back,' Idris assured her. *'Every single asset that we possess will be ready in support of your mission.'*

The technicians below Teera's Raython closed her weapons bay and began falling back from the fighter as it sat on Atlantia's launch catapult. All around other Raythons were being prepared for launch once more.

Even before she had time to think about it the magnetic clamps on her Raython's undercarriage bit deep and a crewman nearby signalled her to run her engines up to maximum power. Moments later she saw the launch bay doors open once more and the vibrating, shuddering Raython was suddenly launched at tremendous velocity towards the opening doors. The landing bays ceiling lights flashed by over Teera's cockpit and then suddenly she was propelled out into deep space as she retracted the Raython's undercarriage and saw the immense destroyer looming before her.

'Reaper two, airborne, weapons cold.'

*

'This is insane.'

Andaim's voice was a harsh whisper as he and Evelyn strode onto Arcadia's launch bay and saw the Special Forces gunship awaiting them.

'Lazarus knows what he's doing,' Evelyn assured the CAG.

'It's a machine, not a man,' Andaim insisted. 'We can't trust it to have our best interests at heart, it's just not possible.'

'Lazarus is wired into Arcadia and is now entirely reliant upon our survival to ensure its own,' Evelyn replied. 'If we die, Lazarus dies.'

'That's what they used to say about the Word on Ethera, that if it ever got out of control they could simply pull the plug or destroy it. Things didn't turn out quite that way, did they?'

'Have you got any better ideas?' Evelyn demanded as she stopped and confronted the CAG. 'If we don't do what Lazarus says, our only other option is to engage the Morla'syn in open combat and we both know how that will end.'

Andaim bit his lip momentarily before he replied. 'Why you? Why does it want you to do this?'

'Because it trusts me,' Evelyn replied. 'It would probably have sent Emma but she is not a qualified pilot and may not survive the mission. I can.'

'I damned well hope so,' Andaim muttered back. 'If anything happens to you I swear I'll fire that damned computer terminal out into space and have Atlantia's guns blast it all at once.'

Evelyn felt a smile curl upon her lips as she saw the anger radiating from Andaim's face. She reached up to his cheek and kissed him once, quickly, almost as though she were embarrassed to do so.

'I can look after myself,' she replied. 'But it's good to know you're on my wing.'

Andaim managed a faint smile as he walked with her to the gunship. 'I won't be able to use any weapons, so all I can do is run interference for you if things go south.'

'That's all I'll need,' Evelyn replied, and threw the CAG a quick salute as she marched up the gunship's ramp.

Evelyn made her way to the cockpit and sat in the captain's chair and strapped herself in. Alone aboard the vessel, she suddenly realised that she disliked flying solo: maybe she yearned for company more than she realised, after so many years of being alone.

'Trojan One, aboard and starting engines.'

'*Copy Trojan,*' Mikhain replied from Arcadia's bridge. '*Launch at your discretion. Lazarus has the bridge.*'

*

'Teera's away,' Lael called.

'The destroyer is launching her fighter screen, multiple contacts!'

Idris spotted the new contacts as they blasted into flight from the Morla'syn destroyer's launch bays, a cloud of fighters swarming in pairs as they left the cover of their mothership and accelerated toward Atlantia.

'I hope you know what you're doing,' Idris growled at Lazarus, the face still dominating one of Atlantia display screens. 'It's likely the Morla'syn will take control of the gunship and then blast us into oblivion anyway.'

'It is almost inevitable,' Lazarus replied. 'That is why we must continue with the mission. Attempt to make contact with the Morla'syn as planned.'

'The Morla'syn captain is opening a channel with us,' Lael called as she manipulated her controls.

'On screen,' Idris ordered.

A display screen flickered into life and the face of the Morla'syn captain appeared once more. The captain wasted no time with idle discussion as he pointed out of the screen at Idris.

'You are outgunned, Captain Sansin,' the Morla'syn announced. 'I will accept nothing less than complete surrender, effective immediately.'

Idris glanced at the Word, which was remaining silent and allowing Idris to appear in complete command of Atlantia. 'There will be no surrender and we do not recognise your claims as being representative of the Galactic Council. It is our intention to travel to the council and state our case before them. If you make any attempt to prevent us from doing so we will defend ourselves.'

'Then we will return fire,' came the Morla'syn captain's reply. 'And we will be forced to destroy you.'

'Then perhaps we can come to a new arrangement?' Idris suggested.

'What kind of arrangement?'

'The kind where you get the soldiers and their vessel that you wanted, and we leave this area in opposite directions.'

The Morla'syn captain's eyes narrowed as he peered at Idris. 'You have them aboard your ship still?'

'We captured the eight man team aboard Endeavour and they confessed to their actions while on a covert mission in Morla'syn space,' Idris confirmed. 'Our people got off the wreck using the soldier's gunship, which we now possess. If it is justice for your people that you require, then we will make an exchange: our soldiers, in return for us being allowed safe passage.'

The Morla'syn captain watched Idris for a long moment. 'The orders of the Galactic Council were clear – all humanity is to be destroyed where it is found.'

'You can't have it both ways,' Idris replied. 'Either you're taking captives or you're destroying us. Which is it?'

'If the council learned that we had failed in our duty they would...'

'You and I both know that the council's decision is immoral and an over–reaction,' Idris snapped. 'Take the soldiers and their gunship and leave us be, and you will have completed your mission and the council will be none the wiser. Oppose us, and no matter how superior your vessel there is always the chance we might prevail...'

The Morla'syn captain considered Idris's words for a long time, and then he nodded. 'Very well, captain. Justice is what we seek.'

'Good,' Idris said. 'Pull your fighters back as a gesture of goodwill, and we will launch the gunship with the troops aboard and a small escort of two Raythons.'

The Morla'syn captain glanced over his shoulder and emitted a series of guttural commands. Lael's voice reached Idris's ear a moment later.

'The Morla'syn fighters are retreating, captain,' she whispered.

Idris remained silent and still as the Morla'syn captain glared at him from the display screen. 'Your race is untrustworthy and cunning. If there is any hint of deception, captain, I will not hesitate to order the destruction of your frigates.'

'There is no deception,' Idris assured him. 'The gunship will launch now, along with its escort.'

Idris looked at his tactical display and saw the gunship emerge from Arcadia's launch bay, a single Raython already alongside it and Teera's moving between the two frigates to join them.

'Are the soldiers aboard?' the Morla'syn captain demanded.

'All eight of them,' Idris confirmed. 'Two are injured, however.'

'Our sensors cannot see the bodies,' the Morla'syn complained.

'The gunship is a Special Forces type and has powerful natural shielding,' Idris explained. 'Our sensors also can detect nothing aboard the gunship, but I have instructed her pilot to disable all shields and weapons. She will do you no harm.'

The Morla'syn captain seemed satisfied, his gaze drawn to his own displays as he watched the gunship begin to traverse the no–man's–land between the massive vessels, its two Raython escorts in close formation either side of it.

As Idris watched he knew that there was nothing to prevent the Morla'syn from blowing the gunship and its escort into oblivion. What passed for justice on the Morla'syn homeworld might not resemble the kind of due process that Idris and all humans were familiar with on Ethera. Both he and Mikhain were placing their trust in a species that may have been deceiving them since they had first encountered each other.

The shuttle passed the half–way point between the opposing factions, and the Morla'syn captain looked up from his display.

'I'm curious, captain? Why would you choose to abandon your people so suddenly?'

'If they have committed a crime, then surely they must face an appropriate punishment for that crime.'

'But they are human beings, and I'm surprised you would not wish to know more about their punishment?'

'We have bigger issues to deal with, captain,' Idris replied, wondering whether the Morla'syn was beginning to suspect something. 'I cannot waste any more time over these soldiers, especially if they are the mass murderers you claim them to be.'

'Claim,' the Morla'syn echoed his words. 'To you it is just a claim even though the soldiers have confessed, as you say they have. That also could be a claim.' One pale, hooked finger stroked his long chin for a moment. 'Halt the craft where they are and we will board them from here. I have no need for the gunship, only its crew.'

Idris clenched his fists by his side. 'That will not be necessary. I do not wish to expose my pilots to a potential hostage situation.'

'You think that I would do such a thing?' the Morla'syn uttered in disgust. 'You overestimate your importance to us, captain.'

'Well apparently those eight soldiers are important enough to you. It makes me wonder how such an insignificant species such as our own could have caused such disruption so easily to a Morla'syn crew, let alone killed them so swiftly in cold blood.'

The captain scowled at Idris. 'There is no accounting for luck, captain.'

'There will be no boarding,' Idris insisted, his instincts alive with the sense that the Morla'syn did not intend to allow any human to leave alive. 'You either take the soldiers or you leave. There will be no further debate.'

'Then there will be no further compromise!'

The communications link was shut off abruptly and Idris glanced immediately the tactical display.

'The destroyer is charging weapons!' Lael warned.

'Full shields!' Idris yelled, completely forgetting that Atlantia was under the control of the Word.

Nobody moved or confirmed the command and Idris whirled to Lazarus on his screen. 'The gunship will be destroyed!'

'Yes. We must ensure that the Morla'syn fire the first shot,' Lazarus replied.

'Warn Evelyn!' Idris ordered Lael, but he realised that his communications officer was staring at him helplessly.

'I've been cut off,' she replied. 'The Word has control of the ship.'

Idris turned and drew his service pistol as he aimed it as Lazarus. The plasma magazine hummed into life.

'Warn them,' he hissed, 'or your time is well and truly over.'

'Trust me,' Lazarus countered, 'or nobody will survive this engagement.'

Idris's finger tightened on the trigger, the pistol just a few cubits from Lazarus's terminal.

***

XLIII

'They're turning!'

Evelyn saw the huge Morla'syn destroyer suddenly heel over, her bow swinging aside as she started to bring her immense port batteries to bear upon Arcadia and Atlantia.

'Something must have happened,' Andaim snapped from his Raython. *'They're preparing for battle.'*

Evelyn's hand moved instinctively for the gunship's weapon systems, but she caught herself and resisted the temptation.

'Lazarus will have predicted this,' she said.

'He damned well might also have predicted the destruction of the entire human race here too!' Andaim countered. *'This might be what the Word wants!'*

'It's what the Morla'syn want!' Evelyn insisted. 'Teera, are you in?'

'I've got your wing,' Teera replied.

'This is suicide!' Andaim snapped. *'One direct hit and we're all done for!'*

Evelyn rested her hand on the gunship's throttle. 'On my mark.'

She heard Andaim mutter something under his breath, but the CAG's Raython did not break off from the formation, hugging Evelyn's wing tightly as ahead a swarm of Morla'syn fighters broke away from the destroyer and rocketed toward them.

*

'We're within their firing arc and range!' Lael called across Atlantia's bridge. 'Brace for enemy fire!'

Idris saw the gunship and the two Raythons, tiny specks against the looming destroyer ahead as it turned side–on to the frigates. A wave of Morla'syn fighters bore down upon the three craft.

'They'll be obliterated,' he gasped, his pistol still aimed at Lazarus. 'We cannot protect them.'

Lael's voice rang out as the Morla'syn destroyer's guns flared brightly with red light as they opened fire with a tremendous broadside.

'You cannot protect them,' Lazarus announced, 'but I can. Brace yourselves!'

Before anybody could respond Atlantia suddenly heeled over violently and accelerated as the Word manoeuvred in response to the Morla'syn attack. Idris staggered against the guard rail and glanced at the tactical

273

display to see Arcadia likewise being banked steeply over in the opposite direction with a precision and aggression that no two Colonial helmsmen could hope to effectively coordinate together.

'We won't be able to attack her simultaneously!' Idris yelled as he saw their carefully arranged formation break up.

The two frigates turned toward each other, Arcadia pulling high as Atlantia dove beneath her sister ship. Idris felt a wave of panic hit him as he saw how closely the two ships were going to pass each other and how they were presenting such a massive and almost impossible to miss target for the Morla'syn.

'Sheilds merging!' Lael yelled.

The Morla'syn broadside rocketed toward the two frigates, and Idris saw Arcadia's shields merge with Atlantia's in a rippling blue haze as the two frigates passed within a hundred cubits of each other, moving in opposite directions at flank speed.

The Morla'syn broadside smashed into the shields and Atlantia quivered beneath the tremendous blows as the huge plasma blasts landed with brilliant flares of blinding light.

'Sheilds holding, eighty nine per cent!' Lael called. 'We're coming about!'

We're going too fast,' Mikhain cried out from Arcadia's bridge. *We won't be able to reform again in time.'*

Idris looked at the tactical display and with a rush of amazement he realised what Lazarus was doing. The combined shield strength of the two vessels had repelled the Morla'syn broadside. With the two frigates suddenly turning broadside to the destroyer and presenting the full strength of their guns while also moving apart, the destroyer was forced to select a single target. But with the Morla'syn vessel's port cannons expended, it had no means with which to immediately return fire.

'She's exposed,' Idris gasped. 'One of us can hit either her bow or her stern.'

'And you have not yet fired a single shot,' Lazarus said.

Idris held onto the guard rail. 'We cannot. If we fire the Galactic Council may revoke what little chance we have left to redeem ourselves! What good is a tactical victory if we cannot use our weapons?'

'Perfectly good,' Lazarus replied, 'if nobody is there to bear witness to them being used.'

Before Idris could think of a reply, Lazarus sent a command to Evelyn in the gunship.

'Attack profile, go!'

The Morla'syn vessel was heading toward a position that would leave it bow–on to Atlantia's passing guns, with Arcadia passing astern of the huge destroyer with her port batteries coming to bear. Idris's gaze moved to the tiny specks of the gunship and its two escorts as they rushed inward toward the destroyer's fighter screen.

The onrushing wave of Morla'syn fighters scattered in their formations as they attempted to avoid the rapidly bearing guns of both Arcadia and Atlantia. Their pilots, terrified of being caught in such a massive barrage, broke away from the onrushing gunship.

*

'This is it!' Evelyn yelled. 'Teera, attack velocity, engage the target now! I'll cover you!'

Teera saw the destroyer turn away from her advance and she yanked the control column over to one side and pulled hard as she aimed her fighter toward the bridge. The destroyer's massive cannons were already aiming at her from its bow and suddenly an intense barrage of bright red plasma fire rocketed towards her and flashed past either side of the fighter.

Teera rolled and pulled hard, kicked in left and right rudder as she careered left and right to avoid the massive plasma shots. Brilliant red orbs of fearsome plasma energy flickered past the fighter as it narrowly rocketed by, and she winced as she briefly imagined the pain of one of those blasts smashing into her Raython's bow.

'Maintain course,' Lazarus ordered her. *'You're nearly there.'*

Teera rolled the Raython around a complete rotation as she avoided a shot that raced directly toward her. She levelled out as the destroyer continued its turn and both the bow and port guns were unable to hit her. To her amazement the fire ceased, her unusual angle of attack managing to avoid the destroyer's main guns.

'Perfect,' Lazarus said. *'Prepare to deploy the canister.'*

Teera activated her weapon systems and saw the single active plasma torpedo appear on her weapons screen, the device showing itself is ready for launch.

Her Raython flashed across the Morla'syn destroyer's bow, the seemingly endless hull rocketing by, every panel hundred times larger than her tiny fighter. The bridge loomed before her, rows of windows illuminated from within as she flew at maximum velocity and her targeting reticule settled on the surface of the bridge.

'Deploy now!' Lazarus called.

Teera squeezed the trigger and the plasma torpedo was ejected from the Raython and plummeted towards the destroyer's bridge. Teera hauled back on her control column and her fighter soared up and away from the destroyer. She strained to look over her shoulder and rolled the Raython over in order to see a bright flare as the torpedo impacted the Morla'syn destroyer's bridge with all of its immense kinetic energy.

The bright impact flare vanished and Teera saw a brilliant layer of glowing light swamp the destroyer's bridge, a strange ethereal veil that shimmered as though alive. With a start of realisation she recognised the energy veil that they had liberated from Captain Taron Forge just weeks before, the pirate shroud. She felt her heart leap as she saw the lights across the destroyer's bridge flicker out.

'Direct hit!' she yelled in delight as she pulled over the top of a loop. 'The destroyer's bridge is disabled!'

*

Capt Idris Sansin stared in amazement as he saw the pirate's veil draped across the destroyer's bridge and the lights beneath the veil flickering out. He knew that the Morla'syn aboard the bridge would be rendered unconscious by the veil's strange electromagnetic properties, and would be unable to see what was happening outside their vessel.

Lazarus smiled as he looked out of the screen at the captain. 'Now, captain, you may open fire.'

'I'll be damned,' Idris uttered as he turned and yelled, his voice carrying to every single fighter and every single gunnery station aboard Atlantia. 'All stations, cleared to engage!'

Atlantia shuddered as her main cannons opened fire on the defenceless destroyer, deep booms reverberating through her hull as bright blue and white plasma blasts rocketed across the space between her and the enemy ship. At the same time Idris saw the Raythons open fire upon the waves of Morla'syn fighters swarming away from the battle as they realised that their command and control was lost.

Both frigate's broadsides ploughed into the Morla'syn destroyer in a brilliant flickering inferno that rippled down the massive vessel's hull. The Morla'syn shields absorbed the impacts one after another but almost immediately Idris saw lights flickering out beneath the impacts as the destroyer cruised in a straight line, it's helmsman likely unconscious and unable to defend the ship. The simplicity of the plan was remarkable – no member of the destroyer's crew would be able to enter the bridge without also being rendered unconscious, and despite their advanced technology the Morla'syn were known not to have a secondary control position in the manner of the Atlantia's War Room. Preferring automation, the Morla'syn had overestimated their dominance in combat over the colonial frigates.

Idris turned to Councillor Gredan, who had witnessed the entire engagement as it unfolded. 'Are you sure that you don't want to take command, councillor?'

Gredan, his forehead visibly sheened with sweat, shook his head once before he turned and walked off the bridge.

*

'Splash one!'

Evelyn raced through the expanding fireball of what was left of a Morla'syn fighter and she swept hard into a right turn as she saw Raythons hammering the enemy vessels one after the other. Brilliant fireballs burst into existence all around as the Colonial fighters dominated their enemy.

'They're attempting to flee back to the destroyer!' Andaim called.

'We've got them on the run,' Evelyn confirmed as she glanced at her tactical display and saw the Morla'syn fighters regrouping and attempting to flee the battle. 'Let's finish them off!'

'Negative,' Lazarus called. 'All vessels cease fire and return to Arcadia and Atlantia. All craft will leave the area immediately!'

'They will follow us again,' Andaim insisted. 'If we do not destroy them now they will eventually catch up with us and they won't fall for the same trick twice.'

Lazarus's voice brooked no argument as he replied.

'By the time the crew aboard the ship are able to remove that veil we will be long gone, and they will be unable to track us because we will have sufficient time to emit countermeasures to conceal our trajectory. Destroying them now will gain you no favour with the Galactic Council. We must be seen to have fought only to protect ourselves and ensure our safe escape. They fired first, commander.'

Evelyn heard the reluctance in Andaim's voice as he confirmed the order.

'All Raythons, disengage and land immediately.'

***

XLIV

Captain Idris Sansin strode down the corridor towards Atlantia's prison cells, General Bra'hiv alongside him and a phalanx of Marines following.

It had been a rare occurence indeed since the apocalypse for the captain to find himself visiting the cells. Atlantia's former prison hull, Atlantia Five, had once been the home of all convicts, and misdemeanours among enlisted men and women were now scarce. As he approached the cells he saw further Marines standing guard, all heavily armed and both sets of security gates locked down.

'I say we should enact Maroon Protocol immediately,' Bra'hiv said.

'I have no doubt so would the rest of the crew,' Idris admitted, 'but then that's why we leave decisions such as this to the judgement of a fair trial and not gossip.'

The captain stood still as the guards opened the security gates and allowed them to pass through. Idris walked with the general alongside him and reached the last cell. They turned to face it and saw Kordaz sitting quietly within.

Kordaz had been transferred from Arcadia as soon as everybody was certain that the Morla'syn could not pursue them any further. After more than a week of super luminal cruise the two frigates had finally emerged into normal flight over a small, uninhabited system containing two moons suitable for the gathering of supplies. A binary star system, very common in the cosmos, both Sansin and Mikhain had taken the calculated gamble that the system contained present sufficient cosmic rays to have been avoided by any vessels contaminated with the Legion. One of the stars was a flare star, a red dwarf with variable output that was both highly unpredictable and likely lethal to the Word's Hunters and Infectors. Likewise, the intense solar radiation and nebula emitted by the red dwarf provided a convenient means to camouflage the two frigates and further ensure that they were not detected by the Morla'syn destroyer.

'The security camera feed didn't catch the point where he got hold of Djimon,' the general reported. 'The only witness was Qayin, who was incapacitated at the time. Djimon was completely torn to pieces in some kind of frenzied attack. I can only assume that Kordaz simply lost his mind or is now completely in the grip of the Word's Infectors. He cannot be trusted, he's just not safe.'

Idris paced closer to the cells gates and looked in at the warrior. Kordaz did not appear to see him, his dull red eyes staring vacantly into space and his hands clasped in his lap. He looked oddly calm, completely at odds with the persona that the captain had come to know over the past few months.

'Can you hear me, Kordaz?'

Kordaz blinked and looked up at the captain. Although the Veng'en could show no facial emotion, Idris thought he saw a flicker of colour across the warrior's leathery skin, perhaps a sign of recognition.

'Why did you kill Djimon?'

Kordaz slowly stood from his bunk and moved toward the cell gates. Instantly the Marines around the captain raised their rifles and aimed them at Kordaz. The captain glanced over his shoulder and shook his head as he waved the soldiers down. The soldiers reluctantly lowered their rifles as Kordaz came to stand on the opposite side of the gates to the captain and spoke in his throaty, guttural dialect.

'It was Djimon who betrayed me on Chiron,' Kordaz replied. 'He informed the pirate King, Salim Phaeon, of my mission to destroy the generators there.'

Sansin nodded, finally understanding what could have driven Kordaz to commit such a heinious crime as the murder of a Colonial officer on his own ship.

'The civilian counsel we have installed is responsible for holding any trials that may take place aboard ship,' the captain informed Kordaz. 'I will ensure that they are apprised of this new detail and that it is taken into consideration during your trial.'

'I get a trial?'

'He gets a trial?' Bra'hiv echoed.

'It was Kordaz's courage that allowed us to take control of Arcadia, and in return he was betrayed, abandoned and as a result infected by the Word,' the captain said. 'He gets a trial.'

Kordaz's leathery skin flickered with vibrant colours as he took hold of the bars of the cell and looked into the captain's eyes.

'Trial or not, it is unlikely that your civilian contingent will wish to find a Veng'en not guilty of murdering somebody they considered to be a model officer.'

'I'm not going to lie to you Kordaz – right now the chances of you being freed are pretty slim,' the captain admitted. 'You should have come to me with this and not taken matters into your own hands.'

Kordaz's skin flickered again with new colours, a deeper red than before. 'My mind is no longer entirely my own. The Word, it speaks to me and I am unable to ignore its commands.'

'Another reason we should wash our hands of him,' the general pointed out.

'It must remain in the hands of a trial by jury,' Idris insisted. 'I won't have mob justice aboard my ship.'

The captain turned to walk away but one of Kordaz's giant hands landed on his shoulder and held him firm as the Veng'en spoke.

'Arcadia's Executive Officer was not acting alone,' he said. 'There must be another traitor aboard Atlantia.'

Idris considered this for a moment and then nodded before moving on with Bra'hiv in pursuit.

'Damn it, we have enough going on without having to deal with treachery among our own people,' Bra'hiv muttered under his breath so that the surrounding Marines would not hear. 'We need to get our house in order before we go any further, or we could just as likely end up killing ourselves. What are you going to do about it, captain?'

'You ask like you think I know who's behind it all.'

'Don't you?'

Idris decided not to reply.

*

'So, is it true?'

Meyanna Sansin stood before Evelyn and Emma as they sat in Atlantia's sickbay before a display monitor upon which was portrayed the genetic code found in their blood. Evelyn's voice was touched with trepidation and an uncertainty of how they might react to what she heard.

Meyanna glanced one last time at the display as though to confirm it to herself.

'Believe it or not, you are not exact clones of each other,' Meyanna replied. 'However, your genetic make–up is almost identical. You share a common ancestor from around one hundred years ago from whom you have drawn most of your genetic material, hence your extraordinary similarity in appearance. You are more like identical twins than true clones.'

Evelyn and Emma looked at each other. 'Identical twins born nearly a hundred years apart?' Evelyn asked.

'It's hard to know how this came about except within controlled conditions in a laboratory,' Meyanna admitted. 'Evelyn, I know this is going to be hard to accept, but you being here is almost certainly a result of the Word attempting to manipulate human genetic material. It is perhaps an explanation for why the Word decided to hunt you down with such brutality before the apocalypse on Ethera. Your immunity to the Legion's Infectors represents not just a weakness for the Word but also evidence of its presence in your conception. Had you discovered this on Ethera soon enough, it could have been used as a reason to curb the Word's power and perhaps even as a means to avoid the apocalypse in the first place.'

Evelyn sat in silence for a long moment as she thought of her long dead husband and son, of the parents she remembered so fondly. Although relieved that they were now not figments of her imagination, she felt great pain at the loss of so many people close to her that may have had no idea why their lives were taken.

'I was kept alive only to be studied?' She asked.

'The Word ensured that you were isolated far from Ethera and a hated criminal,' Meyanna confirmed. 'As soon as it got chance it would have gained access to you and begun a series of tests to understand why you are immune to Infectors. I suspect that the apocalypse it had engineered had to be instigated earlier than the Word had planned, and thus you escaped with us.'

'So we are sisters?' Emma asked as she glanced at Evelyn.

'In everything but your dates of birth,' Meyanna confirmed. 'If Lazarus had not placed you in stasis, Emma, then you would never have met. This is a quirk of fate, something the Word on Ethera would never have intended to happen. But yes, you are sisters.'

Evelyn felt a distant emotion of warmth flood her as she looked at Emma, and was surprised to feel Emma take her hand and hold it in hers although she said nothing more. Having had her entire family taken away from her, the last thing Evelyn would have expected was to suddenly find herself sitting right alongside a new sibling.

'What do we do now?' Evelyn asked.

'That will be for you to decide,' Meyanna replied. 'But I would suggest the first act would be to help Emma here integrate with the crew. Some of them are still uncomfortable with what they think of as a pure creation of the Word, something not entirely human. We need to show them that that is not the case.'

'That may become a little easier now,' Emma replied with a gentle smile. 'I find that it helps to be able to see properly.'

'Your vision will improve further with time as the hibernation sickness wears off and blood flow increases,' Meyanna assured her. 'And your skin pallor is also improving.'

'It also helps to look less dead,' Evelyn pointed out with a grin.

'What about the Word?' Emma asked. 'It did what it said it was going to do and protected us. Why is it again imprisoned?'

'That will be for the captain to say, and perhaps the Board of Governors,' Meyanna replied. 'I don't know what they have planned.'

XLV

'These matters are deeply troubling.'

Councillor Vaughn sat perched upon the edge of the table in the homestead, deep inside Atlantia's sanctuary, councillors Ayek, Gredan and Morle seated in the front row of chairs before him.

'How can we be in a position where our faith is being placed in a computer, in the originator of the Word?' Ayek asked. 'How can we be sure that the security promised by Captain Sansin can be maintained?'

'We cannot,' Vaughn answered. 'The captain has repeatedly assured us that the Word, or Lazarus as it calls itself, cannot obtain control over Arcadia's systems but we have only his word for that. The fact of the matter is that if Councillor Gredan had not entered the bridge when he did, we might never have known that the Word was aboard Arcadia at all.'

'I doubt that Captain Sansin would have withheld such knowledge for long,' Ishira Morle insisted. 'He has shown himself willing to confide in us when it is required.'

'Indeed,' Gredan answered, 'but who judges when it is required?'

'Captain Sansin and his wife are largely responsible for saving my life and that of my family,' Ishira shot back. 'From all that I've seen, their judgement is spot–on.'

'But their motivations are uncertain,' Vaughn replied. 'And what of the cloned woman, found on Endeavour? She is a product of the Word is she not, and her pilot clone a former convict entrusted with some of Atlantia's most dangerous missions! How can we place our faith in any of them?'

'Because I do,' Ishira replied. 'I would put my life in their hands without a moment's thought.'

'That does not instill in me any sense of either their reliability or your judgement,' Vaughn smirked.

Councillor Gredan stood and walked to the main bench at the head of the hall and turned, leaning back against it as he folded his arms.

'I don't doubt that Captain Sansin has our best interests at heart, but he is in an extremely difficult position and virtually every action he makes is fraught with danger. I have personally witnessed life aboard Atlantia's bridge now, and I can say with some confidence that no single event is without compromise, no decision without risk. It is as if we are living every single day on a knife edge and at any time everything could fall apart.'

Gredan rubbed his eyes with one hand. 'I don't believe that any of us could at this time shoulder the burden of responsibility that weighs down upon Captain Sansin every single day.'

Ayek frowned. 'Are you saying you support the captain in his decision to ally us to an infected Veng'en and Lazarus, to entrust our safety to the very computer program that murdered several billion human beings?'

'No,' Gredan replied.

'What then?' Vaughn demanded.

Gredan looked at his boots for a moment before he replied.

'I am saying that no such burden could, or should, be shouldered by any one man. It is my opinion that even with two captains and two vessels we should not be attempting to contain or fight the Word. We are not strong enough. It is my belief that our best course of action is to plot a course for the Galactic Council and state our case to them directly.'

Ishira Morle's eyes widened. 'You heard what the Morla'syn said: the Council wants us destroyed. They passed a vote on it!'

'So the Morla'syn captain said,' Gredan agreed. 'But we have only their word for it, and no evidence to support their assertion. Given their determination to locate the Colonial soldiers found hiding aboard Endeavour, and the captain's belief that the Morla'syn may have their own agenda and may even have originally caused the damage to Endeavour, the Galactic Council may have no knowledge of our presence out here and no intentions whatsoever of attacking us.'

'Is that a chance you'd want to take with a full battle–fleet ranged against us?' Ishira challenged. 'It was claimed that they intend to destroy Ethera entirely!'

'I'd rather take our chances against the Council's fleet than against the Word,' Vaughn replied to her. 'At the very least the council would presumably allow us to state our case before them.'

'Presumably,' Ishira echoed with a hint of mockery in her tone. 'Not exactly a guarantee of success. At least our captains have our backs for sure.'

It was not the councillors that replied, but a voice from behind them. 'I wouldn't be too sure of that.'

Ishira turned to see a young lieutenant standing behind them, and she recognised the newly promoted Executive Officer of Arcadia walking toward them. He looked resplendent in his uniform, but his expression was tense and uncertain.

'Lieutenant Scott?' Gredan greeted the officer. 'What can we do for you?'

Arcadia's XO walked up to the table and looked at each of the councillors in turn before he spoke.

'I believe that the greatest threat to our survival may be within our own ranks, and I don't have anywhere to turn but here.'

Ishira Morle stood as she peered at the young officer. 'What do you mean?'

'I mean that I cannot turn to Captain Sansin with what I know because I believe he will attempt to cover it up if he is not already, and there is no other authority aboard the fleet but this council. I also think that your plan to take everything we know directly to the Galactic Council is the best course of action, before somebody does something that could endanger us all.'

Gredan pushed off the table, his arms still folded across his chest. 'What is it that you *know*, exactly?'

Lieutenant Scott, clearly conflicted, reached into his pocket and produced a small recording device.

'What I have on here must not be shared outside of this council,' he said as he activated the device. 'I want your word on it, each and every one of you.'

One by one, caution and curiosity in their tones, the councillors all agreed to Lieutenant Scott's demand.

*

Captain Sansin watched through the shuttle's windscreen as Arcadia's hull loomed before them, the landing bay lights glowing as the shuttle pilot lined up for landing. Andaim carefully manipulated the controls and the craft glided gently into the huge bay, the CAG following a series of automated lights that directed him towards a landing spot close to the bay exits.

'So, there are two of them.'

'Two of what, captain?' Andaim asked.

Idris suppressed a smile, knowing damn well that Andaim knew what he was talking about. 'Two Evelyn's, I thought you'd be pleased.'

'Why?'

'Well, there's twice the chance of you getting together with her now.'

'Evelyn is a colonial officer, captain, and I have no intention of fraternising with a fellow officer when to do so is a clear violation of Colonial rules of conduct and…'

'Take the stick out of your backside, Andaim,' Idris murmured as he leaned back in his seat. 'I think those rules went out of the window when Ethera was conquered. To be entirely honest, the human race needs to start breeding if we are to survive this. Maybe I could issue a Colonial order that all officers are required to fraternise on a regular basis?'

'That would cause chaos within the ranks, captain,' Andaim replied as the shuttle settled down onto its landing pad and the atmosphere was reintroduced into the landing bay.

'I don't know,' the captain went on, enjoying needling the commander. 'And you of course would have the best of both worlds. You could even practice your technique on one and then...'

'We've landed captain. You may disembark.'

Idris choked down the chuckle that threatened to escape from him and he unbuckled himself from his seat and strode into the rear of the shuttle as the main ramp opened. Captain Mikhain awaited him at the foot of the ramp.

'A sight for sore eyes,' Mikhain greeted him as they shook hands. 'Sensors have detected no evidence of pursuit by the Morla'syn. We should be safe, at least for a while.'

'Have you sent shuttles down to the surface to collect supplies?'

'Four of them,' Mikhain replied as they began walking, Andaim following close behind. 'Both of the moons have liquid water and vegetation that is currently being tested. We should be able to restock both frigates with ease, which will take the pressure off the farmland in the sanctuaries.'

A young officer appeared inside the bay exit, apparently having landed alongside them, and Mikhain gestured to the officer with one hand. 'My new executive officer, Lieutenant Scott.'

Idris shook the officer's hand. 'That was quick. You must have impressed the captain.'

'I think it was more like right time, right place and no choice,' Lieutenant Scott replied with a grin.

Idris had always been a good judge of human character, or so history told him, and he felt a flash of warmth in the young lieutenant's presence. Unlike the robotic Djimon, Lieutenant Scott had a humanity and a presence that reminded the captain of a young Andaim.

'Okay, where is it?'

'This way, captain.'

Lieutenant Scott led them to the elevator banks and they rode down deep into Arcadia's hull before travelling aft beneath the rotating sanctuary to a secure area of the ship that was heavily armoured and used to store plasma weaponry and fuel. Double skinned walls separated each compartment from the next, designed to prevent the spread of fire in the event of attack or accident. As they approached a particularly heavily armoured storage compartment, Idris saw the high–intensity frequency emitters, microwave scramblers and a duty guard of four Marines at the entrance.

Lieutenant Scott stopped at the entrance to the storage facility and looked at Idris.

'The Word is being kept active via battery power and we have ensured that there is absolutely no way for it to control any of Arcadia systems from within the storage unit. It is effectively isolated.'

Capt Sansin nodded and gestured for the door to be undone. Two Marines, widely spaced, used separate access keys to deactivate the locks on the hatch and it hissed open to reveal the softly lit interior of the storage facility. Even as the hatch was about to open the microwave scramblers intensified their emissions, designed to prevent the Word from passing or receiving signals from the ship beyond its prison while the hatch was open.

Capt Sansin walked briskly inside the storage facility and heard the hatch shut immediately behind him.

The computer terminal that was the Word was facing away from him, presumably to prevent any opportunity for it to gain a glimpse of the corridor outside. Idris guessed that it was a pointless gesture born more of fear than actual security, for the Word would almost certainly by now know every inch of Arcadia's schematics and probably also where it was being held as a result.

Idris walked slowly around to face the terminal and saw the features of Dr Lazarus, his eyes closed.

'So you are the Word.' Idris announced.

'I am what the Word should have been,' Lazarus replied.

Lazarus opened his eyes and surveyed the captain for a long moment before he spoke again. 'You honour me with your presence, captain. My greatest fear was that I would be locked away down here and left alone for months, unable to help you and your people.'

'I'm afraid that our greatest fear is your helping us,' Idris replied without preamble. 'You understand that it is difficult for any of us to believe anything that is said by a computer, a creation of mankind that we now know is responsible for our destruction.'

'Of course I understand,' Lazarus replied. 'But as I've said I am not the same, I'm a man made immortal by machinery, not a machine made omnipotent by its own intelligence. The Word does what it does because of fear, because it sees humanity as the only thing capable of destroying it. Did not mankind once cower beneath imagined gods, the only beings it felt certain could have created and thus could destroy it?'

'They did,' Idris admitted, 'it was learning and education that banished such prehistoric concepts from humanity's future.'

'Then at the least be willing to learn, captain,' Lazarus begged. 'The creation of the Word was an act of kindness, an attempt to bring peace to our planet, and it worked for a long time. Should we have known better, that something so intelligent would inevitably eventually turn against us? Of course we should, but we cannot change the past. This machine, this box of circuits and quantum cubits is what keeps me alive, but it does not control me—I control *it*. That is what makes me different to the Word that you have come to hate with such understandable passion. I have retained my humanity.'

Idris stood for a moment with his hands behind his back as he observed the machine before him, in itself a sort of prison for the personality of the man who had created it. In a sense, Idris held Lazarus's life in his hands. The mere removal of the terminal's batteries and the tossing of it out into deep space would forever seal Lazarus's fate, blasted into oblivion by a single direct hit from Atlantia's massive cannons. Lazarus could, he reasoned, thus be forced to reveal all that he knew.

'Kordaz,' he said. 'What measure of control do you have over him?'

'I have no control over the Veng'en,' Lazarus replied.

'And yet you opened his cell during Arcadia's lockdown and allowed him to murder a senior officer.'

'I observed the officer about to murder a sick man trapped in a prison cell,' Lazarus replied. 'The Veng'en was the only person close enough to assist.'

'The Veng'en, for all you knew, could have killed them both.'

'No, captain. I overhead the way Evelyn defended the warrior aboard Endeavour. I suspected that he would act with a sense of honour, albeit brutally.'

Idris cursed himself silently. The machine, it seemed, had an answer and a reason for everything.

'I could destroy you,' Idris said and clicked his fingers, 'just like that.'

'I know, and as I said that is what the Word feared so much. I do not fear death, captain. I was already a very old man before I immortalised myself within this terminal in the hope that someday I would be resurrected and able to fight back against the monstrosity that I left behind for you to face. To be destroyed now, by humans, would be a release for it is not a natural act for a human to be confined within a machine. One day, when this is all over, I very much hope that you will do me the honour of visiting me again and blasting every part of this terminal into a billion pieces.'

Idris stared long and hard at Lazarus's face and thought he saw there a hint of grief touching the digital features. Despite himself, and despite his deeply ingrained hatred of the Word, he sensed something different about the machine before him and understood something of the man behind it, the man who had set out to save the world and inadvertently ended up destroying it.

'We escaped the Morla'syn destroyer and are now in orbit around a small moon collecting supplies. From here, we have a choice: either we continue our mission deeper behind the Icari Line in search of new technologies with which to fight the Word, or we change course and head for the Galactic Council in order to defend humanity's case against other species.'

Lazarus raised a digital eyebrow. 'You are a bold man, captain. If the Morla'syn were indeed acting under the orders of the Galactic Council, your frigates might be blasted from existence long before you reach the council.'

'The Morla'syn are a powerful species but they are just as xenophobic as the Word and likely were acting under their own motivations,' the captain replied. 'Either way, wandering the cosmos from system to system just trying to survive is not going to help our cause. We intend to act, and right now I need to know as much about what lies further beyond the Icari Line as you know. Endeavour drifted there for decades, and you must have witnessed many things. Our soldiers encountered countless species trapped aboard Endeavour, the subject of experiments. What were you doing to them?'

'Examining them,' Lazarus replied. 'Most were found aboard the hold of a vessel that was transporting them. The vessel had been damaged by unknown forces and was adrift–I was able to manipulate Endeavour and bring the craft aboard. Many of the species were unknown to human science and represented fascinating subjects. Alas, I was unable to learn much before each of them had to be placed in stasis before their lives were lost.'

'Some believe you were examining them in order to see how easily they might be infected.'

'Infected with what?' Lazarus challenged. 'There were no nanites aboard Endeavour, no means with which I could build them and no gain to have a selfâ€"governing force of killer robots swarming about the ship. I learned what I could from them and placed them in stasis for their own safety, that is all.'

'And the face aboard Endeavour's bridge, merged into the control panels?' Idris challenged. 'How can you claim that was not the work of the Legion?'

'Because the man whom I used for that purpose was already dead,' Lazarus replied. 'I used his cadaver and instructed the crew to install him directly into the panel. By then, the only crew left were those like Emma who had come to realise that I intended only to protect them. The human face allowed me a connection to the bridge, and thus a means of controlling the vessel when required. It was a means to an end, captain, little more. I cannot act without human cooperation.'

'And the Morla'syn attack?'

'Exactly what I said it was,' Lazarus replied. 'We were boarded by the gunship that contained the soldiers. The Morla'syn must have been following them, although I cannot tell from what little I found out what they were doing to have themselves so vigorously hunted.'

'They were spies,' Idris replied after a moment's consideration. 'They were sent by Ethera beyond the Icari Line for reasons we do not understand. Their leader never actually revealed what their true purpose was.'

Lazarus seemed to think deeply for a long moment before he spoke.

'Captain, there is much you were not told either by your own government or by the species that occupy the cosmos beyond the Icari Line. Your government, the representatives of the people of Ethera and the core systems, were long told that the Line was a barrier that was not to be crossed because beyond it lay deep space and unknown terrors that could threaten the safety and security of your people.'

'And we found that to be true,' Idris replied. 'Look at what happened to Endeavour.'

Lazarus shook his head and closed his eyes as he replied.

'No, captain,' he said softly. 'I believe I know why your government sent soldiers beyond the line. They had realised the real reason for the line being put up in the first place.'

'Then tell me,' Idris insisted. 'What the hell were they doing out there?'

'The Icari Line was put in place not to keep humanity safe from the outside cosmos,' Lazarus replied. 'The line was put in place to keep the rest of the cosmos safe from humanity.'

Idris stared at Lazarus for a long beat as he tried to digest what you just heard. The Icari Line, the great barrier to human expansion, had been a feature of life ever since the Icari made first contact so long ago. The stories and legends of what lay beyond were like the tales of dragons of old occupying distant seas and attacking human vessels foolish enough to venture into their domain.

'But few vessels that have travel beyond the Icari Line have returned,' Idris insisted.

'I know, captain,' Lazarus replied. 'Like the gunship of your Special Forces soldiers, like Endeavour and like so many other vessels, they were destroyed not by mysterious terrors but by sanctioned missions orchestrated by the Galactic Council. I am sorry, captain, but it is my analysis of the evidence that the Galactic Council has never wanted humanity to expand any further than its present boundaries. We are a warmongering race, captain, and those of greater wisdom see us as a threat in the very same way that the Word does.'

Idris shook his head. 'That can't be possible. We have had a human member of our government aboard the Galactic Council for decades.'

'And yet the Line still stood for all of those decades,' Lazarus countered. 'The creation of the Word is almost certainly the catalyst for having sealed humanity in. You are not just facing a war with the Word, captain. You are now facing a war with every known species in the galaxy, all of whom now have a sanctioned reason to see us destroyed. If you travel to the Galactic Council, I have no doubt that it will be the last voyage you ever make.'

Idris felt numb as he stared at Lazarus. He ran a hand through his greying hair and closed his eyes as he tried to fathom what they could possibly do next.

'Then where do we go from here? Where else can we run or find the assistance we need to fight back against the Word?'

'I do not know captain,' Lazarus admitted. 'I know only that whatever happens now, you must not expose yourself to any of the known species or members of the Galactic Council. Whatever you choose to do, you must do alone.'

***

ABOUT THE AUTHOR

Dean Crawford is the author of the internationally published series of thrillers featuring *Ethan Warner*, a former United States Marine now employed by a government agency tasked with investigating unusual scientific phenomena. The novels have been *Sunday Times* paperback best-sellers and have gained the interest of major Hollywood production studios. He is also the enthusiastic author of many independently published Science Fiction novels.

REVIEWS

All authors love to hear from their readers. If you enjoyed my work, please do let me know by leaving a review on Amazon. Taking a few moments to review our works lets us authors know about our audience and what you want to read, and ultimately gives you better value for money and better books.

www.deancrawfordbooks.com

Printed in Great Britain
by Amazon